Silver Pines

Clara Winslow

Published by Clara Winslow, 2024.

This is a work of fiction. Similarities to real people, places, or events are entirely coincidental.

SILVER PINES

First edition. October 8, 2024.

Copyright © 2024 Clara Winslow.

ISBN: 979-8224027224

Written by Clara Winslow.

Chapter 1: Autumn's Embrace

The bell above the door jingles, a cheerful sound clashing with the somber expression etched on Ethan's face as he strides toward me. I can almost hear the creaking of the floorboards beneath his feet, a low groan that seems to echo the discontent brewing in his chest. It's amusing, really, how a man can embody both warmth and frost. His tousled hair catches the light just right, creating an almost ethereal halo above him, yet his furrowed brow grounds him in reality. "You're new here," he states flatly, as if I've just committed a grave offense by stepping foot into his domain.

"And you must be the town's unofficial welcoming committee," I reply, smirking as I stir my latte, watching the foam swirl into intricate patterns. My tone is light, but there's a challenge in my eyes. The truth is, I relish these little encounters, the sparks that fly when two opposing forces collide. It's like watching a summer storm roll in—invigorating, unpredictable, and perhaps a little reckless.

Ethan's lips twitch, betraying the hint of a smile he's trying to suppress. "I run a café, not a social club," he shoots back, crossing his arms, a move that only serves to emphasize the breadth of his shoulders. He's built like the sturdy oaks that line the town square, resilient and imposing. "What brings you to Silver Pines?"

"Curiosity," I say, taking a sip of my latte, allowing the warmth to spread through me. "And a longing for change. You could say I'm searching for inspiration." My eyes flicker around the café, absorbing the eclectic décor—maps of far-off places hanging on the walls, bookshelves crammed with novels begging to be read, and the chalkboard menu announcing the day's specials in whimsical handwriting. "Is it so strange for a traveler to seek out a cozy nook in a new town?"

"It's strange when you've got a camera in hand and a blog that promises to share all the town's secrets," he counters, leaning closer, the tension thickening like fog in the cool morning air. "What secrets do you intend to uncover?"

I lean back in my chair, feigning nonchalance. "Oh, I don't know. Perhaps I'll write about the rich history of this quaint place, or the stories that bubble beneath its surface. Like, say, the charming café owner who's a bit of a mystery." My gaze meets his, and for a fleeting moment, the air crackles with unspoken words.

"Charming, huh?" Ethan chuckles dryly, shaking his head. "Careful with that word. It tends to lose its meaning when applied to someone who'd rather keep to themselves."

"Or perhaps it's just a defense mechanism," I tease, my smile playful, determined to pull him into the banter. "If I were as handsome as you, I'd probably spend my time sulking in corners too."

His eyebrows shoot up, surprise flickering in his eyes before he schools his features into an unreadable mask. "You should know that flattery won't get you anywhere here."

"Ah, but that's where you're mistaken," I respond, leaning forward, my voice lowered as if sharing a delicious secret. "Flattery is merely the key to unlocking people's stories. Everyone has something to share if you know how to ask."

Ethan studies me for a moment, an inscrutable expression on his face. The flicker of interest in his gaze is unmistakable, and I feel a thrill at the prospect of discovering more about him—this man who seems to embody the very essence of Silver Pines, beautiful yet shrouded in mystery.

"Then I suppose you'll be disappointed," he replies, turning on his heel and walking away, leaving me both infuriated and intrigued. My laughter lingers in the air, mingling with the aroma of freshly brewed coffee, as I return to my laptop, fingers poised above the keys.

The café hums around me, an eclectic mix of voices and laughter, but my mind is solely on Ethan. I'm determined to dig deeper, to uncover whatever hidden stories lie beneath that stoic exterior. As I tap away at my blog, painting the scenery of Silver Pines with vivid descriptions and heartfelt anecdotes, I can't shake the feeling that my adventure here has only just begun.

A week passes, each day spent in the warmth of The Maple Leaf Café, my writing flourishing amidst the gentle cadence of life around me. I've grown accustomed to the daily routine—sipping my pumpkin-spice latte, chatting with the regulars, and watching the leaves turn from gold to crimson outside the window. Yet, despite the burgeoning friendships, a piece of me remains tethered to Ethan.

Today, as I type, a familiar shadow crosses my path. He leans against the counter, arms crossed, a skeptical smile playing at the corners of his mouth. "So, what thrilling tale have you penned today, traveler?"

I glance up, heart racing, excitement bubbling just beneath the surface. "You'd be surprised. Today, I wrote about the beauty of autumn in Silver Pines. Did you know the leaves here are like a painter's palette? Gold, amber, and crimson all fighting for attention."

Ethan raises an eyebrow, skepticism creeping back into his features. "And how do you intend to make that interesting?"

"By weaving in the story of a handsome, brooding café owner who acts like he's hiding a treasure map beneath his grumpy demeanor," I reply, daring to meet his gaze.

"Good luck with that," he chuckles, shaking his head as he prepares a fresh batch of muffins. The sound of the mixer whirs in the background, a comforting noise that underscores our repartee. "You'll need it. I have a reputation to uphold."

"Oh, I'll make sure to shine a light on that reputation," I promise, smirking. "Because underneath that scowl, I sense there's a heart of gold waiting to be discovered."

Ethan pauses, the muffin batter nearly spilling over the bowl as he glances at me, surprise evident in his eyes. But I only grin, unafraid of the challenge, ready to navigate the complex landscape of his heart, one witty exchange at a time.

The weeks slip by like autumn leaves caught in a gentle breeze, each day in Silver Pines becoming more familiar, yet no less enchanting. I find myself spending hours in The Maple Leaf Café, where the scent of baked goods mingles with the crisp air seeping through the windows. The chatter of locals has transformed from background noise into a comforting soundtrack, punctuated by laughter and the clinking of coffee cups. I immerse myself in my writing, exploring the stories hidden in every nook and cranny of the town, while my burgeoning friendship with Ethan becomes the highlight of my day.

Ethan, however, remains a puzzle wrapped in mystery. Despite his initial wariness, our banter has morphed into a delightful game of wits, each exchange revealing layers of his character I am eager to uncover. Today, as I sit curled in my corner, my laptop open before me, I notice him behind the counter, effortlessly navigating the bustling café while wearing that ever-present scowl. The man may be grumpy, but I find myself increasingly drawn to the spark of humor that flickers beneath his surface.

I take a sip of my pumpkin-spice latte, savoring the comforting warmth, and call out to him, "Do you ever smile, or is that a strictly forbidden act in your café?"

He glances up, feigning offense as he wipes his hands on a towel. "Smiling is overrated. Besides, I'm saving my energy for when I need to kick someone out for taking up too much space."

I can't help but laugh, the sound brightening the space around us. "I suppose your café policy is strict, then? No joy allowed, only caffeine and crumbs?"

"Exactly. It's a serious business." He leans against the counter, arms crossed, a grin finally breaking through. "But seriously, what have you written about me today?"

"Let's see," I muse, tapping my fingers against my chin as if in deep thought. "I've labeled you the 'Grumpy Guardian of Silver Pines,' a local legend who frightens away unwelcome intruders with just a single glare."

"Charming," he retorts, a smirk tugging at his lips. "Perhaps I should get a t-shirt made."

"Definitely. But I think it needs to say 'Beware: Handsome but Brooding.' That'll keep the tourists at bay."

As the laughter spills from my lips, a warmth spreads through me, and I realize how much I cherish these moments. There's a thrill in the way Ethan's eyes brighten, as if he's finally shedding the weight of his self-imposed solitude, if only for a moment.

Just then, the bell above the door jingles again, and an elderly woman steps in, her presence radiating warmth that almost rivals the café's inviting atmosphere. She moves with a careful grace, a knitted shawl draped over her shoulders. I recognize her as Mrs. Hargrove, a regular fixture in the café, often seen with a book in hand and a gleam of mischief in her eyes.

"Ethan, dear! Have you saved me a blueberry muffin?" she calls out, her voice full of life.

Ethan rolls his eyes, but there's a twinkle of affection in his expression as he responds, "I wouldn't dream of running out before you arrived, Mrs. Hargrove. Your muffin is safe."

She approaches the counter, her gaze darting to me, an inquisitive spark lighting her features. "And who is this lovely young lady? I haven't seen her around before."

"This is my new... friend," Ethan stammers, the word lingering on his lips as he searches for the right term. "She's been... documenting the town."

I grin, feeling the warmth of her attention as she steps closer. "Oh, a writer! How delightful. What stories are you weaving about our little slice of heaven?"

"The kind that showcase all the charming quirks of Silver Pines," I reply, glancing at Ethan. "Especially those tied to a certain café owner who believes he's a misunderstood artist of coffee."

Mrs. Hargrove's eyes sparkle with delight. "Ethan, you should give this young lady a tour of the town. I think she could use a few tales of old!"

Ethan raises an eyebrow, clearly unamused by the suggestion. "I don't do tours, Mrs. Hargrove. I prefer to keep my distance from tourists and their insatiable appetite for snapshots of every flower and fencepost."

"Such a curmudgeon!" she exclaims, waving a hand dismissively. "You'll miss out on a chance to show off the hidden treasures of Silver Pines. Besides, how do you expect her to write a proper story without the inside scoop?"

I sense the playful tension between them, a bond forged through years of familiarity and a shared love for the café. Ethan's reluctance contrasts sharply with Mrs. Hargrove's enthusiasm, and I can't resist chiming in. "It sounds like a perfect idea. Imagine the rich stories I could share with the world if I had a knowledgeable tour guide."

"See?" Mrs. Hargrove grins, clearly enjoying the way the wind is blowing. "It's settled, then! You must take her around, Ethan. I want to hear all about it over coffee next week!"

"Wait—" Ethan starts, but Mrs. Hargrove has already turned to me, her eyes gleaming with excitement.

"Tomorrow, you should meet him here at noon. He knows all the best places! Trust me; it will be worth your while."

"Great! I'll be here," I say, practically vibrating with anticipation.

As Mrs. Hargrove takes her muffin and retreats to a cozy corner with her book, I can't help but feel a thrill at the prospect of spending more time with Ethan, even if it's under the guise of a tour. The idea is both terrifying and exhilarating, a cocktail of excitement and uncertainty that sends butterflies dancing in my stomach.

Ethan, however, seems less than enthused. "You know I can't just wander around with a tourist. I have a café to run."

"Oh, come on. Just think of it as an opportunity to expand your horizons," I tease, leaning in closer. "Besides, you could use a break from behind the counter. Who knows? You might even enjoy it."

"Don't count on it," he replies, shaking his head. But there's a hint of a smile on his lips, and I take that as a victory.

As the evening light spills through the windows, casting a golden hue over the café, I feel a growing sense of hope. Silver Pines is more than just a picturesque town; it's a place where stories weave together, and perhaps, just perhaps, I might be the one to help unravel some of its hidden gems.

Ethan's demeanor softens as he moves closer, his voice lowering to a conspiratorial whisper. "You know, for all your talk about my reputation, you have quite the knack for poking at the edges of my comfort zone."

"Consider it a compliment," I reply, unable to hide my smile. "You're a fascinating subject, and I'm merely doing my job as a writer."

He shakes his head, but I can see the glimmer of amusement dancing in his eyes. "You'll regret it when I take you to the least interesting spots in town."

"Is that a challenge?"

"It might be," he says, feigning indifference, but there's a new energy between us, a shared anticipation that feels electric. The air crackles with possibilities, each moment thick with the promise of discovery and adventure.

Tomorrow, I would dive into the heart of Silver Pines with Ethan as my guide, and who knows what stories would unfurl in the spaces between laughter and banter? With a wink and a grin, I take a sip of my latte, the taste of adventure lingering on my tongue.

The sun hangs low in the sky, casting a warm golden glow over Silver Pines as I arrive at The Maple Leaf Café the next day, anticipation bubbling in my chest. Today is the day Ethan promised to show me around, an invitation wrapped in reluctant charm that has left me buzzing with excitement. I can hardly wait to peel back the layers of this town—and maybe, just maybe, of Ethan himself.

As I push open the door, the familiar jingle welcomes me, and I'm instantly enveloped by the comforting scents of cinnamon and freshly brewed coffee. My heart lifts at the sight of the café, a haven alive with the chatter of regulars and the soft clinking of ceramic cups. I spot Ethan behind the counter, his blue eyes momentarily lost in the grind of the espresso machine. For a heartbeat, I admire the way the sunlight catches his hair, a halo of warm chestnut that almost softens his otherwise serious demeanor.

"Ready for your grand tour?" he asks, barely glancing up as he pours the frothy milk with precision, clearly caught up in his work.

"Absolutely! I brought my notebook, just in case I stumble upon any poetic revelations about you," I reply, slipping into my seat as I set my things down, eager to dive into whatever adventure awaits us.

Ethan finally looks at me, a skeptical eyebrow raised. "You're not planning to write a best-seller based on my life story, are you? Because I assure you, it involves far less drama and far more coffee stains."

"Drama is overrated," I shoot back, my smile playful. "But you must admit, a little intrigue wouldn't hurt. How about a secret hideaway or a scandalous town rumor?"

He laughs, the sound surprising and rich, and I feel a flutter of triumph. "Well, if you're set on secrets, we might need to head to the old library first. There's an ancient story about a treasure hidden somewhere in town, though most people just think it's an old wives' tale."

I lean in, curiosity piqued. "A treasure? Now that's the kind of story I can work with!"

With that, Ethan slips on his jacket, the heavy fabric giving him an air of purpose as we step outside into the crisp autumn air. The town unfolds around us, vibrant and alive. Golden leaves flutter down from the trees like confetti celebrating the season, and I can feel the energy thrumming in the air, a tangible excitement that seems to hum in my bones.

As we stroll down Main Street, Ethan points out little details—each window displays lovingly crafted decorations, and the historical buildings whisper tales of days gone by. I capture snippets of our conversation, the witty back-and-forth serving as the perfect backdrop for the unfolding scenery.

"You know," I say, glancing sideways at him, "I didn't expect a café owner to be so knowledgeable about local lore. Do you moonlight as a historian?"

Ethan chuckles, his hands tucked deep into his pockets. "Only when the coffee rush isn't overwhelming. But the townsfolk love a good story, and I've been around long enough to hear a few."

"Like the one about the treasure?" I press, excitement bubbling to the surface.

He glances at me, a mischievous glint in his eye. "Well, the rumor is that it's hidden somewhere in the old library, but no one's found it yet. Maybe it's protected by ghosts or something."

"Or perhaps it's just a clever ploy to keep curious tourists like me entertained."

"Either way, it sounds like a perfect way to spend a chilly afternoon," he admits, and I can see a hint of eagerness creeping into his expression, as if he's reluctantly beginning to enjoy himself.

As we near the library, the historic building looms ahead, its stone façade draped in creeping vines and moss. It exudes an air of forgotten magic, a sense that something remarkable could linger within. Ethan pushes the heavy door open, and a musty aroma greets us like an old friend.

"Welcome to the treasure trove of Silver Pines," he announces, his tone laced with mock grandeur.

"Where's the map?" I ask, looking around at the towering shelves crammed with books, their spines faded but proud.

"Maps are overrated," he counters, strolling deeper into the room. "Sometimes the best discoveries come when you least expect them."

I follow him, glancing at the titles that line the shelves. History, adventure, romance—all waiting to be explored. The quiet rustle of pages being turned echoes softly, mingling with the hushed whispers of patrons lost in their own worlds.

"Here," Ethan says, pulling a heavy volume from the shelf and brushing off the dust. "This is where the treasure story begins. It's an old journal belonging to one of the town founders." He flips through the pages, his brow furrowing. "It's filled with sketches and notes. Apparently, he was quite the character."

I lean over his shoulder, peering at the delicate ink strokes that tell stories of the town's beginnings. "This is incredible," I breathe, the past feeling close enough to touch. "Do you think anyone's ever tried to find the treasure?"

"People have tried," he admits, closing the book with a thud. "But I think they're missing a crucial detail."

"What's that?"

"The journal speaks in riddles," he says, a smirk forming on his lips. "And riddles have a way of leading you in circles."

"Sounds like a challenge to me!" I declare, a thrill running through me at the prospect of unearthing a mystery. "Let's solve it! What's the first clue?"

Ethan hesitates, the playful glint in his eyes faltering for a moment, a flicker of something darker passing over his face. "You should be careful with riddles. They can lead to unexpected places."

I pause, the weight of his words sinking in. "Is that your way of warning me off this treasure hunt?"

"No, it's a warning to tread lightly." He glances toward the window, where the last rays of sunlight are fading. "Things aren't always what they seem."

Before I can press him further, the door swings open with a loud creak, and a sudden gust of wind sends a shiver through the library. A figure enters, cloaked in shadows, and I instinctively take a step back. The newcomer's eyes sweep over us, an intensity that seems to flicker in the dim light.

"Ethan," the figure says, voice low and gravelly. "We need to talk."

The shift in Ethan's posture is immediate; tension radiates from him like a live wire. "Not now, Jasper. I'm busy."

The air grows thick, the comfortable warmth of the library turning cold. My heart pounds as I watch the two men lock gazes, a silent battle playing out before me.

"You're running out of time. The past isn't as buried as you think," Jasper warns, a chilling undertone threading through his words.

The atmosphere crackles with an urgency I can't quite grasp, and I feel the hair on the back of my neck stand on end. "What's going on?" I ask, stepping closer, unable to shake the feeling that something important is unfolding right before my eyes.

Ethan's jaw tightens, his blue eyes narrowing. "It's nothing you need to worry about," he replies, but the uncertainty in his tone leaves me unsettled.

"Let's go outside and talk," Jasper insists, glancing at me as if gauging whether I'm a threat or a distraction.

"Not in front of her," Ethan says sharply, his protectiveness igniting a rush of adrenaline within me.

"I'll be fine," I interject, desperate to understand the tension crackling between them. "Just tell me what's happening."

But the words die on my lips as Ethan turns to me, the weight of his gaze heavy with unspoken words. "You might want to sit this one out."

And just like that, the warmth of the library fades, leaving me standing on the precipice of a revelation I didn't know I was ready for. I sense that whatever secrets lie between these walls, they are about to unfold, and I'm caught right in the middle of it all.

Chapter 2: A Stormy Encounter

The autumn winds whipped around the quaint town, carrying the crisp scent of falling leaves mixed with the earthy promise of rain. A week had slipped through my fingers since I arrived, and the anticipation for the Harvest Festival filled the air with a vibrancy that danced around the laughter and chatter in The Maple Leaf. I nestled into my usual corner, a cozy nook with mismatched cushions that had long absorbed the whispers and secrets of patrons past. My notebook lay open, pages ready to capture the stories swirling around me, much like the steam curling from my cup of chai.

As I penned a particularly poignant line about the colors of the season, the door swung open with a dramatic flourish, announcing the arrival of a storm that had apparently been waiting just outside, biding its time. The sudden gust sent leaves spiraling in, swirling around like a confetti of chaos. And there he was—Ethan—standing in the threshold, drenched from head to toe, the rain clinging to him like a second skin. His dark hair hung in disarray, a wild mop that framed his sharp features, and the way his eyes narrowed against the storm made him look almost fierce.

I stifled a chuckle, unable to resist the image of a soggy hero making his entrance. But the laughter quickly fled when I caught the fire in his gaze as he stormed to the counter. "What a delightful day," he muttered, voice dripping with sarcasm, as he shook off droplets like a wet dog. I exchanged glances with the barista, who raised an eyebrow and stifled a grin. My heart raced, a wild dance of confusion and excitement. The tension that had marked our previous encounters felt charged in the air, palpable enough to make my skin prickle.

Ignoring my growing curiosity about the man who seemed both infuriating and fascinating, I focused on my notes, hoping to shut out the looming shadow of his presence. But there was something electric about the way he commanded the room, even in his dampened state. It was as if the storm had carried his brooding spirit with it, the promise of thunder rolling in with every terse word he exchanged with the barista.

As the rain beat against the windows, painting a blurred picture of the world outside, I tried to lose myself in my writing. Words flowed in and out like the storm itself—sometimes fierce, sometimes gentle, but always filled with emotion. Then, as if the universe had conspired to entwine our fates, Ethan's dark silhouette loomed closer, and I glanced up, my pulse quickening. He stood before me, holding out a paper-wrapped muffin, warm and slightly crumpled.

"Thought you might like this. A peace offering, or maybe a bribe. Your choice," he said, his tone teasing but softened by an unexpected sincerity. The muffin was chocolate chip, my favorite. How did he know? The tension between us thickened, a taut wire ready to snap, but I couldn't help but smile at the absurdity of it all. Here was this man, who I had sparred with in words and glares, now offering me a simple pastry like a truce had been declared.

"Very generous of you," I replied, my voice lighter than I intended, almost playful. "Does this mean I'm forgiven for, you know, existing?"

"Forgiveness is overrated. Besides, you're the one who keeps interrupting my peace with your relentless chatter about... whatever it is you're writing," he shot back, his lips quirking in a smirk that nearly melted the annoyance I held onto.

I took the muffin, the warmth radiating through the paper, and felt a surge of warmth within me too, an unexpected flicker of attraction. The storm outside raged on, but here, in this little café, amidst the hum of conversations and the scent of coffee mingling with baked goods, the world felt contained, as if we were on our own little island, and for a moment, I allowed myself to revel in the possibility.

"Maybe I'm just trying to inspire you to write something more exciting than your grocery list," I countered, my wry tone matching his. "You might actually enjoy it if you stopped brooding long enough to give it a chance."

He chuckled, the sound rich and genuine, sending a thrill through me. "I assure you, there's a whole world of excitement out there. I'm just choosing to ignore it for now."

"Smart choice. Ignoring the world can often lead to more interesting stories," I replied, raising an eyebrow. "Besides, who wouldn't want to stay tucked away here, avoiding the storm?"

The conversation twisted and turned like the winds outside, each playful jab revealing layers of our personalities. It felt different, lighter. With each passing moment, I found myself drawn deeper into the depths of his dark eyes, which flickered with mischief, revealing a side of him I hadn't seen before. The tension transformed from hostility to something charged, an undercurrent I couldn't quite name but could certainly feel.

As the rain lashed against the café's windows, drowning out the world, I couldn't help but ponder the inexplicable bond forming between us, sparked in the midst of a storm. The taste of the muffin was sweet, mingling with the warmth growing in my chest. The idea that this reluctant friendship could blossom into something more filled my thoughts with a mix of trepidation and excitement.

With the storm raging outside, I suddenly realized that perhaps, just perhaps, this place—and this man—were more than mere distractions from my writing. They could be the very catalyst that turned my life into the vibrant story I had long sought to create.

The storm outside raged like a tempestuous lover, thrashing against the walls of The Maple Leaf as I settled deeper into my seat, the muffin warming my hands as I took small bites, savoring the chocolate melting within. I could almost feel the café's comforting embrace wrapping around me like a soft blanket. The cacophony of raindrops against the windows created a soothing rhythm, a symphony that accompanied my thoughts as I returned to my notes, but my focus kept drifting back to Ethan.

He was perched at the far end of the counter, his brows knitted together as he sipped a steaming cup of coffee, the steam curling around him like an aura of mystique. There was an undeniable charm to his disheveled appearance—clothes clinging in all the wrong places, hair sticking up as if defying gravity itself, and yet it only added to his allure. I shook my head, scolding myself for allowing such thoughts to slip into my mind. This man had proven to be as irritable as a cat with a bath, and yet, something about him was as enticing as the very muffins I was currently devouring.

"You know, you look like you could use a raincoat and an attitude adjustment," I called out, the playful tone escaping my lips before I could rein it in.

He shot me a glance, surprise flickering across his features before he allowed a small smirk to break through. "And you look like you could use a better choice in snacks," he retorted, lifting his muffin-less plate in mock accusation. "What's the point of being here if you're not trying the pumpkin spice special?"

"Oh, please," I replied, feigning indignation. "Pumpkin spice is basically a drink that pretends to be coffee but ends up tasting like a candle. I'm all about the chocolate."

His laughter rolled across the café, deep and warm, sending a jolt through me. I found myself smiling back, the edges of my frustration blurring in the haze of our banter. I leaned back, daring myself to enjoy this unexpected moment of connection.

"Fair point. But if you insist on sticking to the chocolaty delights, at least let me offer you my tried-and-true method for getting through stormy days," he said, leaning in slightly, his voice dropping to a conspiratorial whisper. "It involves coffee, a good book, and absolutely no pumpkin spice. The key is to remain completely unbothered by the elements."

"Unbothered, huh? Sounds awfully optimistic for someone who just walked in drenched," I shot back, gesturing to his wet jeans. "Unless you count the waterlogged dog look as unbothered."

He chuckled, the sound brightening the dim café, and for a moment, we were just two people sharing a moment of laughter, the storm outside forgotten.

"I'd say I'm embracing the wet dog aesthetic," he quipped. "It adds to my mysterious aura, don't you think? Women love a man with an air of danger."

"Danger? I thought you were just a guy with bad hair and a muffin deficit," I replied, arching an eyebrow. "Though I suppose the rain adds an element of unpredictability. Perhaps it's a bit alluring."

"Ah, so you do find me alluring," he teased, leaning back with an exaggerated air of satisfaction.

"Now you're just putting words in my mouth," I said, rolling my eyes, though I could feel a blush creeping up my cheeks. "Besides, allure is subjective. If you're willing to brave the storm for a pastry, you might just be desperate."

"Desperate? Hardly. I'm merely a connoisseur of baked goods," he retorted, his grin broadening. "Now, how about we settle this once and for all? A bake-off—your favorite chocolate muffin against my pumpkin spice. Winner gets bragging rights, and the loser has to buy the coffee."

"Now we're talking! But if you lose, I want that raincoat of yours as a prize," I said, gesturing at the damp fabric clinging to him. "It's only fair."

"Deal," he replied, extending a hand, and I shook it with an air of mock solemnity. A lightness filled the air, a fresh current replacing the earlier tension. For all the irritation I had felt during our previous exchanges, I now recognized a spark of something delightful simmering beneath the surface, transforming our sparring into a kind of game.

As the rain continued to pelt against the windows, I felt a familiar warmth spread through me—not just from the muffin or the steam curling from my cup, but from the possibility of what lay ahead. Perhaps the storm wasn't merely an annoyance but a catalyst, an unexpected twist that could change everything I thought I knew about this small town and about the man sitting across from me.

"Okay, Mr. Connoisseur," I said, leaning forward, my heart racing at the prospect of what this bake-off could mean for us. "Let's get our baking aprons ready. But I should warn you, I'm fiercely competitive. You might want to practice your best puppy-dog eyes for when you inevitably lose."

"I'll be sure to bring my A-game, then," he said, that infuriating smirk returning to his face, igniting something deep within me that felt tantalizingly unpredictable.

The rain began to taper off, the storm's fury settling into a gentle patter. Outside, the world was transformed; puddles reflected the café's warm light, creating a shimmering mosaic that felt like a promise. Just beyond the threshold of our banter and laughter, life continued, and I couldn't shake the feeling that everything was shifting—around me, between us.

Ethan's presence filled the space with an energy that crackled in the air, drawing me closer. I was caught in a web of laughter, muffins, and shared stories, the storm no longer a backdrop but a part of this unfolding narrative. Who knew that within the heart of a tempest, a delightful chaos could unfurl? And as I watched him playfully roll his eyes, I felt a rush of excitement for what was to come.

The atmosphere in The Maple Leaf crackled with a mix of laughter and anticipation, fueled by the promise of the Harvest Festival. After our impromptu bake-off challenge, Ethan and I slipped into a comfortable rhythm, our playful banter taking on a life of its own. The storm that had previously battered the windows now lingered in the background, a distant echo to our spirited exchange. As I savored the last bite of my muffin, I couldn't shake the feeling that something significant was unfolding between us.

"You realize this means war, right?" Ethan said, a mock-seriousness etched across his features. He leaned back in his chair, fingers steepled as if plotting a grand strategy. "My pumpkin spice muffin has won awards, you know."

"Is that so?" I replied, crossing my arms defiantly. "I think you just made that up. Besides, my chocolate muffin is practically legendary. It'll be like David versus Goliath, only tastier."

"Legends are often born from ridiculous challenges," he shot back, his eyes glimmering with mischief. "And if I win, you owe me a coffee date."

I nearly choked on my drink, the unexpectedness of his words sending a thrill through me. "A coffee date? And what if I win?"

"Then I will accept your defeat graciously, but still demand that coffee date," he replied, unabashedly confident.

"Seems fair. But we should raise the stakes a little higher," I proposed, my mind racing with the delicious possibilities. "If I win, you have to agree to help me with my book. I could use a little inspiration, and maybe a few of those dangerously good looks of yours."

"Dangerously good looks? Is that what you think of me?" He leaned closer, the tease in his voice palpable. "I'm not sure I can live up to that kind of hype."

"Oh, please," I replied, waving my hand dismissively. "I'm sure you're well aware of your effect on unsuspecting women. But really, I just need someone to keep me on track. You might just be the perfect distraction."

His gaze lingered on me for a moment, something unspoken passing between us. It was as if he could see through the layers I'd carefully crafted, the hints of vulnerability lurking just beneath my playful façade. I quickly redirected my thoughts. "But if you want to win this bake-off, you might need to brush up on your baking skills. Otherwise, I can't be held responsible for the repercussions."

"Don't worry, I'm a natural at everything," he declared, a laugh dancing in his eyes. "Especially when it comes to impressing stubborn women."

I feigned annoyance, tapping my fingers on the table. "You're going to have to prove that, Mr. Natural. How about we meet at the farmer's market tomorrow? I'll gather my supplies, and you can show up with your... award-winning pumpkin spice mix."

"Challenge accepted," he said, raising his coffee cup in salute. The storm outside had settled into a soft drizzle, but my heart raced with a whirlwind of excitement. I was tempted to indulge in this banter, but as I met his gaze, I felt an undercurrent of something deeper, something I wasn't quite ready to confront.

As our conversation flowed, the café buzzed around us, filled with the comforting sounds of laughter and the aroma of freshly brewed coffee mingling with spices. I felt myself drawn to the warmth in Ethan's laughter, each chuckle bringing us closer together, yet I couldn't ignore the flickering unease bubbling beneath the surface.

Then, as if the universe decided to intervene, the door swung open once more, letting in a rush of cold air. In walked a woman, her presence commanding and electric. She was tall, her dark hair slicked back, and she had a look that screamed confidence mixed with a hint of trouble. I felt a shiver of unease ripple through me as she swept her gaze across the café before locking onto Ethan.

"Ethan," she called out, her voice smooth and enticing, cutting through our playful atmosphere like a knife.

His demeanor shifted instantly, the easy grin faltering as he straightened in his chair. I felt a strange pang of jealousy twist in my stomach, and the warmth between us dimmed, replaced by an uninvited tension.

"Leah," he replied, the single word carrying a weight I didn't quite understand. "What are you doing here?"

"I heard you were back in town," she said, her smile bright but with an edge that hinted at something more. "I thought we could catch up. It's been ages, hasn't it?"

I exchanged glances with Ethan, searching for answers in the sudden shift of his expression. The easy camaraderie we'd shared felt suddenly fragile, as if a storm was brewing not just outside but right here between us.

"I'm... busy," he said, his voice tight, a shadow passing over his features.

"Oh, come on," she pressed, stepping closer. "You know you want to. I've missed our little adventures. Don't tell me you've gone soft on me."

Adventure? The word hung in the air, drawing my thoughts to dark corners I hadn't anticipated. It felt like a challenge, a subtle spark of rivalry igniting in the space between us.

"I have plans," he insisted, glancing at me as if seeking an ally. "I'm meeting someone."

Leah's eyes narrowed, her attention shifting to me with a predatory glint. "Is that so? Must be a very important meeting."

Before I could respond, a flicker of confusion crossed Ethan's face, and I felt the ground beneath me shift. The warmth and comfort of our earlier connection evaporated, replaced by the cold weight of the unknown. Leah's presence felt like an intruder, a storm that had crept in unexpectedly, turning my excitement into uncertainty.

"Yeah, it's important," Ethan replied, a hint of defensiveness creeping into his tone. "But, Leah, maybe we can catch up later?"

"Oh, darling, I'm not going anywhere," she said, her voice sweet but with an underlying sharpness that sent a shiver down my spine. "And you wouldn't want to miss out on what I have planned for tonight, would you?"

An invisible wall seemed to erect itself between Ethan and me, and I could feel the air thickening with tension. I couldn't shake the sense that something was off, that this encounter was far more significant than just a reunion between friends.

My heart pounded, uncertainty clawing at me. Would this new development change everything? I glanced at Ethan, his expression caught somewhere between annoyance and something darker. The connection we'd built felt precarious, teetering on the edge of a cliff, and the storm outside mirrored the tumult within me.

"Listen, Leah—" Ethan started, but she cut him off, a smile still plastered on her face, one that didn't reach her eyes.

I couldn't hold back any longer. "Maybe you should go," I said, surprising even myself with the firmness of my voice. "Ethan and I were in the middle of something."

Ethan looked at me, his eyes wide, as if he hadn't expected my sudden assertiveness. Leah's smile faltered, but she quickly recovered, her gaze flicking between us, calculating.

"Very cute," she said, her tone dripping with sarcasm. "But I think it's time Ethan and I had a little chat."

My heart raced, caught in a storm of emotions as I sensed the tension shifting into something uncharted. What had begun as a playful encounter was rapidly spiraling into something I couldn't quite grasp. And as I met Ethan's gaze, searching for reassurance, I knew one thing for certain—nothing would ever be the same again.

Chapter 3: The Harvest Festival

The town of Maplewood shimmered with the glow of autumn, the leaves a riot of orange and gold as if the trees themselves were dressed for a celebration. The air crackled with the scent of cinnamon and roasted pumpkin, promising a Harvest Festival that would be whispered about for years. As I stepped out of my small apartment above the café, a gentle breeze tousled my hair, carrying with it the laughter of children and the cheerful bellowing of vendors setting up their stalls. I couldn't help but smile; this was the kind of charm I had yearned for when I fled the clamor of the city. But now, I was learning that charm often came with its own set of challenges.

The café had transformed overnight. Ethan had covered the windows with burlap and bright paper cutouts of pumpkins and scarecrows, creating an inviting atmosphere that beckoned passersby inside. I couldn't help but admire his handiwork as I entered, the warm glow of string lights illuminating the cozy room. The barista station was overflowing with all things apple — apple cider, apple pie, and even an apple-infused latte that had become the star of our menu. But beneath the festive surface, the tension was palpable, like the stillness before a storm.

"Are you ready for this?" Ethan asked, leaning over the counter, his brow slightly furrowed. I noticed a sprinkle of flour dusting the tip of his nose, an endearing remnant of his last baking venture. There was something about him that made my heart flutter, but I quickly reminded myself that I was here to work, not to lose my mind over the café's handsome owner.

"Ready as I'll ever be," I replied, flashing a grin that I hoped masked my rising nerves. "What's the plan?"

He chuckled, a deep, rich sound that made my knees feel weak. "Just the usual chaos. We'll start with the cider and then move to the pies. Diane will be hovering like a hawk, so stay sharp."

As if summoned by our conversation, Diane swooped in, her presence as formidable as a summer thundercloud. Clad in a tweed jacket that looked like it had been passed down through generations, she exuded an air of authority that made most people tiptoe around her. "You two, be careful with that," she said, pointing to a stack of pie crusts that I had just laid out. "You don't want the crusts to dry out before the filling is in."

"Thanks, Diane," I replied, forcing a smile that barely concealed my annoyance. "I'll keep that in mind."

Diane's gaze lingered on me, a mix of scrutiny and disdain. "We don't need any of your city slicker ways ruining our traditions. This festival is sacred."

"Oh, please," I shot back, unable to help myself. "If you think I'm here to tear apart the fabric of this quaint little town, you're sorely mistaken. I'm just trying to survive your version of a culinary gauntlet."

Ethan's laughter erupted, echoing around the café. Diane glared, her lips pursing into a tight line, and I felt a surge of satisfaction at having ruffled her feathers. The air shifted slightly, our playful banter acting like a shield against her sharp words.

As the day wore on, the café became a whirlwind of activity. The sound of laughter mingled with the clatter of cups and the scent of baking pies wrapped around us like a warm blanket. Ethan and I worked side by side, stealing glances and quick touches that sent electric shocks through me. Every brush of our hands felt like a dare, a challenge to the unspoken tension simmering beneath the surface.

With each pie that emerged from the oven, I felt my confidence grow. "You know, I didn't think I'd ever enjoy baking this much," I admitted as I tossed a handful of cinnamon into the bowl, my fingers warm and sticky. "Back in the city, everything was about quick fixes and shortcuts."

"Here, we take our time," Ethan said, his voice low and sincere. "It's about the experience, not just the end result."

Just then, the first wave of festival-goers swept through the door, laughter ringing like chimes. Children darted around, their faces painted with bright colors, while couples clutched steaming cups of cider, their cheeks flushed with excitement. I watched as a little girl with wild curls tugged at her mother's sleeve, her eyes wide with wonder at the colorful decorations and the delicious treats.

"Look at them," I said, my heart swelling at the sight. "They're like kids in a candy store."

Ethan leaned against the counter, his eyes warm and glinting with admiration. "This is what it's all about. Community, tradition, and a little bit of magic."

In that moment, everything felt right. The laughter, the food, the vibrant colors swirling around us; it was all part of a tapestry woven from threads of nostalgia and hope. As we exchanged smiles, the atmosphere between us thickened, transforming into something tangible, something I could taste in the air.

But just as I dared to lean into that magic, Diane swooped in again, her sharp voice cutting through the warmth like a winter chill. "I hope you've remembered to stock up on the proper ingredients. We can't afford any mistakes this year."

"Don't worry, Diane," Ethan replied smoothly, his voice steady as he met her gaze. "We've got everything under control."

But I could sense the unease in the air, the unspoken question lingering between us. What if we weren't prepared? What if the festival fell short of everyone's expectations? As I glanced at Ethan, his brow furrowed in concentration, I felt a surge of determination rise within me.

We would make this work. We would prove Diane and anyone else who doubted us wrong. Together, we would create a festival worth remembering.

As the sun dipped low in the sky, casting a golden hue over Maplewood, the atmosphere thickened with anticipation. The festival was more than just a celebration; it was the town's heartbeat, pulsing with the energy of camaraderie and shared history. I stepped outside the café, glancing around at the stalls being set up. There were booths draped in vibrant fabrics, vendors arranging handmade goods, and the tantalizing aroma of roasted corn wafting through the air, mingling with the sweetness of caramel apples. My heart danced at the thought of what lay ahead.

Ethan emerged from the café with an armful of freshly baked pies, a mix of apple, pecan, and pumpkin that filled the air with a buttery, sugary fragrance. He plopped them onto a table outside, the sun illuminating the golden crusts like little works of art. "Just wait until you see the faces when they get a taste of these," he said, his eyes sparkling with enthusiasm.

"I can't believe you're letting me help with this," I said, glancing at the row of pies with both pride and disbelief. "What's next? Am I going to be your official taste tester?"

Ethan smirked, leaning closer, the playful glint in his eyes making my pulse quicken. "You're already the official chaos coordinator. Tasting is just a bonus."

We chuckled, the sound mingling with the distant laughter of children playing in the grassy field nearby. It was a moment filled with warmth and possibility, but just as quickly, it was sliced through by Diane's sharp voice cutting into our lightheartedness.

"Ethan, those pies need to be arranged more strategically. We don't want anyone getting confused. You know how the town can be." She crossed her arms, her brows knitting together in disapproval as she inspected our work. "What would you do without me?"

"Oh, probably just serve the pies in a more relaxed manner," I replied, my tone laced with a faux innocence. "You know, like having fun?"

Diane's glare could have frozen a bonfire, but Ethan's laughter burst forth again, breaking the tension that had momentarily settled over us. "Relaxed is not in the Harvest Festival handbook," he said, shaking his head. "But maybe we could add a little spontaneity, just to keep things interesting?"

Diane rolled her eyes, but I caught a hint of a smile at the corners of her mouth. The weight of her scrutiny felt less suffocating in that moment, and for the first time, I sensed that maybe, just maybe, she wasn't entirely immune to the joy around her.

As the sun continued its descent, the café buzzed with activity. Ethan and I moved deftly between customers, pouring cups of steaming cider and dishing out slices of pie while keeping our playful banter alive. The laughter flowed freely, a beautiful distraction from the underlying tension of Diane's watchful presence. I could see why Ethan loved this place; the vibrancy was infectious, igniting a fire within me that I hadn't realized had been simmering beneath the surface.

"Next up, we need to get the bonfire going," Ethan said, wiping his hands on his apron as he surveyed the gathering crowd. "It's tradition, and nothing brings people together like a good fire."

"I can manage that," I declared, feeling a swell of confidence. "I've done my fair share of campfires. Just don't expect me to sing any campfire songs. My vocal talents are best reserved for the shower."

Ethan chuckled, his gaze softening. "What a shame. I was looking forward to a duet."

"Just wait until you hear my rendition of 'Kumbaya.' It'll be the talk of the festival."

As we strolled toward the designated bonfire area, a chill danced in the air, mixing with the growing excitement of the festival. The flames crackled to life, illuminating the faces of the townsfolk who gathered around. They were a patchwork of smiles and laughter, reflecting a sense of community that had me feeling both welcomed and strangely out of place.

Just as I began to lose myself in the warmth of the fire, a sharp scream cut through the night, shattering the jovial atmosphere. My heart raced as I turned toward the sound, a young girl clutching a half-eaten candy apple, her eyes wide with terror. "Mom! There's a snake!"

A collective gasp rippled through the crowd as heads turned, eyes darting in all directions. Diane's expression shifted from irritation to concern, and I felt an adrenaline rush that drowned out the surrounding chatter. This was chaos.

"Where?" Ethan shouted, his protective instincts kicking in as he scanned the ground. I couldn't help but admire his calmness amidst the sudden panic.

"Over there!" the girl pointed, her finger shaking as she backed away from the bonfire.

Without thinking, I followed her gaze. There, nestled in the grass near the bonfire's edge, lay a long, slender shape that looked more like a garden hose than the slithering creature I dreaded. But as I stepped closer, the unmistakable flicker of scales caught the firelight. "That's definitely a snake," I murmured, glancing back at Ethan, whose face paled slightly.

"Stay back," he warned the crowd, and I could see the townsfolk shift uneasily, their laughter evaporating like morning mist.

"What do we do?" I asked, my heart racing as I wrestled with the urge to flee or to face the creature head-on.

"Call Peter. He'll know how to handle it," he said, motioning to the local animal control officer, who was hovering nearby with his phone already in hand.

Diane, surprisingly, stepped forward, her voice steady. "Everyone, gather around. It's just a snake. We'll take care of this. No need to panic."

To my surprise, a sense of calm washed over the crowd as Diane took charge, her authoritative presence pulling everyone together. I admired her unexpected bravery, and as I watched the townspeople rally, I felt a swell of pride for this community.

With Peter on the scene, we watched in silence as he approached the snake with practiced ease, coaxing it gently before safely securing it in a container. A sense of relief washed over us, the collective tension dissipating like steam from a kettle.

Ethan turned to me, his expression a mix of admiration and amusement. "Well, that was quite the excitement. You handled yourself pretty well back there."

"Just another day in Maplewood, right?" I replied, my heart still pounding but a smile breaking through. "Next time, maybe we'll add 'snake wrangling' to the list of festival activities."

As laughter began to ripple through the crowd again, I realized that the festival was not just about the pies or the bonfire; it was about community and resilience, about moments that brought us together, both sweet and chaotic. I stood beside Ethan, feeling the warmth of the fire and the glow of camaraderie enveloping us like a soft, warm blanket, grateful for the unexpected adventures that made Maplewood feel like home.

The laughter of the festival-goers swelled around us, creating a vibrant tapestry of joy that seemed to blanket the cool evening air. The bonfire crackled in the background, its flames dancing like mischievous spirits, casting flickering shadows that played across the faces of the gathered townsfolk. It was the kind of scene that felt almost cinematic, like something plucked straight from a feel-good movie, and for a moment, I let myself revel in the simplicity of it all.

But as the excitement began to settle back into the familiar rhythm of the festival, I couldn't shake the feeling that something was brewing just beneath the surface. Ethan stood beside me, his eyes reflecting the firelight and a warmth that ignited something deep within me. We exchanged a glance filled with unspoken words, a connection that pulsed like a live wire between us. I could sense the lingering tension from earlier, that almost-kiss hanging in the air like the last note of a song.

"Looks like the snake incident brought everyone together," I remarked, trying to fill the silence with something light, my heart racing with a mixture of exhilaration and apprehension.

"Yeah, who knew that a little crisis could spark such camaraderie?" he replied, his lips curling into that boyish grin that sent my stomach fluttering. "Just imagine the festival without the drama."

"Right? We'd all be standing around discussing pie crust techniques instead of fearing for our lives. Talk about a dull evening," I quipped, my attempt at humor lightening the mood.

The fire crackled, sending up sparks into the night sky as children darted around, their laughter mingling with the sounds of music drifting from a nearby band. I caught sight of Diane, now fully engaged with a group of older ladies, her stern demeanor momentarily softened as she shared a story that drew chuckles from the crowd. Maybe this festival was working its magic on her after all.

"Are you having fun?" Ethan asked, turning to me with genuine curiosity, his brow slightly furrowed as he studied my expression.

I paused, letting his question hang in the air for a moment, savoring the reality that surrounded me—the warmth of the fire, the energy of the crowd, and, most importantly, the connection I felt with him. "I am," I finally replied, the truth spilling from my lips. "More than I expected."

His eyes lit up, a mixture of relief and delight flashing across his features. "Good. Because I was starting to worry I'd dragged you out of the city just to suffer through an autumn gathering."

"Are you kidding? This is way more entertaining than my usual Saturday nights," I said, half-joking. "Usually, I'm on the couch, scrolling through social media, and pretending to care about my neighbor's cat videos."

Ethan laughed, a deep sound that vibrated through the air. "We should make a pact. No more cat videos. Only live-action drama. Like snakes and pie contests."

As we bantered, a sudden commotion erupted from a nearby booth, drawing our attention. A cluster of festival-goers had gathered, their faces lit with excitement as they surrounded a table laden with jars of homemade jams and preserves. I recognized the vibrant red of raspberry and the golden hue of peach, but what truly caught my eye was the old woman standing behind the table, her hands deftly maneuvering a jar filled with a shimmering, deep green concoction.

"What is that?" I asked, curiosity piquing my interest as I leaned closer to Ethan.

"That," he said, his voice laced with caution, "is a mystery jar. No one really knows what's in it. It's a local legend."

I raised an eyebrow, my intrigue deepening. "A mystery jar? Are we sure that's not just a clever way to get people to buy something?"

"Exactly! But you have to admit, it's a little thrilling," he replied, his eyes sparkling with mischief. "Let's go investigate."

Together, we pushed through the throng, weaving our way toward the booth. As we approached, the old woman looked up, her eyes twinkling with a knowing glimmer. "Ah, curious souls, are we?" she croaked, her voice as rich as the preserves she offered.

"What's in the mystery jar?" I asked, unable to contain my excitement. "Is it something supernatural?"

"Only if you're brave enough to taste it," she replied, a sly smile dancing across her lips. "They say it's a blend of the rarest ingredients. Some call it luck; others think it brings mischief."

I shared a glance with Ethan, a mix of trepidation and excitement swirling in my stomach. "What do you think?" I asked, my heart racing at the idea of indulging in something unknown.

"Why not?" he said, stepping forward. "What's life without a little risk?"

Before I could voice my hesitation, the woman handed Ethan the jar, her fingers brushing against his with an intensity that sent a shiver down my spine. "Here, young man. Your fate awaits."

Ethan twisted off the lid, and the pungent aroma wafted up, a blend of sweet and savory that danced tantalizingly in the air. The crowd fell silent, anticipation hanging thick as he dipped a spoon into the jar. He raised it to his lips, eyes sparkling with mischief.

"On the count of three?" he teased, glancing at me, his expression a mix of daring and delight.

"Wait!" I exclaimed, half-laughing, half-worried. "What if it's awful?"

"Then we'll have a funny story to tell. Either way, I'm in," he replied with a wink, his carefree spirit irresistible.

"One... two... three!" he declared, tilting the spoon back as the crowd erupted into cheers and laughter.

His face transformed in an instant, eyes widening as he froze mid-swallow, the spoon hanging perilously from his lips. "What... what is this?" he spluttered, laughter bubbling up around us.

"Do you feel lucky?" I teased, my voice laced with mock seriousness, though my heart raced with worry and delight.

But before he could answer, his expression shifted from confusion to something darker. He staggered back, dropping the spoon as his hand flew to his throat. "Oh no... I think—"

The laughter of the crowd faded into a cacophony of gasps and murmurs as I watched, horrified, as Ethan's face turned pale. "Ethan?" My voice trembled, panic rising in my chest. "Are you okay?"

He clutched the table, his breathing rapid and shallow, and just as I reached out to steady him, a strange stillness enveloped the festival. All eyes were on us, and an electric tension crackled in the air. It felt as though time had stopped, every heartbeat resonating with a foreboding sense of dread.

Then, without warning, Ethan's eyes rolled back, and he collapsed, sending the jars of preserves tumbling to the ground, shattering and spilling their contents across the grass. The festival's laughter turned into chaos, shouts mingling with the crackling of the bonfire, and in that moment, as I rushed to his side, I realized that the Harvest Festival was about to unveil its true, darker nature.

Chapter 4: Secrets Beneath the Surface

The sun hung high in the sky, casting a golden hue over the small town of Maplewood, where the air thrummed with the energy of the annual Harvest Festival. Laughter and the scent of caramel apples mingled in the breeze, creating an intoxicating atmosphere that should have lifted my spirits. Yet, in the midst of the celebration, I felt the sharp sting of tension. Ethan stood at the edge of the square, his eyes fixed on the crowd but clearly miles away. His usual scowl was softened by the gentle warmth of the sun, but the tight set of his jaw suggested that a storm brewed beneath the surface.

I watched him for a moment longer, absorbing the way he was both a part of this town and apart from it. His dark hair tousled by the wind, Ethan looked like a man caught in a storm of memories. I could feel the weight of his presence, a heaviness that dulled the laughter around us. It was as if the festival, with all its vibrant colors and jubilant faces, existed in a parallel universe where he could not find solace. My heart twisted at the sight of him, and I found myself drawn to the shadows lurking behind those troubled eyes.

"Hey there! You're not just going to stand there and mope all day, are you?" Diane's voice, buoyant and cheerful, sliced through my thoughts. She was the local event planner, and today she was dressed in an over-the-top floral dress, her sun-kissed skin practically glowing with excitement. She twirled around, a whirlwind of energy, before grabbing my hand and dragging me toward a nearby booth. "Come on! We need to get you a pumpkin spice latte. You can't enjoy the festival on an empty stomach."

As we approached the coffee stall, the warmth of the crowd swelled around me, but my eyes still found Ethan, who had retreated further into his shell. I could hear snippets of laughter and snippets of conversation—people catching up, sharing inside jokes, and indulging in the festival spirit. Yet, the buzz felt muted as I thought of Ethan's hidden pain, a burden he carried alone. It was a stark contrast to the jubilation surrounding us.

"Julia! Look at that scarecrow competition! They've really outdone themselves this year," Diane exclaimed, oblivious to the turmoil swirling in my mind. I managed a smile, nodding as she dragged me along to admire the goofy, straw-stuffed figures lined up in a row. Each one wore a unique expression, some cheerful, others downright comical, yet none could distract me from the ache I felt for Ethan.

"Hey, I think I'll grab lunch," I said, suddenly craving solitude. "I'll catch up with you later." Before she could protest, I slipped away, weaving through the throng of festival-goers until I spotted Clara at one of the picnic tables, her auburn hair glinting in the sunlight. She was the town's sweetheart, a beacon of kindness who radiated warmth. I took a deep breath, steeling myself as I approached her. If anyone could shed light on Ethan's somber disposition, it was his sister.

"Clara! Mind if I join you?" I asked, sliding onto the bench beside her. She looked up, her green eyes sparkling with surprise and delight.

"Julia! Of course! I could use the company." Clara's smile was infectious, but it faded slightly as she glanced toward the festival, her gaze lingering on Ethan. "How's he been treating you?"

"Complicated," I admitted, rubbing my palms against my thighs. "He seems to carry the weight of the world on his shoulders. I just... I want to understand him better."

Clara's expression shifted, a flicker of something—sadness, perhaps?—crossing her face. "You're right. He's been through a lot, more than anyone here knows." She hesitated, as if weighing her words carefully. "We lost our parents a few years ago. A car accident. Ethan took it the hardest. He feels responsible for so much, even things he couldn't control. He puts on this tough exterior, but it's just a mask."

My heart sank at her revelation. I could see now how his grumpiness was a wall, a fortress built to protect himself from a world that had dealt him an unfair hand. "I'm so sorry, Clara. I had no idea. I thought he was just being difficult."

Clara chuckled softly, shaking her head. "That's just him—he thinks if he pushes people away, he won't get hurt again. But it's exhausting for him. I worry he's going to close himself off entirely." She sighed, her expression becoming serious. "If anyone can reach him, it's you. He needs someone who won't give up on him."

The weight of her words settled over me like a thick blanket, pressing against my chest. I felt a sense of responsibility surge within me, a fierce determination to help him break free from the shackles of his sorrow. "I'll do my best," I promised, feeling the resolve solidify in my bones.

Our conversation turned lighter as we discussed the festival, but my mind raced with thoughts of Ethan. I could picture him now, standing alone beneath the fluttering flags and the joyful sounds of the fair. What would it take to break through the wall he had erected around his heart? I finished my meal with Clara, my heart heavy yet hopeful, and vowed to confront the storm brewing within him.

As we walked back toward the festival, I caught sight of Diane, who seemed to have taken it upon herself to orchestrate a dance-off between some locals, her enthusiasm reaching a fever pitch. The sight of her joy sparked a glimmer of mischief in my heart. Perhaps I could use this lighthearted atmosphere to my advantage.

With newfound determination, I approached Ethan, who stood at a distance, arms crossed over his chest, as if trying to physically ward off the festival's cheer. My heart raced, not just from the anticipation of confronting him, but from the possibility that this could change everything between us. "Hey," I called out, my voice slicing through the laughter surrounding us.

He turned, his brow furrowing slightly, and for a brief moment, I thought I saw a flicker of surprise in his eyes. "What do you want?" His tone was gruff, but there was an undercurrent of curiosity.

"Want to join a dance-off?" I asked, a grin spreading across my face. "I promise it'll be fun. Just one dance—no commitments, no judgments."

Ethan raised an eyebrow, skepticism etched across his features. "You think I'm going to dance?"

"Only if you want to show the world your dazzling moves," I teased, trying to lighten the mood.

He hesitated, and in that moment, I could see the internal battle raging within him. Then, just as quickly, his expression hardened. "No, thanks. I'm not in the mood."

Frustration bubbled within me, threatening to spill over. I had fought hard to reach him, but he was still slipping away. "Ethan, you can't hide forever. You deserve to feel joy, to let go of everything weighing you down."

His eyes darkened, the barrier between us thickening once more. "You don't understand. Joy is fleeting. It doesn't last."

"Then create your own," I shot back, the fire in my belly pushing me forward. "What if you tried? What if you found a way to keep it?"

The tension hung in the air, thick and palpable. A flicker of vulnerability crossed his features, but he masked it quickly. "Not everyone gets that chance," he said, his voice lower now, as if he were revealing something he rarely shared.

I stepped closer, emboldened by the connection I felt. "Ethan, let me in. You don't have to face this alone. You can talk to me."

His gaze softened for a moment, and I felt a tremor of hope. But then the walls returned, and he shook his head. "Just... leave it alone, Julia."

Disappointment washed over me, but I wouldn't give up. Not yet. "I won't. I'll keep trying, whether you like it or not."

And with that, I turned away, my heart heavy but resolute. I would break through his defenses. I would help him find the joy he so desperately needed. The festival roared on around me, a vibrant celebration of life, while beneath the surface, secrets and sorrows lurked, waiting to be unearthed.

The festival's energy surged like a wave, washing over the town square with a relentless tide of laughter, music, and the sweet scent of baked goods wafting through the air. I drifted through the throng, my heart still heavy with the weight of Ethan's struggles, my mind a tumult of thoughts. Each vibrant banner that fluttered overhead seemed to mock his pain, a reminder that while the world around us danced in delight, he remained stuck in a loop of sorrow.

I spotted Diane again, her laughter ringing out like a bell as she attempted to corral a group of children into a makeshift game of tug-of-war. The sight was comical, but it also felt like a beacon of normalcy in my otherwise tumultuous thoughts. She caught my eye, waving me over with her customary exuberance.

"Julia! You have to try this!" she said, thrusting a cotton candy stick toward me. The sugary pink cloud spun delicately on a paper cone, looking utterly irresistible. I hesitated, glancing at the flurry of colors and festivities, then decided to indulge in the moment. After all, if I was to confront the shadows in Ethan's life, I needed to keep my spirits up.

"Thanks, Diane! You're like a walking sugar high," I teased, taking a bite. The sweetness burst on my tongue, a brief distraction from the worries swirling in my mind.

"Sugar makes everything better! You should know that by now." She grinned, nudging me playfully. "But seriously, have you talked to Ethan? I saw you two earlier, and it looked intense."

I rolled my eyes, half amused and half exasperated. "Intense might be putting it lightly. More like a full-blown duel with words. He's so stubborn!"

Diane laughed, her eyes sparkling with mischief. "Stubbornness is just another word for passion. And if anyone can get through to him, it's you. Just channel that inner fierce woman of yours!"

"Channeling fierce is exhausting." I sighed, finishing off the cotton candy, its sugary remnants sticking to my fingers. "I feel like I'm trying to breach a fortress armed with only a butter knife."

Diane leaned closer, her voice dropping conspiratorially. "Okay, but what's the plan? You can't let him wallow in his grumpiness forever. Maybe a little bit of sabotage?"

"Sneaky sabotage?" I raised an eyebrow, intrigued. "What do you have in mind?"

"Oh, I don't know," she said, feigning innocence. "Maybe I could invite him to a spontaneous dance-off? Get him laughing a little. Or perhaps challenge him to a pie-eating contest? Nothing says 'open up' like a face full of blueberry pie!"

I chuckled at the image. "You're delightful, you know that? But I doubt Ethan would take kindly to being ambushed with a pie."

"Then we'll just have to find a way to make him see the fun in it," she replied, determination flashing in her eyes. "You're the charming one; you'll think of something. Just remember, the heart of the festival isn't just the corn mazes and pumpkin patches—it's about connection. And maybe, just maybe, it's time you connected with Ethan beyond those brick walls he's built."

I watched her bounce away, her energy infectious, leaving me with an idea—a flicker of inspiration that danced in my mind. I took a deep breath and scanned the square, spotting Clara chatting with a group of friends nearby. With a renewed sense of purpose, I decided I'd need her help to soften Ethan's defenses.

"Hey, Clara!" I called, striding over. She turned, her face brightening when she saw me. "Can we brainstorm a way to lure Ethan into some festival fun? I need all the allies I can get."

Clara's eyes sparkled with understanding, her earlier conversation about Ethan echoing in my mind. "I'm in! He could use a good distraction. He never lets himself relax."

"Okay, hear me out," I said, leaning closer as we walked. "What if we set up a little 'surprise' activity that involves some laughter? Something unexpected."

"What about a scavenger hunt?" Clara suggested, her enthusiasm palpable. "We could have the town involved. It'll be silly and competitive—Ethan won't be able to resist."

"A scavenger hunt it is!" I clapped my hands together, already envisioning the whimsical lists and the chaotic joy that would unfold. "But we need to keep it light-hearted. Maybe mix in some fun town history with goofy tasks? Like finding the oldest pumpkin or the best scarecrow?"

"And we can add a mystery prize!" Clara beamed, her excitement contagious. "Something ridiculous, like a giant rubber chicken or a silly trophy that says 'Best Town Detective.'"

"Perfect!" The idea warmed my heart. Laughter, competition, and a dash of ridiculousness could create the ideal atmosphere to chip away at Ethan's armor. "Let's get this organized before he slips away into the depths of his grumpy lair again."

We set to work, darting around the festival, rallying townsfolk to participate in our whimsical scavenger hunt. With each person we enlisted, my excitement bubbled up like the sparkling cider in the nearby booth. The anticipation grew as we crafted a list of ridiculous tasks that included taking selfies with a gnome statue and finding someone wearing mismatched socks.

As the afternoon sun began to dip, casting a golden light across the square, we convened the participants and explained the rules. I spotted Ethan lingering at the edge of the crowd, arms crossed and brow furrowed, and my heart raced. This was the moment.

Clara nudged me, a silent encouragement to take the lead. "Time to work your magic," she whispered, her gaze steady on me.

"Alright, everyone!" I called out, my voice cutting through the murmurs of excitement. "Welcome to the first-ever Maplewood Scavenger Hunt! Gather around! Your mission, should you choose to accept it, is to complete the list of tasks and bring some cheer into this glorious day!"

The crowd erupted into laughter, their enthusiasm palpable. "And for the winner," I continued, locking eyes with Ethan as I gestured theatrically, "there's a fabulous prize that will be revealed at the end!"

Ethan's expression was a mixture of skepticism and curiosity, his brow still knitted but his posture slightly less rigid. The sparks of interest ignited a flicker of hope within me. I knew I had to make this work.

"Let's get started!" I exclaimed, thrusting a clipboard into Clara's hands, who flashed me a thumbs-up. The townsfolk scattered in all directions, laughter bubbling up like a wellspring, and for the first time, I saw a hint of a smile tugging at the corners of Ethan's mouth.

I slipped away from the crowd for a moment, my heart racing as I approached him. "You know, you could join us," I said, keeping my tone light. "We could use your keen observation skills to track down the best scarecrow."

He scoffed but didn't immediately dismiss me. "You think I'd waste my time on a scavenger hunt?"

"Not a waste if you make it competitive," I replied, unable to suppress a smile. "Besides, you might just surprise yourself and have fun."

Ethan's lips twitched in what I dared to call a smirk. "Fun, huh? What's that like?"

"It's like cotton candy—sweet and fluffy, but a little sticky when you get too involved," I quipped, winking.

He rolled his eyes, but I caught the glimmer of amusement there. "You're ridiculous."

"I prefer 'delightfully eccentric,'" I shot back, grinning. "So what do you say? One hour of scavenging with us and then you can return to your brooding if you wish."

He hesitated, and I could almost see the gears turning in his head. "Fine. One hour," he finally said, his tone begrudgingly conceding.

"Yes!" I pumped my fist triumphantly, the thrill of victory flooding my veins. "Let's go show these townsfolk what a real team can do!"

As we merged into the bustling crowd, I felt a sense of camaraderie wash over me. Laughter surrounded us, and for the first time, I sensed that the barriers between Ethan and me were beginning to crack. Perhaps this would be the catalyst to unlock the secrets beneath the surface, to peel back the layers of grief and guilt he harbored, and in doing so, we would forge a deeper connection that neither of us could have anticipated.

The scavenger hunt roared to life around us, a vibrant whirlwind of laughter and excitement sweeping through the town square. I felt a rush of adrenaline course through my veins as Clara and I dashed from booth to booth, leading our impromptu team of competitors, eager to uncover the quirky treasures hidden amidst the festival's chaos. Each completed task brought cheers and playful banter, a symphony of joy that resonated in my heart and momentarily drowned out the shadows that clung to Ethan.

As we approached the first challenge—finding the oldest pumpkin—Ethan fell into step beside me, his demeanor shifting from aloof to mildly intrigued. "You know, this is kind of ridiculous," he said, a hint of a smile breaking through his serious facade. "But I'll admit, it's... entertaining."

"See? I knew you had a hidden soft side," I teased, nudging him playfully. "Maybe we should rename you 'Ethan the Entertainer.'"

He snorted, shaking his head. "More like Ethan the Reluctant Participant. I still think this is a waste of time."

"Ah, but the best adventures often come from the most unexpected places," I countered, my eyes sparkling with mischief. "Plus, it's not just about the tasks; it's about camaraderie. You might actually enjoy spending time with us."

Ethan huffed but didn't argue. Instead, he scanned the crowd, his gaze lingering on the participants rushing around, arms filled with pumpkins and laughter echoing in the air. "You're a terrible influence, you know that?"

"I prefer to think of myself as a catalyst for joy," I replied, grinning. "And right now, joy looks good on you."

As the hunt continued, we stumbled upon a team of children huddled around a particularly large pumpkin, their giggles ringing out like music. "You guys found the oldest pumpkin?" I called out, feigning disappointment. "I thought we'd have an edge."

The children beamed, their faces alight with pride. "Nope! This one is just the biggest!" they shouted, their voices bouncing off the festival tents. "But we can share!"

Ethan raised an eyebrow, watching the children with a bemused expression. "You're telling me those pint-sized detectives beat us to the punch?"

"Every time," I laughed. "Their relentless enthusiasm is hard to beat."

"Good point," he conceded, a genuine smile creeping onto his face, warming the chill that had settled in my heart. We moved on to the next task: finding someone wearing mismatched socks. Clara and I rallied our team, and soon we were scouring the crowd, playing a game of hide-and-seek with feet instead of faces.

"Over there!" Clara shouted, pointing at an older man in a tweed jacket and bright orange socks. We sprinted toward him, and I could feel Ethan's presence beside me, his competitive spirit bubbling up. "Sir! We need to inspect your feet for mismatched socks!" I declared dramatically, bending down as if performing a crucial investigation. The man chuckled, lifting his pant leg to reveal the vibrant orange and blue stripes that had clearly been chosen with purpose.

Ethan leaned down, a playful glint in his eyes. "Now that's a fashion statement."

"Does this mean we win?" I asked, straightening up and clapping my hands together in excitement.

"Only if we can convince him to join our team," Clara chimed in. "What do you say, sir? Care to assist us in our quest?"

The man grinned, adjusting his jacket with a flourish. "I'm not just a pretty sock; I'm in!"

With our ranks bolstered, we raced through the remaining tasks, collecting clues and completing challenges, my laughter mingling with Ethan's increasingly genuine chuckles. With each completed task, I felt the ice around his heart begin to thaw, revealing glimpses of the man beneath the surface—the one who longed for connection but was afraid to embrace it.

We reached the final task: a selfie with the town's beloved giant gnome statue. As we posed, Ethan's arm casually draped over my shoulders, and I fought the rush of warmth that spread through me. My heart danced as we snapped the picture, our smiles a testament to the joy we had shared. But just as I leaned back to review the photo, I noticed a flicker of movement behind Ethan—a figure standing in the shadows, watching us.

"Hey, you okay?" Clara asked, nudging me gently as she stepped back to admire our group shot.

"Yeah, I just... thought I saw something." I turned, but the figure was gone, blending into the crowd. "Never mind."

Ethan caught my eye, his brow furrowing. "You're not worried about the gnome being cursed, are you?"

"Only if it means we'll all turn into garden decorations," I quipped, shaking off the unease. "But in all seriousness, I just felt like someone was watching us."

"Maybe it was just your imagination. Or a ghost looking for its gnome," he replied, his tone teasing yet concerned.

As we finished the scavenger hunt, the group congregated to reveal the winner. Laughter erupted, and I could feel the sense of camaraderie wrapping around us like a cozy blanket. But as we huddled together, a chill coursed through the air, an unsettling reminder that not all shadows could be dismissed so easily.

"Alright, folks! The grand prize for our scavenger hunt goes to..." Clara paused for effect, her excitement palpable. "Our eclectic group of mismatched sock connoisseurs!"

Cheers erupted as our team high-fived and celebrated, but just as I turned to Ethan, I saw that same shadow lingering on the edge of the festival. The figure stood just beyond the lights, their silhouette cloaked in darkness, watching intently. My heart skipped a beat, and a shiver ran down my spine.

"Julia?" Ethan's voice pulled me back, his concern palpable as he followed my gaze. "What's wrong?"

"Do you see that?" I asked, pointing toward the darkened corner of the square. "That person... they've been standing there for a while."

Ethan's expression hardened, a protective instinct kicking in as he scanned the area. "Stay close to me," he said, his voice low and serious.

I felt my heart race, the thrill of the hunt dissipating in the face of an unfamiliar danger. Just as I turned to call out to the figure, a sudden commotion erupted from the other side of the square, drawing everyone's attention. The lights flickered ominously, and the joyous festival atmosphere transformed into an uneasy murmur of confusion.

"What's going on?" Clara asked, her eyes wide.

Before I could respond, a loud crash reverberated through the square, a cacophony that shattered the celebratory mood. The ground trembled beneath our feet as I caught sight of the shadowy figure bolting away from the scene. My breath caught in my throat, fear tightening its grip.

"Ethan, we need to—"

But before I could finish my sentence, a deafening scream pierced the night, cutting through the laughter and chatter like a knife. The crowd turned, panic spreading like wildfire, and I knew in that moment that whatever secrets lay beneath the surface of this festival were about to be unveiled in a way I could never have anticipated.

Chapter 5: A Heart Divided

The crisp bite of autumn air wrapped around me like a well-worn scarf, a bittersweet reminder that change was coming. Outside, the trees dressed themselves in flames of orange and red, their leaves drifting down like confetti from some extravagant party no one had been invited to. I leaned against the window of the café, the faint sound of rain pattering against the glass a perfect backdrop to my swirling thoughts. Across from me, Ethan was animatedly recounting a story from his childhood, his eyes sparkling with mischief, and I couldn't help but smile, my heart betraying my better judgment.

"Wait, you really thought you could hide a raccoon in the school playhouse?" I laughed, imagining the chaos that must have ensued.

"Not just any raccoon," he insisted, leaning in closer, the warmth of his breath brushing against my skin. "That raccoon had a name—Mr. Whiskers. He was practically a legend at Maple Grove Elementary."

I shook my head, the laughter bubbling up from somewhere deep within me. The café, dimly lit and cozy, felt like our little sanctuary, a haven from the storms brewing both outside and within my heart. I could lose myself in these moments—his laughter, the way he leaned forward, completely absorbed in the tales of his youth. But with each shared secret, each stolen glance, the shadows of my plans loomed larger, reminding me of the ticking clock.

"Okay, okay. Mr. Whiskers sounds like quite the troublemaker," I said, my tone playful, but there was an edge of sincerity beneath it. "What happened when you got caught?"

Ethan's expression shifted, a flicker of vulnerability crossing his face. "Well, let's just say the principal had a soft spot for raccoons," he replied, his voice tinged with nostalgia. "He even tried to find Mr.

Whiskers a permanent home instead of expelling me. So, I guess it was a win-win?"

We exchanged smiles that lingered longer than they should have, both of us acutely aware of the unspoken bond forming between us. Yet, as the rain drummed softly on the roof, each droplet echoed the reality I couldn't ignore. My heart was straying from my carefully laid plans, and I had to decide if I was willing to divert my course.

The next day, the rain continued its relentless descent, turning the streets of Silver Pines into shimmering rivers. We were huddled together in Ethan's living room, a blanket draped over our laps, the scent of coffee wafting through the air. The comfort of being together felt electric, yet I could feel the tension coiling tight in my stomach, an uninvited guest at our gathering.

"I've been thinking," I ventured, breaking the silence. "What if you joined me in Paris? You know, for a little adventure?"

Ethan raised an eyebrow, an amused grin playing at the corners of his mouth. "And what exactly would I do in Paris? Compete with street artists for the best croissant?"

I chuckled, but my heart thudded loudly in my chest. "Why not? I hear the pastries are to die for, and we could explore the city together. Imagine—"

"Wait, are you suggesting we turn our charming little town into a Parisian escape?" he interrupted, his eyes dancing with excitement. "I can see it now: baguettes and berets all around. It'll be like an American in Paris but with a lot more mud and fewer romantic rooftops."

"You have to admit, it's a tempting offer," I said, my tone teasing yet layered with hope.

But the laughter faded when the reality hit me—the reason for my plans in the first place. A small part of me longed to stay in Silver Pines, to let myself be swept away in the charm of the town and in Ethan's easy laughter. However, the weight of Diane's rumors hung heavy in the air, a constant reminder that my presence here was tenuous at best.

"Let's make a pact," Ethan suggested, his voice suddenly serious. "No matter what happens, we promise to chase our dreams—together or apart. Just no raccoons in the mix, okay?"

The sincerity in his gaze made my heart ache, an unspoken promise that somehow made the weight of my decision heavier. I nodded, my throat tight with emotion. "Deal. But we have to face reality, Ethan. I don't want to uproot you from your life here, nor can I ignore my own ambitions."

"Why can't we have both?" he replied, his determination palpable. "You could find a way to balance both worlds."

As the words left his lips, I felt a flicker of hope ignite in my chest, like the first rays of sunlight piercing through a cloudy sky. Perhaps it was possible to weave my dreams with the reality of Silver Pines, to let love and ambition coexist in harmony. Yet, just as quickly, the shadow of Diane crept back into my thoughts, her sharp words echoing like a chilling breeze.

"You think it'll be easy?" I asked, my voice barely above a whisper.

"No, but I think it'll be worth it," he said, his conviction steady.

Outside, the rain continued to fall, a soft, rhythmic lullaby. I took a deep breath, tasting the bittersweet tang of uncertainty. In that moment, I realized my heart was divided, torn between the safety of my plans and the exhilarating chaos of new love. And though I didn't know where this path would lead, I felt a flicker of courage igniting within me, daring me to take a leap of faith.

The rain continued its relentless drumming, a soothing backdrop to our conversations as we sprawled comfortably in Ethan's living room. The scent of freshly brewed coffee mingled with the faint notes of cinnamon from the pumpkin muffins we had baked together. It was a small kitchen victory, an endeavor that felt deceptively simple, yet transformed into a comical disaster when we realized half the flour had been swapped with powdered sugar.

"That's a sweet surprise," Ethan chuckled, holding a muffin half-heartedly. "Not what I expected when I volunteered for 'the great muffin bake-off.'"

I rolled my eyes, unable to suppress my laughter. "At least we're keeping things interesting! It's like a surprise party for your taste buds. Who doesn't love a good twist?"

His laughter mingled with mine, filling the room with warmth, a stark contrast to the gloomy world outside. I could feel the atmosphere thickening with unspoken words, desires, and doubts, but in that moment, we were two friends entwined in the sweet thrill of spontaneity. We were cocooned in our little world, where nothing else mattered—until it did.

"Okay, what's next on our cooking adventures? I could be persuaded to try some outrageous pasta dish," he said, leaning back on the couch, a playful glint in his eye.

"Oh, you're going to regret that suggestion," I warned, crossing my arms in mock seriousness. "I once attempted homemade fettuccine that ended with me covered in flour and pasta goo."

"Flour and pasta goo? That sounds like a masterpiece waiting to happen," he retorted, laughter bubbling in his voice.

Just then, my phone buzzed on the table, cutting through our banter like a sudden gust of wind. I glanced at the screen, my heart sinking as I saw Diane's name flash across the notification. A tight knot twisted in my stomach, a reminder that our joyful escapades were shadowed by the reality of her schemes.

"Everything okay?" Ethan asked, his voice dipping with concern.

"Yeah, just... a reminder of why I can't let myself get too comfortable here," I replied, forcing a smile that felt brittle at best. "You know, life is complicated."

"Tell me about it. I'm currently embroiled in a fierce battle against my own cooking skills," he quipped, but the lightness of his tone did little to alleviate the tension hanging between us.

I took a deep breath, the decision weighing heavily on my heart. "Diane seems to think my time in Silver Pines is over. She's been... well, relentless."

"Relentless how?" Ethan leaned forward, his expression shifting from amusement to something more serious, an intensity in his gaze that made my pulse quicken.

"Whispers, rumors—nothing too out of the ordinary for someone who thrives on chaos," I admitted, my voice barely above a whisper. "But it's not just me. She's targeting anyone who gets too close to me, trying to isolate me."

His expression hardened, and I could see the protective fire ignite within him. "What's her angle? I mean, why go after you in the first place?"

"Maybe it's because I'm a newcomer," I said, shrugging off the weight of her animosity with a forced casualness. "Or maybe it's because she sees me as a threat to her precious status quo."

Ethan's jaw clenched, and for a moment, I felt a rush of gratitude mixed with fear. Gratitude that he cared enough to react, and fear that my presence might indeed disrupt the balance of the community. "You know," he began, his tone low and steady, "you should stand up for yourself. Don't let her drive you out."

"I appreciate that, but standing up doesn't mean I can just ignore the reality of my plans. Paris is still waiting," I replied, my heart aching with the weight of what I knew I had to do.

"Paris or not, it doesn't mean you have to sacrifice who you are. We can fight back together," he said, his voice laced with determination. "I refuse to let some petty jealousy chase you away."

As the words hung in the air between us, I felt a wave of warmth wash over me. This was more than just friendship. He was offering something deeper, a connection that felt as real and vital as the autumn air filling our lungs. But the moment was shattered when I heard a loud thump outside, followed by a chorus of laughter.

"What was that?" I asked, peering through the rain-splattered window.

Ethan rose, a curious look on his face. "Let's find out."

We stepped outside, the chilly air wrapping around us like a shroud. The laughter grew louder as we approached the source, which turned out to be a group of kids launching themselves into a pile of leaves, squealing as they tumbled and rolled. The sight tugged at my heartstrings, nostalgia washing over me like the rain cascading from the eaves.

"Remember when we used to do that?" Ethan asked, grinning as he watched the children.

"Yeah, I think I may have gotten a few leaves stuck in my hair," I laughed, the memory lighting up my face.

"Good times, huh?" His gaze shifted from the children to me, an intensity flickering in his eyes. "You know, you could create some good times here too."

"Maybe," I said, my heart heavy with uncertainty. "But what if I'm just a fleeting moment in this town's story?"

"Maybe so, but fleeting moments can leave lasting impressions," he said, his voice a low rumble that sent a thrill through me. "And who knows? Sometimes those moments lead to something bigger."

Before I could respond, a familiar figure emerged from the shadows of the trees—Diane, her expression smug and calculating. The kids fell silent, sensing the tension in the air.

"Out playing in the rain? How quaint," she called out, her voice dripping with sarcasm.

"Just enjoying the beauty of autumn, Diane," Ethan shot back, standing tall beside me, a wall of steadfast support.

Her gaze flicked between us, a hawk assessing its prey. "You'd do well to remember your place in this town," she warned, her voice low, almost conspiratorial. "Not everyone is as welcoming to newcomers as others."

"I don't need your welcome," I said, surprising even myself with the firmness in my tone. "I'm here to stay, at least for now."

Ethan's arm brushed against mine, a silent reassurance. For a fleeting moment, I felt invincible, buoyed by the strength of our connection.

"Oh, darling, I'd watch your step if I were you," Diane said, her smile sharp as glass. "You don't want to find yourself lost in the woods without a map."

As she turned and strode away, her laughter trailing behind like a fading echo, I felt the breath leave my lungs. The weight of her words lingered, a dark promise that loomed over us, but Ethan's presence beside me felt like a beacon of hope.

"You handled that well," he said, his voice low, filled with admiration.

"Let's just say I'm learning from the best," I replied, allowing a flicker of a smile to grace my lips.

"Together," he said, his gaze steady on mine. "We'll figure this out."

As the rain softened to a gentle drizzle, I found myself clinging to that hope, realizing that even amid chaos and uncertainty, there was strength to be found in vulnerability, and perhaps, just perhaps, in the warmth of a shared journey.

The clouds hung heavy above Silver Pines, their dark bellies threatening another downpour as I made my way to the town square. Ethan's laughter still echoed in my ears, a sweet sound that had managed to pierce the gloom of my worries. Yet, as I stepped out, the biting wind reminded me that the world beyond our little sanctuary was still a battleground. Diane's words lingered like the scent of burnt coffee, impossible to shake.

The square was bustling with the usual weekend activity, a farmer's market brimming with the vibrant colors of autumn. Pumpkins and gourds in hues that looked plucked from a painter's palette adorned the stalls, while the scent of freshly baked bread wafted through the air, mingling with the laughter of families enjoying the crisp day. I walked past a group of children gleefully darting between stalls, their laughter filling the air with warmth, but I couldn't shake the chill of uncertainty clinging to my bones.

"Hey! Are you going to just stand there, or are you coming to help me with these?" Ethan's voice cut through the haze of my thoughts. He was struggling to juggle several bags of apples, his brows furrowed in mock concentration.

"Trying to channel my inner grocery bag lady?" I teased, moving closer to lend a hand. "If only I had a plaid skirt and some sensible shoes."

"Don't sell yourself short; you'd rock the plaid," he grinned, his eyes twinkling. "And you might want to add a cape for dramatic flair, given our current situation."

With a laugh, I helped him with the bags, our fingers brushing occasionally, sending warmth racing through my chest. Each accidental touch was electric, the spark between us both thrilling and terrifying.

As we navigated the crowd, Ethan stopped to chat with the local vendors, his charm lighting up each interaction. I watched, a soft smile tugging at my lips, as he bantered effortlessly. But then I saw her—Diane, standing a few stalls away, her sharp gaze cutting through the laughter and joy like a knife. My heart sank. It was impossible to enjoy this moment while she loomed like a dark cloud.

"Ethan," I whispered, tugging on his sleeve, "we should—"

"Not let Diane ruin our day?" he finished, a fierce determination in his eyes. "You're right. Let's get what we need and head to my place for a cooking session. How about homemade apple pie?"

"Only if you promise to let me handle the dough. I have a reputation to uphold," I replied, my voice light, even though my mind raced with worries.

We made our way through the market, picking up ingredients for our pie, the air around us filled with a delightful mix of chatter and laughter. But as we moved, I felt Diane's eyes on me, a palpable weight that made the apples in my bag feel heavier. I steeled myself against the unease, reminding myself of the pact we had made—to stand tall against whatever chaos she would conjure.

Once we arrived at Ethan's place, the familiar warmth enveloped me like a cozy blanket. The smell of cinnamon still lingered from our previous baking adventure, intertwining with the fresh scent of apples as I began to peel and slice them. Ethan leaned against the counter, watching me with an amused smile.

"Ever consider a career as a professional apple slicer?" he asked, feigning seriousness.

"I'd need a snazzy uniform," I shot back, grinning. "How about one with lots of pockets for all the treats I'll be sampling?"

As we worked side by side, the rhythm of our movements felt instinctive, our banter flowing easily, wrapping us in a bubble of comfort. But beneath that surface, the tension was still there, lurking in the shadows.

"Do you think we can face her?" I asked, my voice quieter than I intended. "Diane's not going to back off easily. What if she tries to get everyone to turn against me?"

Ethan stepped closer, his brow furrowed with concern. "We will deal with that together. You're not alone in this, remember? If she thinks she can intimidate you, she's got another thing coming."

"Famous last words," I muttered, stirring the apple filling as if it could magically whisk away my fears.

He reached out, his hand resting lightly on my shoulder, grounding me. "I mean it. We can come up with a plan. If we stand firm and let the truth speak for itself, Diane's power diminishes. We can't let her poison our experiences."

"Right. Stand firm," I echoed, the mantra settling in my mind. But just as the words left my lips, my phone buzzed insistently on the counter. I glanced at the screen, and my heart plummeted.

It was a message from one of my friends back in the city, and her words were sharp: Just heard some interesting gossip about you in Silver Pines. People are talking...

I turned my phone to Ethan, my hands trembling as I showed him the screen. "I can't keep doing this. It's exhausting."

He frowned, studying me intently. "What does it say?"

"That Diane is spreading rumors that I'm only in town to sabotage the local businesses. Like, who does that?" My voice rose with frustration. "She's painting me as the villain here!"

Ethan's expression hardened, and I could see the gears turning in his mind. "We need to confront her. Face to face. She can't keep getting away with this."

I shook my head, anxiety clawing at my chest. "You don't understand, Ethan. She has everyone wrapped around her finger. What if they believe her?"

"Then we make them see the truth. Together." His voice was resolute, the spark of determination in his eyes igniting something within me.

"Together," I repeated, my resolve growing stronger.

But as the tension crackled in the air, the doorbell rang, interrupting our moment. I glanced at Ethan, a question in my eyes. "Who could that be?"

He shrugged, moving toward the door, but my gut twisted with unease. As he opened it, I was met with the sight of Diane standing on the threshold, a picture of feigned innocence, her smile perfectly curated but devoid of warmth.

"Surprise! Just wanted to check on my favorite new resident," she said, her voice syrupy sweet, a façade that made my skin crawl.

"Not sure I'm your favorite," I retorted, crossing my arms defensively.

Her gaze darted between us, a predator sizing up its prey. "Oh, I was just passing by and thought I'd drop in. I hope I'm not interrupting anything too... cozy?"

Ethan stepped in front of me, protective and unyielding. "We were just about to start baking. Why don't you join us?"

Diane's smile widened, but I could see the flicker of annoyance beneath her perfect exterior. "Oh, how sweet. But I actually came here with a message. There are some people who believe a certain newcomer might be trying to play both sides."

A chill shot down my spine as her words hung ominously in the air, a clear warning that the battle lines were drawn. I opened my mouth to respond, but before I could utter a word, she continued, her voice dripping with insincerity.

"Just wanted to remind you both that this town has a way of revealing true colors." With that, she stepped back, her laugh echoing as she walked away, leaving a shadow that seeped into the room like an unwelcome fog.

I turned to Ethan, my heart racing as the weight of her message settled in. "What does she mean by true colors?"

Ethan clenched his jaw, frustration etched across his face. "We're going to find out. She won't win, not while we're standing together."

But as the door closed behind Diane, an uneasy silence enveloped us, and I couldn't shake the feeling that the real battle was just beginning.

Chapter 6: Underneath the Stars

The night air was a tapestry of cool whispers and warm laughter, woven together under a sky so dense with stars that it felt like we were nestled in the heart of the universe itself. The Harvest Festival had transformed our quaint little town into a vibrant carnival of color and sound, each booth and string of lights humming with life. The scent of caramel apples mingled with the crispness of autumn leaves, and the faint echoes of a fiddle played somewhere in the distance, coaxing a carefree rhythm from the heart of the crowd.

I leaned against the wooden railing of the festival's main stage, the rustic texture cool against my back, my gaze drifting across the sea of faces. Everywhere I looked, people were laughing, dancing, and lost in the joy of the moment. Yet, despite the celebration swirling around me, a heaviness settled in my chest, an anchor that threatened to drag me into deeper waters. My decision to leave felt like an invisible weight, pressing down on my shoulders, while the flickering lights danced like fireflies, teasing me with their fleeting glow.

"Hey, you," Ethan's voice broke through my thoughts, warm and familiar. I turned to find him stepping out of the crowd, his dark hair tousled by the gentle breeze, eyes sparkling with mischief and a hint of concern. The way he looked at me, like I was a puzzle he was desperate to solve, made my heart flutter. "You're missing the best part of the festival. Come on, let's go dance!" He reached out a hand, his palm open and inviting, as if daring me to take a leap of faith.

"I don't know, Ethan. I'm just..." My voice trailed off, caught between the exhilaration of the night and the heaviness in my heart. I wanted nothing more than to lose myself in the rhythm of the music and the warmth of his touch, but the weight of my decision loomed large.

"Just what? Afraid you might have fun?" He raised an eyebrow, a playful challenge in his gaze. "Trust me, it's impossible not to smile when you're surrounded by all this," he gestured broadly to the laughter and lights, "even if you're trying to play the reluctant heroine."

His teasing pulled a reluctant smile from my lips, a flicker of brightness amidst the shadows in my mind. "I'm not a heroine, Ethan. Just a girl trying to figure out what to do with her life."

He stepped closer, the distance between us narrowing, his expression softening. "And what is that life, exactly? Running away to chase... what? A dream that might not even be there?" The sincerity in his voice resonated with the ache in my heart, and I felt my defenses begin to crumble.

"Maybe it's more like a nightmare I'm trying to wake up from," I admitted, feeling an unexpected rush of vulnerability. "I'm scared, Ethan. Scared that if I stay, I'll never find out what I'm capable of. But if I leave... I might lose everything that matters."

His eyes searched mine, a flicker of understanding passing between us, and in that moment, the cacophony of the festival faded into the background. The world around us shrank to the space we occupied, filled only with the tension of unspoken words and shared fears.

"Sometimes you have to take risks, even when the stakes are high," he said, his voice low and steady. "But you don't have to do it alone." He reached out, his fingers brushing against mine, sending a jolt of electricity coursing through me.

"I know," I breathed, the honesty of the moment washing over me like a wave. "But I'm not sure I'm ready to face all of this." I gestured around us, the festival lights twinkling like stars in a vast, unknown sky.

"Ready or not, the world keeps spinning. Just remember, I'm here," he replied, his voice rich with sincerity. The warmth radiating from him enveloped me, and the moment felt charged with possibilities, ripe and intoxicating. I could sense the pull between us, an undeniable gravity that drew me closer to him.

"Why do you make it so hard to leave?" I murmured, my voice barely above a whisper. The question hung in the air, heavy with meaning.

"Maybe because I don't want you to," he admitted, his voice thick with emotion. "But I also know you have to do what's right for you. Just don't forget... you'll always have a home here." His gaze held mine, a soft promise nestled within the depths of his eyes.

As if drawn by an invisible thread, I leaned closer, the world fading away until it was just us. "You're infuriating," I said, a teasing lilt in my voice, breaking the tension that had built between us. "You know that, right?"

"Only when you're being indecisive," he shot back, the corner of his mouth quirking up in that infuriatingly charming way that always made my stomach flutter.

"Fine, I'll own that. But you're still infuriatingly charming," I teased, feeling lighter, a smile breaking free as the banter filled the space between us.

"Good to know I have some redeeming qualities," he laughed, but then his expression shifted, turning serious once more. "In all honesty, you deserve to be happy. Just... don't shut me out completely."

In that moment, the weight of my indecision felt heavier than ever, and the fragile connection we shared flickered like a candle in a storm. "I promise I won't. Just give me a little time," I replied, feeling the sincerity of my words wrapping around us, binding us in that moment of honesty.

He nodded, his gaze unwavering, and for the first time, I felt a sense of clarity wash over me, softening the edges of my fears. Just then, the laughter from the nearby dance floor swelled, drawing our attention back to the festival, the vibrant colors swirling like a beautiful tapestry around us.

As if sensing the shift, Ethan took a step back, his hand reluctantly slipping from mine. "Dance with me," he urged, a hint of mischief returning to his eyes. "Let's forget everything for a little while. Just you and me under the stars."

With a breathless smile, I nodded, the heaviness in my heart momentarily lifted as I surrendered to the music, the rhythm, and the promise of what the night could hold.

The music swelled, a lively blend of fiddle and drum that beckoned us toward the center of the festival, where a makeshift dance floor had emerged. Lanterns hung from trees, their soft glow casting a golden hue over the sea of faces, every one of them alive with joy. As we stepped into the crowd, the air thickened with warmth and camaraderie, laughter spiraling up into the night like wisps of smoke. I could feel the pulse of excitement wrapping around me, drawing me into the moment, yet I remained tethered to the weight of our conversation.

"See? Not so bad, right?" Ethan grinned, pulling me into the throng. His confidence was infectious, and I found myself smiling back, the earlier heaviness lifting just a bit. We twirled and swayed, our movements clumsy yet exhilarating. His hand found the small of my back, grounding me as the music urged us into a dizzying whirl.

"You're a terrible dancer!" I exclaimed, laughing as he stumbled slightly, his foot catching mine.

"Speak for yourself! I'm just trying to channel my inner star," he replied, winking dramatically as he lifted his arms and swayed like a peacock.

"More like a flailing fish," I countered, my laughter mingling with the cheerful sounds around us. But there was a spark in his eyes, something fierce and unyielding that pushed back against the shadows lurking in my heart.

The crowd pulsed around us, people merging into a collective celebration of life. The rhythm vibrated through the soles of my shoes, and for a moment, I allowed myself to forget the tangled knots of my future, the decision waiting in the wings like a storm cloud. With each twirl, Ethan spun me deeper into the whirlwind of festivity, his laughter bright and intoxicating, a soothing balm against my unease.

"What's the matter?" he asked, his tone shifting, the teasing edge fading as he pulled me closer, his expression turning serious. "You still look like you've got a storm brewing inside."

"I'm just... processing," I replied, trying to muster a smile that wouldn't quite reach my eyes. "Everything feels so intense tonight, and I'm not sure if I can handle it all."

"Processing? That sounds dangerously close to overthinking," he teased, but I could see the concern in his gaze. "Don't you know that life is a series of beautifully chaotic moments? You can't control everything. Sometimes, you just have to jump in."

"Easy for you to say," I quipped, rolling my eyes, but his earnestness chipped away at my defenses. "You've got it all figured out, don't you?"

"Not even close," he replied, a hint of vulnerability creeping into his tone. "You think I'm just a carefree guy who dances through life? I've got my own shadows to contend with."

I raised an eyebrow, intrigued. "Shadows? I've seen plenty of dancing, but I don't recall any shadows."

"Believe me, they're there, lurking behind the smiles." He met my gaze, and I sensed a flicker of something deeper, a story waiting to be unearthed. "Sometimes, it's harder to dance when you're dragging your past along with you."

The words hung in the air between us, laden with unspoken truths. I was surprised at how easily I found myself wanting to know more about him, to peel back the layers of the charming facade he presented. "What do you mean?"

"Let's just say I've had my fair share of things that still weigh on me," he admitted, his eyes momentarily distant, lost in memories I could only imagine. "But that's why moments like this matter. They remind me that there's beauty amidst the chaos, even if I can't always see it."

"Do you ever feel like it's too much?" I asked, my voice softer, less guarded. "Like the weight of everything is just too heavy to bear?"

He paused, the world around us fading into a gentle hum as he considered my question. "All the time," he finally said, his voice steady yet laden with emotion. "But I've learned that the key is to find joy in the small moments. Like dancing under the stars. They remind me that I'm still here, still fighting."

The sincerity in his words resonated within me, a quiet echo of my own fears and desires. "And what if those small moments are overshadowed by bigger decisions?" I challenged gently, searching his eyes for clarity.

"Then you need to make a choice," he replied, his expression resolute. "But don't let fear dictate that choice. Embrace it, whatever it may be."

His words wrapped around my heart, a lifeline in the swirling chaos of my emotions. Just then, the music shifted, morphing into a slower, more melodic tune. The crowd began to sway, and without thinking, Ethan pulled me closer, his arms encircling my waist, drawing me into the warmth of his body.

As we moved, I could feel the heat radiating between us, an intoxicating blend of comfort and tension. I let my head rest against his shoulder, inhaling the familiar scent of cedar and something uniquely Ethan. For a moment, the worries that had been clawing at me faded into the background, leaving only the rhythm of our hearts in sync with the music.

"I could get used to this," I murmured, feeling the pulse of the moment wash over me like a warm tide.

"Good. Because I'm not letting you out of my sight tonight," he replied, his voice low and playful. "I refuse to let you go back to being all serious. You're way too fun when you're laughing."

"Flattery will get you everywhere," I joked, but the warmth in my chest wasn't just from his words; it was the connection we shared, an unspoken understanding woven into the fabric of the night.

Just then, the spell was broken. Diane, her presence as imposing as ever, stalked toward us, her expression a storm cloud that promised rain on our parade. "Well, isn't this cozy?" she drawled, her voice laced with condescension, eyes narrowed as she took in our closeness.

I straightened, the warmth of the moment evaporating like mist under the harsh light of her judgment. "Diane," I greeted, forcing a smile that felt more like a mask. "What brings you here?"

"Oh, just keeping an eye on the locals," she replied, her gaze flitting between Ethan and me. "Some of us have responsibilities, you know. Unlike some people who just dance around their problems."

Ethan's grip on me tightened slightly, a protective gesture that sent a flicker of warmth through my veins, but I felt the coolness of Diane's words seeping into the atmosphere.

"Maybe you should try it sometime," I shot back, a little more fire in my tone than I intended. "It might do you some good to loosen up."

Diane's lips pursed, and for a moment, I could see the gears turning in her mind, evaluating the potential for a comeback. But before she could respond, Ethan spoke up, his voice steady and firm. "We're just enjoying the night, Diane. Maybe you should try that too."

Her expression shifted, momentarily thrown off balance by his unexpected retort. "Charming as always, Ethan," she said, her voice dripping with sarcasm. "Just remember, some of us have to deal with reality. Enjoy your little dance while it lasts."

With that, she turned on her heel and disappeared back into the crowd, leaving a chill in her wake. I felt the tension radiate from Ethan as he released a slow breath, the atmosphere around us shifting back to something warmer, but it didn't completely dissipate the unease in my chest.

"Sorry about that," I said, shifting uncomfortably, unsure if I wanted to talk about what just happened or let it slide. "She knows how to kill the mood."

Ethan shook his head, a wry smile creeping back onto his lips. "She really does, doesn't she? But you handled that like a champ. I'm impressed."

"Impressed? You should have seen me earlier. I was a mess," I admitted, laughing lightly to dispel the lingering tension.

"You're still here, though, aren't you? That says a lot," he replied, his gaze piercing yet warm, and suddenly, I felt as if he could see through all the layers I had carefully built around my heart.

"Yeah, I guess so." I swallowed hard, the earlier weight returning as I thought about my impending decision. "But sometimes I wonder if being here is really where I'm meant to be."

"Just remember, life is full of surprises," he said softly, a hint of something deeper in his tone. "Don't be afraid to embrace them."

As the night wrapped around us, the music began to swell once more, a vibrant heartbeat that mirrored the pulse of our conversation. I wanted to let go, to surrender to the magic of the moment, but Diane's words echoed in my mind, the reality of my choices still looming like a shadow over our starlit dance.

The moment hung suspended, the remnants of Diane's icy presence lingering like a shadow that refused to lift. I watched as she melted back into the crowd, leaving behind a charged silence that felt heavier than the flickering lanterns overhead. Ethan's hand remained at my waist, a reassuring anchor in the whirlwind of uncertainty, but the warmth from that brief kiss began to feel distant, like a fading memory I was desperately trying to cling to.

"Forget her," he said, his voice low but firm, as if he could sense the unease crawling beneath my skin. "This is our night. Let's not let anyone ruin it."

"Right. Our night," I echoed, trying to reclaim the spirit of the celebration while suppressing the knot of anxiety twisting in my stomach. I could feel the anticipation of laughter and dancing urging me to let go, yet the impending decision loomed like a dark cloud, threatening to burst. "But what if she's right? What if I'm just dancing around my problems?"

Ethan tilted his head, a thoughtful frown crinkling his brow. "That's a pretty morose way to look at it. Dancing can be a way of facing your problems head-on. Sometimes you just have to shake off the weight, even if it feels like you're fooling yourself."

"Or pretending everything's fine when it's not," I countered, the words slipping out before I could catch them. I wasn't here to wallow in self-doubt; I was supposed to be embracing this moment. I could feel a tension building, the kind that skated dangerously close to an argument.

"Look, I get it," he replied, exasperation flickering across his face. "But don't you think that by leaving, you're just running away? You said yourself that this place matters to you."

"It does! It really does." The fervor in my voice surprised me, and I felt my cheeks flush as I spoke. "But what if I never find out what else is out there? I can't just stay here forever, tethered to something that could hold me back."

"Or you could be missing out on something amazing right in front of you," he shot back, a mixture of passion and concern evident in his eyes. "You're smart and capable, and you could do incredible things—here or anywhere. But you have to make that choice for yourself, not because someone else thinks you should."

The music pulsed again, and with it came the laughter of revelers lost in the magic of the night. I wanted to drown out the doubt, to simply surrender to the moment. But even as we swayed together, I felt my heart divided, caught between the safety of the familiar and the thrill of the unknown.

"Maybe you're right," I murmured, feeling the weight of his gaze. "But I can't help but wonder if I'm making the biggest mistake of my life by even considering leaving."

"You won't know unless you try," he replied softly, the intensity of his eyes sending a rush of warmth through me. "You owe it to yourself to explore. And if you decide to go, just remember that it doesn't have to mean saying goodbye forever."

The air between us thickened, my heart racing in response to the depth of his words. "You make it sound so easy," I said, an incredulous laugh escaping my lips. "You really think it's that simple?"

"Simple? No. But life rarely is. Just look at us—here we are, two people who couldn't be more different, caught in a moment of awkward dancing and deeper truths," he said, a hint of a smile returning to his lips. "But maybe that's what makes it all worthwhile."

I felt a warmth bloom in my chest, a spark igniting amidst the swirling doubts. "So we're just going to keep dancing around the issue until one of us trips?" I teased, lifting an eyebrow playfully, trying to lighten the mood.

"I'd say that's a fair assessment," he chuckled, the sound wrapping around us like a cozy blanket. "But let's hope neither of us falls flat on our faces. I don't think my ego could take it."

"Please, as if you have an ego," I replied, rolling my eyes. "But I wouldn't mind if you fell if it meant getting a good laugh out of it."

"Challenge accepted," he grinned, then suddenly, his expression shifted. "But really, whatever you decide, just know that I'm here for you. No matter what."

His words struck a chord deep within me, sending tremors of warmth coursing through my veins. It was rare to find someone so willing to stand by me amidst the swirling chaos of life, and that realization made my heart swell with both gratitude and fear.

Before I could reply, a sudden ruckus erupted nearby, breaking the spell that had woven itself between us. The laughter and music faded into a startled hush, and I turned to see a group of festival-goers gathered around a makeshift stage, their excited chatter growing louder.

"What's happening?" I asked, my curiosity piqued.

"Looks like someone's about to take the mic," Ethan said, his eyes scanning the crowd. The energy shifted again, vibrant and electric as the crowd buzzed with anticipation.

Just as I opened my mouth to respond, a familiar face broke through the throng. It was Mia, my childhood friend, her hair a wild halo around her beaming face, eyes sparkling with mischief. "You won't believe what just happened!" she exclaimed, bouncing on her heels like a kid on Christmas morning.

"What is it?" I pressed, the excitement in her voice infectious, momentarily distracting me from the weight of my earlier conversation with Ethan.

"I found a hidden stash of cider and—oh! You're going to want to see this," she said, grabbing my hand with an urgency that sent a jolt of energy through me. "Come on, it's amazing!"

With a glance at Ethan, I hesitated, torn between following Mia and staying in the comforting warmth of our conversation. But as she pulled me into the throng, I felt the pulse of the festival calling me back into its embrace, drawing me away from the shadows of uncertainty that had threatened to consume me.

Ethan fell into step beside us, and I could feel the connection between us shifting as we melded into the crowd. The anticipation was palpable, and I couldn't help but wonder what surprise awaited us just beyond the horizon of the revelry.

As we reached the edge of the crowd, the energy crackled in the air like static electricity. I looked over at Ethan, and he flashed me a grin that sent a warm shiver down my spine. "Whatever it is, I'm ready for it," he said, his tone light but his eyes betraying a hint of deeper curiosity.

"Just trust me," Mia urged, her excitement contagious. "You're going to love this."

We rounded a corner, and what I saw left my heart racing. A makeshift stage had been set up, adorned with twinkling fairy lights, and a local band was tuning their instruments. But that wasn't the surprise. No, it was the figure stepping up to the microphone that left me breathless.

"Good evening, everyone!" boomed a familiar voice that sent a rush of emotions coursing through me. "I'm back!"

There, standing in the spotlight, was Sam—my older brother, who had left town years ago, leaving behind an empty space that had never quite filled. I hadn't expected to see him here, not tonight, not ever.

The crowd erupted into cheers, and the joy that washed over me was both exhilarating and terrifying. As my heart raced, I glanced at Ethan, who was watching me with an expression I couldn't quite decipher.

"Hey, you okay?" he asked, his voice barely audible above the din.

"Yeah, I just—my brother is back," I managed to reply, a whirlwind of emotions crashing over me. I had so many questions, so many unresolved feelings.

Before I could gather my thoughts, Sam caught my eye, and for a brief moment, it felt like the entire world faded away. He waved, a bright smile on his face, and I knew in that instant that nothing would ever be the same again.

But just as the weight of my joy began to settle, I felt a tug on my heart—an echo of the decision that still loomed over me, waiting to be addressed. The night had transformed into a canvas of new beginnings, but with it came the looming question of what I was willing to sacrifice in order to embrace this unexpected twist in my life.

As the music began to play and the crowd erupted into a jubilant celebration, I stood there, caught between the thrill of reunion and the uncertainty of my own path. In that moment, with the stars shining bright above us and my heart racing like a drum, I realized that sometimes, the answers we seek are hidden in the chaos. And just like that, the world shifted around me, setting the stage for a new adventure—one that I couldn't yet see but felt was hurtling toward me at full speed.

Chapter 7: The Reckoning

The soft hum of the town settled back into its familiar rhythm, the echoes of the festival still lingering like a sweet, forgotten song. Silver Pines was a place of pastel sunsets and wood-smoked mornings, where the pines whispered secrets and the townsfolk exchanged knowing glances over steaming cups of coffee. Yet beneath this idyllic surface, a storm brewed, and it all revolved around a kiss—a stolen moment that shattered the peace and sent ripples through the community.

Each morning, as I walked to the café, the weight of my decision settled like a thick fog around my heart. The sunlight filtering through the trees cast dappled patterns on the cobblestone path, but no amount of beauty could dispel the uncertainty that gnawed at me. My thoughts spiraled—what would happen if I stayed? What if I left? The kiss with Ethan lingered like the scent of freshly baked cinnamon rolls, sweet yet suffocating, each breath I took tasted of cinnamon and confusion.

I found solace in the café, the comforting clatter of dishes and the aromatic embrace of coffee beans pulling me into a semblance of normalcy. Here, the scent of vanilla wafted through the air, a promise of warmth amidst the chill that had settled in my bones. It was a small haven where I could pretend the outside world didn't exist, but that illusion shattered the moment Diane sauntered in, her presence as unwelcome as a winter chill in early spring.

Diane was a force of nature, a storm wrapped in a tailored coat, and her eyes glinted with the sharpness of freshly sharpened knives. She had taken it upon herself to paint me as an outsider, a rogue wave threatening the fragile peace of Silver Pines. "You're just a temporary guest, aren't you?" she had sneered at the town meeting, her voice dripping with disdain. "What do you know about our way of life?"

The townsfolk, who once greeted me with polite smiles, now turned their backs, murmurs swirling like autumn leaves caught in a whirlwind. I could feel the eyes of the community on me, a thousand weighty glares pinning me in place. I was losing my footing in this town that had once embraced me like a cozy blanket, and with each passing day, Diane's influence grew like an unwelcome weed.

"Don't let her get to you," Ethan urged one evening as we sat in the café, his hand warm over mine, grounding me in the chaos. His deep-set eyes, usually filled with warmth, flickered with determination. "You belong here, and I'll make sure everyone knows it."

His words ignited a fire within me, but doubt clung to my heart like a shadow. "What if they don't want me here?" I asked, fear curling around my voice. The thought of being a pariah, an interloper in a town that once felt like home, sent tremors through my core.

"Then we'll fight for it," he replied, a fierce resolve lighting up his features. "You're worth it. I'm not going to let Diane tear us apart."

His confidence seeped into me, mingling with my desire for acceptance. But with every passing day, Diane's campaign grew louder, echoing through the narrow streets and climbing the town's hills. Whispers in the wind turned into shouts at the market, where I overheard snippets of conversation about "outsiders" and "keeping Silver Pines safe." The once-friendly smiles turned to cold glares, leaving me feeling like a ghost haunting my own life.

The turning point came on a crisp autumn evening, the sunset painting the sky in hues of orange and purple, when tensions erupted in the town square. A gathering had been called, and the air was electric with anticipation. I stood with Ethan at the edge of the crowd, the energy palpable as townsfolk clustered around, murmurs rising and falling like the tide.

Diane stood at the front, her arms crossed, a self-appointed guardian of the town's traditions. "We cannot let someone like her disrupt our way of life!" she bellowed, her voice cutting through the murmurs. "This is our home, and we need to protect it!"

The crowd shifted uncomfortably, eyes darting between her and me. I could feel my heart hammering in my chest, a wild drumbeat of fear and resolve. It was now or never. Ethan squeezed my hand, a silent promise that we were in this together.

"Diane," I called, my voice shaking but resolute, "this isn't about me being an outsider. This is about understanding and acceptance. Silver Pines has always been a place of community. I came here for a fresh start, just like so many others before me."

Diane scoffed, her dismissive laugh echoing through the square. "A fresh start at our expense? You think you can waltz in here and change everything? You don't know us!"

"I'm learning," I shot back, the words tumbling out before I could rein them in. "I care about this town, its people. I've invested in your community. I've poured my heart into the café, into the stories shared over coffee. But it's not enough for you, is it?"

The crowd held its breath, caught in a moment of suspended disbelief. I could see flickers of doubt on some faces, but Diane wasn't done yet. "You're manipulating them with your charm and your coffee!" she yelled, her voice sharp as a winter wind.

"Maybe it's time we stop seeing each other as enemies and start understanding what we can create together," Ethan interjected, stepping forward, his presence a steady anchor. "We're all human here. We've all got stories that matter. Isn't that what this town is supposed to be about?"

A silence hung in the air, thick and tangible. I could feel the pulse of the crowd, the tension building like the pressure before a storm. Would they choose to stand with Diane's narrow vision, or could they embrace a broader view, one that welcomed diversity instead of shunning it? I was terrified, but more than that, I was resolute. I'd fight for the life I had begun to build, for the love blossoming between Ethan and me, and for the hope that Silver Pines could indeed be a place where we all belonged.

The crowd seemed to ripple like a living organism, breathing in sync with the tension thickening the air. Ethan's words hung suspended, an invocation to a higher understanding that seemed to resonate with a few, while others remained rooted in their discomfort. I could see the expressions on the townsfolk's faces shifting, the gears of thought turning, and for a fleeting moment, I dared to hope that perhaps the tide could turn in our favor.

Then Diane struck back, her voice sharper than the autumn chill. "And what's your plan, Ethan? To turn our quaint little town into a circus? To let anyone and everyone walk through our doors without so much as a nod to who we are?" Her eyes darted around the crowd, seeking allies in her crusade. "We can't let our traditions dissolve into chaos just because someone with a charming smile thinks they know better."

I took a breath, feeling the warmth of Ethan's hand grounding me. "This isn't about tradition; it's about community. You can keep your traditions alive while still allowing new voices to join the conversation. Isn't that what makes a place vibrant?"

"Vibrant?" Diane laughed, a sound devoid of warmth. "Vibrant is just another word for disorder. We're not here to host an open mic night for every lost soul that wanders in."

"I'm not lost," I shot back, heart pounding with indignation. "I'm here, and I'm trying to build something. Something that honors the past while embracing the future." I could see the uncertainty on some faces—the whispers of doubt that rippled through the crowd. I pressed on, sensing a small opening. "Do you really want to live in a place that shuts its doors to growth? That fears what's outside instead of celebrating it?"

SILVER PINES

Diane's face flushed, a storm brewing behind her eyes. "And what happens when growth means losing everything we hold dear? We become a shell of what we once were!"

A tall man in the back spoke up, his voice surprisingly calm amidst the brewing chaos. "But what if this place could be more? What if we could bring new life to Silver Pines? It doesn't mean we lose our identity." He glanced at me, and I saw a flicker of understanding in his gaze. "Maybe we need a little chaos sometimes to remind us of what's worth protecting."

Diane scoffed, but the undercurrent of support began to swell. "What's next?" she demanded, her tone icy. "Are we going to invite city folk to come in and change our way of life? Have you seen what they did to Maplewood?"

"I'm not from Maplewood," I replied, my voice steadying. "And I'm not here to bulldoze anyone's way of life. I'm here because I love this place—the spirit of it, the people. I want to learn and grow with you, not against you."

The murmurs shifted, and I could feel a few more faces soften. Ethan stepped closer, his presence radiating strength. "We're asking for openness, not for everyone to abandon their roots. What if we can keep the heart of Silver Pines while embracing what's new?"

A woman near the front nodded, her face lit by the warm glow of the setting sun. "I don't want to lose what makes this place special. But I see what you mean. It can be hard to share, to let new voices in."

Diane turned, incredulous. "Are you all really considering this? Letting a newcomer dictate how we live?"

"This isn't about dictating," Ethan said, his voice rising above the din. "It's about finding common ground. It's about respect." He paused, his gaze sweeping the crowd. "This town has survived because of its ability to adapt. Why shouldn't we continue that tradition?"

Suddenly, the crowd erupted in overlapping conversations, the tension shifting, swirling like leaves caught in a gust of wind. My heart raced as I caught glimpses of support building among the townsfolk. Perhaps there was a chance to turn this around, to foster understanding instead of division.

But then, with a triumphant glint in her eye, Diane launched her final strike. "Fine! But let's see how well you fare when push comes to shove. Let's see if your ideals hold up against real problems. I dare you to put your so-called community to the test!"

"Are you suggesting a challenge?" I asked, barely suppressing a smirk. It felt like a trap, but there was a spark of something within me—a challenge I couldn't resist. "What kind of problems are we talking about?"

"Oh, let's make it interesting," she said, her lips curling into a sly grin. "A town project. Something you think you can manage better than us locals. How about revitalizing the old community garden? If you can turn that dead space into something valuable by the harvest season, I'll consider your place here legitimate."

I blinked, caught off guard by her audacity. The community garden was nothing more than a tangle of weeds and memories, long since forgotten. It would be a massive undertaking, and I could see it in the crowd's shifting expressions—some were eager, while others looked skeptical.

"Are you serious?" I asked, my heart thumping louder than the murmurs. "You think we can just... fix it?"

"Absolutely," Diane said, crossing her arms defiantly. "Show us you can take a run-down patch of dirt and turn it into something worthwhile, and maybe I'll change my mind. But if you fail..."

The threat hung in the air like a dark cloud, threatening to burst. The stakes had been raised, and I could feel the weight of the challenge pressing down. The crowd was watching, their curiosity piqued, and I knew this was no longer just about me; it was about the town's future.

"I'm in," I said, surprising myself as much as anyone. "But I won't do it alone. This is a community effort, and if we're going to do this, we do it together." I turned to the crowd, adrenaline coursing through me. "Who's with me?"

A few hesitant hands went up, then a few more. Slowly, one by one, the townsfolk began to nod and murmur their agreement. The energy shifted, and for the first time, I felt a sense of unity, a shared purpose blossoming among us.

"Looks like we have ourselves a project," Ethan said, a proud smile lighting up his face as he squeezed my hand tighter. "Now let's see what we can do together."

As the crowd began to disperse, excitement mixed with apprehension. The town had been split, but in that moment, something new began to forge. I could feel it in my bones—a fire ignited within me, fueled by the thrill of the challenge and the hope of acceptance. Perhaps the kiss was just the beginning of something far more significant, something worth fighting for.

The days that followed our public declaration felt like a peculiar dance on a tightrope, suspended between hope and the looming threat of disaster. I threw myself into the challenge of revitalizing the community garden with a fervor that surprised even me. The air was tinged with autumn's crispness, each morning greeting us with a sharp clarity that mirrored my growing determination. I could almost hear the rhythmic pulse of the town, a heartbeat that quickened with each decision, each small victory.

The first meeting we held at the café was a motley collection of townsfolk, some curious, others skeptical. I stood at the front, armed with enthusiasm and a whiteboard that promised transformation. "All right, everyone! Welcome to the Garden Revival Committee!"

I announced, my voice more buoyant than I felt. "We're here to breathe new life into this old patch of dirt, but I can't do it alone."

A chuckle rippled through the room, and I spotted Mr. Hargrove, a retired teacher with a twinkle in his eye, leaning back in his chair. "A patch of dirt, eh? Looks more like a war zone to me," he said, feigning concern.

"It's a canvas waiting for a masterpiece," I countered, throwing him a mock-serious glance. "And I happen to have a few ideas that might surprise you."

With Ethan's support, we laid out a plan that included workshops on gardening techniques, local flora to plant, and even a weekly farmers' market that would not only benefit the garden but the community as a whole. There was a newfound energy in the room, a sense of collaboration that had been sorely missing since Diane's tirade. As people signed up to help, I caught glimpses of familiar faces among the crowd—people who had once greeted me with indifference, now stepping forward to lend their hands.

One evening, as the sun dipped low and painted the café in shades of gold, Ethan and I stood shoulder to shoulder outside, surveying the garden's neglected expanse. "You're really doing it," he said, a note of admiration in his voice. "I didn't think you'd jump in headfirst like this."

"Neither did I, honestly," I admitted, running my fingers through my hair. "It feels good to have something to fight for, something that connects us all." The tension of the last few weeks began to ease, the prospect of working together uniting us in a way that felt both exhilarating and terrifying.

But with each passing day, the undercurrent of animosity that Diane had stirred remained palpable. The older residents still whispered as they passed by, glancing sideways as if afraid of catching the enthusiasm that had begun to bloom among the younger crowd. I knew it would take more than just a garden to win their trust. It was a long road ahead, and as we dug up weeds and cleared out debris, I found myself digging deeper into my own insecurities as well.

"Do you think they'll ever accept me?" I asked Ethan one night, the stars bright against a backdrop of indigo, while we gathered discarded branches into a bonfire. "Or will I always be the outsider?"

Ethan turned, his expression earnest, lit by the flickering flames. "You've already changed things, you know. People are starting to see you for who you are, not just who they think you are. Just give it time."

His faith in me warmed my heart, but as we settled into the rhythm of late-night conversations, the unease continued to gnaw at my gut. Each laugh shared was a temporary salve, a distraction from the storm brewing on the horizon.

Then came the day of our first big community event—the Garden Revival Festival. Anticipation buzzed in the air as we set up tents, arranged tables, and laid out colorful displays of fresh produce and handmade goods. I could hardly contain my excitement as neighbors stopped by, exchanging smiles and lively chatter. For a moment, the garden felt alive, like it was finally awakening from a long slumber.

But just as we began to feel the warmth of community, the chill of reality crept back in. Diane arrived, flanked by her loyalists, her presence looming like a shadow over our festivities. She surveyed the scene with a critical eye, arms crossed tightly over her chest. "Is this really what you're calling a revival?" she scoffed, her voice sharp enough to slice through the laughter. "A few flowerpots and some crafts don't make you a community."

A hush fell over the crowd, the cheerful atmosphere draining away like a receding tide. I felt the blood rush to my cheeks, anger and fear colliding in a whirlwind within me. This was not the moment I wanted to be undermined, not when we had worked so hard to bring everyone together.

"Actually, it's a celebration of our efforts to bring the community closer," I replied, my voice steadier than I felt. "This garden represents more than just plants; it's a symbol of unity, of our shared commitment to improving Silver Pines."

She smirked, but a ripple of support from the crowd began to emerge, murmurs of agreement breaking through the tension. I could see a few of the younger faces nodding, emboldened by my response.

"You think this is unity? This is nothing but a distraction!" Diane shot back, her voice rising in pitch. "And when it fails—and it will—you'll have nothing left but regret."

"Why are you so determined to destroy this?" I challenged, my frustration bubbling over. "Is it that hard for you to see us working together?"

A dangerous glint sparkled in her eyes. "Because I've seen too many outsiders come in and think they know what's best. You don't belong here."

Before I could respond, a commotion erupted on the other side of the tent, drawing our attention. Panic rippled through the crowd as someone shouted. A dark figure darted between the tables, the chaos unsettling everyone. In a heartbeat, a collective gasp echoed as the figure slipped and fell, crashing into the display of fresh vegetables, sending them scattering like marbles across the ground.

I pushed through the throng, adrenaline surging as I approached the fallen figure. It was one of the younger volunteers, Marcus, his face pale and eyes wide with fear. "They... they're coming!" he gasped, his breath hitching in his throat.

"What do you mean?" I asked, panic gripping my chest. The laughter of our gathering evaporated, replaced by confusion and dread.

"Diane... she's behind this!" he stammered, his eyes darting towards her. "She called them!"

A wave of horror washed over me, and I turned to face Diane, but the look in her eyes was a mix of satisfaction and defiance, as if she relished the chaos unfurling around us. "You wanted to test your little community project, didn't you?" she taunted, her words dripping with malice. "Let's see how it really holds up under pressure."

The air crackled with tension, the festival we had worked so hard to create teetering on the brink of collapse. In that moment, the stakes rose higher than I could have imagined, the warmth of unity threatened by the shadow of betrayal. The future of Silver Pines hung in the balance, and the realization struck me like a thunderclap—this was far from over, and the reckoning was only just beginning.

Chapter 8: Choices

The aroma of freshly brewed coffee enveloped me like a warm hug as I settled into my usual corner at The Crooked Mug, a quaint café nestled on the cobblestone streets of Silver Pines. The clatter of cups and the low hum of chatter filled the air, but all I could hear was the frantic thumping of my heart, the rhythm of my anxiety echoing through my bones. I looked down at my notebook, the pages still stark white, waiting patiently for my thoughts to spill forth. It felt like every word I penned was a boulder in my chest, heavy and unwieldy, just like the burden of the confrontation I had faced with Diane.

I could see her, a specter haunting the edges of my mind, her piercing gaze and venomous words still echoing in the cavern of my thoughts. She thrived on chaos, each jibe and jab calculated to draw blood. I had come to Silver Pines seeking solace, a chance to breathe and rediscover my voice, only to find myself ensnared in a web of petty rivalries and small-town politics. I thought I was resilient, but with every attack, my confidence crumbled a little more. Yet here I was, a moth drawn to the flame of my ambition, but the heat was starting to feel like a scorched reminder of what I might lose.

"Hey there, wordsmith," came a familiar voice, warm and teasing, like sunlight filtering through the clouds. Ethan slid into the seat across from me, his easy smile chasing away the shadows lingering around my heart. "You look like you've been fighting off a herd of stampeding moose. What's on your mind?"

I chuckled, the sound almost foreign to my ears. "More like an angry mob of local gossipers. Diane is back at it again, and I'm running out of ways to dodge her."

His brow furrowed, and the warmth in his eyes flickered with concern. "You know, you don't have to take this on alone. I can—"

"No," I interrupted, a little too sharply. I didn't want him to sacrifice his place here for me, for my battle. Silver Pines was his home, a tapestry woven from family and friendships. I could feel the tension hanging between us, an invisible string pulling tighter as I wrestled with the weight of my own choices. "I appreciate it, really, but I have to handle this myself. I came here to reclaim my voice, not lean on someone else's strength."

Ethan leaned back, crossing his arms, a mix of admiration and frustration playing on his features. "It's not leaning on someone's strength if they want to help. You're not a burden, you know. You're the spark this place needs."

"Easy to say when you're not the one facing down a dragon," I shot back, the corners of my mouth betraying me with a grin. "Or in this case, a very sharp-tongued real estate agent."

His laughter bubbled up like a cool breeze on a hot day, and I felt my tension ease just a fraction. "Maybe you just need a sword," he quipped, raising his coffee mug as if it were a knight's weapon. "I'll defend your honor against the evil Diane with nothing but caffeine and charm!"

"Charming, yes," I mused, stirring the remnants of my coffee absentmindedly. "But I don't think that'll cut it."

"Try me," he replied, leaning forward, his blue eyes sparkling with mischief. "What's your battle plan? You can't just let her push you around."

My gaze drifted to the window, where a light drizzle began to tap dance on the glass, blurring the edges of the world outside. The town was alive, bustling with people moving about their daily routines, oblivious to the turmoil swirling inside me. It was beautiful, and I wanted to be part of it, but I also wanted to shield it from the storm brewing within me.

"I think I need to confront her," I said, the words slipping from my mouth before I could reel them back in. "Face her directly, demand she stop her petty harassment. It's time I stand up for myself."

Ethan nodded slowly, his expression shifting from amusement to something more serious. "That sounds like a plan. Just make sure you've got your shield up, okay? She won't back down easily."

As I absorbed his words, a rush of empowerment surged through me. This was my moment—no longer the timid newcomer trying to find her footing. I could feel my resolve hardening, a new sense of clarity emerging from the fog of self-doubt that had clouded my mind for weeks.

Later that day, I found myself standing outside Diane's office, the small sign swinging slightly in the breeze, her name etched in an elegant script that felt far too inviting for the storm that was about to unfold. My palms were sweaty, heart racing like a runaway train. But with every breath, I reminded myself of the power I wielded, the dreams I had nurtured and fought for.

"Just be bold," I whispered to myself, stepping across the threshold. The door creaked open, and I entered, the familiar scent of freshly printed brochures and polished wood welcoming me like an unwelcome friend. Diane looked up, her eyes narrowing as she recognized the intruder.

"Why, if it isn't the aspiring author. What brings you to my kingdom today?" Her voice dripped with faux sweetness, the kind that made my skin crawl.

I straightened my spine, determination surging through me like a battle cry. "We need to talk, Diane. I want you to stop. Your harassment is unacceptable, and I won't tolerate it anymore."

The silence that followed felt electric, the tension crackling in the air like an impending storm. She opened her mouth to respond, but I held up my hand, my voice steady as I pressed on. "You may think your words have power over me, but they don't. I'm here to stay, and I won't let you chase me out of a place I've come to love."

Diane's smile faltered, her eyes flashing with something darker. "Oh, sweetheart, you have no idea what you're getting into. This is Silver Pines. You're either with us, or you're against us. Choose wisely."

With those words hanging ominously in the air, I felt the world shift beneath my feet, the stakes rising higher than I had ever anticipated. The fight had just begun, and the realization was both terrifying and exhilarating. I had stepped into a battle I hadn't fully understood, but there was no turning back now.

The confrontation with Diane left a jagged edge on my heart, a wound that throbbed with uncertainty. As I stepped back into the bustling streets of Silver Pines, the chatter around me felt muted, like the world was spinning in slow motion while I was caught in a whirlwind of emotions. The townspeople's curious glances were like daggers, and I could almost hear the whispered speculation following me like a shadow. Had I really just declared war on the queen bee of the town?

I found myself wandering aimlessly, the crisp autumn air nipping at my skin, the scent of damp earth mingling with the sweetness of fallen leaves. My thoughts spiraled, caught in a relentless cycle of doubt and determination. What had I done? Standing up to Diane felt empowering, yet the looming threat of her retaliation hung over me like a storm cloud ready to unleash its fury. I needed to regroup, to find my footing again.

Back at The Crooked Mug, I settled into my favorite nook, the corner where the sunlight poured in like liquid gold, illuminating my notebook's blank pages. I pulled out my pen, the familiar weight grounding me as I began to write, but the words eluded me like elusive fireflies on a summer night.

"What's the matter? Cat got your tongue?" Ethan's voice cut through my thoughts, laced with that playful teasing I had grown to adore. He slid into the seat across from me, a steaming cup of coffee in hand, his blue eyes dancing with mischief.

"More like a dragon," I replied, forcing a smile as I closed my notebook. "Diane's officially declared me public enemy number one. I think she might be plotting my demise as we speak."

Ethan raised an eyebrow, amusement playing at the corners of his lips. "You? Really? I thought you were the brave knight charging into battle, sword drawn and everything."

"Oh, please. If I were a knight, I'd be the one hiding behind the castle walls, peeking out just to check if the dragon had gone home for the night." I sighed, running a hand through my hair, the weight of the world settling heavily on my shoulders. "I just wanted to come here and write my story, not get entangled in a local drama."

"Writing's not just about putting words on a page, you know," he countered, leaning forward, his expression earnest. "It's about living your story, too. And sometimes, that means facing the dragons head-on, even if it scares the living daylights out of you."

"Is that your roundabout way of saying I should embrace my inner warrior?" I smirked, my heart fluttering at the earnestness in his gaze.

"Only if that warrior knows how to wield a coffee cup like a pro." His laughter was infectious, drawing a genuine smile from me. We shared a moment of lightness, the weight of the confrontation easing, if only for a heartbeat.

Yet, as the laughter faded, the reality of my situation crept back in. "What if I lose? What if Diane gets her claws into something that puts me in a corner? I came here for a fresh start, and now it feels like I'm stuck in a never-ending battle for acceptance."

Ethan leaned back, contemplating my words. "You're not the only one fighting here. This town needs you, your voice. Sure, it might feel like you're battling a dragon, but sometimes the toughest battles lead to the best victories. You might inspire others to stand up against their own monsters."

"You make it sound so noble," I replied, the skepticism creeping back in. "But what if I'm just making things worse?"

"Then you'll know you fought for what you believe in. And who knows? You might just surprise yourself." He paused, an amused smirk appearing. "Besides, you've got me in your corner, and I've been known to scare off a dragon or two."

Our banter lightened the heaviness in my chest, but as I gazed into the depths of my coffee, I felt the ground shift beneath me. I was grateful for his unwavering support, yet the stakes had never felt higher. The division in town loomed like a shadow over my aspirations. Diane had made it clear that my presence was an unwelcome storm in her perfectly manicured garden, and as much as I wished to stand my ground, the thought of being the cause of chaos in this town churned my stomach.

The following days were a dance of tension and uncertainty. I became a ghost of sorts, slipping through the town while avoiding conversations that might ignite the spark of gossip. I found solace in my writing, pouring my thoughts into the pages as if I were bleeding my soul onto the paper. The café had become my sanctuary, a place where I could hide from the swirling drama outside.

But the safety of my refuge began to feel suffocating. With each passing day, I could sense the energy in the town shift. The whispered conversations grew louder, the looks from passersby sharpened into pointed glares, and the air crackled with the unspoken tension that had seeped into Silver Pines. It was as if I had stepped into a carefully woven tapestry of rivalry, and my very presence threatened to unravel the threads holding it all together.

Then one chilly afternoon, as the sun dipped low and the sky turned a vibrant orange, I made my way to the park, hoping for a moment of clarity. The crunch of leaves underfoot punctuated my thoughts as I strolled along the path, the scent of damp earth and fallen foliage filling my lungs. The park was quieter than usual, and I relished the solitude, allowing my mind to wander through the possibilities of my future.

Just as I reached a secluded bench, I spotted a familiar figure on the other side of the park. Diane, perched like a hawk, her eyes scanning the area. My heart raced, instinctively wanting to retreat, to hide from her prying gaze. But I knew I couldn't keep running. If I was going to reclaim my narrative, I needed to confront this chapter head-on.

I took a deep breath, steeling myself as I crossed the distance between us, the sunlight casting long shadows behind me. "Diane," I called out, my voice steady despite the fluttering in my stomach.

She turned, surprise flickering in her eyes before her expression settled into that familiar smirk. "Well, if it isn't the aspiring author. What a pleasant surprise. Come to regale me with tales of your latest literary escapade?"

I squared my shoulders, refusing to let her condescension shake me. "No more games, Diane. I'm here to talk about what happened the other day. I'm not backing down, and I need you to stop spreading rumors."

Her laughter rang out, sharp and biting, echoing through the park. "You really think you can dictate how I run my business? This isn't a fairytale where you get to slay the dragon and claim victory. This is real life, and I'm not going anywhere."

The anger bubbled within me, hot and fierce, but I took a moment to breathe, to ground myself in the truth of who I was. "Maybe you're right. But I'm not going to let you bully me anymore. I came here to build a future, not to be your punching bag."

Diane's smile faded, her eyes narrowing with something akin to respect mixed with disdain. "You're brave, I'll give you that. But bravery doesn't always win the day. This town has its way of keeping things... orderly."

The challenge in her tone was unmistakable, a subtle warning laced with veiled threats. I felt the tension thicken in the air, the weight of the moment pressing down on us. It was a showdown I hadn't anticipated, a clash of wills beneath the fading light.

"Maybe," I replied, my voice firm, "but sometimes, all it takes is one determined heart to change the course of a story. And I'm not afraid to fight for mine."

With that declaration hanging between us, I turned on my heel and walked away, my heart racing. The path before me stretched out like an uncharted territory, filled with uncertainties, but I felt a flicker of hope igniting within me. I had chosen my fight. Now, all that remained was to see if I could write my own ending in this unpredictable tale.

The confrontation had acted like a catalyst, and as I walked away from Diane that day, the winds of change howled around me, a stark contrast to the calm facade I tried to maintain. My mind raced, the town's divided atmosphere swirling around like a tempest, and I found myself standing at the precipice of something monumental. I was tired of living in the shadows of others' expectations, ready to stake my claim on this narrative. Yet, the weight of that decision settled heavily on my chest, each breath a reminder of the stakes.

I returned to The Crooked Mug, hoping to find solace in my writing, but the familiar buzz of the café felt different now. The cozy warmth and the soft chatter of patrons no longer felt like a refuge; instead, it felt suffocating, a reminder of the growing rift between me and the people of Silver Pines. I slipped into my usual seat, where sunlight poured in through the window, illuminating the dust particles dancing in the air. I stared at my notebook, the blank pages challenging me to fill them with something profound, something worthy of the battle I was waging.

"Back for round two?" Ethan asked, his voice cutting through my reverie as he approached with two steaming mugs, one of which he slid in front of me. "This one's on me. A little pick-me-up for the warrior queen."

I chuckled, the corner of my mouth lifting despite the heaviness in my heart. "More like the queen in a perpetual state of bewilderment. What have I done, Ethan? I feel like I'm playing chess with a master strategist, and I just knocked over my own king."

Ethan settled across from me, his expression softening. "You're not alone in this game, you know. And sometimes, knocking over a king is just a part of strategy. It might create an opening for you to move in another direction."

"Right. Or it could get me checkmated in the next turn," I muttered, lifting the warm mug to my lips, letting the heat seep into my palms. "Diane's not just some pawn; she's the whole chessboard."

He leaned in, eyes glimmering with encouragement. "Then redefine the game. You've got the pieces; now it's time to play your hand. Besides, have you considered that maybe her power is only as strong as the fear she instills? If you stop letting her intimidate you, you might just see the board differently."

I pondered his words, my heart swelling with hope. "You're right. Fear can be a powerful force, but it can also be a prison. I need to break free, not just for myself, but for everyone she's trying to intimidate."

"Exactly," he said, grinning like a child who'd just solved a riddle. "So, what's your next move?"

Just then, my phone buzzed on the table, a jarring interruption to our moment of camaraderie. The screen lit up with a message that sent my pulse racing. It was a group text from the local book club, a gathering I'd been avoiding since the fallout with Diane. They wanted to discuss the recent events in town and invited me to join them at the community center that evening. The irony was not lost on me; the very people who might rally around me were the same ones I had sidestepped, hoping to escape the chaos.

"I have to go," I said, determination flickering to life within me. "If they want to talk about Diane, I can't hide anymore."

"Are you sure you're ready for that?" Ethan asked, concern shadowing his features.

I nodded, the gravity of my choice settling in. "I need to confront the reality of my situation, and who better to face it with than people who understand the stakes?"

With that decision made, I fortified myself with another sip of coffee before heading to the community center. The late afternoon sun dipped low, casting long shadows on the ground as I walked. Each step felt heavier than the last, the weight of the town's judgment palpable in the crisp autumn air.

Upon arriving, I was greeted by a mixture of curious glances and warm smiles, the ambiance charged with a tension that mirrored my own. The room was a vibrant tapestry of personalities, each thread woven into the fabric of Silver Pines. I scanned the faces, looking for allies among the sea of unfamiliarity.

"Glad you could make it!" Ruth, a sprightly woman with curly gray hair and an infectious smile, waved me over. "We were just discussing the latest happenings in town. Sit down, we could use your insight!"

I took a seat, my pulse quickening as I prepared to speak. "Thanks for inviting me, Ruth. I wanted to hear what everyone thinks about...well, everything. The recent tensions have been difficult."

The murmurs of agreement rippled through the group, and as the conversation flowed, I felt the room shift. Voices rose and fell like the tides, each wave bringing new perspectives. Stories were shared—some of resentment against Diane, others of courage in the face of adversity. With each account, I felt the embers of my resolve ignite.

"Diane has been a thorn in our sides for far too long," one woman declared, her voice rising above the rest. "We can't let her dictate how we live our lives in Silver Pines!"

"Exactly!" another chimed in, enthusiasm sparking in her eyes. "It's time we take a stand."

Their passion stirred something deep within me, igniting a fire I hadn't realized I needed. "I agree," I said, my voice steady. "But it's not just about standing against her. It's about creating a community where we all feel safe and supported. If we let fear dictate our actions, we lose sight of what this town truly is."

Cheers erupted around the room, the sound wrapping around me like a warm embrace. My heart soared, buoyed by the camaraderie and shared conviction.

As we began to strategize, forming plans for a community meeting to address the growing tensions, the door swung open. A figure stepped into the room, a chill sweeping in with the gust of wind that followed. The moment I locked eyes with the newcomer, my stomach dropped. It was Diane, her presence darkening the room like a thunderstorm rolling in.

"Thought I'd drop by," she announced, her tone dripping with mockery. "Looks like you've all gathered for a little pity party. I hope you're not planning to cast any spells against me. You'll need more than mere words to send me packing."

The atmosphere shifted, tension spiraling into the air like a coiled spring. The group fell silent, eyes darting between Diane and me, the air thick with uncertainty. I felt every heartbeat reverberate through the room as all eyes turned to me, waiting to see how I would respond to this unexpected twist.

I took a deep breath, channeling every ounce of courage I could muster. "You may think you can intimidate us, but we're not backing down anymore."

Diane stepped closer, her eyes narrowing as she looked at me with a mix of fury and intrigue. "Oh, sweetheart, you have no idea what you're getting into. You might want to think carefully about this little rebellion of yours."

A shiver ran down my spine, the warning implicit in her tone. I glanced around the room, my heart racing as the reality of the moment crystallized. It was no longer just about me standing up for my dreams; it was about the entire town facing a force they had long feared. As the tension hung in the air, poised on a knife's edge, I realized this was just the beginning of a much larger battle, one that would test not only my resolve but the very fabric of Silver Pines.

With my heart pounding and adrenaline coursing through my veins, I prepared to face Diane, knowing that the outcome of this confrontation could change everything. The stakes had never felt higher, and the world around us seemed to hold its breath, waiting for the next move.

Chapter 9: The Heart's Path

The sun hung low in the sky, casting a warm, golden glow over Silver Pines, painting the quaint town in hues of nostalgia. As I packed my things, each item felt like a piece of my heart, each moment stitched into the fabric of this place. Memories of laughter and late-night confessions echoed in my mind like the sweetest melodies, pulling at the strings of my soul. I had arrived in Silver Pines a stranger, but I was leaving as a part of something—a community that had welcomed me with open arms and, more importantly, a heart.

The café, a hub of life and chatter, was a second home. Its rustic wooden tables bore witness to countless conversations, secrets shared over steaming cups of coffee, and dreams whispered into the air like dandelion seeds. I could almost hear the laughter of the locals mingling with the aroma of freshly baked pastries, the scent wrapping around me like a comforting embrace. I had spent so many hours tucked away in a corner with my laptop, crafting articles that spilled my heart onto the page, while the world continued to whirl around me in a blissful cacophony. Yet, amidst all this vibrant chaos, it was Ethan's laughter that had become my favorite soundtrack.

With each day, he had chipped away at my walls, his easy smile and playful banter drawing me into his orbit. I could still remember the first time I had seen him—leaning against the café counter, tousled hair catching the light, eyes sparkling with mischief as he recounted a story to a group of friends. I had felt an instant connection, an inexplicable pull that had rooted itself deep within me. He had become the sun, brightening my days, and now, the thought of leaving him behind felt like a cruel twist of fate.

My heart raced as I gathered my belongings, the urgency of the moment pressing against my chest like a weight. This was it. I was meant to walk away, to step into an uncertain future, yet I felt tethered to this place, to him. The letter, which I had left unopened on the table, loomed large in my mind. Ethan had poured his soul into those words—words that had the power to ignite a flame or extinguish it entirely. I hesitated, glancing back at the café, the windows reflecting my internal struggle.

The wind danced through the streets, carrying with it the scent of autumn leaves and the promise of change. My breath caught as I imagined what lay ahead. The bustling city, with its relentless pace and shimmering skyline, seemed so distant now, like a fading dream. I had been so certain that leaving was the right choice, that pursuing my career was paramount. But as I looked out over the town square, where the fountain bubbled joyfully and children played, laughter ringing out like music, my resolve wavered.

What if this was where I was meant to be? What if my heart had already chosen its path, and I was simply too afraid to follow? I turned on my heel, the impulse bubbling up from within, urging me to reclaim what I was about to lose. The café door swung open with a creak, the bell above announcing my departure—or, perhaps, my return. I stepped outside, my heart thundering, searching for Ethan.

The street was alive with the buzz of conversations, but all I could focus on was him. My eyes scanned the crowd until they landed on a familiar silhouette leaning against the side of the café, his expression a mixture of hope and worry. My breath hitched at the sight, the realization washing over me like a warm tide. He had been waiting, as if he had sensed my inner turmoil, his very presence a beacon guiding me home.

"Lily!" His voice broke through the noise, pulling me closer. "I thought you had left." Relief flooded his features, and it sent a rush of warmth through me, a reminder of the connection we shared.

"I was about to," I admitted, my voice barely above a whisper, "but I—"

Before I could finish, I found myself enveloped in his arms, the world falling away as I melted into him. The embrace felt like an unspoken promise, a declaration that no words could encapsulate. He pulled back slightly, searching my face for answers, his brow furrowed with concern. "What's wrong? You look like you've seen a ghost."

"More like I've seen my future," I replied, the truth spilling out before I could contain it. "I just read your letter."

His eyes widened, a flicker of vulnerability dancing across his features. "And?"

"And it made me realize that I don't want to leave. Not now. Not without giving us a real chance." The words rushed out, my heart pounding with the weight of honesty.

Ethan's expression shifted, the worry melting away, replaced by a dawning hope. "So, what does that mean for us?"

"It means I choose you, Ethan. I choose Silver Pines." The certainty in my voice surprised even me. I could feel the wind pick up, swirling around us, echoing the shift within me.

His grin was infectious, spreading across his face like sunlight breaking through clouds. "You just made my day," he said, laughter lacing his words. "You sure know how to keep a guy on his toes."

"Just trying to keep things interesting," I teased, the playful banter spilling forth as we both took a breath, allowing ourselves to savor the moment.

He stepped closer, our fingers intertwining, grounding me in the reality of this new path. "So, what now?"

"Now, I'm going to stick around and see where this journey takes us. Together."

In that moment, surrounded by the familiar sights and sounds of Silver Pines, I knew the road ahead would be paved with challenges. But for the first time in a long while, I felt an exhilarating thrill at the thought of facing them side by side. The whispers of change swirled around us, and as we stood there—hearts aligned, futures intertwined—I realized this was just the beginning.

The autumn breeze danced around us, carrying the crisp scent of falling leaves and something more—the exhilarating spark of possibilities. As we stood on the sidewalk, the world around us faded into a blur, leaving just the two of us caught in this moment of newfound clarity. Ethan's smile was infectious, brightening my thoughts like a sunbeam breaking through a cloudy sky. The café doors swung shut behind me, sealing away my past decisions while ushering in an unexpected future.

"Okay, so if you're sticking around, I suppose I should probably give you a proper tour of Silver Pines," he said, his voice light and teasing, but his eyes were serious, searching mine for confirmation. "You know, the kind that doesn't involve you hunched over your laptop in the café all day."

I chuckled, playfully nudging him. "What, you mean you don't want me to just live off caffeine and scones?"

"Not if I can help it," he replied, feigning exasperation. "Come on, there's so much more to this town than baked goods, even if they are extraordinary."

With that, he took my hand, and we set off down the winding street, the sun casting long shadows as it dipped lower in the sky. I had always thought of Silver Pines as quaint, but now, as I walked beside Ethan, it felt vibrant and alive, every corner filled with potential.

He led me first to the town square, where a fountain gurgled happily, surrounded by benches and a sprawling maple tree shedding its leaves in a brilliant display of orange and gold. Children chased one another, laughter ringing out like bells. "See that tree?" Ethan pointed, his voice warm with nostalgia. "I climbed it when I was eight and promptly got stuck. My dad had to come rescue me. I still can't look at it without feeling a mix of pride and embarrassment."

I laughed, the sound bubbling up effortlessly. "And here I thought you were the daring type, scaling mountains and leaping from cliffs."

"Only when I have a great safety net," he quipped back, his grin wide. "But the real adventures happen in the quieter moments. Like sharing this town with someone who appreciates it."

His words lingered, igniting something deep within me. We strolled through the square, stopping to watch a street musician playing an acoustic guitar, the melody weaving through the air, adding to the ambiance. The music wrapped around us, each note a thread pulling us closer, making me acutely aware of how different my life felt in this moment.

"So, what's next?" I asked, curious about the life Ethan envisioned for us. "Do you have a grand plan to make Silver Pines the next big tourist destination?"

He chuckled, rubbing the back of his neck. "Only if it involves a lot of ice cream and no commitment to actual work."

I rolled my eyes dramatically. "Ice cream, huh? You're really aiming high."

"Well, I could always throw in a few 'local delicacies'—like my mom's famous blueberry pie."

"Now that's a tempting offer," I said, my heart fluttering at the thought. "What do I need to do to earn a slice?"

"Just be my partner in crime. Help me deliver a few pies around town and charm the locals. And who knows? I might even throw in some homemade vanilla ice cream as a bonus."

"Are you trying to bribe me?" I teased, but inside, a warmth spread, igniting the idea of shared adventures—simple yet profound.

As we wandered deeper into Silver Pines, Ethan led me to a small bookshop tucked between two larger buildings, its windows filled with stacks of colorful novels and quirky decor. "This is my favorite place," he said, pulling the door open with a gentle creak.

The bell above chimed, and a familiar scent of old paper and fresh coffee enveloped us. The interior was cozy, with mismatched chairs, and a cat lazily draped across a stack of books. "Welcome!" a cheerful voice called out from behind the counter. It was Lily, the shop owner, her glasses perched at the end of her nose. "Ethan! Good to see you! And you must be the famous new resident!"

I felt a blush creep up my cheeks, not used to being referred to in such a way. "I wouldn't say famous, but I'm trying to make my mark."

"Fame is overrated," Lily declared, waving a dismissive hand. "But finding a good book? Now, that's a journey worth taking."

Ethan winked at me, his playful nature shining through. "See? Even the locals agree. It's not about how many followers you have; it's about the stories you create."

We browsed through the aisles, my fingers dancing over the spines of novels, each one whispering secrets of worlds untold. I could feel Ethan's presence beside me, his energy infectious as he pointed out his favorite reads. "This one changed my life," he said, holding up a well-worn copy of a classic novel. "I read it every summer, and somehow, I find something new in it each time."

"Like life," I mused, and he nodded, a thoughtful look on his face.

The atmosphere shifted slightly as we moved towards the back of the shop, where a small reading nook beckoned with overstuffed chairs and warm lighting. It felt like a secret haven, a perfect spot for two souls to escape the outside world.

"So, do you think you can handle living in a town where the biggest gossip revolves around blueberry pie recipes and book recommendations?" he asked, plopping into a chair, leaning back with an exaggerated sigh.

"Honestly? It sounds like paradise," I replied, sinking into the chair opposite him, our eyes locking in that electric way that made my stomach flip. "I could get used to this."

"And me?" he pressed, curiosity lacing his tone. "Could you get used to me?"

The question hung in the air, charged with potential. My heart raced at the thought, and I realized how much I wanted to say yes, to embrace this unexpected turn of fate. "Ethan, you're the best part of this town. If I'm choosing Silver Pines, I'm definitely choosing you."

His face lit up like the stars that would soon twinkle above us, and he leaned closer, a playful glint in his eye. "Well, then, I guess I'll have to keep you entertained. How about a pie-baking contest this weekend? Loser has to wear a ridiculous costume to the next town event."

"Challenge accepted," I shot back, my competitive spirit igniting. "But you should know—I'm a culinary disaster in the making."

"Perfect! I love a good underdog story."

The laughter bubbled between us, and I felt a sense of belonging seep into my bones, mixing with the excitement of the unknown. There was magic in the air, the kind that transformed ordinary moments into extraordinary memories. As I sat there, enveloped by the warmth of Ethan's presence and the charm of Silver Pines, I knew I was exactly where I was meant to be.

The sun dipped lower in the sky, painting the horizon with shades of pink and orange, as if the world itself was celebrating my decision. I watched Ethan, his expression softening with every passing moment, and realized that I had never truly allowed myself to embrace the joy of now. "So, pie-baking contest it is, then?" I said, breaking the comfortable silence. "What's the worst that could happen?"

"Oh, just the loss of our dignity, perhaps," he replied, raising an eyebrow with mock seriousness. "But you know, I've heard that humiliation is good for the soul."

"Great! Just what I need—more soul-searching while I'm covered in flour and blueberries."

"Flour is an excellent exfoliant. Consider it a two-for-one deal."

Laughter bubbled between us, the kind that made everything else fade into the background. But beneath the playful banter, I felt a thread of uncertainty tugging at my heart. The fear of failure, of not measuring up, of losing the very thing I was just starting to grasp.

As we left the bookshop, the evening air grew cooler, sending a delightful shiver down my spine. Ethan draped his jacket over my shoulders, the warmth enveloping me like a soft hug. "I hope you don't mind the lack of formality around here," he said, his tone teasing. "We don't do fancy, especially when it comes to pie."

"Fancy is overrated," I replied, slipping my arms into the sleeves. "Besides, I'm here for the chaos, not the etiquette."

"Perfect. Chaos is our specialty."

We walked hand in hand, weaving through the streets of Silver Pines, our conversation flowing freely like the river nearby. The twinkling lights strung above us danced with a life of their own, casting a warm glow that highlighted the charm of the town. I realized I was falling in love not just with Ethan, but with every corner of this quaint place, where every face was familiar, and every moment felt like a page from a story waiting to unfold.

As we approached the small park where a few benches dotted the landscape, Ethan halted. "Let's sit for a moment. I want to show you something."

Intrigued, I followed him to a bench nestled beneath a towering oak. The leaves rustled softly in the breeze, creating a soothing symphony. He reached into his pocket and pulled out a small, crumpled piece of paper.

"I've kept this for a long time," he said, his voice low. "It's a list."

"A list? Of what, exactly? Best pie flavors?"

"Better," he said, his eyes gleaming with mischief. "Things I want to do with someone special. You're the first person I've ever wanted to share this with."

He unfolded the paper, revealing a series of handwritten bullet points. I leaned closer, reading aloud. "Go hiking at sunrise. Attend a music festival. Try every ice cream flavor in town... Wait, this last one says 'conquer my fear of karaoke.'"

He blushed, the color rising to his cheeks. "Okay, fine. That's on there, too. But don't think it's an invitation! I'm no rock star."

"Who says you can't be? You might be a hidden gem."

"Or a total disaster waiting to happen," he quipped, feigning a dramatic sigh. "But I'm willing to risk it if you are."

"Count me in, but only if I get to hear your rendition of 'Livin' on a Prayer.'"

His laughter was contagious, the sound filling the evening air with warmth. "Only if you promise to back me up on those high notes."

As we exchanged banter, a sudden chill crept through the air, shifting the mood from light-hearted to something more profound. My thoughts began to swirl with all the possibilities we had just unleashed, but a small voice nagged at the back of my mind—what if the life I had left behind clawed its way back into my present? What if my decision to stay came with unforeseen consequences?

Just as I was about to voice my concerns, a shadow passed overhead. A man approached, his silhouette cutting sharply against the glow of the streetlamps. Something about him felt off—his gait was hurried, his demeanor tense. I exchanged a glance with Ethan, whose smile faltered slightly.

"Can I help you?" Ethan called out, his tone polite but wary.

The stranger stopped in front of us, a flicker of recognition flashing in his eyes before settling into an expression I couldn't quite read. "Ethan?"

"Yes?" Ethan replied, standing a little taller, instinctively protective.

The man hesitated, as if weighing his words. "You need to come with me. It's important."

"Important? Who are you?" I interjected, a shiver of anxiety snaking down my spine.

He glanced at me briefly before turning back to Ethan. "You don't have time for this. We have to go now."

Ethan's eyes narrowed, his hand tightening around mine. "I'm not going anywhere with you. What's this about?"

"It's about your father. He—"

The man's voice cut off abruptly, as though he had said too much. A sudden, ominous silence settled over us, the laughter and warmth of the evening dissipating into the night. Ethan stiffened beside me, tension radiating from him like a storm gathering force.

"What about my father?" Ethan pressed, a mixture of confusion and anger boiling beneath the surface.

The man took a step closer, his urgency palpable. "He needs you. There's been an accident."

The words hung in the air like a heavy fog, thick with dread. My heart raced, pulse quickening with the weight of what I just heard. Ethan's grip on my hand tightened, and I could feel the raw panic emanating from him. "What kind of accident?"

"I can't explain here. Just trust me."

Trust. The word echoed in my mind, heavy with implications. Just when I had begun to feel grounded, to create a life that I cherished, fate was pulling the rug out from under us. Ethan's face hardened, resolve settling into the lines of his expression, and I knew that whatever came next would change everything.

He turned to me, searching my eyes for answers, his vulnerability laid bare. "I have to go," he said, his voice low. "But I'll be back."

"Ethan—"

"Stay here. Please."

With one last look, he turned and followed the stranger into the shadows, leaving me alone on the bench beneath the oak, the weight of uncertainty crashing down like a tidal wave. In that moment, I understood that the journey we had just begun was about to take a detour I had never anticipated. As the cool night settled around me, I knew I would do anything to bring him back safely, no matter the cost.

Chapter 10: A New Dawn

The sun rises over Silver Pines, draping the town in a soft golden glow that dances over the colorful leaves, painting the world in hues of amber and ruby. I stretch in my cozy little apartment, the smell of fresh coffee wafting through the air, mingling with the crispness of autumn. Today feels different—almost electric. I've made my decision, and as I throw open the window, a brisk breeze sweeps in, rustling the pages of my half-finished novel sprawled across the table.

With renewed energy, I slip into my favorite sweater, the one that feels like a warm hug, and grab my canvas tote bag, adorned with little pine trees—a small tribute to the town that had surprisingly woven itself into the fabric of my life. As I step outside, the crunch of fallen leaves beneath my boots is a symphony of nature celebrating my newfound resolve. Silver Pines is awakening, and so am I.

The path to The Maple Leaf Café winds through the heart of town, and as I walk, I can't help but admire the charming houses, each with its unique quirks and colors. There's the old Victorian with its creaking porch, the quaint cottage draped in climbing ivy, and the modern abode with its sleek lines and glass windows reflecting the morning light. It's a mishmash of styles, each telling a story that resonates with my own. I glance up at the sky, a brilliant blue canvas streaked with wisps of white, and I feel the anticipation bubbling within me, urging me onward.

When I finally push open the café's door, the familiar jingle of the bell announces my arrival, and the aroma of freshly baked pastries envelops me like a comforting blanket. Ethan is behind the counter, and the sight of him sends a flutter through my chest. He's been my anchor in this whirlwind of change, his grumpy exterior hiding a heart that beats with kindness and depth. Today, however, there's a light in his eyes that ignites something within me.

"Morning, sunshine," he greets, his lips curling into a smirk as he notices my beaming smile.

"Just enjoying the beautiful day," I reply, stepping closer to the counter, my heart racing slightly as our fingers brush when he hands me a steaming cup of coffee. The connection lingers, a spark igniting the air between us, and for a moment, it feels like the rest of the world fades away.

"Guess you decided to stick around, huh?" he says, his voice laced with a teasing edge.

"Yeah, I think Silver Pines has grown on me," I admit, taking a sip of the rich brew. It's perfect, just like I remembered, and warmth spreads through me, a reflection of the way I feel about this town and the people in it.

Ethan leans against the counter, his gaze searching mine. "You know, if you're staying, you'll have to help me out more with the café. I can't run this place alone."

"Is that your way of saying you can't live without me?" I counter, raising an eyebrow, a playful smile dancing on my lips.

He chuckles, the sound low and rich, and I can't help but feel like I've won a small victory. "Maybe. Or maybe I just need someone who doesn't look at me like I'm a miserable old bear all the time."

"Old bear? Please, you're more like a grumpy kitten who occasionally lets a smile slip through," I tease back, my heart soaring as his lips twitch into a genuine smile.

Just then, the bell above the door rings, and the morning crowd starts trickling in. Regulars greet us, their voices filling the café with a sense of home. I look around and realize that this isn't just a stop along my journey; it's where I belong. The laughter, the shared stories, and the warmth of community weave a tapestry that draws me deeper into its folds.

As I sip my coffee, I spot Mrs. Henderson at her usual table, knitting needles clicking away as she crafts yet another vibrant scarf.

Across from her, the Peterson twins are already hatching some new mischief, their giggles infectious. Each familiar face feels like a thread connecting me to this place, and I can't help but smile. I am part of this fabric now, not just a visitor observing from the sidelines.

"Hey, Ethan, what's the special today?" I ask, glancing over the menu on the chalkboard.

He raises an eyebrow, a glint of mischief in his eyes. "Guess you'll have to stick around to find out."

I laugh, my heart dancing with delight. "You know I will. What else do I have to do?"

The playful banter continues, our words flowing effortlessly as we navigate the early morning rush together. But amidst the laughter and chatter, an underlying tension simmers, a current of unspoken feelings weaving through our exchanges. It's like a game of chess, each word a strategic move, each glance an invitation to step closer.

As the café fills with warmth and laughter, I can't shake the feeling that today marks the beginning of something significant. I feel it in the air, the way the sun pours through the windows, casting golden beams across our shared space. There's a rhythm to life here, and as I settle into it, I know that I am ready to embrace whatever comes next.

Ethan leans closer, his voice dropping to a conspiratorial whisper. "So, what's next for the great adventurer in Silver Pines?"

I glance around, the laughter of the townsfolk wrapping around us like a warm embrace. "I think I'm ready to explore everything this town has to offer," I say, determination etching my features. "Starting with you."

His eyebrows raise, surprise flickering across his face, but it's quickly replaced by a knowing smile. "Well, buckle up, because Silver Pines has more surprises than you can imagine."

The tension between us thickens, a palpable energy that hints at what might be waiting just beyond the horizon.

As I settle into the vibrant chaos of The Maple Leaf Café, the world around me pulses with life. Ethan leans back against the counter, arms crossed, a smirk playing on his lips as he watches the morning unfold. His eyes, bright and mischievous, dart to the door as more patrons arrive, each bringing their own stories and quirks, transforming the café into a tapestry of warmth and laughter.

"Ready for another day of chaos?" I ask, taking another sip of my coffee, feeling its heat radiate through me like the sun outside.

Ethan rolls his eyes in exaggerated fashion. "If by chaos you mean listening to Mrs. Henderson complain about the weather for the next hour, then yes, I'm absolutely ready."

I laugh, knowing how much he secretly enjoys her rants. "She means well; it's just her way of connecting with the world."

"Or a way of scaring away the tourists," he replies, a twinkle in his eye. "They never come back after hearing her opinions on the 'impending doom' of winter."

Our banter flows easily, an unspoken rhythm that feels familiar and comfortable. As I lean against the counter, I catch snippets of conversations swirling around us, the café buzzing with life. The sound of laughter and the clinking of cups create a symphony that envelops me, wrapping me in its embrace. The smell of cinnamon rolls baking in the oven tickles my senses, and I can't resist the urge to take a peek at what's coming out next.

"Are you plotting a sugar heist?" Ethan quips, catching me eyeing the pastry display with more interest than is polite.

"Just admiring your work," I reply, my eyes wide with mock innocence. "I can't help it; those pastries are practically singing my name."

"Don't worry; I'm sure you'll earn your keep here with just one or two," he says, leaning closer, a conspiratorial glint in his eye. "Besides, Mrs. Henderson has offered to help me with the baking—imagine the chaos if that happens."

I chuckle, imagining Mrs. Henderson decked out in an apron, flour dusting her hair like some culinary fairy godmother. "I'll bring the fire extinguisher."

The door swings open, and in walks Leo, a regular with a penchant for dramatic entrances. His tousled hair and brightly patterned scarf give him an artist's flair that immediately draws attention. "Good morning, fine citizens of Silver Pines!" he announces, arms spread wide as if he's just returned from a grand adventure.

"Ah, the sun has risen on another day of your theatrics," Ethan teases, rolling his eyes.

"Better than another day of your brooding!" Leo shoots back, winking at me. "I see you're in good company, though. Has Ethan finally warmed up to the idea of human interaction?"

"Very funny," Ethan mutters, but I can see the corners of his mouth twitching.

Leo plops down at the table next to us, grinning like a Cheshire cat. "You know, I was just telling Mrs. Henson how this café should host an open mic night. We could showcase local talent and let the world bask in the glory that is Silver Pines!"

"Or scare them away," Ethan retorts, folding his arms across his chest.

"Think of it as a chance to show off your—how do I put this gently?—unique singing voice."

"Thanks, but I'll spare everyone the trauma."

I snicker, watching their playful exchange, feeling a warmth spreading in my chest. This is what I've been searching for—a sense of belonging, a place where laughter drowns out worries.

As the morning rush settles into a comfortable hum, I decide to help Ethan clear some tables, relishing the opportunity to contribute to the chaos that is his life. As we work side by side, our movements become synchronized, and the air around us crackles with an energy that's hard to ignore.

"Hey," I say, leaning against the counter as I stack the dishes, "what do you do for fun around here? Besides, you know, glowering at customers."

Ethan raises an eyebrow, a grin tugging at his lips. "Oh, I have a secret life you'd never guess."

"Really? Do tell."

"I'm actually a master of origami," he replies, deadpan. "By night, I craft paper cranes and occasionally save the world from boredom."

I laugh, the sound bubbling up effortlessly. "You've officially peaked my curiosity. I'm picturing you in a dark alley, folding paper under the moonlight."

"Now you've made it weird," he says, shaking his head but unable to suppress his smile. "But if you're looking for fun, we have the annual harvest festival coming up. That's usually a good time."

"Harvest festival?" My interest piques. "What's that all about?"

"Picture this: hayrides, pie-eating contests, and more pumpkins than you can shake a stick at," he explains, his eyes lighting up with the prospect. "And of course, Leo will be leading the festival's musical entertainment. It'll be a beautiful cacophony."

"Sounds like my kind of chaos," I muse, already envisioning the colorful decorations, the laughter of children, and the scent of cinnamon and nutmeg wafting through the crisp autumn air. "Count me in."

Ethan's expression softens, and I see a flicker of something unspoken in his eyes. "You should come with me. I mean, not just as a café employee but as my—"

"Partner in crime?" I suggest, a grin spreading across my face, hoping to lighten the moment.

"Yeah, something like that." His voice trails off, and for a heartbeat, the air hangs heavy with possibility.

Before I can respond, Mrs. Henderson approaches, her knitting needles clacking together. "Excuse me, young lady," she says, her gaze sharp yet warm. "I hear you're sticking around."

"Yes, ma'am," I reply, straightening slightly under her scrutiny.

"Good. You've got spunk, and we need more of that around here," she declares, her tone leaving no room for argument.

"Thank you, Mrs. Henderson. I'll do my best to bring the chaos you love."

"Oh, I have no doubt. Just remember, if you're joining this community, you're in for the long haul. We'll keep you busy."

"I can handle it," I say, a wave of determination surging through me.

As she walks away, I share a look with Ethan, both of us caught between amusement and the weight of her words. In this small town, where the past and present entwine, I realize that my journey is just beginning. Silver Pines feels like home, and I'm ready to embrace all that it has to offer.

The day unfurls like a vivid painting, every brushstroke bringing Silver Pines to life in a way that makes my heart race. The café hums with chatter, a warm hum of camaraderie that settles around me like a favorite blanket. I steal glances at Ethan as he moves through the café, deftly taking orders and sharing easy laughter with the customers. His easy charm is palpable, and I can't help but admire how he navigates this bustling world, making everyone feel like they're the only one who matters in that moment.

"Hey, I need a hand here!" Leo calls out from across the café, his voice exaggerated and playful. He's balancing a tray of scones that look precariously close to a catastrophe.

I dart over, a grin plastered on my face. "Looks like you're in over your head, Leo."

"Just a bit of a balancing act," he replies, feigning nonchalance as one of the scones teeters on the edge. "A little help would be appreciated, though, unless you'd rather watch me become a pastry casualty."

"Don't worry, I won't let you fall. That would ruin your artistic flair," I tease, steadying the tray while he rearranges the scones with a flourish.

"Ah, yes, my 'pastry masterpiece,'" he says, rolling his eyes. "If only the world could appreciate the nuances of baked goods as I do."

Just then, Mrs. Henderson reappears, a look of intense concentration on her face as she holds up a lopsided scarf she's been knitting. "Young lady, what do you think? Is this the latest trend or a fashion crime?"

I take a moment to study it, biting back a laugh. "I'd say it's a unique statement piece, perfect for making an impression," I reply diplomatically.

"An impression? Ha! That's just a fancy way of saying it's awful!" Leo interjects, snorting with laughter.

Mrs. Henderson narrows her eyes, and I hold my breath, half-expecting her to launch into a tirade. Instead, she just shakes her head, a smirk creeping onto her lips. "You boys are lucky I'm a good sport."

"I think you mean lucky that you're too talented to care about our opinions," I add, lightening the mood as I hand her a cup of coffee.

Her laughter mingles with the chatter around us, and I can feel the warmth of community wrap around me like a hug. It's moments like this that make me realize how much I've come to love Silver Pines. Each character adds their own color to this beautiful tapestry, and I feel grateful to be woven into it.

After a few more moments of playful banter, the café begins to empty as the morning rush subsides. Ethan's expression shifts as he turns to me, a serious note threading through his usual mirth. "So, what's next on your adventure list?"

I lean against the counter, feeling the energy between us crackle. "I'm not sure. Maybe I'll explore the trails or check out that little antique shop down the street."

"Ah, yes, the treasure trove of bizarre finds and questionable items," he says, chuckling. "You might come back with a Victorian doll that gives you nightmares."

"Hey, I'd take that risk for a good story," I reply, grinning. "Besides, I could use something interesting to fill my shelves."

"Or something to scare off intruders," he counters, crossing his arms as he studies me, a spark of mischief in his eyes. "But if you're really looking for adventure, you should join me for a hike. The view from the cliffs is breathtaking."

"A hike? You? Mr. Grumpy Bear?" I tease, raising an eyebrow. "I didn't peg you for the outdoorsy type."

He shrugs, the corner of his mouth twitching up. "You'd be surprised. I can be charming in the wild—like a bear in a top hat."

I laugh, the image taking root in my mind, and nod. "Okay, I'm in. Let's explore this so-called charm of yours."

As the café clears, Ethan and I begin closing up, the familiar routine unfolding like a well-rehearsed play. We sweep floors and stack chairs, the rhythm of our movements syncopating with the fading light streaming through the windows.

"I'm glad you're here," he says quietly, his voice low and earnest. "It's been... different."

"Different good or different bad?" I ask, trying to read his expression.

"Good. I mean, it's always chaotic around here, but you add something I didn't know I needed."

A warmth spreads through me, igniting a flicker of hope. "You're not too bad yourself, you know. You just need someone to draw out your inner sunshine."

"Or my inner bear," he jokes, but the sincerity behind his words is evident, creating an atmosphere thick with unspoken possibilities.

The sun dips lower in the sky, casting long shadows that dance across the wooden floor. Just as we finish up, Leo bursts back through the door, breathless and wide-eyed. "You won't believe what I just heard!"

Ethan and I exchange amused glances, bracing ourselves for whatever theatrical tale Leo is about to spin. "Do enlighten us," Ethan says, rolling his eyes in anticipation.

"Apparently, there's a rumor going around that the old Thompson estate is haunted," Leo declares dramatically, leaning in closer as if sharing a state secret. "You know, the one at the edge of town?"

I feel a shiver race down my spine. "Haunted? Seriously?"

"Yeah! And they say if you're brave enough to go there at midnight, you might catch a glimpse of the ghost of Clara Thompson, who still roams the halls looking for her lost love," he explains, his eyes glinting with excitement.

Ethan snorts, crossing his arms. "Great, just what we need—more ghost stories to scare the tourists."

"But think of the adventure!" I counter, my heart racing at the idea of exploring the estate. "We could investigate."

"Now who's sounding like a grumpy bear?" Leo shoots back, bouncing on the balls of his feet.

Ethan raises an eyebrow, a smirk on his lips. "Are you sure you're ready for that kind of adventure? Ghosts can be pretty clingy."

"Clingy ghosts? Just my luck," I tease back.

As the conversation continues, the air around us thickens with excitement, my mind racing at the thought of wandering through the haunted estate. But beneath the thrill lies a growing tension, a whisper of something lurking just beyond our laughter—a curiosity that calls to me, urging me to explore the shadows.

"What do you say? A late-night expedition to the Thompson estate?" I propose, glancing between Ethan and Leo, my heart pounding with anticipation.

Ethan's expression falters for a moment, the weight of my suggestion hanging in the air. "Are you sure about that? You never know what might be waiting for you in the dark."

"Like a bear?" I quip, but there's a seriousness in his eyes that sends a shiver through me.

"Exactly."

Before I can respond, the door swings open again, this time revealing a figure cloaked in shadow. The café falls silent, and a chill wraps around us as the stranger steps inside, their presence an uninvited disruption that feels both exhilarating and foreboding.

"Did someone say adventure?" the figure murmurs, a voice low and sultry, sending a shiver down my spine.

The atmosphere shifts, thickening with an intensity that leaves me breathless.

Chapter 11: Strained Ties

The sun hung low in the sky, casting a golden glow over Silver Pines, the quaint town I had finally begun to call home. My cozy cottage was bathed in warmth, the scent of freshly brewed coffee mingling with the delicate aroma of lavender wafting from the garden. I had spent the morning indulging in my favorite ritual: sipping coffee on the porch, surrounded by blooming flowers, each petal vivid against the backdrop of a clear blue sky. It was a far cry from the honking cars and crowded sidewalks of the city, a retreat I had desperately needed after years of relentless ambition. Yet, the tranquility I had fought so hard to establish felt as fragile as the porcelain teacups I had inherited from my grandmother.

Just as I began to relax into the rhythm of my new life, the unexpected sound of tires crunching on gravel shattered the peaceful atmosphere. I squinted at the driveway, my heart sinking as a familiar car pulled in. Claire. The mere thought of her arrival sent a jolt through me, a mix of excitement and dread. We hadn't spoken in months, our once inseparable bond frayed by unspoken words and simmering resentment. With a swift motion, I brushed a strand of hair behind my ear, hoping to mask the surprise that colored my cheeks.

The door swung open, and there she was—my sister, vibrant and full of life, as if she had stepped straight out of a magazine. Her hair, a cascade of golden waves, bounced with every step as she rushed toward me, arms wide open. "Look at you! You've turned into a blooming flower!" she exclaimed, her voice a harmonious blend of warmth and teasing. I embraced her, the scent of her floral perfume washing over me like an unwelcome wave, stirring memories of our childhood, laughter echoing through sunlit rooms.

"Thanks, I think?" I replied, stepping back to appraise her. Claire looked like she had just returned from a whirlwind tour of Paris, dressed in a tailored blazer that clung perfectly to her form and a pair of chic ankle boots. She was the epitome of a New Yorker—confident, brimming with ideas, ready to take the world by storm. And there I stood, in my paint-splattered overalls, the remnants of my latest DIY project still lingering on my hands. A stark contrast, indeed.

"Oh, come on! This place is lovely, but we both know you belong in the city, sipping lattes in some trendy café," she chided, sweeping her arm toward the picturesque view behind me. "You can't tell me this quiet life is what you really want."

"Claire, it's not about what I want," I protested, feeling the heat rise in my cheeks. "I needed a break. A chance to breathe."

Her laughter rang out, a musical sound that reminded me of happier days. "Breathe? Please. You've traded the pulse of the city for the chirping of crickets. You'll get bored, I promise you."

As we wandered through Silver Pines, I couldn't shake the feeling that Claire was determined to drag me back into a life that no longer felt like mine. The townsfolk greeted us with friendly waves, their smiles genuine, yet Claire's expression darkened slightly with each nod. It was as if she was searching for something to criticize, some flaw in this idyllic facade.

"Look at this place," she remarked, eyes narrowing. "I mean, who needs a bakery that closes at four in the afternoon? And why is everyone so... relaxed? You're going to turn into one of them, sipping herbal tea and chatting about garden gnomes."

A laugh bubbled up from my throat, but I quickly stifled it. "It's not so bad. The bakery has the best muffins. And I like garden gnomes."

"Of course you do," she retorted, rolling her eyes playfully. "But what about adventure? Spontaneity? Ethan—does he really light your fire, or are you just settling?"

My heart skipped a beat at the mention of Ethan, the man who had unexpectedly entered my life, bringing with him laughter and a sense of belonging I hadn't anticipated. I could feel the heat creeping back into my cheeks, a blush creeping up on me that I couldn't quite suppress. "Ethan is... different. He's kind and genuine."

Claire's brows shot up. "Kind? Genuine? Those are your standards now?" Her tone was teasing, but I could detect the edge of concern beneath it, like a pebble under the soft surface of a freshly mowed lawn.

"Honestly, Claire, it's refreshing to be around someone who doesn't demand perfection. I'm not looking for excitement for excitement's sake. I've had enough of that."

She glanced at me, her expression softening for a moment, but the tension returned, tightening like a noose around our conversation. "You're not happy, are you? I can see it. This place, it's not you. It's just... so quiet."

We turned a corner, the charming little bookstore coming into view. The smell of old pages and coffee wafted toward us, a sweet distraction from the growing discomfort between us. I loved that place, its worn wooden floors and shelves crammed with stories waiting to be discovered. "I am happy, Claire. Maybe you just don't understand what that looks like for me anymore."

"Oh, I understand happiness. I'm not so sure this is it."

The words hung in the air, heavy with implication. I felt the tension simmering beneath the surface, a churning storm ready to break. This wasn't just about my life choices; it was about the choices that had led us here, to this fractured relationship.

With every step we took through the town, I felt the dichotomy of our lives—the fast-paced chaos she thrived in, and the tranquil charm I had embraced. My heart tugged in two directions, caught between loyalty to my sister and the undeniable connection I had with Ethan, a man whose warmth and understanding felt like a balm to my weary soul.

The day wore on, the golden hues of afternoon slipping into a more muted palette as we strolled through Silver Pines. My sister's laughter echoed off the quaint storefronts, but the lightness of it felt slightly brittle, like a sugar sculpture, ready to shatter with the slightest tremor. I led her to my favorite coffee shop, a cozy nook where the barista knew my order by heart. The aroma of roasted beans and the gentle hum of conversation enveloped us, a warm blanket against the growing chill in the air.

"What will it be? The usual?" I asked, trying to inject some normalcy into the moment, but Claire waved her hand dismissively.

"I'll take a double shot of your small-town charm with a side of something extravagant. You know, something with a name longer than my last relationship." Her eyes sparkled with mischief, a teasing grin breaking through her earlier seriousness.

I chuckled, but the comparison hung heavily in the air. I ordered my usual—a caramel macchiato, sweet but balanced—and Claire, with her typical flair, requested a matcha latte adorned with lavender petals and a drizzle of honey. She always had a flair for the dramatic, a tendency to make even the simplest moments feel like a performance.

As we settled into a small table by the window, I caught a glimpse of Ethan just outside. He was walking his dog, a fluffy golden retriever bounding alongside him, tail wagging like a metronome. My heart gave a little flutter at the sight. Ethan's laugh was infectious; it wrapped around me like a hug on a chilly day. He had this way of making me feel as if every ordinary moment held magic—like my life was worthy of being lived with excitement and joy. I waved, my smile brightening at the thought of him joining us.

Claire followed my gaze, her expression shifting from playful to scrutinizing. "So, that's Ethan?" she said, her voice cool, almost calculating. "He looks... outdoorsy. What is he, a hiking guide?"

"Something like that," I replied, a defensive edge creeping into my tone. "He works at the local outdoor gear shop. He's passionate about nature."

"Passionate about nature," she repeated, her eyebrow arching with skepticism. "Charming. And what about you? You're stuck here in this... what did you call it? A 'peaceful haven'?"

"It's more than that," I shot back, frustration bubbling just beneath the surface. "It's a fresh start. A place where I can breathe and think without the constant pressure to keep up with the city."

"Breathe? Sweetheart, you're not a yoga instructor. You're an accomplished woman who should be running circles around the competition, not baking pies in a cottage!"

I clenched my jaw, biting back a retort. Claire didn't get it. She thrived on ambition and the adrenaline of city life. The hustle. The grind. But for me, that had all become suffocating. I preferred the gentle rustle of leaves to the blaring of horns. "I'm happy here. I'm building something real," I insisted, my heart pounding in my chest.

"Building what? A flower shop? Is that your grand plan?" Her laughter was light, but the jab stung.

Just then, Ethan approached, his golden retriever bounding ahead, tongue lolling, full of exuberance. "Hey there!" he called, his voice warm and inviting. "I saw you from across the street. Is that Claire?"

I introduced them, a tiny knot of anxiety tightening in my stomach as I watched Claire's smile fade slightly at the sight of him. "Nice to meet you, Claire," Ethan said, extending his hand. "I've heard a lot about you."

"Really?" Claire's tone dripped with sarcasm, her smile not quite reaching her eyes. "I hope it was all good things."

"Only the best," he replied, unfazed, his smile genuine as he turned to me. "You should have invited me sooner. I would've loved to help you two plan a sisterly adventure."

"Adventure?" Claire scoffed, folding her arms across her chest. "You mean a stroll through the town? Exciting."

"Adventures come in all shapes and sizes," I interjected, a little more defensively than I intended. "Sometimes they're about finding beauty in the mundane."

Ethan glanced at me, his expression encouraging, as if he understood the turmoil swirling beneath the surface. "How about I take you both on a hike tomorrow? Show you the real beauty of Silver Pines?"

"Or maybe I can just show you how to grab a latte that doesn't taste like tree bark," Claire quipped, a smirk playing on her lips.

I shot her a look, hoping she'd dial down the sarcasm. "You might actually enjoy it, Claire. The view from the ridge is breathtaking, especially at sunset."

"Sunset, huh? I guess I could tolerate a little nature for a good view," she conceded, though her tone remained teasing.

We spent the rest of the afternoon in a delicate dance, Claire continuing her gentle probing about my life choices while Ethan chimed in with genuine interest. His easy demeanor soothed my fraying nerves, but each time Claire scoffed or dismissed him, I felt a pang of frustration.

When the conversation drifted toward my art—my passion for painting the landscapes around us—Claire leaned back, crossing her arms again. "I'm not sure this is enough for you, but if you're happy, who am I to judge?"

The undercurrent of her words hung heavy between us. "It's not just about enough," I replied softly, my voice barely above a whisper. "It's about fulfillment."

Ethan, sensing the tension, shifted the focus back to the town, sharing stories about the quirky characters we had both met since I had moved here. I watched Claire's expression soften, the walls around her heart gradually crumbling as she leaned in, genuinely laughing at his tales.

Yet, beneath the laughter, I felt a chasm widening—a rift that stemmed not just from our differing lives but from the unresolved tension that lingered like smoke after a fire. It was as if the distance between our choices was a physical barrier, one that threatened to engulf us in a storm of resentment and longing.

As the sun dipped lower in the sky, painting the world in hues of pink and orange, I realized that this moment would not merely be a fleeting encounter between sisters but a reckoning of sorts. We were two sides of the same coin, destined to clash yet undeniably intertwined, each of us grappling with what it meant to be free.

The air around us crackled with unspoken words as we settled into our chairs, Ethan's infectious laughter fading into a comfortable silence. The café buzzed with the soft murmur of patrons, and the hum of the espresso machine provided a steady backdrop as I felt the weight of Claire's gaze lingering on me. I could sense the impending storm; it hung thick in the air like the humidity before a downpour.

"Tell me more about this art thing you're doing," Claire began, her tone deceptively casual. "I hear the local art show is coming up. Are you planning to enter?"

I hesitated, stirring my coffee absently, watching the creamy swirls blend into a caramel dream. "I might, but it's more about exploring my creativity right now. Not everything has to be a competition, you know."

Her brow furrowed, and I could almost see the wheels turning in her mind. "But you're talented, aren't you? You should be showcasing that talent to the world, not hiding it away like a secret recipe."

"Who says I'm hiding it? Just because I'm not in some fancy gallery doesn't mean my work is any less valid," I shot back, trying to keep my voice steady. I knew she meant well, but her words felt like tiny darts aimed at my insecurities.

Ethan, sensing the tension escalating, tried to interject. "I've seen some of your paintings, and they're fantastic. You have a unique perspective on the beauty around here."

"Thanks," I said, grateful for his support, but Claire rolled her eyes. "Is that your official endorsement? Or are you just trying to win brownie points with her?"

"Actually, I'd prefer cookies," he quipped, a lopsided grin breaking the tension. "Chocolate chip, fresh from the oven."

Claire chuckled but quickly masked it with a cough, her expression shifting back to seriousness. "Look, I'm not saying you need to jump back into the rat race, but you've got talent that deserves recognition. You're wasting it in this sleepy little town."

The words stung like a cold wind biting at exposed skin. "I'm not wasting anything. I'm trying to find out who I am without the pressure of deadlines or the constant hum of the city."

"What if you've forgotten who you are?" Claire's voice was softer now, almost conspiratorial, as if she were letting me in on a secret. "What if this version of you is just a mask? You might think you're happy, but what if it's just... convenient?"

I felt my breath hitch, her words hitting closer to home than I cared to admit. Was this new life merely a façade? Had I traded ambition for comfort? I didn't want to explore that too deeply, not now, not with Claire sitting across from me, her sharp eyes like searchlights.

Ethan leaned in, trying to defuse the moment. "How about this—let's focus on the hike tomorrow. It'll be a chance for all of us to get some fresh air and enjoy the views. Claire can see why this place means so much to you."

She raised an eyebrow, skepticism etched across her features. "Sure, if I don't end up stuck in some muddy field with no cell service."

"Trust me, the views will be worth it," I replied, my excitement bubbling up despite the tension. "There's a spot on the ridge where you can see the entire valley."

"I guess I'll have to put my trust in your idea of beauty," Claire said, smirking.

As our conversation shifted back to lighter topics—Ethan's antics at the gear shop and Claire's latest adventures in the city—the underlying tension remained, simmering just beneath the surface. Claire's presence felt like a wave crashing against the quiet shore of my life, threatening to disrupt the delicate balance I had finally found.

The sun dipped lower, casting a warm glow that turned the café golden, yet the warmth didn't quite reach my heart. I caught Ethan's gaze, and in that fleeting moment, the connection we shared felt electric, a lifeline amid the brewing storm. But Claire was still here, her watchful eyes a constant reminder of the choices I had made and the path I was forging.

When the conversation finally began to wind down, and Claire's impatience bubbled to the surface again, she leaned back, crossing her arms with a sigh. "You know, I worry about you. This life—" she gestured dismissively at the café, the flowers outside, "—isn't going to fill the void left by our family."

"Family?" I echoed, the word tasting bitter on my tongue. "You mean the family that barely speaks? The one that feels more like a competition than a support system?"

Claire's expression tightened, but I pressed on. "You left. You chose the city over us, over everything. And now you're here, telling me I should do the same. That's rich."

For a moment, her eyes flashed with something unreadable—hurt, anger, maybe a touch of guilt. "It's not like that. You know I've always wanted the best for you."

"Is this your version of 'the best'?" I shot back, my heart pounding in my chest. "Because it feels more like a power play, like you're trying to drag me back into your world instead of accepting that I'm happy here."

The silence that followed was deafening, the tension palpable. It felt like a bubble ready to burst, and I half-expected the ground to open up and swallow us whole.

Suddenly, Ethan broke the silence, his voice low but steady. "Maybe we should focus on tomorrow, let Claire see what makes this place special. It's about time she experiences a different kind of adventure."

Claire's lips twitched into a smile, but it didn't quite reach her eyes. "Adventure, huh? Fine. But don't be surprised if I end up with a new appreciation for coffee shops over hiking trails."

"Fair enough," Ethan said, grinning. "But prepare to be amazed."

As we stood to leave, I felt a pang of reluctance. Part of me wanted to stay wrapped in this little bubble of laughter, where the world outside seemed far away. But Claire's presence loomed like a storm cloud, threatening to burst.

We stepped out of the café, the cool evening air wrapping around us. I took a deep breath, inhaling the scent of impending rain mixed with blooming jasmine, but my senses were interrupted by the sound of tires screeching. A car careened around the corner, its headlights cutting through the dusk.

"Watch out!" I shouted instinctively, pushing Claire aside just as the vehicle swerved toward us, barely missing my sister. The world seemed to slow as I braced for impact, heart racing as I reached out, hoping to protect her from the chaos unraveling in front of us.

The screech of brakes echoed in my ears, but all I could focus on was the fear that twisted in my gut. The car skidded to a halt, but it wasn't the vehicle that caught my attention. It was the figure stepping out, a familiar face with an expression that sent shivers down my spine.

"Claire," I breathed, but the warning hung heavy in the air, unspoken yet crystal clear. The evening, once filled with laughter and promise, had morphed into something darker, a shift I could feel deep in my bones.

The confrontation was just beginning, and I couldn't shake the feeling that nothing would ever be the same again.

Chapter 12: The Dinner Party

The warm glow of candlelight flickered across the dining room, casting soft shadows against the walls decorated with an eclectic mix of art, each piece a fragment of my life's journey. I arranged the table meticulously, each setting a small testament to the bridging of my two worlds. The china, a delicate floral pattern that once graced my childhood home, was juxtaposed with the rustic simplicity of Ethan's handcrafted wooden serving dishes. I wanted the night to be a celebration, a fusion of urban sophistication and small-town charm. My heart raced with anticipation, but the growing knot in my stomach whispered reminders of the inevitable clash looming on the horizon.

Ethan arrived first, his presence a comforting balm against my fraying nerves. His unruly curls were tousled in that effortlessly charming way, and he wore a navy blue shirt that brought out the color in his eyes. "Hope you didn't go overboard with the decorations," he teased, leaning in to plant a soft kiss on my cheek, leaving behind a trace of his familiar coffee scent. "I can already tell you're trying too hard to impress Clara."

"Clara," I corrected, a smile tugging at my lips. "And I wouldn't dream of trying too hard." But inside, I felt the weight of expectation; I wanted both of them to see the beauty of the lives we'd built.

We chatted in the kitchen as I stirred a pot of creamy risotto, the aroma of garlic and parmesan wafting through the air. Ethan leaned against the counter, watching me with an amused expression. "You're in your element, aren't you? Cooking like this? It's practically a scene from a rom-com. All you need is a little music in the background."

I chuckled, the tension easing just a little as I turned to grab a bottle of white wine. "And a charming love interest who offers unsolicited cooking advice?"

"Clearly, I'm an expert," he said, feigning seriousness. Just then, the doorbell chimed, and my heart lurched. Clara was punctual as always, the kind of person who believed that time was a construct meant to be honored. I wiped my hands on a towel and straightened my hair, attempting to smooth out the flutter of nerves.

When I opened the door, Clara stood there, radiant and commanding, her auburn hair cascading in waves down her back, her sharp eyes taking in the scene before her. "Wow, you've gone all out, haven't you?" she remarked, stepping in with an air of superiority that made my heart sink. "Just don't let Ethan burn the place down while you're trying to impress me."

"Just you wait," I said with a grin, leading her to the kitchen where Ethan stood, a playful smirk on his face. "I'm sure he can do more than just brew coffee."

The evening began with light conversation, laughter punctuating the air like delicate chimes. I served the risotto, the creamy texture and subtle flavors eliciting approving nods from both sides. Clara regaled us with stories from her latest project, her tone vibrant and animated, and Ethan chimed in, offering his own anecdotes from the café that somehow seemed to echo with a kind of homespun warmth.

But soon, the conversation turned, as it often does, toward the uncomfortable edges of life. Clara leaned back, a glass of wine swirling in her hand, her smile turning sharper. "So, Ethan, how's the business? I can't imagine a small-town café is all that thrilling."

The shift in the atmosphere was immediate. Ethan's expression hardened, his brow furrowing as he set his glass down a little too firmly. "It's not all about thrill, Clara. It's about community. You wouldn't understand that, living in your high-rise bubble."

I felt the tension crackle in the air like static, the kind that precedes a summer storm. Clara's lips tightened, the playful banter replaced by something colder. "Community, right. I suppose when you're in a town that's stuck in the past, it's comforting to cling to whatever traditions you can find. But wouldn't it be nice to aspire to something more? Something bigger?"

Ethan's jaw clenched, and I could see the vulnerability in his eyes turning to defensiveness. "Bigger isn't always better. We have a good thing going. People come in for more than just coffee; they come in for the warmth and the connection. Can you say the same about your—" he gestured dismissively toward the city, "whatever that is?"

I felt a pang of disappointment; the night was spiraling, the two worlds I had hoped would harmonize clashing instead. Clara's gaze turned icy, and I could feel the disappointment pooling in my stomach, a mixture of anger and sadness.

"Ethan, I don't think it's fair to dismiss my life just because it's different from yours," Clara snapped, the sharpness of her words slicing through the room. "I've worked hard to get where I am, and if you can't respect that, then perhaps you shouldn't be at this dinner."

"Respect? You think you deserve respect when you can't even acknowledge that not everyone wants to live in a constant rush to the top?" Ethan retorted, his voice rising. "You don't know the first thing about what it means to build something meaningful."

I watched in helpless horror as their exchange escalated. My heart raced, and I wanted to shout, to interject, to make them see how their words were pulling apart the fabric of the evening I had woven with care. I opened my mouth, but no words came, only the oppressive weight of realization that I had underestimated the complexities of my choices.

As the clamor of their voices filled the air, I felt the warmth of the room dissipating, the candlelight flickering as if sensing the tension. I sat back, feeling both of their eyes on me, the expectations of what this dinner was supposed to represent crashing down around us like fragile glass. In that moment, I realized I couldn't keep hiding behind the comfort of my past; I had to confront the truth of my life, the choices that had led me to this collision of worlds.

With their voices still echoing in my mind, I took a deep breath, searching for a way to guide the conversation back to calmer waters, to remind both of them of the common ground we once shared. But the shadows were closing in, and I could already feel the distance stretching between us, a chasm I wasn't sure I could bridge.

The air in the dining room felt electric, thick with the kind of unspoken words that often loom heavier than the ones that are exchanged. I could sense Ethan's hurt simmering beneath his surface, a tempest brewing beneath the façade of a steady smile. Clara, on the other hand, appeared to thrive on the tension, her eyes flashing with that familiar spark of mischief that often masked her more ruthless critiques. As the conversation began to crumble around us, I wanted nothing more than to grab both of them by the shoulders and shake them until they saw the absurdity of it all.

The laughter from earlier had dwindled to strained smiles, and the sound of silverware clinking against porcelain felt jarring. I placed the wine bottle down with an exaggerated flourish, desperate to reclaim some semblance of control. "How about a toast?" I suggested, my voice slightly too bright, hoping to illuminate the darkness creeping into the evening.

Ethan raised an eyebrow, skepticism written all over his handsome face, while Clara's gaze softened ever so slightly, as if she were contemplating the sincerity behind my effort. "To...?" Ethan prompted, leaning forward with curiosity.

"To the beauty of our differences!" I declared, attempting to inject humor into the moment. "After all, what's a party without a little conflict?"

Clara snorted, a genuine laugh that momentarily broke through the tension. "I suppose you're right. My life is one conflict after another."

"And mine is all about coffee and croissants," Ethan countered, rolling his eyes playfully. "Truly riveting."

As the tension began to wane, I dared to hope we could steer this ship back onto calmer waters. The laughter that followed felt tentative yet genuine, a delicate truce amidst the chaos. I poured another glass of wine, letting the deep, crisp notes wash over us, blending flavors and personalities in the way I had hoped the evening would unfold.

"Honestly, though," Clara continued, her voice dropping to a conspiratorial whisper, "how do you handle the small-town life, Ethan? It must be mind-numbingly boring."

Before he could respond, I jumped in. "You know, sometimes I think it's refreshing. There's a simplicity to it that's rare in this whirlwind we call life."

Ethan nodded, clearly grateful for the reprieve. "Exactly. It's not about the glamour; it's about connection. The café isn't just a place to grab a coffee; it's where people come together, share stories, and build relationships. It's about community, Clara."

Clara scoffed lightly, rolling her eyes. "Community is great and all, but have you ever experienced a rooftop party in Manhattan? That's the kind of connection that really energizes you."

"Right," Ethan replied, his sarcasm sharpened. "Because nothing says 'real connection' quite like shouting over loud music and overpriced cocktails."

"Hey, at least there's good food," Clara shot back, a playful glint in her eyes. "You can't argue with that. Unless your café serves truffle oil fries."

Just as I was about to interject, shifting the conversation toward something less combative—perhaps Ethan's infamous banana bread recipe—my phone buzzed insistently from the table, startling me. I glanced at the screen, and my heart sank. It was my mother, her name blinking ominously. I hesitated, a wave of anxiety washing over me, wondering whether to answer or ignore it. My mom's calls usually led to the kind of drama I was trying to avoid tonight.

Ethan caught my eye and nodded toward the phone, silently encouraging me to take the call. "Go ahead, it's fine," he said, though I could hear the slight edge in his tone, an unspoken understanding that this was just another layer to our already complicated evening.

"Excuse me for a moment," I said, standing up and stepping into the hallway, the distant hum of their banter following me like a shadow.

I answered the call, my heart racing. "Hey, Mom."

"Sweetheart! I just wanted to check in," she said, her voice bright but somehow fraught with concern. "How's the dinner going? Are those friends of yours treating you well?"

I swallowed hard, glancing back at the dining room. "It's... going," I managed, my tone betraying me.

"Is Clara being difficult? You know she always has those opinions," she replied, her tone dipping into that familiar maternal worry.

"Actually, it's Ethan who—" I began, but the words caught in my throat. Would I really share the reality of the evening? I wanted to paint a picture of peace and harmony, not the fractious atmosphere that had enveloped us.

"Listen, sweetheart," my mother interrupted, "I just think it's important that you don't lose yourself in these people. You're doing great things. Just remember where you came from, okay?"

Her words stung, the hint of disappointment echoing in the back of my mind. "I know, Mom. I promise I'm handling it."

"Alright, well, I just wanted to remind you that family is the most important thing."

The conversation trailed off, and I hung up feeling heavier than before, a weight settling in my chest. I returned to the dining room, where Clara and Ethan were both deep in conversation, the tension temporarily forgotten.

"Everything okay?" Ethan asked, concern flickering across his features.

"Yeah, just a quick check-in," I replied, forcing a smile. "Let's dive back in. What's the best part of living in a small town?"

"Definitely the gossip," Clara replied with a teasing grin. "I hear your café is at the center of all the drama."

Ethan laughed, his earlier defensiveness melting away. "You have no idea. We had a chicken fiasco last week that involved a raccoon, a broken door, and Mrs. Whitaker's prized tomatoes."

"What? You can't leave me hanging like that!" Clara leaned in, intrigued.

And just like that, the evening began to shift again, laughter threading through the air, knitting us back together. I relaxed, relishing the warmth of their camaraderie, the cracks in the façade beginning to fill with a sense of understanding.

Yet even as I found solace in their banter, a whisper of unease lingered at the edges of my thoughts. I was reminded of the conversations I needed to have, the truths that still sat between us like an uninvited guest. But for now, we laughed, and I clung to that joy, hoping that perhaps, just perhaps, there was a way to bridge the divide without losing myself in the process.

The dinner table, once a sanctuary of warmth and laughter, now felt like a battlefield littered with unspoken words and fractured glances. As the jokes resumed, the air was thick with tension, each punchline landing with the weight of unsaid frustrations. Clara's playful banter flowed, but beneath the surface lay an edge sharper than any knife I had laid out for our meal. I leaned back in my chair, surveying the scene before me—two worlds colliding like tectonic plates, and I was caught in the middle, a reluctant referee in a match I never wanted to witness.

"Do you have any plans for the weekend, Ethan?" Clara asked, her voice a touch too sweet, the kind that made my insides twist. "I hear there's a festival in town. That must be... quaint."

Ethan's jaw tightened. "Quaint isn't a word I'd use. It's a gathering of local artists, music, and food. It's actually quite vibrant."

"Vibrant, huh? A far cry from your everyday grind, I assume." Clara leaned in, her expression mischievous, but I saw the spark of something darker behind it.

"Everyday grind?" he echoed, his tone suddenly colder, almost as if he were issuing a challenge. "I think you'd be surprised at how many people come out to enjoy it. It's not all about neon lights and skyscrapers, Clara."

"Not everyone needs the thrill of city life to feel alive, you know," I added, attempting to throw a lifeline to Ethan. "There's something refreshing about embracing the simpler things."

"Ah, embracing the simpler things," Clara scoffed, rolling her eyes with theatrical flair. "How very... charming. But tell me, what happens when you tire of charm? What's the plan then?"

Before I could respond, Ethan shot me a sideways glance, a silent plea for support, but Clara's piercing gaze trapped me in a web of expectation. "What happens when the café closes? Will you pack up your quaint life and run back to the city, tail between your legs?" she taunted, her words laced with a toxic sweetness.

The laughter had evaporated, replaced by the stark reality of her challenge. I felt a cold sweat prick at my temples, the sudden heaviness of what we were doing hanging like a storm cloud above us. "That's not really fair," I said, my voice barely above a whisper. "Ethan's café is more than just a business; it's a lifeline for many in our town."

"Oh please," Clara waved a dismissive hand, as if swatting away a fly. "I can't believe you want to cling to that idea. You have so much potential, yet you're stuck in this—this dream of a slow life with artisan coffee and local artists."

"Local artists are people too," Ethan shot back, his eyes flashing with indignation. "You think being an artist means you can only exist in the city? It's people like you who overlook what really matters. Community isn't defined by location, Clara."

"Community is defined by ambition!" she snapped, her voice rising. "You're both just hiding in your little bubble, pretending that it's enough."

"I'm not pretending," I said, feeling my pulse quicken as the room grew tense. "I'm choosing this. I'm creating a life that feels genuine to me."

"Creating a life?" Clara laughed, but there was no humor in it, only derision. "More like playing house. How long until you realize it's all a game? There's more out there, you know?"

"I'm not playing," Ethan interrupted, his voice steady but fierce. "This is real for us. It's not some fantasy escape from reality."

"Sure, if you call waiting for the next town meeting 'real,'" Clara replied, sarcasm dripping from her tone.

The tension between them exploded, the air thick with unspoken truths and resentments that had been festering just beneath the surface. I felt the weight of disappointment settling in my stomach, a heavy anchor dragging me down. I had invited them both here, believing I could bridge this gap, but instead, I was watching my two worlds tear apart at the seams.

In that moment, I realized I could no longer straddle the line between them. It was time to choose a side, and the realization hit me with the force of a freight train. The energy in the room shifted; the laughter had gone, replaced by a palpable ache that stretched between us like an invisible barrier.

"Maybe it's not about where you are, but what you make of it," I said, my voice shaky but resolute. "Life isn't just about the hustle and bustle. It's also about connection, about finding joy in the everyday."

Clara leaned back in her chair, arms crossed, a smirk curling at her lips. "Is that what you tell yourself? That this life is enough?"

Ethan leaned in, a hint of frustration creeping into his voice. "It's enough for me. Maybe if you spent a little more time in the real world, you'd see it too."

The words hung in the air, thick and heavy. Clara narrowed her eyes, a flicker of disbelief crossing her features. "And maybe if you stepped out of your cozy café, you'd understand what real ambition looks like."

"Ambition doesn't have to look a certain way," I interjected, feeling the tension bubble over. "What's the point of pursuing a life that makes you miserable? If you're unhappy, what's the use of ambition?"

"Wow, you really don't get it, do you?" Clara said, her voice rising as her frustration peaked. "You think because you've found a slice of happiness, it means you've achieved something? That's just a comfortable illusion."

"I think you're the one who doesn't get it," Ethan shot back, his voice cracking with emotion. "You're so busy chasing some ideal that you're missing the beauty right in front of you."

The two of them were on the brink of a full-blown argument, and I felt the walls closing in. I glanced out the window, the fading light casting long shadows across the room, mirroring the darkness that had begun to settle in my heart. What had started as an evening filled with promise was spiraling into chaos, and I found myself caught in the crossfire.

"Enough!" I shouted, surprising myself with the force of my voice. Both Clara and Ethan paused, their eyes wide, and for a moment, the air was still.

"Maybe we should just stop pretending we can all fit together," I said, the words spilling out before I could stop them. "Maybe it's time to recognize that we're all just grasping at something different."

The silence that followed was suffocating. I could see the realization wash over Ethan's face, and Clara's expression shifted from surprise to something resembling understanding, though it was laced with hurt.

"I didn't mean to—" I began, but the sound of a door slamming outside cut me off, startling us all.

My heart raced as I turned to the sound, instinctively fearing the worst. I opened the door, the cool evening air rushing in, and saw a figure standing at the edge of the porch. The silhouette was familiar, but the tension surrounding it was a storm all its own.

As the figure stepped into the light, I felt my breath catch in my throat. It was someone I hadn't expected to see, someone whose presence threatened to unravel the fragile threads of my carefully constructed life even further.

"Surprise!" they exclaimed, a grin spreading across their face. The laughter and lightheartedness from before felt like a distant memory as I stood frozen, the reality of my dinner party shattered by an unforeseen arrival.

Chapter 13: A Turning Point

The fallout from the dinner party lingers in the air like the fading scent of autumn leaves, sharp and bittersweet. The café hums with its usual chatter, but the warmth of the steaming cups before us contrasts sharply with the chill that has settled between Ethan and me. I can see it in the way he stares into his coffee as if seeking answers in the swirling depths instead of meeting my gaze. His usual spark—those witty comments that used to dance like confetti between us—is now muted, as though the world had pressed a soft filter over his vibrant personality.

"Ethan," I begin, my voice barely above a whisper, "we need to talk." The words slip out, each one a pebble dropping into the silence, reverberating softly as they settle. I can almost feel my heart thrumming against my ribs, anxious and eager for the dialogue that seems to hang just out of reach.

He looks up, and for a moment, I catch a glimpse of the man I adore—eyes bright and alive, a thousand jokes waiting to tumble from his lips. But then that flicker dies, replaced by a solemnity that weighs heavy on my chest. "Yeah," he replies, his voice low, like the last echo of a song fading away.

I take a deep breath, the warm aroma of coffee enveloping me, trying to draw courage from its comforting embrace. "I can't pretend like everything is fine anymore. That dinner... it didn't go the way I hoped. It's like I can feel the walls closing in, and it scares me." My fingers wrap around my mug, grounding myself as I lay my heart bare on the table between us, each word a thread woven into the tapestry of my fears.

Ethan leans back, his posture a fortress I'm desperate to breach. "It was a disaster, wasn't it?" he muses, a hint of humor creeping back into his voice, though it feels fragile, like glass on the brink of shattering. "I thought I was ready for your world, but maybe I'm not cut out for it."

"Don't say that." My heart twists at the thought of him retreating further. "You're more than capable, Ethan. You're brilliant and funny. It's just... it's complicated."

"Complicated doesn't even begin to cover it." He chuckles, though the sound lacks its usual warmth. "Your family is like a well-scripted reality show, and I'm just the poor sap who wandered in without a cue card."

I can't help but smile at that—Ethan's wry humor, even when tinged with sadness, always cuts through the gloom like a sunbeam breaking through a storm. "You're not just some extra, you know. You matter to me, and I don't want to lose you."

For a moment, the tension in the air shifts, and I can feel the barriers begin to crack. "It's not just your family, either," he says, his voice turning serious, drawing me in with its sincerity. "I've got my own issues to sort through. The past... it has a way of haunting you, doesn't it? Like a shadow you can't quite shake."

The admission hangs between us, heavy and raw. I nod, my chest tightening with understanding. "I get that. We all have ghosts, Ethan. Sometimes, they whisper in your ear, telling you that you're not enough. I've felt it every time I've doubted myself, every time I've worried that I'll never fit into your world."

He stares at me, the silence crackling like a live wire, and then he speaks, voice low and earnest. "I think we've both been afraid. Afraid of the truth, afraid of getting hurt."

"I've been terrified," I admit, my heart racing as I sift through my own vulnerability. "I thought I could be brave, but I feel like I'm stumbling in the dark, just hoping to find my way."

Ethan leans forward, the distance between us closing, his eyes locking onto mine with an intensity that sends shivers down my spine. "But what if we faced the dark together? What if we stopped hiding from each other?"

The heat from our mugs begins to seep into my fingertips, and I take a moment to breathe, letting the moment sink in. There's something beautifully terrifying about vulnerability, and it blooms between us, filling the empty space with possibilities. "Together," I echo, the word a promise, a pact.

"I don't want to run away from this," he says, and for the first time since the dinner, there's a flicker of hope in his voice. "I want to be here with you, all the messy, complicated parts included."

And just like that, the ice begins to melt, dropping away to reveal something raw and real beneath. "You know, I've always admired how you confront the chaos," I say, a smile breaking through. "Even if it makes my family seem like a bunch of well-meaning, slightly mad puppies."

"Mad puppies?" He raises an eyebrow, a smirk finally dancing back onto his lips, and for a moment, we're lost in laughter. "I can handle that. I've faced worse. Remember the time I tried to bake cookies? That was a real disaster."

"Ah, yes. The great flour explosion of twenty-twenty-three," I tease, my heart swelling as we bask in the warmth of shared memories. "I thought I was going to have to call in the SWAT team to clean up."

Ethan's laughter fills the air, and it feels like the first rays of sunshine after a long storm. The walls that had been closing in now feel like they're expanding, breathing life back into our connection. As we sit there, two souls tethered together by our flaws and fears, I realize that this moment—this turning point—is where our journey truly begins.

The air between us crackles with the remnants of our laughter, yet an underlying tension still simmers beneath the surface. I can see the shadows of doubt still dancing in Ethan's eyes, flickering like candle flames caught in a breeze. His smile, though genuine, doesn't quite reach the corners of his eyes, and I know we're not out of the woods yet. But for now, we're in this together, and it feels like a fragile truce, one that has the potential to bloom into something beautiful—if only we can nurture it.

"Okay, enough about my cookie disaster," Ethan says, taking a sip of his coffee, his brows furrowing in mock seriousness. "Let's talk about your family instead. What's the verdict? Are they plotting to send me to the moon, or is there still a chance for me to stick around?"

I can't help but chuckle at his nervous energy. "Well, there's always a risk. They do have a thing for the dramatic." I lean in, dropping my voice to a conspiratorial whisper. "Last week, my aunt Judith showed up with a family tree that had more branches than a sprawling oak. I thought she was trying to pull me into some sort of genealogical cult."

Ethan's laughter bubbles up, and in that moment, the tension begins to dissolve. "That sounds like a great opening for a reality show: 'Family Trees and Twisted Roots.'"

"Right? Imagine the tagline: 'Where family secrets grow as wild as the branches!'"

"Next season, starring us as the unsuspecting victims," he grins, the warmth in his gaze rekindling the spark between us. "But in all seriousness, I'd like to meet them someday. I know it sounds terrifying, but I'm willing to face the family circus."

"Good luck with that," I tease, but inside, his words flutter through me like the wings of a trapped butterfly. The thought of him stepping into my world, of weaving his life with mine, sends a shiver of excitement down my spine. "They're a handful, but once you get past the surface chaos, they're fiercely loyal."

He tilts his head, a playful smirk gracing his lips. "I'll keep that in mind. Just remind me to bring some popcorn and a safety net."

As we share more laughter, I can feel the walls around my heart beginning to crumble. Ethan's willingness to face my family, to confront the chaos head-on, feels like a promise—a testament to his commitment. I take a sip of my coffee, letting the warmth seep into me, pondering the layers of vulnerability and strength we've uncovered.

"Can I ask you something?" I say, shifting my tone as a more serious note creeps back in.

"Hit me," he replies, leaning forward, his interest piqued.

"What were you so afraid of, really? After everything we talked about, what's holding you back from fully diving into this?"

His gaze flickers away for a moment, a cloud of uncertainty passing over his features. "I guess I've never been good at relationships. Every time I let someone in, it feels like I'm handing them a loaded gun—dangerous and unpredictable."

"Ethan, you're not dangerous," I protest gently, but he shakes his head.

"Not like that. I mean, I'm a mess. I have a history—issues with commitment, with trusting people. I just don't want to ruin what we have by dragging my baggage into it."

"That's the thing, though," I say, my voice steady, though my heart races at the admission. "Everyone has baggage. What matters is whether we're willing to help each other carry it. I'm here for you, and I need you to be here for me, too."

His expression softens, and the vulnerability between us shifts again. "You're right. It's just... scary. I want to be the person you deserve, not the broken version of myself that I keep hiding behind."

"Then let's work on it together." I reach across the table, our fingers brushing against one another, and the electricity zings between us, igniting a spark I didn't realize I was missing. "You don't have to be perfect. Just be honest. That's all I need."

"Honesty, huh?" He chuckles lightly, squeezing my hand. "Then let's be honest about the fact that I might need a little extra practice when it comes to navigating family drama."

"I'll put you in a crash course," I promise, grinning at the thought. "By the end of it, you'll be negotiating peace treaties over Thanksgiving dinner."

"Thanksgiving?" He raises an eyebrow, and I can see the glint of mischief in his eyes. "So there's a chance I could survive the family holiday gauntlet? Sounds like a challenge I'm willing to accept."

With the banter flowing, I can feel the tension between us transforming into something lighter, more buoyant. The fears that once felt like shadows loom less threatening now. As the conversation sways, I catch glimpses of the man I fell for—brave, funny, and surprisingly sweet beneath his sometimes rugged exterior.

"Okay, so what's next for us?" I ask, genuinely curious, my heart pounding in my chest like a drumbeat. "Are we going to set some sort of guidelines for this adventure we're on?"

"Guidelines, huh?" He considers, tapping his finger against his chin dramatically. "How about we start with rule number one: no more avoiding conversations? Honesty only."

"Agreed. And rule number two: coffee dates are mandatory. At least once a week."

"I can work with that." He grins, his eyes sparkling. "And how about a rule for spontaneity? We need to make room for the unexpected."

"Spontaneity sounds dangerous," I tease, though I can feel the thrill of excitement welling up inside me. "What do you have in mind?"

"Oh, just something simple—like a random road trip or an impromptu karaoke night."

My laughter rings out, a sweet melody in the warm air. "Karaoke? You're really going to throw down the gauntlet, aren't you? Just so you know, I have a hidden talent for belting out 'I Will Survive' with great passion."

"Now I'm sold. We're doing this."

As our laughter intertwines with the café's ambiance, I feel a sense of freedom blossoming within me. With each shared joke, each raw confession, we're forging a new path together. The road ahead is uncertain, but I can see the promise of joy shimmering on the horizon, just waiting for us to embrace it.

The warmth of the café wraps around us like a familiar blanket, a sanctuary from the world outside. The rhythmic clinking of cups and the barista's cheerful banter create a comforting backdrop to our unfolding connection. I watch as Ethan leans back in his chair, a spark of determination igniting in his eyes. There's a newfound energy between us, a promise of what's to come, and I can't help but feel like we're on the precipice of something extraordinary.

"Okay, so we've established the coffee date rule, the honesty rule, and the spontaneity clause," he declares, grinning as he takes a sip of his drink. "What else do we need? A rule about dessert?"

"Dessert is non-negotiable," I reply with mock seriousness. "Life is too short to skip dessert. That should be rule number one."

Ethan chuckles, shaking his head in feigned disbelief. "So we're just going to throw caution to the wind and indulge like there's no tomorrow? I'm in. But I might need a wheelbarrow for the aftermath."

"Fair warning: I take my chocolate cake very seriously."

He leans closer, his voice dropping to a conspiratorial whisper. "What if I told you I'm more of a pie person?"

The mock horror on my face sends us both into fits of laughter. "A pie person? You might as well have declared your allegiance to the dark side!"

"Hey, don't knock the pie until you've tried it. I'm pretty sure there's a place in my heart for both cake and pie."

"Compromise, then. I'll introduce you to the wonders of cake while you lure me into the sweet embrace of pie."

"Deal."

Just as we settle into a comfortable rhythm, the bell above the café door jingles, slicing through our bubble of warmth. I turn to see a figure standing at the entrance, drenched in the muted light of the autumn afternoon. It's Mia, my younger sister, her expression a curious mix of excitement and concern. I can already sense the brewing storm that tends to follow her whenever she shows up unexpectedly.

"Mia!" I exclaim, genuinely surprised. "What brings you here?"

She saunters over, her usual confidence evident in the way she carries herself. "I was in the neighborhood and thought I'd drop by. Looks like I'm interrupting a moment."

Ethan straightens, shooting me a glance that dances between concern and amusement. I wave my hand dismissively, silently assuring him that this isn't the end of the world. "Not at all! We were just discussing pie and cake and the complexities of dessert diplomacy."

Mia raises an eyebrow, a teasing smile creeping across her face. "Ah, sounds riveting. But really, I need to talk to you."

Ethan's expression tightens slightly, and I can feel the shift in the air as Mia's presence draws me back into the orbit of family obligations. "Is everything okay?" I ask, my instincts kicking in.

She hesitates, glancing around as if the walls are closing in. "Well, not really. It's about Mom."

My stomach drops at the mention of our mother. "What about her?"

"She's planning something, and it might involve you. Like, really involve you."

The playful banter evaporates, replaced by a sudden heaviness that settles like a fog in the café. I lock eyes with Ethan, searching for some reassurance, but his expression mirrors my concern. "What do you mean?" I ask, my voice barely above a whisper.

Mia shifts uncomfortably, her fingers fidgeting with the strap of her bag. "She wants to throw this big family gathering. Something... formal. You know how she is. And I think she expects you to bring a 'plus one.'"

My heart races. A formal gathering means introductions, expectations, and the potential for chaos—particularly if Ethan's in the mix. "A plus one?" I echo, trying to process the whirlwind of emotions. "What does she think this is, a wedding?"

"Honestly, I think she's trying to orchestrate a matchmaking event, and you're the star of the show."

Ethan raises his eyebrows, clearly amused by the absurdity of it all. "Wow, sounds like your mom is the head of an unsolicited dating service."

"Exactly!" I exclaim, a mixture of laughter and disbelief bubbling up within me. "As if my love life needs more spotlight."

"Is that what you want?" Mia presses, her tone suddenly serious. "You can't keep pretending like this is all easy. It's going to get messy, and I don't want you to feel cornered."

Ethan leans forward, sensing the gravity of the situation. "You're not cornered. You have a choice, right?"

"Choice? That's rich. This is my family we're talking about," I say, frustration bubbling to the surface. "When has choice ever been a real thing at one of our gatherings?"

"Then let's shake things up," Ethan says, his eyes lighting up with mischief. "You know, show them what a wild ride your love life can be. Bring me as your date, and we'll turn this whole matchmaking fiasco into the best night ever."

I blink at him, caught between panic and excitement. "Wait, you're serious?"

"Why not? It could be fun. We'll make it a game—like a scavenger hunt for awkward family moments. I'll take notes."

"Why would you want to subject yourself to that?" I ask, half-laughing, half-horrified at the idea.

"Because I want to be part of your world, even the chaotic parts," he replies, his voice steady and sincere. "And I promise to handle any embarrassing family stories with grace."

My heart swells with appreciation, but a flutter of anxiety still lingers. "It's not just embarrassing stories. My family doesn't do subtle."

"Subtlety is overrated. Besides, we can make a pact—if we both survive, we'll treat ourselves to dessert for the rest of the month."

"Now that's a plan I can get behind," I say, feeling a grin break across my face. "But if we're doing this, we need to prepare. I'm not losing my sanity for a slice of pie."

Mia's laughter cuts through the tension, and for a moment, I allow myself to bask in the lightness of it all. But just as I'm about to embrace this unexpected adventure, my phone buzzes on the table, the screen lighting up with a message from my mother.

"Speak of the devil," I murmur, my heart racing as I glance down at the screen. The words swim before my eyes, turning the vibrant atmosphere of the café into something suffocating. "We need to talk about the gathering," it reads, and the air grows thick with uncertainty.

Ethan leans closer, concern etched on his face. "What does she want?"

"She says it's urgent."

In that moment, as I glance between the text and Ethan's anxious expression, I realize the stakes have just risen. The idea of facing my family, of unraveling the truth about my feelings for Ethan amidst their scrutiny, suddenly feels like a tightrope walk over a chasm of uncertainty.

"Okay," I say, my voice shaky but resolute. "Let's do this. But I need you to promise me one thing."

"Anything," he replies, his gaze steady, unwavering.

"No matter what happens, we stick together."

He nods, and the weight of his promise settles over me like a comforting blanket, even as the world beyond the café walls swirls with chaos and impending confrontation. As I type out a response to my mother, my heart pounds in anticipation, each keystroke echoing with the weight of decisions yet to be made.

And just as I hit send, the door swings open again, and a gust of wind rushes in, carrying with it the scent of impending rain and a sense of foreboding. In that moment, I realize that no matter how prepared I think I am, the storm that lies ahead may not just be a family gathering—it might be a reckoning, with shadows lurking at the edges of our lives, ready to pounce when we least expect it.

Chapter 14: Winds of Change

Leaves pirouetted from their branches, caught in a dance that felt both deliberate and whimsical, as if nature had decided to put on a show just for us. The air was crisp, imbued with that particular October chill that made you want to curl up with a good book or, better yet, a warm drink. The Maple Leaf café, nestled on the corner of Main Street, pulsed with the energy of Leaf-Peeping Weekend preparations. I stood behind the counter, a steaming mug of spiced cider cradled in my hands, my eyes flitting to Ethan, who was adjusting a string of fairy lights above the entrance.

"Not bad for a couple of amateurs, huh?" I remarked, taking a sip. The heat wrapped around me like a blanket, the sweetness laced with hints of cinnamon and nutmeg.

Ethan turned, his dark hair tousled, a smudge of caramel from our earlier endeavor dusted across his cheek. "If by 'amateurs' you mean culinary wizards, then yes, we're practically Michelin-starred chefs." He winked, his smile genuine and bright, and for a moment, the bustling café faded away.

"Culinary wizards? I think that title belongs to the grandmothers of this town," I teased, leaning against the counter, my heart fluttering as I caught his gaze. "I'm just the apprentice, stealing their secrets one pie at a time."

He chuckled, the sound deep and warm, sending a thrill through me. "Apprentice or not, your storytelling event is going to be the highlight of the weekend. I can already see the crowds lining up for their turn."

A surge of pride swelled within me. It wasn't just about the storytelling; it was about bringing people together, sharing the unique tales that made Silver Pines more than just a dot on the map. As I looked around, the café buzzed with life—patrons chatting, the hiss of the espresso machine, and the delightful clinking of cups filling the air.

But beneath the vibrant surface, shadows loomed. Diane, the self-proclaimed guardian of tradition, was stirring the pot once again. Word had reached me through the grapevine that she was busy spreading tales of discontent, muttering about how my newfangled ideas threatened the very soul of our quaint town. The fact that she had taken it upon herself to gather a small troupe of like-minded individuals to rally against me was disheartening.

"Isn't it just lovely," I said, rolling my eyes as Ethan watched me with an amused expression. "Diane is out there peddling her discontent like it's a hot commodity."

"She's not as bad as you make her out to be," Ethan replied, leaning against the counter, his arms crossed. "I think she's just scared of change."

"Scared or stubborn? There's a fine line." I sighed, frustration lacing my voice. "It's like trying to turn a freight train around. No amount of enthusiasm will budge her."

"Maybe you just need to show her that change can be good." His gaze held mine, earnest and unwavering. "Invite her to the storytelling event. Let her see the community's support firsthand."

I considered his words, the flicker of hope igniting a spark within me. Perhaps inviting Diane was an outlandish idea, but sometimes the most unexpected gestures could shatter walls. "Maybe you're right," I conceded, though doubt gnawed at me. "It's worth a shot."

As preparations progressed, the sun dipped lower in the sky, painting the world in hues of gold and crimson. I felt the pull of the festival, the magic that enveloped Silver Pines during this time of year. We strung up decorations, our laughter weaving a tapestry of memories that seemed to stick to the walls like the scent of cinnamon in the air.

In the days that followed, the café transformed into a wonderland. Pumpkins adorned the tables, each one a canvas for a different artist in town, from the delicate strokes of a child's hand to the intricate carvings by our local sculptor. Ethan and I worked side by side, and every shared glance sent a rush of warmth through me.

"Do you think the townsfolk will like the story theme?" I asked one afternoon, my fingers stained with paint as I added final touches to a pumpkin display.

"Of course they will," Ethan assured, his eyes glimmering with confidence. "You've tapped into something special. People crave connection, and your stories will give them that."

"Let's just hope they don't throw tomatoes at me if I mess up." I laughed, my heart a little lighter at the thought of stepping into the spotlight.

The night before the festival, anxiety tangled with excitement, wrapping around my stomach like a vine. I found myself pacing the café, rehearsing my introduction in the empty room, the glow of the fairy lights casting a gentle glow over the tables. Every creak of the floorboard echoed my apprehension, but as I practiced, a small voice inside me whispered that this was my moment.

With each word I spoke to the empty chairs, I could see faces coming alive, smiles and laughter intertwining with the tales I shared. The excitement of the weekend loomed just beyond the door, and with it came the potential for something new, something vibrant that could change the course of Silver Pines forever.

But as I closed up that night, a chill swept through the air, carrying with it the faint echoes of Diane's discontent. I took a deep breath, ready to face whatever storms lay ahead, determined to weave my narrative into the fabric of this town. After all, change is often the wind that carries us toward unexpected horizons, and I was ready to soar.

The morning of Leaf-Peeping Weekend dawned with a vibrant clarity, the sun spilling its golden rays over Silver Pines like warm honey drenching a crisp apple. I stood at the entrance of The Maple Leaf, hands on my hips, surveying the world with a mix of exhilaration and trepidation. The café was transformed into a cozy haven, with colorful decorations and the enticing aroma of baked goods wafting through the air. It felt like the town had been wrapped in a quilt of autumn colors, each leaf fluttering with the promise of joy and connection.

"Look at this place!" Ethan exclaimed, stepping outside with a stack of freshly baked pumpkin muffins. "We're practically a postcard." He grinned, his enthusiasm infectious as he handed me a muffin still warm from the oven.

I took a bite, the rich flavor bursting in my mouth, and nodded in agreement. "Definitely postcard material. If only we could sell this muffin recipe; we'd be millionaires."

"Why stop at millionaires? We could be the next great culinary duo—fighting off the forces of evil with baked goods!" He posed dramatically, muffin in hand like a weapon, and I couldn't help but laugh.

"Only if I get to wear a cape," I shot back, feigning seriousness. "We could call ourselves the Muffin Avengers. Saving the world one muffin at a time!"

Ethan feigned deep thought. "We might need to work on the branding. Muffin Avengers sounds more like a bakery-themed superhero team than culinary geniuses."

"Geniuses with flair, I'll have you know!" I replied, feeling my spirits lift despite the undercurrent of anxiety bubbling beneath the surface. This weekend was about more than just muffins and decorations; it was my chance to prove that change could be good, that storytelling could connect us in ways that we had forgotten.

As the sun climbed higher, the town buzzed with energy. People strolled through the streets, their laughter mingling with the sounds of fiddles playing nearby. Families gathered at stalls selling artisan crafts and local produce. Children chased each other, their faces smeared with the remnants of caramel apples, while elderly couples reminisced over steaming cups of cider. Silver Pines had turned into a playground, vibrant and alive.

"Ready for the storytelling event?" Ethan asked, wiping his hands on a towel as we prepared for the first session.

I nodded, though my heart raced. "I'm as ready as I'll ever be. Just need to remember to breathe."

"Breathing is overrated," he quipped, a twinkle in his eye. "What's the worst that could happen? They boo you off the stage? Start a food fight?"

"Let's not tempt fate," I replied, trying to suppress my nerves. "But if they do throw muffins, I hope they're fresh."

As the hour approached, I arranged chairs outside under a grand oak tree that had taken on a riot of colors—golds, reds, and burnt oranges—its leaves whispering secrets in the autumn breeze. The townsfolk began to gather, their chatter weaving a comforting tapestry of anticipation. My heart swelled with gratitude at the sight of familiar faces—neighbors, friends, and even a few newcomers who had found their way to our corner of the world.

"Okay, everyone!" I called out, my voice steadier than I felt as I stepped onto the makeshift stage. "Welcome to the first ever Leaf-Peeping Storytelling Session at The Maple Leaf! Let's share tales of adventure, of love, of what makes this town so special!"

A warm cheer erupted from the crowd, and I caught sight of Diane lurking at the back, arms crossed and her expression skeptical. My stomach twisted at the sight of her, but I pushed the feeling aside. This was about connection, not confrontation.

As the first storyteller took the stage, I listened intently, captivated by a tale that wove together laughter and nostalgia, each word painting vivid pictures of days gone by. The audience was rapt, their attention hanging on every syllable. With each story shared, I felt the fabric of our community strengthen, the bond of shared experiences knitting us together in a way I had hoped for.

But just as the sun dipped lower in the sky, casting a warm glow over the gathering, Diane finally made her move. "Isn't it charming?" she called out, her voice dripping with sarcasm as she stepped forward, drawing all eyes toward her. "But what happened to the good old days, when we didn't need gimmicks to enjoy ourselves?"

A murmur rippled through the crowd, tension crackling in the air. I could feel my heart race, adrenaline surging as I stepped forward. "Change is not a gimmick, Diane," I replied, trying to keep my tone light despite the weight of her words. "It's an opportunity for growth and connection. This weekend is about celebrating our stories, not erasing them."

"Celebrating or commodifying?" she shot back, her gaze piercing. "You've turned our town into a circus. Is this really what Silver Pines stands for?"

Ethan moved closer, his presence a solid anchor beside me. "What we stand for is community. It's about sharing what we love and creating new traditions together. Isn't that worth celebrating?"

The air thickened with anticipation, and for a moment, I thought we might just tip over the edge into a full-blown confrontation. But before Diane could respond, a little girl, no more than six years old, raised her hand. "I want to tell a story!" she declared, her voice bright and clear, cutting through the tension like a knife.

Everyone turned to her, the atmosphere shifting from confrontation to curiosity. Diane's brow furrowed, but the girl's innocent enthusiasm was impossible to resist.

"Alright! Come on up!" I beckoned, my heart swelling with relief. As the child scampered to the front, the crowd erupted into applause, and the moment of potential conflict dissolved into something sweet and hopeful.

As she shared her tale of a magical pumpkin that could talk, laughter filled the air, and I glanced at Ethan, who wore a proud grin. The little girl's story ignited joy, reminding everyone of the power of imagination and community.

With each tale that followed, the warmth of connection enveloped us, and even Diane seemed to soften, her scowl fading as the laughter rose. I felt a flicker of hope igniting within me; perhaps I could reach her, could help her see that change wasn't a threat but an invitation to embrace the future.

As the sun dipped below the horizon, painting the sky with a tapestry of pinks and purples, I realized that this moment, this gathering of hearts and stories, was a triumph. The townsfolk applauded enthusiastically, and for the first time, I felt the weight of Diane's discontent lift just a little, like the clouds parting to let the sun through.

Maybe, just maybe, I could help Silver Pines find its way to a new chapter—one filled with stories old and new, united under the brilliant canopy of autumn leaves.

The sun slipped lower in the sky, bathing Silver Pines in a warm, golden glow that felt almost magical. The storytelling event had surpassed my expectations; laughter echoed in the crisp air, and the scent of fresh cider mingled with the leaves falling around us like confetti. I felt the collective heartbeat of the town pulsing with every tale shared, and it was as if the air was thick with the warmth of community.

As the last storyteller wrapped up, applause erupted, and I glanced around to catch Ethan's eye. He was leaning against the counter, arms crossed, with that endearing smile that made my heart race. "You did it," he mouthed, and I beamed back at him.

But just as the joy began to settle in my chest, Diane cleared her throat, her voice cutting through the laughter like a knife. "This was all very charming," she began, her tone dripping with the same syrupy sweetness as the caramel apples we'd served. "But I wonder how long this... festival spirit will last."

A hush fell over the crowd, tension coiling like a snake ready to strike. I felt the warmth of the moment dissipate, replaced by a chill. "What do you mean?" I asked, trying to keep my voice steady.

She stepped forward, eyes flashing. "You've introduced a series of distractions, and while they might be entertaining, they don't address the real issues facing our town. What about our traditions?"

"Traditions can evolve," I countered, feeling a flush creep up my neck. "We can honor the past while also inviting new stories to join the tapestry of our community."

"Or you can dilute it to nothing," she shot back, her tone biting. "If you're not careful, Silver Pines will become just another tourist trap."

Ethan's presence beside me steadied my resolve. "Diane, what matters is how we come together. Look at the joy today has brought. Isn't that worth something?"

The murmurs of agreement rippled through the crowd, but Diane stood firm. "Maybe so, but it's not sustainable. What will happen when the tourists leave, and we're left with nothing but hollow events?"

"Diane, we can't live in fear of change," I replied, my heart racing. "This is our chance to build something new."

"New or not, I will fight for the soul of this town," she declared, her voice ringing with conviction. "And I won't let one misguided idea undermine what we've built."

I braced myself as her gaze swept over the crowd, searching for allies, but instead, a murmur of support flowed in my direction. A few nods, a couple of raised hands. The townsfolk were beginning to see the potential in the change I was championing.

"Let's not turn this into a debate," Ethan intervened, his tone diplomatic yet firm. "We're all here because we care about Silver Pines. Can we agree to disagree and focus on enjoying this beautiful weekend?"

Diane opened her mouth to retort, but before she could speak, a gust of wind swept through the gathering, sending a flurry of leaves dancing into the air. It was as if nature itself was stepping in to break the tension. The momentary distraction caught everyone off guard, laughter bubbling up once more as leaves whirled around us.

"Let's take a break and enjoy the festivities," I suggested, seizing the moment. "We have music, food, and plenty more stories to share. How about we let our feet guide us for a bit?"

With a reluctant nod, Diane stepped back, allowing the warmth of the moment to creep back in. The crowd dispersed, laughter and chatter rekindling the sense of community I had fought for. I grabbed Ethan's hand, pulling him toward the edge of the gathering, a smile on my face.

"Thank you for stepping in like that," I said, feeling the warmth of his grip, a grounding presence amid the chaos.

"Just doing my part," he replied, a teasing glint in his eye. "Besides, I couldn't let you handle her alone. I'm not ready to lose my favorite storytelling partner."

I rolled my eyes, trying to suppress a grin. "Flattery will get you everywhere, you know."

He leaned in, a playful smirk on his lips. "Good thing I'm an expert at it, then."

We wandered through the crowd, stopping at a stall selling handmade trinkets, laughing over silly knickknacks and sipping on cider. But despite the festivities around us, a nagging worry nestled in the back of my mind. Diane's words hung heavy in the air, a reminder that not everyone was ready to embrace change.

The sun began its descent, painting the sky with streaks of pink and orange. As we made our way back to the café, the crowd thickened, a tapestry of familiar faces and new visitors. I caught snippets of conversation—people were buzzing about the stories shared, the laughter, the warmth.

Just as I felt a swell of hope, the atmosphere shifted. A commotion broke out at the edge of the gathering. I squinted through the crowd, trying to see what was happening, but the mass of bodies obscured my view.

"Stay here," Ethan instructed, concern etched across his face. "I'll check it out."

Before I could protest, he slipped through the crowd. My heart pounded as I strained to hear what was happening, and then I caught snippets of frantic voices.

"Something's wrong!"

"Did you see her? Where did she go?"

Panic surged through me, a wave of dread washing over as I fought my way closer to the source of the disturbance.

"What's happening?" I shouted to no one in particular, but the rising tide of voices drowned out my question.

Then I saw Ethan, his expression a mix of confusion and alarm as he gestured toward a small group of people gathered around a bench. My stomach dropped as I pushed my way through the crowd, the world around me fading into a blur of colors and sounds.

When I finally reached the front, the scene before me froze my heart. A woman sat on the bench, pale and trembling, clutching her chest. Around her, faces were drawn with concern, and I recognized her—it was Lydia, the local florist.

"Call an ambulance!" someone shouted, and my pulse quickened, the air suddenly thick with tension and fear.

"What happened?" I managed to ask, my voice shaking.

"She collapsed," a woman replied, her eyes wide with panic. "I don't know what's wrong."

Ethan knelt beside Lydia, his hand resting on her shoulder, his voice low and calming. "Lydia, can you hear me? Just breathe, okay? Help is on the way."

As I stood there, the festive atmosphere of Leaf-Peeping Weekend shattered, leaving only uncertainty and dread in its wake. I could feel the weight of Diane's earlier words pressing down on me; change was inevitable, but it often came at a price.

And in that moment, as the sounds of celebration faded into the background, I realized that the winds of change were more powerful than I had ever imagined. What would the fallout be? What storm had I unwittingly invited into our beloved town?

The questions swirled in my mind, unanswered and haunting. I opened my mouth to speak, but the words caught in my throat as the sirens wailed in the distance, a harbinger of the chaos that lay ahead.

Chapter 15: Shadows of Doubt

The sun dipped low in the sky, casting a warm golden hue over Silver Pines as I maneuvered through the bustling market, my senses alive with the scent of baked bread and roasted coffee beans. Stalls were adorned with vibrant produce, the earthy aroma of freshly picked herbs mingling with the sweetness of ripe berries. Children's laughter echoed as they darted between stalls, their joy an infectious melody that filled the air. I reveled in the lively atmosphere, the kind that made my heart swell with a mix of gratitude and dread. With the festival only days away, the anticipation was palpable, like the charge before a summer storm. But beneath that excitement lay an undercurrent of anxiety, a whisper of unease that came from one source: Diane.

She had always been a thorn in my side, but lately, she seemed hell-bent on sharpening that thorn into a dagger. I had heard the hushed tones of her gossip, the way it slipped through the market like a shadow, darkening the corners of friendly conversations. "She doesn't belong here," they'd say, their voices tinged with uncertainty. "The town was fine before she came." Those words dug into me like the sharp edges of a blade, slicing through my resolve. Each rumor was a thread in a web she was spinning, and I could feel myself caught in it.

As I turned a corner, I spotted her—a blonde streak, a flash of designer jeans that didn't quite fit the rustic charm of the town. Diane stood at the fruit stand, her laughter ringing out like a bell, drawing the attention of anyone within earshot. It struck me then, an undeniable truth that pulled at my heartstrings: she was more than a rival; she was a force of nature, relentless and unwavering.

"Look who it is," she called out, her voice dripping with mockery as she spotted me. The small crowd around her turned, their eyes flickering between us like moths drawn to a flame. "The town's very own charity case." Her words danced in the air, sweet on the surface but laced with venom.

A wave of heat washed over me. I fought the urge to turn and walk away, but something deep inside refused to back down. I had worked too hard to make Silver Pines my home, to carve out a space for myself. The festival was meant to celebrate community, a gathering of familiar faces and shared stories, not a battleground for personal vendettas. I squared my shoulders, feeling a surge of adrenaline as I stepped closer.

"Why don't you share what you really think, Diane?" I shot back, my voice steady despite the tremor in my heart. "Or are you afraid the truth might ruin your carefully crafted image?"

The tension crackled between us, a palpable energy that seemed to draw the onlookers in closer. They were silent now, the thrill of drama electrifying the air. For a brief moment, I reveled in the spotlight, the exhilaration of standing up for myself overshadowing the fear of judgment. But Diane was quick to regain her composure, a glimmer of amusement dancing in her eyes.

"Oh, sweetie," she said, a mocking smile stretching across her face. "You think you're a part of this town? You're just a tourist who got lost and decided to stay. Silver Pines is better without your kind."

Gasps flitted through the crowd like startled birds. My breath caught in my throat, the sting of her words hitting harder than I anticipated. This wasn't just about me anymore; it was about my connection to a place that had slowly started to feel like home. The cheers and laughter of the festival seemed to fade into a muffled echo as the weight of Diane's words settled on my shoulders.

"Maybe I don't fit your perfect little mold, but I care about this town and its people," I fired back, my voice gaining strength. "You may have everyone fooled with your charm, but I know what you're doing. You're using your influence to create divisions. This isn't just a rivalry; it's toxic."

"Goodness, who knew you could be so dramatic?" Diane feigned a gasp, rolling her eyes theatrically. "This is a small town, darling. People love a good story, and you just handed them the best one."

With each word, I felt the town's eyes on me, a mix of sympathy and judgment swirling like a tempest. My heart raced, an erratic beat against the backdrop of whispers that bounced off the market stalls. I caught a glimpse of Ethan standing a few paces back, his expression unreadable but his posture tense. The world around us narrowed, the vibrant colors fading to a dull blur as the focus shifted solely to us.

"I may not have grown up here, but I'm here now," I said, forcing the words out despite the crack in my voice. "And I refuse to let you turn this community into your playground for spite."

With that, a sudden silence enveloped the market, as if the very air had thickened with tension. My heart raced as I realized the weight of my words, the implications rippling through the crowd. I could feel the judgment, a collective gaze scrutinizing my every move. In that moment, I understood how much this place meant to me, how deeply I had rooted myself within its heart.

But before Diane could retaliate, I turned on my heel and strode away, the bustling market fading behind me. I needed to escape the suffocating stares, the weight of their expectations pressing down like a heavy shroud. The café loomed ahead, a comforting haven amidst the chaos. I pushed through the door, the familiar aroma of coffee wrapping around me like a warm embrace.

But as I stepped inside, my resolve crumbled. I felt defeated, my shoulders heavy with the burden of uncertainty. And there, in the corner, I spotted Ethan, his presence a calming anchor in the storm of my emotions. He looked up, concern etched in the lines of his brow, his eyes warm and understanding.

"Hey," he said softly, his voice a soothing balm against the jagged edges of my day. "I saw what happened. You okay?"

In that moment, the world outside melted away, leaving just us. I took a deep breath, allowing the tension to ebb as I sank into the chair opposite him. The weight of the market felt lighter, the judgment of the townsfolk drifting like clouds after a storm. With Ethan's understanding gaze upon me, I felt a flicker of hope spark within, a fragile light against the encroaching shadows of doubt.

The aroma of freshly brewed coffee wrapped around me like a soft quilt, its rich scent mingling with the sweet undertones of pastries lining the display case. I sat across from Ethan, his presence radiating warmth, a stark contrast to the chill that had seeped into my bones after my confrontation with Diane. The café, usually my sanctuary, felt like a bubble where reality couldn't reach me, if only for a moment.

"Do you want to talk about it?" Ethan asked, his voice gentle but steady, cutting through the fog of my thoughts. He leaned forward, his hazel eyes searching mine, as if he could decipher the storm brewing just beneath the surface.

"Honestly? I'd rather not," I replied, offering a faint smile that didn't quite reach my eyes. "I'm tired of giving her the satisfaction of knowing she gets to me."

Ethan chuckled softly, the sound low and rich like the coffee swirling in my cup. "That's the spirit. Just let the town think what it wants. You know they love a good scandal."

"Scandal? Is that what I am now?" I leaned back, the chair creaking beneath me as I crossed my arms defensively. "I came here to build a life, not to be the star of a reality show."

"Oh, you're much more than that," he teased, a smirk dancing on his lips. "You're like the plot twist everyone didn't see coming—unpredictable and slightly chaotic."

"Unpredictable and slightly chaotic," I echoed, rolling my eyes but unable to suppress a smile. "Now that's a title I can work with."

As we laughed, I felt the tension in my shoulders ease. In that moment, the weight of the world began to lift, but it was only temporary. Just as I was starting to feel lighter, the café door swung open, and in walked Diane, a whirlwind of confidence and couture. She strutted in like she owned the place, her designer heels clicking sharply against the wooden floor, a cacophony of arrogance that sent a ripple through the café.

"Fancy seeing you here," she called out, her voice smooth as silk but coated in a thin layer of disdain. The café fell silent, eyes darting between her and me, as if waiting for the next act in our little drama.

"Nice of you to drop by," I shot back, attempting to project an air of nonchalance. The tension coiled tighter in my stomach, a snake ready to strike.

Ethan remained silent, his gaze flicking between us, the amusement in his eyes dimmed to something more cautious. I could feel the heat of the crowd's attention like a spotlight illuminating every crack in my façade. Diane advanced, her smile saccharine, deceptively sweet.

"Still trying to play the town hero?" she asked, tilting her head as if I were a particularly amusing painting in a gallery. "You know, it's exhausting to watch you attempt to fit into a mold you weren't designed for."

"Oh, and you'd know all about that, wouldn't you?" I countered, my voice firmer than I felt. "The last person I'd take advice from is someone who thrives on gossip and drama."

Her laughter rang out, sharp and mocking. "Gossip? Oh, honey, I'm simply a concerned citizen. Someone needs to protect the charm of Silver Pines from the likes of you."

With every word she tossed my way, I felt a surge of anger bubbling beneath the surface. But beneath the anger lay a deeper current of hurt, a pang of insecurity. What if she was right? What if I didn't belong here?

"Concerned citizen, huh?" I managed, forcing a smile that felt more like a grimace. "If you're so concerned, why not do something productive instead of making my life a living hell?"

"Productive?" Diane raised an eyebrow, a sly smile playing at the corners of her mouth. "Sweetheart, I'm just getting started. But who knows? Maybe you'll surprise us all and actually prove you have a place in this town."

"Enough!" Ethan's voice cut through the tension, sharp and unwavering. "This isn't a game, Diane. If you have something to say, say it like an adult."

Her expression shifted, surprise flashing across her face before it hardened. "Oh, is the golden boy coming to the rescue? How noble."

I glanced at Ethan, grateful yet wary. "I can handle this, you know," I said, my voice softer but steady.

"Yeah, I know you can," he replied, his eyes locked onto mine, silently urging me to stand my ground. "But you shouldn't have to. She's playing dirty."

Diane flicked her hair over her shoulder, an exaggerated gesture dripping with disdain. "Dirty? Please, this is Silver Pines. We all know it's about playing your cards right. Some people just don't know how to fold."

My heart raced as the crowd remained hushed, the air thick with anticipation. I could feel their eyes boring into me, waiting to see how I would respond.

"Look, Diane," I said, taking a step forward, my voice steadier than I felt. "If you want to play games, fine. But I refuse to be your pawn."

"Pawns can become queens, darling. I'd watch your back if I were you."

Her words hung in the air like smoke, acrid and suffocating. I turned to Ethan, whose expression mirrored my growing frustration and confusion.

"Come on, let's get out of here," he suggested, rising from his seat. The café felt stifling, the walls closing in around me, every judgmental gaze a reminder of my insecurities.

With one last glare at Diane, I followed Ethan outside, the cool air hitting me like a splash of cold water. We stood on the café's porch, the din of the market fading behind us.

"Thanks for that," I said, exhaling deeply. "You didn't have to step in."

"Maybe not, but I couldn't just sit back and watch her tear you down," he replied, his tone firm yet gentle. "You deserve to be here, and she's just threatened by how much you've accomplished."

"I'm not sure about that," I muttered, my confidence teetering. "What if she's right? What if I don't belong here?"

"Every single person in this town has their own doubts, trust me. What matters is how you handle them," he said, his gaze unwavering. "And you handle yourself like a damn queen."

I chuckled softly, the tension easing slightly. "A pawn turned queen, huh? Maybe I should take that as my motto."

Ethan grinned, the corners of his mouth crinkling adorably. "I think it suits you."

As the market buzzed behind us, I felt a flicker of something bright and hopeful. Perhaps the shadows of doubt wouldn't consume me after all. Together, we stood on that porch, a small island in the tumultuous sea of Silver Pines, ready to face whatever storm came next.

The vibrant market buzz continued to hum in the background as I leaned against the café railing, savoring the cool breeze that swept through Silver Pines. The lingering warmth of the sun brushed against my skin, creating a strange sense of solace, even amidst the chaos of emotions swirling inside me. Ethan stood beside me, his shoulder brushing against mine, a silent assurance that I wasn't alone in this tangled web of small-town drama.

"Are you really okay?" he asked, his voice low, as if he feared the answer would shatter the moment.

"Honestly?" I paused, taking in the colorful stalls bustling with life and laughter. "I'm still trying to convince myself I belong here."

"Anyone with a heart for this place belongs," he replied firmly. "You've poured so much into it, and the townspeople see that, even if Diane wants to spin it otherwise."

His words hung in the air, softening the sharp edges of doubt I had been grappling with. The café, a quaint little spot filled with mismatched furniture and the scent of coffee beans, felt like a refuge. Yet, that comfort was tempered by the ever-looming threat of Diane's disdain.

"Is she always this... insufferable?" I asked, my gaze drifting to the market where Diane stood, flanked by her minions, the very embodiment of a high school queen bee who had never graduated.

Ethan chuckled, a sound rich and warm. "Oh, she's a pro at it. If she had a trophy for it, she'd probably have a whole shelf dedicated to her 'Most Dramatic' awards."

"Lucky for her, I'm not here for a competition." I smirked, but the undercurrent of anxiety still lingered.

"Look," he said, turning serious, "you can't let her overshadow everything you've worked for. You're here to make a difference, and you are. Just focus on what you love about this place."

"Like the coffee?" I quipped, gesturing to the barista who was expertly crafting a latte.

"Sure, the coffee. But I was thinking more about the community, the people." He hesitated, then added, "And maybe a certain someone who makes even the weirdest town politics seem somewhat bearable."

I felt my cheeks warm at his compliment, a flutter of something electric dancing through the air between us. "Oh, now you're just buttering me up."

"Guilty as charged," he laughed, his eyes crinkling with sincerity. "But seriously, don't let Diane push you around. She's just scared that you might actually do something good for this town that she can't control."

I turned to him, the weight of his encouragement solidifying a flicker of resolve deep within me. "I won't give in to her. She can spread her rumors all she wants; I'm going to show the town what I can really do."

"Now that's the spirit!" he said, a spark igniting in his eyes. "We should plan something—something big for the festival. Show her that Silver Pines is more than just a set of whispers."

"Like what?" I asked, intrigued.

"I don't know, but we could start with a community event. Something that brings people together. You're great at that."

"Are you suggesting I lead a town-wide bake sale?" I asked, feigning horror.

"Hey, don't knock it! Nothing brings people together like baked goods." He grinned, leaning closer. "Or we could do a charity fundraiser. Maybe a talent show? You know, reveal some hidden gems among the townsfolk."

The idea began to form in my mind, twirling like a dervish. "A talent show could work! I could get people involved, share their skills—music, dance, crafts—anything to showcase what makes this community unique."

"Exactly! And while we're at it, we could even get local businesses to sponsor prizes. A little competition could add some spice."

"Okay, now you're just trying to convince me that this is a good idea because it sounds fun," I teased. "But I do love the idea of bringing everyone together, especially after everything that's been happening."

His eyes sparkled with excitement. "Let's do it, then! We can start planning tonight."

Just as the weight of anticipation settled in, a shrill voice pierced the air, cutting through our moment like a knife. "There you are!" Diane appeared at the café entrance, her tone dripping with sarcasm. "Planning another little event to distract everyone from how poorly you're doing?"

I sighed, tension creeping back into my muscles. "What do you want, Diane?"

"Can't a girl stop by to check on her favorite rival?" She smirked, crossing her arms. "You know, I'm all for community events—maybe I should host one myself."

"Right," I shot back, my heart racing. "And I'm sure you'll have it planned around your schedule and whims."

"Oh, sweetie," she said, batting her eyelashes, "it'll be a grand affair. With a theme like 'Elegance Over Eccentricity.' And it will show exactly what Silver Pines needs: a little refinement."

Ethan stepped forward, his body a protective wall beside me. "This isn't a competition, Diane. Maybe if you invested your energy in something positive, you'd see the benefits of community spirit."

"Community spirit?" she scoffed, rolling her eyes. "Let's see how long that lasts. I'm all about efficiency, darling. We both know the best way to win this town's heart is through style, not those dreary bake sales."

I took a breath, steadying myself against the brewing storm. "You think charm is all that matters? The people of this town have been through enough drama already. They deserve something genuine."

"Genuine?" Diane laughed, the sound harsh and condescending. "Genuine doesn't win awards. But if you'd like, I could help you with your little talent show."

Her suggestion hung in the air, ripe with suspicion. "Help? Since when have you ever offered help?"

"Consider it an olive branch," she said sweetly, yet the undertone was anything but sincere. "After all, I wouldn't want to see you fail. Not that you could do it without me."

"I'd rather not," I replied, my voice steady. "I think I can handle it on my own, thanks."

Diane stepped closer, her gaze sharp. "You really think you can? This town is a fragile thing, and you're not as untouchable as you believe."

Ethan shifted beside me, a protective stance emanating from him. "Leave her alone, Diane. She's done nothing but try to uplift this town."

With a smirk, she stepped back, arms wide as if presenting a theatrical exit. "I'm just here to remind you both: the festival is a double-edged sword. It can cut both ways."

"Why do you always have to make everything a threat?" I shot back, anger surging through me.

"Because I care about the town," she said, faux sincerity dripping from her words. "And I want it to be its best self. Maybe you should ask yourself: who do the people really want leading their celebrations?"

She turned and walked away, leaving behind a heavy silence that lingered like smoke from a dying fire. I could feel the air thicken with doubt, but I was determined not to let her words seep into my resolve.

"Don't let her get to you," Ethan said quietly, watching Diane's retreating figure. "She's just trying to rattle you. You're stronger than that."

"Stronger? Maybe," I replied, glancing back at the market, now buzzing again with the chatter of eager patrons. "But I need to get this talent show rolling before she has a chance to sabotage it."

Ethan nodded, a fierce look of determination on his face. "Let's meet tonight to brainstorm. We can tackle this head-on, and if Diane tries to meddle, we'll show her that Silver Pines is better when it comes together."

A plan started to form in my mind, one that buzzed with excitement and potential. But just as I felt the spark of determination igniting within me, my phone buzzed in my pocket. Pulling it out, I glanced at the screen, my heart dropping as I read the message.

It was from the town mayor, and the words glared back at me: We need to talk. It's about the festival and the recent rumors. Please come to my office ASAP.

"Ethan," I said, my voice shaking, "I think things just got a lot more complicated."

His expression shifted, concern etching deep lines into his brow. "What do you mean?"

I glanced back at the market, at the people who were supposed to be supporting me, and suddenly, the weight of the world felt heavier than ever. "I think Diane's threats have reached the mayor."

As I turned to leave, a sudden sense of foreboding washed over me, the air thick with anticipation and uncertainty. The weight of Silver Pines pressed down like an impending storm, and as I stepped off the porch, I couldn't shake the feeling that something was about to change forever.

Chapter 16: The Festival Unfolds

The festival erupted in a riot of colors, the kind that only autumn could conjure—a kaleidoscope of fiery reds, burnt oranges, and sunny yellows enveloping Silver Pines. Each leaf seemed to dance in the crisp air, their delicate rustle echoing the laughter spilling from the bustling café. I could barely keep up with the flow of customers clamoring for spiced cider and warm apple tarts, the sweet aromas wrapping around me like a comforting embrace. Ethan moved with an effortless grace beside me, his laughter punctuating the air, a melodic contrast to the clinking of coffee mugs and the hum of cheerful chatter. We were a well-oiled machine, each glance and nod a silent agreement, our teamwork as natural as the seasonal transition outside.

The storytelling event had drawn a crowd larger than we could have imagined. Each tale spun from the lips of local storytellers was laced with the warmth of nostalgia and sprinkled with just enough humor to keep the audience in stitches. I watched the way Ethan's eyes sparkled with enthusiasm as he interacted with the townsfolk, his charisma drawing them in like moths to a flame. It was hard to believe that just a few weeks ago, I had met him, my heart heavy with uncertainty. Now, the lightness between us felt tangible, electric, charged with possibilities that made my breath catch in my throat.

As the sun dipped below the horizon, the festival took on a magical quality, the sky painted in hues of deep purple and soft gold. Lanterns swayed gently in the evening breeze, casting a warm glow over the cobblestone street. The bonfire awaited us, a majestic blaze flickering like a giant beacon, drawing everyone in. I could see families gathered around, children's faces illuminated by the firelight, their eyes wide with wonder.

"Do you think we should roast marshmallows?" Ethan suggested, a playful glint in his eye.

"Only if you promise to make a s'more that won't send me into a sugar coma," I replied, grinning back at him.

His laughter rang out, mingling with the crackling flames. There was something deeply satisfying about sharing this moment, our playful banter mixing seamlessly with the energy of the festival.

Yet, in the back of my mind, a familiar tension flickered like the fire's glow. Diane's presence loomed, a shadow that darkened my thoughts. I hadn't seen her today, but the air was thick with her unspoken words, the weight of her disdain palpable even from afar. I had grown accustomed to the way her gaze could slice through laughter and light, leaving behind an uncomfortable chill. She was an uninvited guest at my celebration, a reminder that not all stories had a happy ending.

As we settled by the bonfire, a few other townsfolk joined us, their faces aglow with excitement. I could feel the warmth of the flames on my skin, but it was the closeness of Ethan beside me that ignited something far more exhilarating. "You know," I began, a playful smirk crossing my lips, "they say the best way to bond is through firelight and sweets. We could be creating a legendary love story right now."

"Is that so?" he replied, his voice low, teasing. "What's the first line of our epic saga?"

"Oh, I'm sure it starts with two strangers trapped in a café, only to discover their shared destiny amidst marshmallow madness."

"Just wait until I introduce you to the s'mores of destiny," he said, winking before turning to gather sticks for our marshmallow-roasting adventure.

The townsfolk joined in, laughter rising around us as we prepared our treats. I savored each moment, wrapping myself in the warmth of camaraderie. But just as I began to let my guard down, an unsettling feeling crept in, like a sudden chill in the air.

"Have you seen Diane today?" I asked casually, my voice steady despite the tremor beneath.

Ethan paused, the stick in his hand hovering over the flames. "No, but I've heard whispers. They say she's been plotting something."

My heart sank, the weight of his words pulling me back into the shadows of worry. "Plotting what?"

He shrugged, but I could see the concern flickering in his eyes. "Who knows? But she's never one to stay quiet for long."

The laughter around the fire took on a hollow quality, the warmth of the moment dimmed by the specter of her intentions. I wanted to shake off the unease, to focus on the joy surrounding me, but Diane's shadow loomed larger with every passing second. Just as I thought I could push the thoughts aside, the festival's vibrancy seemed to dim, the flickering flames casting longer shadows, echoing the uncertainty that sat heavy in my chest.

I tried to divert my attention, engaging with the townsfolk and sharing tales of past festivals, but my heart wasn't fully in it. It felt as if the air was thick with tension, each laugh and cheer more fragile than the last. As the bonfire blazed, the firelight illuminating Ethan's features, I could almost convince myself that everything was perfect, that the festival was the fairy tale we'd crafted. But in the back of my mind, the nagging worry lingered like smoke in the air, and I couldn't shake the feeling that the night was only just beginning.

The bonfire crackled with energy, the flames leaping higher as if eager to join the stars that began to twinkle in the deepening sky. I leaned into Ethan, the warmth of his shoulder grounding me against the weight of uncertainty that still clung to my heart like an unwanted coat. Around us, townsfolk had gathered, their faces glowing in the firelight, exchanging stories and laughter, a chorus of voices rising in harmony against the night's embrace.

"Okay, here's the deal," Ethan announced, his eyes sparkling with mischief. "For every marshmallow that catches fire, you have to share an embarrassing secret. Deal?"

I laughed, my initial hesitation evaporating in the face of his enthusiasm. "Fine! But you'll regret this, mister. I've got some doozies in my back pocket."

"Bring it on," he challenged, reaching for a fresh marshmallow. The way he leaned in, that playful glint in his eye, made my heart flutter. I couldn't help but wonder what secrets lay behind those captivating eyes, hidden beneath the confident exterior.

As we roasted our marshmallows, I couldn't help but feel that this was the perfect moment—candy-colored leaves floating down around us, the crisp air tinged with smoke, and the delicious scent of caramelizing sugar filling my nostrils. I could almost forget about Diane lurking like a thundercloud over our fun. Almost.

Ethan turned to me, a perfectly golden-brown marshmallow speared on his stick. "Okay, your turn first. What's the most embarrassing thing that's ever happened to you?"

I rolled my eyes dramatically, pretending to mull it over. "Well, there was that one time I tried to impress my crush by showing off my baking skills. I accidentally substituted salt for sugar in the cookie recipe. Let's just say those cookies were definitely... salty."

His laughter was infectious, bright and rich against the backdrop of the fire. "That's gold! I can't believe you survived that one. What did your crush say?"

"Oh, he politely pretended to enjoy them," I replied, chuckling at the memory. "Then he spent the next hour chugging water like he was training for a marathon."

"That's the kind of dedication I respect," Ethan quipped, a playful smirk on his lips. "Your turn to roast."

"Alright, but if my marshmallow catches fire, you'll have to come up with a doozy of your own," I warned, extending my stick over the flames.

As if on cue, the marshmallow ignited, sending a plume of smoke curling into the air. "Guess I'm in trouble," he said, his grin widening. "Okay, here goes nothing. Back in college, I tried to impress a girl by pretending I could play the guitar. I couldn't even strum a simple chord, but I put on a show anyway. I ended up playing 'Smoke on the Water' like a dying cat. She left halfway through."

We both dissolved into laughter, the tension of the evening melting away like the marshmallows between the graham crackers and chocolate. As I took a bite of my s'more, the gooey sweetness enveloped my senses, a moment of bliss punctuated by the rhythmic pulse of the festival around us.

"Hey, you've got marshmallow on your nose," Ethan teased, his fingers brushing against my cheek as he wiped it away, his touch lingering just a heartbeat too long. I felt a jolt of warmth shoot through me, a flash of something deeper, something that felt like a promise whispered just between us.

Before I could respond, the laughter and joy surrounding us shattered like glass. A familiar figure appeared at the edge of the firelight—Diane, her silhouette sharp against the glow, her expression a mask of disdain. I could feel my stomach drop, the joy of the moment dimmed as her presence seemed to suck the warmth from the air.

"Nice gathering," she called out, her voice cutting through the merriment like a knife. "I didn't realize this was the 'let's roast marshmallows and pretend everything is perfect' event."

A chill settled over the group, the atmosphere shifting as her words hung heavy in the air. I forced myself to meet her gaze, trying to project confidence despite the turmoil bubbling inside me.

"Diane, we're just having some fun," I said, keeping my tone light. "You should join us. It's a great night."

"Fun?" she scoffed, rolling her eyes. "You mean a distraction from reality. Nice to see you've made a cozy little nest here, but you won't always have your head in the clouds. Eventually, you'll have to face the truth."

Ethan stepped closer to me, his posture protective. "We're all allowed to enjoy ourselves, Diane. Maybe you should try it sometime."

Her laugh was sharp, devoid of warmth. "Oh, I'll enjoy myself. Just not here, surrounded by... whatever this is." She gestured dismissively at the gathering, her gaze landing on me, then Ethan. "But keep playing house; I'll be here when you're ready for a reality check."

Before I could respond, she turned on her heel, leaving a heavy silence in her wake. The fire crackled awkwardly, the merriment feeling distant and out of reach. I could sense the townsfolk shifting uneasily, the energy dimmed by her harsh words.

"I'm sorry about that," I murmured, glancing at Ethan, who wore a look of irritation mixed with concern. "She always seems to know how to ruin a moment."

"Don't let her get to you," he said firmly, his hand resting on my shoulder, grounding me. "She's just bitter because she's not part of this community like you are."

I nodded, but the unease lingered like a bitter aftertaste. Just as I thought the evening might be overrun by her negativity, someone from the crowd broke the silence.

"Hey, how about another story?" a cheerful voice called out, and the townsfolk rallied, shifting the mood back to one of lightheartedness.

Ethan turned to me, his expression softening. "What do you say? Another tale or two? I think we can drown out Diane's comments with enough laughter."

"Absolutely," I replied, feeling a spark of determination. "Let's show her that we won't be shaken."

As the stories flowed, I found my laughter mingling with the rest, slowly piecing together the joy that had been momentarily snatched away. I could feel the warmth of community wrapping around me again, each story a reminder that we were stronger together. Ethan's gaze never strayed far from mine, and with every shared laugh, I felt a flicker of hope. Perhaps tonight wouldn't end in shadows, after all.

The warmth of the bonfire returned like a long-lost friend, chasing away the chill that had crept into the atmosphere after Diane's unwelcome interruption. The townsfolk resumed their tales, laughter bubbling forth like the cider simmering in the nearby pot, each story an antidote to the poison she had injected into the evening.

"Alright, who's got a ghost story?" someone called out, excitement rippling through the crowd like a breeze. My heart quickened at the suggestion; I loved a good ghost story, especially with the leaves swirling around us like spirits released from their autumn prisons.

Ethan leaned closer, a playful glint in his eye. "Only if you promise to tell one yourself after."

"Deal!" I said, my competitive spirit flaring up. "But be warned, I have a knack for the spooky."

The first storyteller, a wiry old man with a shock of white hair, took center stage. He spun a tale about the old mill on the outskirts of town, claiming it was haunted by the spirit of a miller who had mysteriously vanished decades ago. As he wove his story, I found myself leaning forward, captivated, as the crackling flames danced to the rhythm of his voice.

"And if you listen closely on quiet nights," he said, lowering his voice for dramatic effect, "you can hear the mill wheel turning, even though it hasn't operated in years."

The crowd gasped collectively, their imaginations ignited. I glanced at Ethan, who was watching the storyteller with an intensity that made my heart flutter. His eyes sparkled like the flames, and I felt a rush of warmth that had nothing to do with the fire.

"Okay, it's my turn," I declared after the old man finished, standing up with exaggerated confidence. The townsfolk turned to me, eager and expectant. "So, gather 'round, and prepare to be terrified!"

I launched into a tale about the ghost of a lonely widow who roamed the woods near Silver Pines, forever searching for her lost love. As I painted the picture of her ethereal form gliding through the mist, I caught Ethan's gaze, and the look in his eyes made me feel invincible.

"Legend has it," I said, my voice dropping to a conspiratorial whisper, "if you see her, she'll ask you a question: 'Have you seen my heart?' If you answer her truthfully, she'll leave you be. But if you lie... well, let's just say you might find yourself lost in the woods forever."

The crowd shuddered at the last line, a mix of delight and dread coursing through them. I took a breath, the rush of storytelling filling me with a sense of power. But as the applause faded, I felt the weight of Diane's earlier words creeping back in.

"You think you're safe here, but you're just a moment away from reality crashing down," she had said, and suddenly, my heart raced. I didn't want reality to intrude on this perfect night.

"Okay, who's next?" I called, trying to shake off the unease, and another townsperson stepped up to share a hilarious tale of misadventures in their own childhood. The laughter returned, and for a moment, I surrendered to the joy, letting the spirit of the festival wash over me.

But the air shifted again when I noticed a commotion at the edge of the gathering. A group of teenagers was whispering and pointing, their laughter taking on an ominous tone. I squinted through the flickering light, the shadows playing tricks on my eyes. What had captured their attention?

Then, I saw her—Diane, standing slightly apart from the group, her expression unreadable. My heart sank. Had she really come back for more?

"Maybe she's decided to join the fun after all," Ethan said, trying to lighten the mood. I could sense the tension still lingering between us, a reminder of her earlier interruption.

"Or she's plotting her next move," I muttered, more to myself than to him.

"Let her plot," Ethan said, his voice steady. "We're here to enjoy the festival, and I won't let her ruin it."

Just as I was about to respond, a loud scream shattered the evening. The laughter died instantly, replaced by gasps and murmurs. The teenagers had backed away, their faces pale. My stomach dropped as I turned to see what had happened.

In the dim light, I could make out a figure slumped on the ground—a girl, her dark hair cascading around her like a curtain, her eyes wide in shock. My heart raced as I rushed forward, Ethan close at my side.

"Is she okay?" I called out, pushing through the crowd that had gathered around her.

Diane was there too, her face inscrutable, and I felt a mix of fear and anger churning in my gut. "What happened?" I asked, my voice rising above the murmurs.

"She just collapsed!" one of the teenagers exclaimed, pointing at the girl. "We were just messing around, and then—"

"Just messing around?" I echoed incredulously. "What does that mean?"

SILVER PINES

Before anyone could answer, the girl stirred slightly, her eyes fluttering open. "What... what happened?" she whispered, her voice barely audible above the hushed crowd.

"Just breathe," I urged gently, kneeling beside her. "You're okay. Can you tell me your name?"

But just as she opened her mouth to speak, a strange shadow flickered behind her, and Diane stepped closer, her gaze fixed intently on the girl. "What's wrong, dear?" she purred, her tone syrupy sweet yet somehow sinister.

The girl's expression shifted, her eyes narrowing as if sensing something unsettling about Diane's presence. "Stay away from me," she said, her voice gaining strength. "You're not supposed to be here."

A ripple of unease passed through the crowd. Diane's lips curled into a smile, but it didn't reach her eyes. "Oh, I'm exactly where I need to be," she replied, her voice smooth as silk but laced with a chill that sent shivers down my spine.

I looked between them, confusion and fear swirling in my mind. What was happening?

"Someone should call for help," Ethan said, pulling out his phone, but the moment felt fragile, teetering on the edge of something dark and unknown.

As I knelt there, adrenaline coursing through my veins, I realized that the festival's warmth had evaporated, replaced by a tense energy that seemed to thrum with unspoken words.

Diane's gaze shifted back to me, an unreadable expression on her face, and in that instant, I felt a connection between her and the girl—one that sent a shiver of foreboding racing through me.

The laughter and joy of the evening faded away, replaced by the uncertainty that now loomed large. I could feel it in the air, thick and heavy, like a storm waiting to break. And just as the first drops of rain began to fall from the darkening sky, I knew one thing for certain: the night was far from over, and the real story was only just beginning.

Chapter 17: Heartstrings

The sun hung high in the sky, draping Silver Pines in a golden hue that turned every blade of grass into a glistening emerald. The laughter of the festival still echoed in my mind, a joyous reminder of fleeting moments that felt too perfect to hold onto. But now, standing at the edge of the hidden waterfall, surrounded by towering pines, my heart thrummed with a mixture of excitement and apprehension. Ethan was by my side, his presence as comforting as the sun warming my skin, yet I couldn't shake the feeling that the shadows of Diane loomed close, whispering doubts that threatened to unravel the delicate threads of our connection.

The trail to the waterfall had been a journey in itself, filled with lighthearted banter and playful jabs that felt like a dance we had perfected. Each step brought us closer, and the laughter we shared over tangled roots and slippery stones felt like a prelude to something monumental. Ethan was not just a companion; he was the kind of man who made me feel seen, like I had finally stepped into the spotlight after years of fading into the background. His easy grin and the way he rolled his eyes at my terrible jokes were intoxicating, and as we reached our destination, I couldn't help but think this was what happiness was meant to feel like.

Water cascaded down the rocks in a frothy embrace, sparkling like a million diamonds in the sunlight. The sound of the waterfall was a symphony, its rhythm soothing my racing heart as I took in the scene before me. Ethan stepped closer to the edge, the mist from the water curling around us like an embrace, drawing me into its coolness. "You know," he said, leaning against a nearby boulder, "I think this is the most beautiful spot in all of Silver Pines. It's like nature just threw a party and forgot to send out invitations."

I laughed, the sound mingling with the rush of the water. "Well, I'm glad we crashed. Otherwise, it would just be a pretty view and a bunch of lonely trees."

He turned to me, his expression suddenly serious, the lightheartedness slipping away like the water slipping over the rocks. "You make everything better, you know that? Even a secret spot like this feels more alive with you here."

The sincerity in his voice wrapped around me like a warm blanket, and for a moment, the world fell away. The weight of uncertainty lingered in the air, but it was overshadowed by the gravity of the moment. I could feel the words pressing against my lips, ready to tumble out like the waterfall before us. My heart raced, caught between exhilaration and fear. And then, without fully understanding the leap I was taking, I said it: "I love you."

The silence that followed was thick, almost tangible. Ethan's eyes widened, a blend of shock and wonder transforming his features. It was as if I had taken the air from his lungs, suspended in a moment that felt both infinite and fleeting. I cursed the vulnerability that washed over me, the sheer terror of exposing my heart laid bare before him. What if he didn't feel the same? What if the shadows I feared were already consuming us?

But then his lips curved into a smile, one that sent a wave of relief washing over me. "You know," he said, stepping closer, "I thought I was going to be the first one to say it. I love you too."

The way he said it made the world around us shimmer with possibility. The gravity of our confessions ignited a warmth that melted away the chill of uncertainty, wrapping us both in a cocoon of safety. We moved closer until there was no space left between us, the rush of the waterfall echoing the rapid beating of my heart. In that moment, the world felt expansive, a canvas stretching infinitely before us, painted in shades of love and trust.

But as our lips met, the kiss charged with everything we had both held back, a gust of wind swept through the trees, a whisper that felt like a warning. I couldn't help but remember Diane, the specter of our past hovering just beyond the veil of this beautiful moment. She was a reminder that love, while exhilarating, often came with chains that could bind or break us.

As we pulled apart, breathless and glowing, I glanced at the waterfall, its endless flow a stark contrast to the stillness that now filled the air between us. "This is perfect," I said softly, trying to shake off the lingering doubt.

"Yeah," Ethan replied, his fingers brushing against mine, grounding me in the present. "It is. But what do we do now? I mean, where do we go from here?"

His question hung in the air, a testament to the reality we were stepping into. I could see the flicker of worry in his eyes, and I wondered if he too felt the pull of Diane's influence. She was a shadow in the back of my mind, her voice insistent, demanding that I question the sincerity of this moment. But in the warmth of Ethan's gaze, I found my answer.

"We take it one day at a time," I said, summoning all the confidence I could muster. "We enjoy this. We explore together. Let's not rush into anything we're not ready for."

He nodded, his expression easing, the tension in his shoulders relaxing. "That sounds perfect. Just like this place."

And for a moment, it felt like we had created our own little bubble, a world where the chaos of reality could not intrude. Yet deep down, I could sense the storm brewing on the horizon. The winds of change were gathering, and I couldn't help but wonder how long our joy could withstand the impending deluge. Would we be able to navigate the turbulent waters ahead, or would the tides pull us under, leaving us gasping for air?

The days unfurled like a vibrant tapestry, each thread a moment woven into the fabric of our newfound love. Silver Pines had become our playground, a stunning backdrop where laughter mingled with the rustle of leaves and the song of distant birds. We roamed the quaint streets, our shoulders brushing as we strolled past local cafés and shops that boasted handmade trinkets and the mouthwatering scent of fresh pastries. Every corner felt like an adventure, and every shared glance sent warmth curling through me like the softest cashmere.

It was on one such day, with the sun filtering through the branches and casting playful patterns on the path ahead, that I found myself at the local bakery, the air thick with the aroma of cinnamon and sugar. Ethan had insisted on treating me, his eyes sparkling with mischief as he suggested we sample everything. "How else will we know what we like?" he said, flashing that signature grin that made my heart skip.

I rolled my eyes but couldn't help laughing. "Are you trying to make me gain ten pounds before we even start hiking again?"

"Life is short! We'll burn it off later, I promise. Plus, have you ever tried their apple turnover? It's like a hug from a grandma who actually knows how to bake."

As we stood at the counter, Ethan's playful banter filled the space between us, and for a moment, the world outside faded into the background. The baker, a kind woman with flour dusting her apron, overheard our chatter and chimed in, "You two are the sweetest thing! Lovebirds, are we?"

Ethan turned to me with a teasing glint in his eye. "Looks like we're officially a thing now. Should we get matching T-shirts that say 'Ethan and [Insert Your Name Here]: Bakery Connoisseurs'?"

"Oh please, let's not get carried away. But maybe just one turnover to start?" I said, feigning disinterest while my stomach rumbled at the thought.

After our indulgence, we found a cozy bench outside, the sun warming our faces as we savored the flaky pastry, my taste buds exploding with the sweetness of baked apples and cinnamon. "Okay, you were right. This is incredible," I admitted, licking the crumbs from my fingers.

"See? I'm full of good ideas. Next, I propose an ice cream detour. You can never have too much sugar, especially when you're in love."

"Is that a scientific fact, or are you just trying to butter me up?"

"Why not both? It's all about balance." His laughter was infectious, and I couldn't help but mirror it, the ease between us feeling like a dance I never wanted to end.

Yet, even as we laughed and enjoyed each other's company, I felt the tendrils of doubt creeping back in, gnawing at the edges of my joy. Diane's shadow lurked behind every smile, a reminder that the path we were carving out could easily be marred by the past. I glanced at Ethan, his face alight with mirth, and wondered how long we could maintain this illusion of bliss.

That evening, as we settled in for a movie night at his cozy cabin, the flickering light from the screen illuminated our faces, creating a bubble of warmth in the cool night air. Ethan had picked a classic rom-com, the kind that made my heart flutter and my cheeks ache from smiling too much.

"This is the kind of movie that'll make you believe in love, isn't it?" he said, snuggling closer to me on the couch, his arm draping around my shoulders.

"Or make me question my life choices," I replied, a teasing note in my voice. "I mean, why does love always have to be so complicated in these things? Can't someone just have a nice dinner without all the drama?"

He chuckled, his breath tickling my ear. "Where's the fun in that? A little drama adds spice. And besides, wouldn't it be boring if everyone just got along all the time?"

I sighed dramatically. "Fine, you win. But I still want a happy ending—preferably with snacks."

The movie played on, but my mind began to drift, contemplating the balance between what we were and what could be. I found myself stealing glances at Ethan, the way his brow furrowed in concentration or how his smile would break through during the funnier scenes. Each detail was etched in my memory like a perfect snapshot, but with each glance, the weight of uncertainty returned, threatening to overshadow our playful banter.

"Hey, are you with me?" Ethan's voice broke through my thoughts, and I realized I had been silent for far too long. He looked at me, a hint of concern in his eyes. "You've gone quiet. What's going on in that beautiful head of yours?"

I hesitated, the words caught in my throat like a stubborn fish. "Just... thinking about us. This feels incredible, but I can't shake the feeling that something's looming. Diane is still part of my reality, and I don't want her to—"

"Hey." His voice was soft yet firm, cutting through the air like the sharpest knife. "We can handle this together. Whatever shadows come, we'll face them. You're not alone in this."

I leaned into him, the warmth of his body grounding me. "I want to believe that. I really do. But it's hard not to look over my shoulder."

"Then don't look," he said, his tone playful yet serious. "Keep your eyes on the prize. Us. This."

His words wrapped around me like a protective shield, and I felt the heaviness of doubt begin to lift, if only slightly. "Okay, no more looking back. Just forward."

"Exactly. And forward looks pretty good, doesn't it?" He winked, and I couldn't help but laugh.

The movie continued, but I felt lighter, a spark of hope igniting in my chest. Maybe love was like this—an ongoing dance, filled with laughter, a little drama, and plenty of snacks. As the credits rolled and the last echoes of laughter faded, I knew that whatever challenges lay ahead, I was ready to embrace them, hand in hand with Ethan, together against the world. The shadows may still linger, but for now, we had carved out a pocket of happiness that was undeniably ours.

The following week slipped by in a blur, each day melting seamlessly into the next like soft butter on warm toast. Ethan and I slipped into a rhythm that felt comfortable yet electric, filled with inside jokes and the kind of laughter that echoed against the mountains surrounding Silver Pines. Each morning, I would wake up to the faint aroma of coffee wafting through the air, courtesy of Ethan, who seemed to have taken it upon himself to become my personal barista.

"You know," I teased one morning, my voice still thick with sleep as I sank into the warmth of my blanket, "if you keep this up, I might start thinking you want to win some kind of 'Best Boyfriend' award."

He chuckled, pouring the steaming brew into a cup decorated with tiny dancing bears. "Oh, I absolutely do. You should see the competition. Ted down the street is quite the contender with his scones."

I took a sip, letting the rich flavor dance on my tongue. "Alright, I'll give you this one, but I'll need you to step up your game if you want to keep the title. How about some homemade pancakes next?"

"Homemade? Are we sure we want to take that risk?" He raised an eyebrow, a playful smirk tugging at his lips. "Last time I checked, I might have mixed up the salt and sugar."

"Exactly! I'm here for the chaos, remember? Life is more fun when we're both borderline incompetent in the kitchen."

"Okay, challenge accepted," he replied, a gleam of determination in his eyes. "But don't blame me if we end up with a pancake that could double as a doorstop."

And just like that, we launched into a day filled with laughter, the worries about Diane and the shadows of my past momentarily forgotten. But deep inside, I could feel the undercurrents of uncertainty still swirling, waiting for a moment of weakness to drag me under.

Later that week, we ventured to the local farmer's market, a lively affair bursting with color and noise. The air was rich with the scents of fresh produce, fragrant herbs, and sizzling street food that made my mouth water. As we navigated the stalls, I felt the tension from earlier days fade, replaced by a sense of community and warmth that Silver Pines seemed to radiate.

"Look at these!" Ethan exclaimed, gesturing toward a display of plump tomatoes that glistened under the sunlight like tiny jewels. "We should make a caprese salad. With your impeccable taste in cheese, I can guarantee it'll be a hit."

"You really think I have impeccable taste? It's just cheese. I've never met a dairy product I didn't like."

"Exactly. That's why you're perfect for this. Plus, I promise I won't mix up the salt and sugar this time. How about we get some basil while we're at it?"

We moved from stall to stall, filling our basket with fresh ingredients and stolen bites of local delicacies, the atmosphere charged with a vibrant energy. As we reached the final stall, a woman with wild curls and a broad smile beckoned us over, offering samples of her homemade jams. "Try this one! It's my secret recipe—strawberry and rosemary. It's like summer in a jar!"

I exchanged a glance with Ethan, and we both dove in. The taste exploded in my mouth, a delightful contrast of sweetness and herbal freshness. "Oh my God, this is amazing!" I exclaimed, wiping the back of my hand over my mouth.

"Right? Perfect for breakfast on those pancake mornings!" he said, grinning ear to ear.

"Okay, but don't think you can escape from the pancake challenge just because we found some good jam. We're still making a disaster in the kitchen, and you're not getting out of it."

"Fair enough. Let's grab a jar then and commit to our culinary chaos."

As we made our purchase and turned to leave, the joyous atmosphere began to shift. I noticed a familiar figure at the edge of the market, standing under the shade of an old oak tree. My heart dropped. Diane.

I froze mid-step, my blood running cold as anxiety coiled in my stomach. What was she doing here? My mind raced with possibilities. Had she come to confront me? To disrupt this fragile happiness I had built?

Ethan felt my sudden stillness and turned, concern flickering in his eyes. "What's wrong?"

"Look over there," I said, nodding toward Diane. "She's here."

He turned, his expression morphing from curiosity to a hard line of determination. "What does she want?"

"I don't know, but I don't want to find out," I replied, a knot of dread tightening in my chest. "Not today, not now."

Ethan reached for my hand, his grip steady and reassuring. "Then let's just keep walking. We don't owe her anything."

I wanted to believe that, but as we moved to slip past the stalls, I felt a ripple of unease dance up my spine. My instincts screamed that she wouldn't let this go so easily. And just as we were about to slip into the crowd, her voice sliced through the air, smooth as silk yet sharp as a knife.

"Going somewhere?"

I turned slowly, my heart pounding like a drum. Diane stood there, her expression unreadable but her eyes glinting with mischief. She had a way of turning casual encounters into full-blown battles, and I couldn't shake the feeling that she had come armed with something much sharper than words.

"Diane," I said, forcing a smile that felt brittle on my lips. "What a surprise. We were just... shopping."

She stepped closer, her gaze flickering between Ethan and me, a calculating smile playing on her lips. "I see you've found a new friend. How quaint."

Ethan's stance shifted protectively beside me, his body tense with unspoken words. "We don't want any trouble, Diane."

"Oh, I don't want trouble either. But I have to say, it's amusing to see you two playing house while you've still got unfinished business."

The air thickened with tension, and I could feel the weight of her words pressing down on me, smothering the joy that had just blossomed between us. My heart raced, caught in a whirlwind of emotions—anger, fear, and a fierce urge to protect what I had with Ethan.

"Whatever you think you know," I replied, my voice steadying with each word, "it's none of your business. I'm happy now, and you can't take that away from me."

"Happy?" she laughed, the sound cold and biting. "It's cute that you think that. But let's be honest—happiness is a fragile thing. One gust of wind, and poof—it's gone."

With that, she stepped back, her eyes glinting with satisfaction as if she had just pulled the first card from a carefully constructed house of cards. I could feel the churning in my stomach, a mix of anger and fear, but I refused to let her win. Not today.

But as I opened my mouth to respond, the ground beneath us shifted, a tremor running through the earth that sent a ripple of unease coursing through the crowd. Gasps erupted, and the joyous market transformed into a chaos of shouts and scattering feet.

"Did you feel that?" Ethan shouted, gripping my hand tighter, eyes wide.

"Yeah, but what was that?" I managed to say, my heart racing as I scanned the crowd, now in disarray.

Diane's expression shifted, surprise flashing across her face, before her lips curled into a knowing smile. "I guess that's life, isn't it? Full of unexpected turns."

And with that, she turned to vanish into the throng of people, leaving me standing there, heart pounding, uncertain of what had just unfolded.

The ground shook again, more violently this time, and the world around us felt like it was tipping off its axis. As panic rose in the crowd, I turned to Ethan, dread pooling in my stomach. Whatever was happening, it felt like a storm was brewing on the horizon, one that would test the fragile foundations of our happiness. And I had no idea how much time we had before everything changed.

Chapter 18: Cracks in the Foundation

The morning sun filtered through the sheer curtains, casting a warm, golden glow across the small kitchen table where I nursed my coffee, savoring the rich aroma that mingled with the lingering scent of freshly baked scones. The warmth of the sun felt like an embrace, and for a moment, I allowed myself to sink into the delicious comfort of my new life, the hum of the town outside a gentle reminder of my own happiness. My little corner of the world in Briarwood had taken on a new rhythm, a melody of laughter, community events, and the quiet intimacy of shared moments. Ethan had become my favorite note in that symphony, his presence like the soft strum of a guitar, steady and reassuring.

I had just begun to imagine a future laced with possibility when the sharp trill of the doorbell shattered the tranquility. I set my coffee down, puzzled. Who could it be? The only visitors I usually received were those intent on borrowing a cup of sugar or gossiping about the latest town drama. With a slight frown creasing my forehead, I padded to the door, opening it to find a small envelope lying on the welcome mat. It was addressed in Claire's hurried, sprawling script. My heart dropped, a lead weight settling in my chest as I picked it up.

As I tore it open, my fingers trembled slightly, a flutter of anxiety rippling through me. Claire's words tumbled out in frantic loops, her distress palpable even through the paper. She was desperate for me to come home, pleading with me to abandon this life I had carved out for myself in Briarwood. My heart raced as I read her words, each sentence a reminder of the complicated tapestry of love and expectation that bound us. Claire, ever the big sister, had always borne the brunt of our family's chaos, and now it seemed she was reaching for me, needing me in a way that felt almost suffocating.

I stood in the doorway, my mind a tumultuous whirlpool of emotions. The tranquil scenes I had painted in my mind were now fraying at the edges, the vibrant colors dulling to gray. I could almost hear the echoes of our childhood, the nights spent sharing secrets and fears, and the burden of loyalty that had long rested on my shoulders. I stepped back inside, closing the door with a soft click, as if sealing off the outside world to give myself a moment to breathe.

The warmth of the kitchen seemed to mock me now, the scones a sweet reminder of the life I was trying to build. I sank into a chair, cradling the letter like a fragile bird, my heart aching for my sister but torn by the life I had begun to embrace here. The town had wrapped me in its charms, each interaction weaving a thread of connection. And Ethan—he was a radiant burst of joy, his laughter filling the corners of my mind with light, pushing away shadows that had lingered too long.

Ethan had sensed the shift in me that morning when I had finally shared my feelings about Claire's letter. "It's just a piece of paper," he had said, leaning against the kitchen counter, his arms crossed, an expression of concern shadowing his handsome face. "You have to do what's best for you. What do you want?"

His question lingered in the air, heavy with implications. What did I want? I wanted to reach out and pull Claire into my embrace, to assure her that everything would be okay, yet that desire felt like a chain binding me to a past I had begun to break away from. "I want to be here," I had whispered, and it was true, each word buoyed by the warmth of my feelings for him and the town that felt like home.

Ethan nodded, his eyes searching mine. "Then you need to make that clear. You can't keep bending to her will, not if it means sacrificing your happiness."

But sacrifice was woven into the fabric of sisterhood, wasn't it? As I looked into his steadfast gaze, I felt the weight of my indecision pushing down on me. I needed to confront Claire, to untangle the threads of expectation and obligation that had bound us for so long. But what would that look like? The thought of facing her discontent felt like standing on the edge of a precipice, the churning waves of our past threatening to pull me under.

The door swung open unexpectedly, and in walked Claire, her presence as imposing as the summer storm clouds that sometimes rolled over the hills. I barely had time to process her arrival before she filled the space with a whirlwind of energy, her eyes wide and frantic. "You got my letter!" she exclaimed, her voice cutting through the stillness. "You need to come back home. I can't do this without you!"

The room thickened with tension, each heartbeat a reminder of the chasm that had grown between us. As Claire's words spilled over into the kitchen, I felt the walls closing in, her discontent washing over me like a sudden downpour, drenching the bright moments I had shared with Ethan.

"I... I'm happy here, Claire," I stammered, the words tasting foreign on my tongue.

"You're happy?" She scoffed, the sound sharp like shattered glass. "You think this little town is enough? You've run away from everything!"

Ethan stepped forward, his protective stance a silent assertion that he would stand by me. "No one's running away. She's building a life here."

Claire turned her piercing gaze on him, dismissing his presence as if he were nothing more than a passing breeze. "This isn't about him! It's about us—about family!"

The crack in our foundation echoed ominously, each accusation shattering the fragile peace I had fought so hard to maintain. My heart raced, the weight of loyalty tugging me one way while the burgeoning love for my new life pulled me another. I stood at the crossroads, aware that every choice would ripple out, reshaping the landscape of my existence.

The air thickened with tension, Claire's presence electrifying the room, crackling with unsaid words and pent-up emotions. I glanced at Ethan, whose brow furrowed in concern, but I knew better than to lean on him for support just yet. This wasn't his battle; it was mine. I needed to find my voice, to articulate the conflict swirling in my heart.

"Claire," I began, my voice steadier than I felt. "I love you, but you need to understand that this is my life now. I can't just drop everything because you're feeling overwhelmed."

Her eyes blazed with indignation, a wildfire igniting in the dim light of the kitchen. "Overwhelmed? Is that what you call it? You've turned your back on everything we worked for! Do you even know what it's like without you?"

With each word, I felt the foundation of our sisterhood shaking beneath me. I had left, yes, but it was never about abandoning her; it was about finding my place in the world, a place where I didn't have to wear the heavy cloak of responsibility that had been stitched to me since childhood.

"Claire, I didn't run away. I've found a home here," I said, keeping my tone even despite the swell of anger rising within me. "I've built friendships, a routine, and... and I've built a relationship with Ethan."

At the mention of his name, she stiffened, her disdain for him bubbling to the surface. "Oh, so it's him now? This small-town romance? You think he can fill the void of family? You're making a mistake!"

I felt my chest tighten, a mix of defensiveness and guilt. "He's not just a fling, Claire. You can't diminish what we have. You don't know him!"

Her laughter was sharp, slicing through the atmosphere like a knife. "And what is he? A guy who thinks he can sweep you off your feet with sweet talk and charming smiles? You're smarter than this!"

Ethan stepped closer, his voice calm yet firm. "I may not know your family dynamics, Claire, but I do know that a sister should support her sibling's happiness, not try to dictate it."

"See? He's already getting in your head!" Claire shot back, her voice rising, practically vibrating with frustration. "You're throwing away everything just for some guy!"

The unspoken weight of expectation crashed against me, a tidal wave threatening to pull me under. "No, Claire," I insisted, my voice trembling with intensity. "I'm choosing to embrace a life that makes me happy, something I've longed for since we were kids. Don't you want that for me?"

"Of course I do!" she snapped, her expression morphing from anger to desperation. "But you're doing it wrong. You're running away from your responsibilities, and you're leaving me to pick up the pieces. Do you think I wanted to be the one taking care of everything?"

The guilt stabbed at me, sharper than any knife, twisting into the core of my heart. I thought of the nights Claire had spent trying to hold our family together, the sacrifices she had made, and the dreams she had shelved for the sake of others. But I couldn't continue to carry that burden on my shoulders. "I didn't choose this life because I wanted to escape you. I chose it because I needed to find out who I am outside of our family's expectations."

Claire took a step back, the anger in her eyes flickering momentarily, replaced by something softer, more vulnerable. "And what if that person isn't enough? What if you find out you've given everything up for nothing?"

"Then I'll face it. I'd rather risk failure than live a life dictated by fear." My words hung in the air, heavy with the truth I'd been avoiding.

For a moment, silence enveloped us, thick and charged, as if the world outside had faded into oblivion. Claire's features softened, the fierce resolve in her eyes giving way to uncertainty. "You really believe that, don't you?"

"I do," I whispered, my heart pounding with the weight of my conviction.

Just then, the door swung open again, this time revealing Clara, the feisty barista from the café who always brought a burst of sunshine with her. "Did I hear someone say 'life dictated by fear'?" she chimed, her voice light and playful, instantly diffusing some of the tension.

"Uh, well, you're a bit late for the pep talk," I quipped, half-grinning, grateful for the reprieve.

"Hey, I'll have you know I'm a pro at interrupting existential crises!" Clara declared, winking as she tossed her apron over her shoulder. "What's the drama, my friends? You're not in some ridiculous rom-com, are you?"

I couldn't help but chuckle at her antics, the weight on my shoulders lifting ever so slightly. "More like a family tragedy," I replied, and as I caught Claire's eye, I saw a flicker of humor beneath the surface of her tension.

"I'm sensing a potential sequel to 'Sisterly Squabbles'—with a side of caffeine, of course," Clara teased, oblivious to the emotional storm that had just erupted.

"Maybe we should pitch it to a streaming service," I shot back, smirking, but as I glanced at Claire, I noticed the corners of her mouth twitching, hinting that perhaps the barriers were starting to crumble.

"Do you know what I could really go for right now?" Clara continued, her excitement bubbling over. "A huge slice of your infamous double chocolate cake! It might help ease the drama. I hear chocolate solves everything."

"Except my sister's discontent," I muttered, but the playful banter had injected a much-needed dose of levity into the room.

Ethan leaned against the counter, his expression one of amusement as he watched the back-and-forth. "You've got your work cut out for you if you're going to bake your way into her good graces," he said, a teasing glint in his eye.

"Trust me, the cake is my secret weapon," I replied, and even Claire couldn't suppress a chuckle at that.

With Clara's contagious energy infusing the space, the tension shifted. "I'm in," Claire finally said, her voice softer, her eyes brightening a fraction. "But only if I can help. I've got my own secret recipes."

"Oh, now we're negotiating?" I shot back, unable to hide my smile.

"It's what sisters do," Claire replied, and for the first time that day, I felt a spark of hope flickering in the air between us. The storm wasn't over, but maybe the clouds had begun to part.

As we moved toward the kitchen, our laughter mingling with the aroma of coffee and chocolate, I realized that perhaps this was the beginning of a new chapter. A fragile but hopeful thread weaving us back together, and while the cracks in our foundation might still be visible, it felt like they were beginning to reshape into something stronger, something more resilient.

The kitchen had morphed into a flurry of flour, chocolate, and the occasional witty retort, with Claire and me attempting to negotiate the intricacies of baking as Clara stood by, her laughter bubbling like the yeast we had forgotten to activate. The aroma of melting chocolate wrapped around us like a warm hug, the earlier tension slipping away as if it had never been there. My sister, who had stormed in like a summer tempest, was now rolling out dough with a ferocity I hadn't expected, her brows furrowed in concentration.

"I have to admit," she said, glancing at me with a glimmer of competitiveness in her eyes, "the only thing I've ever baked was an epic disaster involving an explosion of eggs and a smoke alarm that still haunts me."

"Welcome to the club," I quipped, recalling my own early misadventures in the kitchen. "The first time I tried baking, I mistook baking powder for powdered sugar. Let's just say the results were unforgettable."

"See? We could start a support group for disaster bakers," she replied, a smirk pulling at the corners of her mouth. "Though I suspect you'd outshine me."

Ethan leaned against the doorway, arms crossed, an amused expression playing on his lips. "I'm just here for the cake. Just remember, if it turns out half-baked, I still love you both."

"Oh, the pressure's on now!" I exclaimed, mock horror on my face. "What if it's an utter failure? You might be forced to come to terms with your questionable taste in women."

"Touché," he replied, raising an eyebrow. "But I still think you're worth the risk."

We chuckled as Claire rolled her eyes, but I noticed the faintest blush creeping up her cheeks. Maybe there was still a flicker of warmth beneath the icy exterior she had presented when she first walked in. We set to work, our laughter mingling with the sounds of mixing and whisking, the ingredients binding us together in this moment of fragile harmony.

"Okay, so what's the next step?" Claire asked, a hint of trepidation threading through her voice as she adjusted her apron.

"We need to fold in the chocolate chips," I instructed, gesturing toward the bowl brimming with gooey chocolate goodness.

"Fold? As in, be delicate? In the kitchen? Not happening," Claire declared, brandishing a spatula like a sword. "I don't do delicate."

"Welcome to my life," I chuckled, watching her haphazardly mix the ingredients as if she were wielding a paintbrush instead of a spatula.

Amidst the laughter and flour dusting the air, I felt the walls of tension between us crumbling further, each joke chipping away at the misunderstanding that had settled like a fog between sisters. Yet, just as I began to believe we had turned a corner, a familiar darkness crept back into my thoughts. Claire's arrival had brought with it the weight of our unresolved issues, the unspoken expectations that had lingered in the corners of our relationship.

As the cake baked in the oven, a pleasant aroma wafting through the kitchen, I pulled Claire aside. "Listen, we've made a lot of progress here, but I don't want to ignore what's really bothering you. I need to know what's in your heart."

Her face hardened momentarily, the playful energy of our earlier exchanges fading. "It's just... hard, you know? I feel like I'm losing you, and everything feels chaotic back home. I need you there, especially with Mom and Dad being, well, them."

The air thickened with the heaviness of her words. I swallowed hard, knowing our family dynamics were more complicated than a double-chocolate cake recipe. "You aren't losing me, Claire. I promise I'm not going anywhere. But I can't go back to the old ways of doing things. I need to forge my own path, and you need to trust that I can handle my life."

"I just don't want to be the one left holding the pieces," she confessed, her voice barely above a whisper.

"And you won't be," I replied, heart aching for her. "But we can't be tied down by the past. It's time to break the cycle."

Just then, Clara poked her head into our quiet conversation, a devilish grin on her face. "Hey, can we have a moment of silence for the cake that's almost ready to sacrifice itself to the oven gods?"

"Right!" Claire said, snapping back to her former self. "Cake first, deep conversations later. I can't believe I almost got all emotional! Let's focus on the sweet stuff."

Ethan rejoined us as we pulled the cake from the oven, steam rising and the smell enveloping us like a comforting blanket. "Wow, it looks amazing!" he exclaimed, and for a moment, the simple joy of baking brought us together, our shared laughter filling the space like the warm sunlight streaming through the windows.

As we adorned the cake with frosting, a sense of unity began to settle in the kitchen. The earlier conflicts felt less daunting, less threatening. But just as I started to believe we could navigate this, the door swung open once again, and in walked my mother, her face stormy with a mix of concern and disappointment.

"Why didn't you tell me Claire was here?" she demanded, her eyes darting between us like a hawk. "I called you earlier! You need to come home now!"

The sudden shift in atmosphere was palpable. All the warmth and laughter drained from the room, replaced by a chill that seemed to creep into my bones. I opened my mouth to respond, but no words came. The balance we had just begun to establish felt precarious, teetering on the edge of something chaotic.

"Mom, I—" Claire began, but our mother cut her off.

"No! You both need to listen to me!" she said, her voice rising. "This isn't a game. There are things happening back home you don't understand. You need to take this seriously!"

"What kind of things?" I finally found my voice, though it came out more demanding than I intended.

Mom's gaze shifted to me, a mixture of urgency and fear in her eyes. "Things that involve your father. You need to come home, all of you. It's time to face what's been left unsaid."

With her words, the air grew heavy, the weight of our family's unresolved issues crashing down on us like an avalanche. I felt Claire's hand brush against mine, a silent plea for solidarity. In that moment, I realized that the cake, the laughter, the fleeting warmth—everything that had seemed so perfect—could crumble in an instant.

"What's going on?" I demanded, heart pounding as the room fell silent.

Mom took a deep breath, her face a mask of uncertainty. "There's no easy way to say this, but your father... he's in trouble."

And with those words, the ground beneath us felt like it was shifting, the cracks in our foundation widening into chasms that could swallow us whole.

Chapter 19: The Reckoning

The golden leaves, already starting to crumple under the weight of autumn, cast an enchanting spell over Silver Pines. The crisp air carried the sweet, earthy scent of fallen foliage mingling with the sharp tang of woodsmoke. The town transformed into a kaleidoscope of fiery reds and deep oranges, but even the beauty of the season couldn't mask the tension in our home. As I stood at the kitchen counter, my hands lost in the familiar rhythm of chopping vegetables, I felt the ground shifting beneath me.

"Claire's only here for a couple of days," Ethan reassured me, his voice a low rumble from the living room. I could hear the warmth in his tone, the way it wrapped around the words like a protective blanket, but it did little to soothe the fluttering unease in my stomach. My knife sliced through the last carrot, and I sighed, wishing I could share his optimism. In my mind, Claire was more than a guest; she was a tempest, an uninvited storm that threatened to uproot everything we had cultivated together in this quaint corner of the world.

"Right. Just a couple of days," I muttered under my breath, hoping my voice wouldn't betray the turmoil churning within. I tossed the chopped vegetables into a bowl, their bright colors a stark contrast to the gloom I felt creeping in. I had never thought of Claire as an antagonist, but her arrival in Silver Pines had shifted something in our delicate balance. I stole a glance out of the window, where she stood on the porch, her silhouette framed by the fading sunlight. There was a boldness to her, an ease with the world that felt foreign to me, as if she thrived on the energy of a bustling city while I was made for the gentle cadence of this sleepy town.

"Claire, what are you doing?" Ethan's voice broke through my thoughts, rising in pitch, laced with an edge I hadn't heard before. I dropped the spoon, a sudden jolt of adrenaline coursing through me as I hurried to the living room, where I found them standing toe-to-toe. The air between them crackled, thick with unspoken words.

"I'm just saying this place isn't worth settling for," Claire shot back, her arms crossed defiantly. "You're wasting your potential here, Ethan. There's a whole world out there." Her dark hair, tousled by the wind, framed her face like an artist's brushstroke, and her eyes sparkled with conviction that bordered on arrogance.

Ethan's brows knitted together, the muscles in his jaw tightening. "This isn't just a place to me, Claire. It's home. It's where I grew up, where my family is. You wouldn't understand." His voice, usually so calm and steady, cracked under the weight of his emotions. My heart ached at the sight of him like this, caught between two worlds, and I felt the distance between us yawning wider with every passing second.

"Of course, I wouldn't understand," she countered, her voice rising to a crescendo. "You've never let me in on that. You live here like it's a cage, and I'm not going to let you convince me it's something beautiful. You need to see what's out there."

"I'm not looking for something bigger, Claire! I'm happy here," Ethan shot back, his voice now tinged with desperation. I watched helplessly, a silent observer as their argument spiraled into chaos, echoing through the walls of our cozy home.

"Happy?" she scoffed. "Is that what you call it? Going through the motions? You think this is what life is meant to be?" The bitterness in her tone cut through the air, and I could see the disbelief etched into Ethan's features, a shadow of hurt crossing his face.

"Claire, that's not fair," I finally said, stepping into the fray, my own voice shaky but determined. I had to intervene, had to pull them back from the precipice before they fell into a chasm of hurtful words. "Ethan loves this town. There's more to happiness than chasing some ideal."

"And what about you?" Claire shot back, her gaze piercing through me. "Are you content being tied to a man who's content with mediocrity? Are you really happy, or are you just settling?"

The accusation hit me like a slap. My heart raced, an unwelcome twist of anxiety knotting my stomach. Was that what I was doing? I opened my mouth to respond, but no words came. I felt exposed, like the sun had suddenly pierced the comfortable fog of my existence, revealing all the insecurities I'd tucked away under the guise of tranquility.

Ethan turned to me, his eyes wide, searching. "That's not true, is it?"

"I..." I hesitated, the truth lying heavy on my tongue. Claire's words echoed in my mind, stirring something deep within me. I had always prided myself on being rooted, on finding beauty in the everyday, but perhaps I had also ignored my own desires, my own ambitions, in the name of love.

"Look, I didn't mean to make it personal," Claire said, her tone softening slightly, but the damage was done. I could see the way her words had etched doubt into Ethan's expression, the flicker of frustration on his face shifting to something more vulnerable.

"No, you did," he replied, his voice now a low growl. "You don't get to come here and tear down everything I've built just because it doesn't fit into your idea of success."

And in that moment, I felt the air shift again, this time colder, like a winter gust rolling through the autumn leaves. The room filled with a palpable silence, a vacuum of uncertainty and unresolved tension.

"Maybe you both need to take a step back," I said quietly, my heart racing as I sensed the walls closing in around us. "This isn't just about you two. It's about me, too."

Claire and Ethan turned their gaze to me, their expressions a mix of surprise and apprehension. "What do you mean?" Claire asked, her voice softer now, as if she sensed the shift in the atmosphere.

"I mean... I've been trying to keep the peace, to make everyone happy," I confessed, my voice barely above a whisper. "But in doing that, I've ignored my own feelings, my own path. And maybe it's time for me to figure out what I really want, even if it means upsetting the apple cart."

The tension hung thick in the air, a charged moment that felt both frightening and liberating. I could feel the weight of their gazes on me, and in that instant, the truth was undeniable. It was time to confront the reality of my own life, to reclaim my voice from the shadows of others' expectations.

The silence lingered like a held breath, heavy and tense. I could feel the weight of my words settle between us, creating an invisible wall that demanded attention. Claire shifted slightly, her expression morphing from confrontation to contemplation. Ethan, however, was still caught in the throes of disbelief, his brow furrowing deeper, eyes searching for clarity amidst the chaos.

"You're not happy?" he finally asked, the words slipping from his lips like a fragile secret, vulnerable and raw. The room felt smaller, as if the walls were inching closer, eager to hear the truth laid bare. My heart thundered in my chest, each beat a reminder of the weight of expectations I'd been carrying.

"I don't know," I admitted, the words tasting foreign on my tongue. "I thought I was, but maybe I was just afraid of wanting something more." I glanced at Claire, her posture relaxing, the sharpness in her demeanor softening as she regarded me with something akin to understanding.

"You have every right to want more," she said gently, her tone shifting as she stepped away from the argumentative edge.

"Small-town charm can feel like a gilded cage when you dream of bigger things."

Ethan crossed his arms tightly, a fortress built of his own insecurities. "So, you're saying you want to leave Silver Pines?" The hurt in his voice felt like a knife to my heart, and I wanted to reach out, to reassure him that my feelings for him were still vibrant and real, but the truth was tangled in a mess of confusion.

"I'm saying I want to explore what that 'more' could be," I replied carefully. "I love this town, and I love you, but I also feel like I'm only part of myself here. And maybe that's okay."

A silence followed, thick with unspoken words, as if we were all waiting for something to shatter the moment. Claire's gaze flitted between us, an uncharacteristic gentleness in her eyes. "Maybe you need to take some time for yourself, figure out what you really want without anyone else's influence."

Ethan's reaction was immediate. "So, what? You're just going to run away?" The disappointment was palpable, a cold rush that brushed against my skin.

"It's not running away, Ethan. It's... stepping away," I replied, my voice steadier now, fueled by a sudden burst of determination. "I need to figure out what I want, not just what others expect of me."

"But you'll come back, right?" His eyes locked onto mine, filled with a mix of hope and fear.

"I don't know," I whispered, feeling the truth resonate within me, a sharp pang of liberation mingled with fear. The realization that I had been waiting for permission to dream, to desire, washed over me like a sudden rain.

Claire took a step forward, her expression shifting to something softer. "Look, I get it. I love my city, the pulse of it, the chaos. But I also get that sometimes you have to leave to understand what home really is."

Ethan ran a hand through his hair, frustration etched across his features. "But why does it have to be all or nothing?"

"Maybe it doesn't," I suggested. "Maybe there's a middle ground we haven't explored. What if I took a short trip? Just a week or two?"

"Who are you?" Claire teased lightly, a mischievous grin creeping onto her face. "You sound like a true adventurer."

"I'm not an adventurer," I protested with a light laugh, the tension beginning to dissipate under the warmth of her words. "I'm just... trying to figure out how to live for myself without stepping on anyone's toes."

"Or breaking your own heart," Claire added, her voice turning serious again. "But sometimes you have to do that to find out what truly makes you happy."

Ethan's gaze softened as he turned to me, the armor he'd been wearing starting to crack. "I don't want you to leave," he said quietly, the vulnerability in his voice disarming.

"I don't want to leave you," I replied, my heart aching with the weight of unfulfilled desires and promises. "But I also can't ignore this feeling any longer."

The conversation lingered in the air, each of us grappling with the enormity of the moment. I caught a glimpse of Claire, her face illuminated by the fading light, and in that instant, I realized she was more than just an intruder in our lives; she was a catalyst, a spark igniting a long-buried desire to seek out the unknown.

"Let's take a walk," Claire suggested suddenly, her voice brightening with spontaneity. "The sunset is going to be stunning over at the lake."

Ethan glanced at me, uncertainty flickering in his eyes. "You don't have to—"

"No, I want to," I interrupted, a sudden urge to embrace the moment taking hold. "I think it would be good for all of us."

So, we set out into the cool evening, the air fresh and invigorating against our skin. The path to the lake wound through a grove of trees, their leaves rustling softly, whispering secrets that felt sacred. I felt lighter with every step, the heaviness of the confrontation behind us, replaced by the thrill of possibility.

Claire took the lead, her stride confident and bold, while Ethan fell slightly behind, his presence a comforting shadow. "You know," Claire said, her voice playful, "when I suggested a visit, I didn't think I'd be stirring the pot like this. I just wanted to catch up."

I chuckled, my heart warming. "Well, you certainly managed to mix things up."

"It's my specialty," she replied, throwing a glance over her shoulder. "Besides, if you're going to break free, you might as well do it in style."

As we reached the lake, the sky stretched above us, a canvas of swirling oranges and pinks. The sun dipped low on the horizon, casting a golden shimmer across the water. It was breathtaking—almost surreal—reminding me of the beauty that still existed in my world, even amid the turmoil.

"I can't believe I never came here before," I breathed, taking in the moment, the shimmering reflections dancing on the surface of the lake like laughter caught in a gentle breeze.

"Sometimes you need a nudge to find the magic around you," Claire said, her eyes sparkling with mischief. "Or, in your case, an explosive confrontation."

Ethan chuckled, and for a brief moment, the tension faded, replaced by laughter that echoed softly through the trees. As we settled on a weathered bench overlooking the water, I felt the weight of my decisions pressing on me, but now it felt lighter, like I was finally beginning to understand the path I needed to take.

"Whatever you decide, I just want you to be happy," Ethan said, his voice sincere, and I could see the glimmer of hope in his eyes.

"Thank you," I replied, my heart swelling with affection. "I promise I'll figure this out."

Claire leaned back, a satisfied smile on her face. "And I'll be here to help, whether you want me to or not."

As the sun slipped below the horizon, painting the sky with fading hues, I felt a renewed sense of purpose. The road ahead was uncertain, but for the first time in a long while, I felt the exhilarating pulse of possibility, a flicker of adventure that whispered to me, urging me to embrace the unknown.

The sun dipped low, casting a warm golden glow over the lake, and the world around us felt both suspended and alive. The moment hung heavy with possibility, and I drank it in like sweet cider, the warmth settling deep within me. Claire leaned back against the bench, her expression unreadable, while Ethan stared out over the water, the soft waves lapping at the shore mirroring the restless currents of our conversation.

"Okay, so what's the plan?" Claire asked, her voice breaking through the serene quiet. "You can't just say you're going to explore the world and then not do it. That's like saying you want dessert and then sticking to salad."

"Right, because who wants to be stuck in the 'salad' of life?" I quipped, unable to hide the smile that tugged at my lips. The tension from earlier had faded, replaced by a comfortable camaraderie, a lightness that felt almost foreign yet utterly welcome.

"Exactly! You need a little reckless abandon," Claire replied, her eyes sparkling with mischief. "What's stopping you from taking a leap? Are you just going to sit here and watch the sunset every evening, or are you going to go out and make some stories worth telling?"

Her words struck a chord, resonating deep within. What was stopping me? I had spent so long caught in the web of expectation—first my parents, then Ethan, and now Claire, as if they were all pieces of a puzzle I was desperately trying to fit together. "I suppose I've always played it safe," I admitted, my voice almost a whisper.

Ethan turned to me, his brows furrowing slightly. "You don't have to justify anything to anyone, you know. You deserve to chase what makes you happy."

I glanced at him, and for a moment, I could see a flicker of understanding, of acceptance, even in the midst of our earlier conflict. "What if that happiness takes me far away?" The words felt heavy, like stones in my pocket, yet I couldn't hold back the honesty spilling from my heart.

Claire stretched her arms wide as if to embrace the horizon. "Then so be it! Imagine the stories you'll have to share when you come back. What if you discover you're meant for something completely different? What if you want to stay away?"

Ethan's expression darkened, a shadow passing over his face. "And what if you don't come back?" he asked, his voice barely above a whisper. It was a question that hung in the air like a thundercloud, darkening the beautiful evening.

The weight of his words hit me, and I felt a pang of guilt. Did I really want to risk everything I had here? The laughter shared over kitchen tables, the warmth of lazy Sunday mornings, and the smell of fresh-baked bread from the local bakery? The life I'd built was good, yet there was this gnawing restlessness that would not let go.

"I don't want to lose you," Ethan continued, his voice breaking through my spiraling thoughts. "But I can't hold you back, either. Just... promise me you'll think about it."

"I promise," I said softly, but in my heart, the promise felt vague and uncertain. The sunset painted the sky in shades of pink and orange, a breathtaking spectacle, yet I couldn't shake the sense of foreboding that lurked beneath the surface.

As the sun dipped below the horizon, casting a long shadow over the water, Claire leaned forward, her eyes sparkling with mischief again. "Okay, let's make a pact. For every day you stay here, you write down one thing you want to explore outside Silver Pines. Then, when you feel ready, you'll pick a destination and go. Simple, right?"

"Simple," I echoed, but the notion felt like stepping off a cliff into the unknown.

"Deal?" she pressed, her tone teasing yet earnest.

"Deal," I said, more to appease her than out of certainty. Still, the thrill of it sent a shiver of excitement coursing through me. What could I possibly want?

Before I could get lost in thought, Ethan interjected, his tone suddenly serious. "And what if you don't want to come back at all?"

"That's the risk, isn't it?" Claire replied, her expression unwavering. "You can't find out what makes you happy without taking a leap."

I opened my mouth to respond, but a sudden rustling in the nearby bushes interrupted us. The sound sliced through the conversation like a knife, and my heart raced as I turned to see what it was.

A figure stepped into view—a man, tall and broad-shouldered, dressed in a rugged flannel shirt and faded jeans. His face was shadowed, but I could see the glint of mischief in his eyes as he approached, a grin spreading across his lips. "Didn't mean to intrude on your little heart-to-heart," he called out, his voice smooth as whiskey.

"What are you doing here?" Claire asked, her surprise evident.

"I was just passing through," the stranger said, leaning casually against a tree, his eyes darting between us. "But I couldn't help but overhear your discussion about adventure. And let me tell you, I'm all about adventure."

"Who are you?" Ethan asked, his protective instinct flaring.

"Name's Jake," he replied with a wink. "And if you're looking for adventure, you've got to be willing to go off the beaten path."

My heart thudded at the unexpected intrusion, a wild flutter of intrigue mingling with caution. I could sense the air shift, the dynamic among us altering. I hadn't expected anyone else to join us at this pivotal moment, and I wasn't sure how I felt about it.

Ethan's brow furrowed as he stepped forward, putting himself between me and Jake. "And what exactly do you mean by 'off the beaten path'?"

Jake chuckled, unphased by Ethan's protectiveness. "I'm talking about taking chances, living life on your terms. I saw you guys at the lake and figured you could use some company—someone who knows the ins and outs of the area. There's a lot more to Silver Pines than meets the eye."

I glanced at Ethan, who looked both intrigued and wary. My heart raced as Jake continued, "You want stories? I've got plenty. And who knows, maybe I can show you a side of this place you've never seen."

The air buzzed with uncertainty, the potential for something new looming on the horizon like a gathering storm. I could feel Claire's excitement bubbling beneath the surface, while Ethan's protective instinct surged. The conversation took a turn, unexpected and electrifying, and in that moment, I felt the world shift beneath me, opening up in a way I hadn't anticipated.

"Adventure doesn't wait," Jake said, his eyes glinting with a promise of excitement. "What do you say? Are you ready to take the leap?"

Before I could respond, a sudden rustle from the bushes interrupted our moment again, and out stepped another figure, this one familiar but with an air of unpredictability. It was Sam, my childhood friend, his expression serious, eyes wide with urgency.

"I need to talk to you. It's important."

The weight of his words hung heavily in the air, and as I glanced back at Ethan and Claire, the stakes felt higher than ever. Choices loomed before me, each path fraught with uncertainty, and I couldn't shake the feeling that my life was about to change in ways I couldn't yet comprehend.

Chapter 20: Paths Diverging

The scent of cinnamon and steaming milk wafted through The Maple Leaf, wrapping around me like a cozy blanket, the kind that beckoned you to stay just a little longer. I stirred my chai latte, the rich, spiced aroma intertwining with the soft jazz playing in the background. A few patrons dotted the café, lost in their own worlds, their voices a gentle hum that faded into the walls. It was a sanctuary of sorts, a pocket of warmth against the chill that had crept into my life since the arrival of Claire and the weighty history she carried like a shield.

As I sat at my usual table, the sunlight streamed through the large windows, casting a golden hue over the rustic wood furniture. I had set out to write down my thoughts, hoping to unravel the knots in my mind, but every attempt ended in a jumble of words that didn't quite capture the turmoil brewing within me. I took a sip of my latte, letting the warmth spread through me, but even the comforting drink could not thaw the icy grip of uncertainty that clutched my heart.

Ethan walked in, his tall frame silhouetted against the doorway, a familiar figure that now felt like both home and a storm on the horizon. His usual charm seemed dimmed, replaced by a gravity that made my stomach churn. I waved him over, forcing a smile that felt more like a mask than a welcome. As he slid into the chair opposite me, the air thickened, filled with the tension of unspoken words and lingering doubts.

"Hey," he said, running a hand through his hair, a habit I had come to find endearing. But today, it felt more like a sign of frustration. "You're deep in thought. What's on your mind?"

"Just trying to sort through some things," I replied, my voice wavering slightly. "You know how it is."

He leaned forward, a frown etched across his handsome features. "It feels like you're carrying the weight of the world on your shoulders. It's okay to talk about it, you know."

The sincerity in his eyes warmed me, yet it also stirred the pot of conflict simmering inside. "It's complicated, Ethan. With Claire here, everything feels different. I don't know how to navigate this without hurting someone."

His expression darkened, the lines of worry deepening. "I can see that. It's like there's this invisible wall growing between us. I don't want to lose you, but I also don't want to push you into a corner."

The truth of his words struck me like a slap. I had felt the distance, the subtle shifts in our dynamic, as Claire's presence transformed everything around us. The once effortless conversations felt strained, each word wrapped in layers of hesitation. My heart ached at the thought of losing what we had built, but the reality was that my life had become a balancing act, teetering dangerously between two worlds.

As I searched for a way to express my turmoil, my phone buzzed on the table, cutting through the moment like a knife. The screen lit up with Claire's name, and an involuntary dread settled in my stomach. I had forgotten about our planned 'family meeting,' a gathering that felt more like an intervention with every passing day.

"I should—" I started, but Ethan's hand reached out, gently resting on mine, an anchor in the storm.

"Wait," he urged, his voice low and firm. "Just a minute. Whatever she wants, we can deal with it together."

A small part of me was grateful for his support, but another part felt a swell of guilt. I knew Claire needed me, and the pull of familial loyalty was strong. I had never been one to abandon those I cared about, yet with each passing day, the divide between my obligations and my desires seemed to widen.

The phone buzzed again, a reminder of the urgency that couldn't be ignored. "I have to go," I finally said, pulling my hand away from his.

"Just... promise me you'll think about us," he said, a hint of vulnerability breaking through the facade he wore.

"Of course," I replied, my voice barely above a whisper as I stood to leave, the weight of his gaze following me like a heavy cloak.

I made my way to the door, my heart pounding in rhythm with the unsteady drum of uncertainty. The cool air hit me as I stepped outside, a stark contrast to the warmth of the café, as if the universe itself was trying to shake me from my reverie. I took a deep breath, preparing myself for the conversation ahead, but each step felt heavier than the last.

Claire was waiting at the park, the trees around us shifting in the autumn breeze, their leaves a vibrant tapestry of reds and golds. I had always loved this time of year, the way it felt like nature was setting the stage for change, but today it only reminded me of the impending storm between my two lives.

"Thanks for coming," Claire said, her voice laced with a seriousness that made my stomach drop. She gestured to a nearby bench, the familiar comfort of the park feeling foreign today.

I sat down, my mind racing as I braced myself for what was to come. The unspoken words hung in the air, thick and heavy. "What did you want to talk about?" I finally asked, trying to keep my tone even, but my heart was a tumultuous mess beneath the surface.

She took a deep breath, her eyes shimmering with something unidentifiable. "I want you to know that I'm here for you, no matter what happens with Ethan. Family means everything to me, and I just... I don't want to lose you."

Her vulnerability pierced through my defenses, and the sincerity of her words made me question everything I had thought about loyalty and love. Here we were, caught in a web of our own making, where every choice felt like a path diverging into uncharted territory, and I was standing at the crossroads, paralyzed by indecision.

The air around us felt electric, a tense dance of words unspoken and emotions barely contained. Claire's gaze held mine, searching for reassurance in the depths of my confusion. "You know I love you, right?" she said, her voice thick with an emotion I couldn't quite place. "Family is everything to me. But I don't want to put pressure on you. I just need to know where we stand."

A thousand thoughts swirled in my mind, a tempest of loyalty and desire. "I love you too, Claire," I managed, each word heavy with the weight of my commitment. "But this situation with Ethan... it's complicated. I don't want to hurt you or lose him."

She sighed, a sound that echoed the weight of the world on her shoulders. "It's not fair, is it? To be caught in the middle?"

"No," I said, my voice barely a whisper as I turned my gaze to the ground. The leaves crunched beneath my feet, the vibrant colors reminiscent of the chaos swirling within me. "But I feel like I'm being torn in two. Every choice feels monumental."

"Then let's make this easy," Claire suggested, an unexpected determination glinting in her eyes. "We both know that you need to choose what makes you happiest. I can't dictate that for you. Just be honest with yourself, and with us."

I met her gaze, and the sincerity radiating from her momentarily silenced the storm within. Yet beneath that honesty lay an unspoken challenge, a dare to confront the truth. As she spoke, a light breeze rustled through the branches overhead, reminding me that change was not only inevitable but necessary.

"I'll think about it," I promised, though the resolve felt tenuous at best.

As we parted ways, the crisp air filled with the earthy scent of fallen leaves, I felt the sharp bite of reality. My heart was divided, and every step I took felt like navigating a minefield, each choice fraught with the potential for explosion. I headed back to The Maple Leaf, where Ethan awaited, unaware of the internal battle I was facing.

He looked up as I walked in, his expression a mix of concern and hope, and I felt my heart stutter. "Everything okay?" he asked, his voice low, as if afraid to disturb the fragile peace that hung between us.

"Just... talking," I replied, attempting to keep my voice steady. "Claire wanted to clear the air."

His brow furrowed, a flicker of unease passing over his features. "And? What did she say?"

"Nothing that hasn't been said before. Just that family is important to her." I hesitated, choosing my words carefully. "She's willing to let me choose what makes me happy."

"Easy for her to say," Ethan replied, his tone sharper than I expected. "But it doesn't make this any simpler for you."

The tension in the air thickened, and I could almost hear the unspoken words echoing between us. "No, it doesn't," I agreed, sitting down again, suddenly aware of how monumental this conversation felt. "But I don't want to lose you, either."

Ethan leaned back in his chair, running a hand over his face in a gesture of frustration. "This feels so much like a game, and I don't want to play anymore. I thought we were on the same team."

"Team? It feels more like a standoff," I countered, my frustration bubbling to the surface. "I wish we could just... make sense of this mess."

He met my gaze, and I could see the wheels turning in his mind, the lines of his jaw tightening. "You know, maybe we need to redefine the rules."

"What do you mean?"

"I mean, what if we just set the stakes down? Forget Claire for a moment and just focus on us. Let's not think about the complications, the family obligations, or what we're 'supposed' to do. Just... us."

A part of me wanted to agree, to dive headfirst into the simplicity he offered, but the weight of reality pulled me back. "Ethan, you know it's not that simple. Claire's family is a huge part of my life."

"And I get that," he replied, his voice gentle but firm. "But that doesn't mean you have to sacrifice your happiness for it. You deserve more than to be caught between two worlds."

I wanted to believe him, to trust that we could carve out a space where our needs intersected. But the nagging fear that I was teetering on the edge of a precipice kept me rooted in place. "I don't want to hurt Claire, and I can't ignore what we have."

He sighed, the sound heavy with resignation. "Maybe it's time you decide what 'we' means. I'm willing to fight for us, but you have to want it too."

Just then, a familiar figure entered the café—Claire, her eyes scanning the room before they landed on me. The moment hung suspended in time, the air charged with the potential for confrontation. I felt my stomach twist, and a cold wave of anxiety washed over me.

"Looks like she's here for round two," Ethan muttered, his eyes narrowing slightly.

"Ethan, please..." I started, but he raised a hand, silencing me.

"Let's face it head-on," he said, determination flaring in his gaze. "Whatever happens next, we deal with it together."

Claire approached, her demeanor calm yet undeniably tense. "Can we talk?" she asked, the weight of her words unmistakable.

"Sure," I replied, though my heart raced, knowing this conversation would shift the course of everything.

Ethan shot me an encouraging look, a silent promise that he was in my corner. As Claire sat down, I felt the tension coalesce into a palpable force, and the café around us faded into the background.

"Can we just be honest for a moment?" Claire began, her tone steady yet laced with vulnerability. "I don't want to lose you, and I don't want you to feel trapped between us."

"Neither do I," I said, my voice shaking slightly. "But I can't ignore the way things are changing."

Claire nodded, her expression softening. "Then let's be brave together. I want you to feel free to choose your path, even if it leads you away from me."

Ethan and I exchanged glances, the air thick with uncharted territory. My heart raced as the walls I had built began to crumble, leaving a raw, open space for truth. Whatever lay ahead, I knew this moment would define the paths diverging before us.

The atmosphere in the café shifted as Claire took her seat across from us, her presence commanding attention like a lighthouse in a tempest. I could see the determination etched on her face, framed by the unruly curls that danced around her shoulders. "Okay, let's cut to the chase," she said, her voice steady yet tinged with an urgency that made my pulse quicken. "I know things are complicated, but we can't keep dancing around this. It's exhausting."

Ethan leaned back, crossing his arms, his posture radiating defiance and protectiveness. "That's one way to put it," he replied, the tension in his tone mirroring the atmosphere. "But it's not just about you or me anymore. It's about what she wants, too."

I felt caught in a crossfire, two sides of my life colliding in a way I had never anticipated. "What I want," I began, my voice shaking slightly, "is for us to be honest with each other." I could feel my heart pounding in my chest, a drumbeat that echoed the turmoil swirling inside. "Claire, you said you wanted me to feel free. But I don't want to lose either of you in the process."

"Losing you would be the worst kind of freedom," Claire replied, her gaze steady. "I love you, and I want you to be happy, even if that means stepping back."

Ethan's brow furrowed. "That's not what I want," he interjected, his voice sharper. "I want you to choose what makes you happy—with us. But if you decide to step back from us both, then we need to know."

The weight of their expectations pressed down on me like a heavy fog, obscuring my vision of a clear path forward. "It's not that simple," I said, frustration bubbling to the surface. "I feel like I'm on a tightrope, and every step I take is precarious."

Claire's expression softened, and she leaned in, her elbows resting on the table. "You're not alone in this. We're both here, and we can figure it out together. What if we establish some ground rules? Something that allows you to explore your feelings without pressure?"

Ethan's eyes narrowed, and he shifted in his seat. "Ground rules? Is that really the solution? It sounds more like a temporary fix for something that's about to blow up."

"Maybe blowing up is what we need," Claire shot back, her voice rising slightly. "If we keep pretending everything is fine, we're only going to hurt each other more."

A tense silence fell over us, the weight of their words hanging in the air. I could feel the gravity of the moment, the kind that twisted your stomach into knots. "What if I just want a moment to breathe? A moment where I don't have to decide anything?" I implored, my voice rising in pitch.

Claire glanced at Ethan, her eyes pleading. "Is that so wrong? Can't we agree to take a step back for now?"

Ethan's jaw tightened, his gaze unwavering. "But that doesn't solve anything. You can't just avoid the decision. It's looming over us like a dark cloud."

The café felt stifling as the reality of our situation enveloped me. I pushed back my chair, the sound echoing like a gunshot in the tense silence. "I need air," I blurted, rising from the table. I didn't want to run away, but the walls felt like they were closing in, and I needed to escape before I suffocated under the weight of their scrutiny.

"Wait, where are you going?" Claire called after me, her voice laced with concern.

"Just outside," I replied, my heart racing as I rushed through the door and into the crisp autumn air. The chill bit at my cheeks, invigorating me as I inhaled deeply, trying to regain my bearings. The world outside felt different—clearer somehow, as though the chaos had been muffled just moments before.

I wandered along the nearby path, the crunch of leaves beneath my feet grounding me in reality. I had to think. I had to decide what I truly wanted.

As I walked, I felt the weight of their eyes on me, even from a distance. Each step seemed to amplify the storm brewing in my mind. I paused at the edge of the park, staring at the vibrant display of leaves. Nature had its own way of embracing change, and yet here I was, paralyzed by fear of the unknown.

"Hey, you okay?" Ethan's voice broke through my thoughts, startling me. I turned to find him a few paces behind me, concern etched into his features.

"I don't know, Ethan. I feel like I'm losing control," I confessed, my voice trembling. "Every decision I make just leads to more confusion."

He closed the distance between us, his expression softening as he reached for my hand. "You're not losing control; you're just navigating a complicated situation. It's okay to feel overwhelmed."

I met his gaze, searching for the reassurance I craved. "But how do I know what's right?"

"Sometimes, you just have to trust your gut. What does it tell you?" he asked, his thumb brushing over my knuckles in a gesture that made my heart flutter despite the heaviness in my chest.

"I don't know if my gut is the best advisor right now," I admitted with a wry smile, trying to lighten the mood. "It feels like it's doing somersaults."

His chuckle eased some of the tension, but I could still feel the impending storm looming over us. "Okay, then let's try this: close your eyes for a moment. Picture your life a year from now. What does it look like?"

I hesitated, the idea of envisioning my future both tantalizing and terrifying. But I closed my eyes, focusing on the sound of my breath mingling with the rustle of the leaves. I imagined the possibilities stretching before me, each path diverging from the last. Would I see Claire smiling at me, secure in our relationship? Would Ethan be standing beside me, our hands intertwined as we faced whatever challenges lay ahead?

"Tell me what you see," Ethan urged gently, his voice anchoring me.

"I see... happiness," I breathed, the word tasting bittersweet on my tongue. "But it's not just one picture; it's like a collage of everything I love."

"Then maybe that's your answer," he suggested, hope flickering in his eyes. "You don't have to choose one over the other. You just need to figure out how to make it all fit."

I opened my eyes, the world around me sharper, more vibrant. "You make it sound so easy," I said, a soft smile breaking through my uncertainty.

"Nothing worthwhile ever is," he replied, a glint of mischief dancing in his gaze. "But I'm willing to face the chaos if you are."

Just as the tension began to ease, a familiar figure emerged from the distance. Claire approached, her expression resolute, her body language conveying a mix of urgency and determination. "There you are," she called out, a hint of relief breaking through her tension. "I've been looking for you."

Ethan's grip on my hand tightened slightly, and I felt the world shift once more. "What's going on?" he asked, a warning note in his voice.

"I think we need to talk about what happens next," Claire said, her eyes darting between us. "We can't keep dancing around the truth."

Before I could respond, Claire pulled something from her pocket, a small piece of paper crumpled and worn. "I found this earlier," she continued, her voice trembling slightly. "And I think it's time we address what's really at stake here."

I glanced at Ethan, confusion rippling through the air between us. The moment felt suspended, the weight of her words hanging in the balance, and I could sense the ground shifting beneath my feet. Whatever she was about to reveal could change everything, and as I braced myself for the unexpected, I felt a spark of fear ignite within me.

"Claire, what is it?" I asked, my heart racing as she unfolded the paper, revealing something that would shatter the fragile equilibrium we had fought so hard to maintain.

Chapter 21: Family Ties

The storm clouds gathered as I pulled into the parking lot of the café, the familiar blue-and-white sign swinging gently in the wind like a lighthouse beacon in a tumultuous sea. Just last week, I had envisioned this place as a refuge—a sanctuary where laughter mingled with the scent of freshly brewed coffee and warm pastries. Now, as I stepped inside, the air was thick with a tension that made my stomach twist. Ethan sat at our usual corner table, his handsome features shadowed by the dim light, brow furrowed, a stark contrast to the easygoing charm I had come to adore. I hesitated at the door, taking a moment to absorb the scene: a couple shared a slice of chocolate cake while another group animatedly debated the best hiking trails in Silver Pines. I longed for that kind of lightness, but my heart was heavy with Claire's words, still echoing in my mind like a ghost that wouldn't let go.

"Hey," I said, forcing a smile as I approached, though it felt more like a grimace than anything close to joy. "You're early."

"I had a feeling you'd need me today," he replied, his voice low and rich, yet tinged with an undercurrent of concern. He gestured toward the half-empty cup in front of him, the latte now lukewarm, a mirror of my own lingering doubts.

I slid into the chair opposite him, instinctively tucking a loose strand of hair behind my ear. "Sorry for the delay. Family meeting turned into an... ordeal." My words stumbled out, hesitant, like I was navigating through a field of hidden traps. "Claire was... well, she didn't hold back."

"Is she still against you staying?" Ethan asked, his gaze unwavering, penetrating. He leaned forward slightly, as if he could physically bridge the gap between us, siphoning off some of the weight that hung in the air.

"She thinks I'm making a huge mistake," I said, the knot in my throat tightening as I recalled my sister's fiery speech. "That I should be focusing on my career in the city, not wasting my potential here in Silver Pines." The last word felt like a betrayal, a heavy stone dropping into a still pond, sending ripples of conflict through my thoughts.

Ethan's lips pressed into a thin line, his brow furrowing in that way that made my heart flutter despite everything. "But you don't feel that way, do you? You love it here."

"Love? It's complicated." I looked away, past the clinking of silverware and the muted chatter of patrons. "This place has history for me, for us. I grew up here, Ethan. But I can't help but feel... stagnant. Claire's right, in a way. Maybe I'm just clinging to the past."

"Or maybe you're afraid to embrace your future," he countered gently, his eyes softening as he studied me. "You can have both, you know. You don't have to choose. You can find a balance."

"Balance." The word hung in the air between us, tantalizing yet elusive. Claire had made me feel like a tightrope walker, one misstep from falling into a pit of disappointment. "I wish it were that easy." I sighed, letting the weariness seep into my voice. "Every time I think I'm carving out a niche for myself, she swoops in with her concerns, and I'm left questioning everything."

"Family can be a lot." He nodded, understanding etched in his expression. "But Claire's not you. She doesn't know what it's like to live in your shoes. Maybe she's projecting her fears onto you."

"Maybe." I toyed with the edge of the tablecloth, feeling the fabric's roughness beneath my fingers, grounding me as I fought against the tide of uncertainty. "But she's my sister. I've always been her cheerleader. How can I just ignore her?"

"By listening, and then doing what feels right for you," he said, leaning back slightly as if to give me space to breathe. "At the end of the day, this is your life. Your happiness matters too."

The truth of his words resonated deeply within me, stirring up memories of shared laughter with Claire, summer nights filled with whispered secrets under the stars. But it also dredged up the resentment of feeling like I was the one always bending to her will. "You make it sound so easy, like I can just wave a magic wand and everything will be okay."

"Wands are overrated," he replied with a smirk, the corners of his mouth lifting, and I couldn't help but smile back despite my turmoil. "Maybe what you need is a little chaos. Shake things up a bit."

"Chaos sounds... exhausting." I chuckled lightly, but there was truth in his playful tone. "You know me too well. I prefer my life like a perfectly brewed cup of tea—balanced, smooth, comforting."

"Sometimes the best teas come with a splash of something unexpected," he teased, and I felt a warmth spread through me, a reminder of the connection we shared.

"I can't argue with that." The spark in his eyes made me reconsider everything—maybe embracing the unknown didn't mean abandoning my roots. Maybe it was the next step in my journey.

The café buzzed around us, and for a moment, the world outside faded into a gentle hum. I felt lighter, as if Ethan's words had peeled away some of the layers weighing me down. "You're right. I need to confront Claire, to show her that I'm not just some wandering leaf in the wind."

He smiled, a proud glimmer in his gaze that made my heart swell. "There's that fire I like to see. Just remember, you're not alone in this. You have me."

I nodded, feeling the weight of his support. I wasn't just fighting for my future; I was ready to reclaim my voice, to stand firm in the storm of familial expectations. The path ahead may be winding and unpredictable, but I was ready to step into it, with Ethan by my side, ready for whatever chaos came our way.

I found myself pacing the cobblestone paths of Silver Pines, the cool air brushing against my cheeks, each step echoing with uncertainty. The café was behind me, a cocoon of warmth and familiarity now tainted by the heaviness in my heart. My mind churned with fragments of the conversation I had with Claire, her words sharp and unyielding like the winter frost. "You're choosing comfort over ambition," she had said, and each syllable clung to me like the last vestiges of summer, fading too fast to grasp.

The quaint town was alive, its autumnal hues spilling over the trees like spilled paint, each leaf a tiny protest against the encroaching chill. I paused to inhale the rich scent of burning wood from nearby chimneys, reminding me that even the coldest days could bring warmth if you looked closely enough. But here, amidst the picturesque scenery, I felt like a ghost—a specter drifting between two worlds, neither fully mine.

It was time to confront Claire. I needed to show her that staying in Silver Pines didn't mean I was abandoning my dreams. But first, I needed to clear my head. I made my way to the park, where the small pond reflected the golden light of the setting sun. I sat on a weathered bench, the wood cool against my skin, and closed my eyes, letting the soothing sounds of nature wash over me. I pictured Ethan's face, his unwavering support grounding me. It was a balm against my sister's skepticism, a reminder of why I was choosing this path.

Just as I began to find my center, the sound of laughter pulled me from my reverie. A group of children chased each other around the pond, their shrieks of joy piercing through my thoughts. I cracked a smile, a genuine one that pushed back against the shadows of doubt. Watching their carefree antics was a moment of clarity—life was too short to let fear dictate my choices.

Suddenly, a familiar voice broke through my peaceful bubble. "Hey, you! Are you going to keep sitting there looking like a lost puppy, or are you going to join the fun?" It was Olivia, a friend from high school, her wild curls bouncing as she approached. She'd always had an infectious energy, one that could brighten the gloomiest days.

"Just trying to sort out my life over here," I replied, managing a laugh as she plopped down next to me. "What about you? Shouldn't you be, I don't know, working on your next big project or something?"

"Oh please, you know how I feel about those projects. They can wait." She rolled her eyes dramatically, her carefree spirit unfazed by the world's expectations. "Right now, I'm all about living in the moment. Life's too short for spreadsheets and deadlines."

"Is that your way of saying you're avoiding adult responsibilities?" I teased, nudging her lightly with my shoulder.

"Absolutely!" She grinned, her eyes sparkling. "But really, what's got you all mopey? You look like you just lost a game of Monopoly."

"Family drama," I said, rolling my eyes as I recounted Claire's insistence that I was making a mistake by staying in Silver Pines. "It's like I'm stuck in this tug-of-war between my sister's expectations and what I actually want."

Olivia's expression turned serious, her light-hearted demeanor giving way to a more contemplative look. "That sounds rough. But you have to do what's right for you. Have you talked to Ethan about it? He seems like the type who'd support you no matter what."

"Yeah, he does." A warmth spread through me at the thought of him. "But I don't want to drag him into my family's mess. It's... complicated."

"Complicated is my middle name," Olivia quipped, nudging me again. "Seriously, though, sometimes you need a little chaos in your life. Maybe Ethan's the chaos you need. You're like peanut butter and jelly—better together, right?"

I chuckled at her analogy, appreciating her relentless optimism. "I think you're reaching a bit with that one, but I get what you're saying. Maybe I'm just afraid of what it'll mean if I choose to stay."

"Or maybe you're scared of what it'll mean if you leave?" she countered, her gaze unwavering. "You're trying to balance loyalty to your sister with your own dreams, and that's tough. But it doesn't mean you have to sacrifice your happiness. Remember, you can't pour from an empty cup."

I mulled over her words, the truth of them settling deep within me. "You're right, of course. It's just hard to break those expectations, especially with family. I want to support Claire, but I also need to find my own path."

"Then take the leap," Olivia urged, her voice passionate and invigorating. "You don't have to make all the decisions at once. Start with one small step—have that conversation with Claire. Let her know you're not abandoning her or your roots. Show her that your journey can include her, too."

The idea ignited a spark of determination in me. Maybe I could bridge that gap, weaving together my own ambitions with Claire's hopes. "You know, you're right. I need to stop avoiding the conversation and just face it."

"That's the spirit!" Olivia grinned, and I felt the warmth of her encouragement seep into my bones, making me feel less alone in this. "And if you need backup, I'm your girl. We'll take on Claire together."

"Thanks, Liv. I appreciate that more than you know." I stood up, feeling a renewed sense of purpose. "But I think I need to do this on my own. It's time to be brave."

We walked together toward the edge of the park, the sun dipping lower, casting long shadows on the ground. The world felt alive, vibrant with possibilities. I could almost taste the freedom on my tongue, the tang of uncertainty mingling with the sweetness of hope. My heart raced with the thrill of what lay ahead.

As I turned to say goodbye to Olivia, I spotted Ethan across the street, his silhouette framed against the fading light. He was deep in conversation with a couple of locals, his laughter ringing out like a bell, and my heart swelled with affection. This was what I wanted—this blend of chaos and comfort, the intertwining of paths that felt so impossibly right.

With each step, I felt more anchored in my decision, ready to face the storm that awaited me at home. It wouldn't be easy, but it would be my choice, and for the first time in a long time, I felt ready to embrace it all.

The sun dipped below the horizon as I approached Ethan, his laughter fading into a contemplative silence that filled the space between us. He spotted me, the corner of his mouth lifting in a soft smile that sent a flutter through my chest. Yet, I could feel the unspoken questions lingering in the air, a delicate tension weaving between our thoughts.

"How was the family meeting?" he asked, his voice low, careful as if probing the surface of a fragile lake.

"Like stepping into a wrestling ring without a helmet," I replied, half-joking but entirely serious. "Claire had some strong opinions, and I came out more bruised than I went in." I leaned against the wooden railing of the café's porch, the sun casting long shadows that seemed to echo my doubts. "It's hard to shake the feeling that I'm letting her down."

"You're not letting anyone down by choosing to be happy," he said, a warmth in his tone that felt both comforting and challenging. "But it's easier said than done, right?"

"Exactly," I sighed, running a hand through my hair. "It's not just about me; it's about the history we share. I can't just ignore that."

"History doesn't define your future," Ethan countered, crossing his arms. The posture was strong, and I found myself wishing I had that same resilience. "You can build a new chapter while still honoring the past."

I studied him, the way the fading light danced in his dark hair, illuminating the contours of his face. There was a strength about him that I admired, a certainty I desperately sought. "How do you stay so grounded?" I asked, a genuine curiosity slipping through. "Don't you ever feel like you're caught in someone else's whirlwind?"

"Every day," he admitted, his expression turning serious. "But I've learned that the best way to handle chaos is to lean into it. Embrace it, even. You can't control the wind, but you can adjust your sails."

His metaphor struck a chord deep within me. Perhaps it was time to adjust my sails, to find a way to blend Claire's expectations with my own desires. "Maybe I'll take a page out of your book," I mused, feeling a flicker of determination ignite within me.

"Good. Just promise me you won't drown in the storm." His eyes sparkled with that familiar mischief. "I'd hate to have to dive in after you."

"Deal," I laughed, the sound lifting the weight in my chest, if only for a moment. "Now, let's head back. I need to face the music."

As we walked side by side, a comfortable silence enveloped us, the kind that felt like a shared secret. I appreciated how effortlessly we could slide between levity and seriousness, how Ethan's presence acted like a balm to my racing thoughts.

The streets of Silver Pines, bathed in the amber glow of streetlights, felt welcoming yet foreign. The cozy homes lined the street, their windows glowing with warmth and laughter, a stark contrast to the turmoil swirling within me. I could hear Claire's voice in my head, a constant reminder of the tightrope I was about to walk.

When we reached the front porch of my childhood home, the familiar scent of pine and the sound of Claire's laughter wafted through the open window, inviting and foreboding. I took a deep breath, the crisp air filling my lungs with courage. "Here goes nothing," I muttered, glancing at Ethan.

"Remember, you're not alone. You've got this," he said, giving my hand a reassuring squeeze before stepping back.

I knocked on the door, each rap sounding louder than the last, reverberating through the air like a drumroll before a performance. The door swung open, revealing Claire, her expression shifting from joy to concern in an instant.

"Hey! You're back," she greeted, but her eyes narrowed slightly, as if gauging my mood.

"Yep. Just came to clear the air," I said, trying to inject some levity into the moment. "I'm not here to argue, I promise."

"Good, because I really don't want to fight right now," she replied, stepping aside to let me in. The cozy living room was filled with the remnants of a dinner gathering: half-finished wine glasses and plates littered with the last dregs of pasta.

I could feel the tension rising, a tangible force that wrapped around us like a thick fog. "So, um, can we talk?" I ventured, shifting my weight from one foot to the other, suddenly aware of how small I felt in this space that once felt so safe.

"Of course," she said, her voice softening as she gestured toward the couch. "What's on your mind?"

I sank into the cushions, feeling the fabric beneath me, the familiar wear of years whispering stories of our shared past. "I've been thinking a lot about what you said. About my future here versus in the city. I get that you're looking out for me, but—"

"I just don't want you to settle," she interrupted, her eyes flashing with concern. "You deserve so much more than this small town can offer."

"Maybe it's not about settling. Maybe it's about finding joy in the here and now," I countered, feeling the urgency of my words rise like a tide. "I love it here, Claire. I don't want to leave. I want to build something for myself, and that includes you."

Her expression softened, but I could still see the shadows of doubt flickering in her eyes. "And what if that something doesn't work out? What if you regret it?"

"What if it does?" I challenged, feeling a rush of adrenaline. "What if staying here is what I need to find my true self? To figure out who I am outside of your expectations?"

Silence hung between us, a chasm filled with years of unspoken words and shared memories. The tension was palpable, thick enough to slice through with a knife.

"Sometimes I feel like you're suffocating under my shadow," she finally said, her voice a mere whisper. "Like you're not allowed to shine unless I approve."

"No, it's not that!" I protested, desperation creeping into my voice. "I want to shine, Claire. But I also want you to be proud of me."

At that moment, a loud crash echoed from the kitchen, followed by a chorus of startled voices. Claire's expression shifted from concern to alarm as we both stood up, the conversation momentarily forgotten in the chaos.

"What was that?" I asked, my heart racing.

"I don't know!" Claire rushed to the kitchen, and I followed, dread curling in my stomach like a snake.

As we entered the kitchen, I froze, my breath caught in my throat. The sight before us was like something out of a nightmare: shattered glass lay scattered across the floor, and in the middle of it all, a figure stood, their back to us.

"Who are you?" Claire demanded, her voice steady despite the chaos.

The figure turned, revealing a masked face and dark clothing that seemed to swallow the light. "You shouldn't have stayed," they said, their voice smooth but menacing.

The air turned electric, my heart pounding like a war drum. In that instant, every fear, every doubt I had faced, coalesced into a singular moment of terror. I was no longer just fighting for my future; I was fighting for my life.

Chapter 22: Defending My Heart

The scent of freshly brewed coffee wafted through The Maple Leaf, a cozy café tucked away between a quirky bookshop and an artisanal bakery. It had become my sanctuary, where the chatter of locals mingled with the clinking of cups and the comforting hum of a well-loved espresso machine. Today, however, the warmth of the atmosphere felt like a thin veil over the tension coiling in my stomach. I had invited Diane here, not for pleasantries, but to confront her about the insidious whispers I had heard—the rumors, half-truths, and outright lies that seemed to trail behind me like a persistent shadow.

As I settled into my usual corner table, the sunlight filtering through the window cast a golden hue over the pages of my well-worn notebook. I could see her approaching, a whirlwind of brisk confidence and disdain. Diane was not one to be trifled with; her reputation for cutting words was well-known. She slid into the chair opposite me, her expression a mask of polite curiosity tinged with a hint of condescension.

"Nice place you've picked," she remarked, her voice smooth like a silk scarf, yet with an undercurrent of sharpness that made my skin prickle. "I suppose it's fitting for someone trying to blend in."

I leaned forward, forcing my hands to remain steady on the table. "Diane, I didn't invite you here to discuss decor. I want to talk about what you've been saying."

She arched an eyebrow, a smirk playing on her lips. "Oh? And what would that be? I'm curious about what new drama you're fabricating."

"Don't play coy," I shot back, my voice rising slightly. "You know exactly what I mean. You've been spreading lies about me—about my past, my intentions. It needs to stop."

The café seemed to quiet around us, as if the very walls were leaning in to eavesdrop. Her eyes narrowed, a flicker of surprise giving way to a cool disdain. "Lies? Honey, I'm merely voicing my opinions. Isn't that what you wanted? To be part of this community?"

"I wanted to be part of this community," I emphasized, my heart racing as I fought to keep my tone steady, "not a target for your jealousy or insecurities. I'm not here to threaten anyone's place; I'm just trying to find my own."

Diane leaned back, crossing her arms, her posture radiating confidence. "And what makes you think you deserve that? You think you can just stroll into Silver Pines and—what? Become one of us?"

Her words stung, but they only fueled my resolve. "I'm not just strolling in. I've worked hard to build a life here, to create connections. And if you'd take a moment to listen instead of assuming the worst, you might see that I'm not the enemy."

For a heartbeat, the tension stretched between us like a taut string, and I could feel the weight of the café's atmosphere, each patron acutely aware of the brewing storm. Then Diane laughed, a cold sound that felt like a slap. "You're naive if you think this is just about you. Silver Pines has its ways, its rules, and newcomers rarely fit in seamlessly."

"Maybe it's time for those rules to change," I replied, my voice firmer than I felt. "I refuse to be defined by your perceptions or anyone else's. I'm here to carve my own path, and I won't let you or anyone else dictate what that looks like."

Diane's smile faded, replaced by a calculating gaze. "You really believe that? This town has a way of chewing people up and spitting them out. You might find that your determination is misplaced. It's not that easy."

"Maybe not," I acknowledged, my heart pounding. "But it's my battle to fight, and I'm not backing down."

With that, I stood, leaving my half-finished coffee behind as I walked out of The Maple Leaf. The door chimed softly, a stark contrast to the tumult of emotions swirling inside me. Outside, the crisp air filled my lungs, and I felt a flicker of something unfamiliar—empowerment. I had stood up for myself, and even though the confrontation had left me shaken, there was a simmering strength within me that refused to be extinguished.

Later that evening, I found Ethan in his workshop, the warm glow of overhead lights illuminating the chaos of tools and wood shavings scattered about. He was engrossed in a project, a piece of furniture taking shape beneath his skilled hands. The familiar scent of sawdust and the faint notes of oil paint wrapped around me like a comforting embrace as I stepped inside.

"Hey," I said, my voice barely above a whisper. "Can we talk?"

He looked up, his expression shifting from concentration to concern. "Of course. Everything okay?"

I took a breath, gathering the words I had practiced in my mind all day. "I confronted Diane about the rumors. I'm done letting her dictate how I feel or what I can achieve here."

Ethan put down his tools, his gaze steady and encouraging. "That's big. How did it go?"

"It was fiery," I admitted, feeling the remnants of the confrontation bubble to the surface. "She tried to undermine me, but I held my ground. I won't let her push me around anymore."

I searched his eyes for judgment, but all I found was admiration, a spark that ignited something deep within me. "I'm proud of you. It takes courage to stand up to people like her."

"I just want to belong here," I confessed, my voice softer now. "But it feels like such a battle, and I can't help but wonder if it's worth it."

"It is," he replied, stepping closer, the space between us shrinking. "You belong here. You're bringing something fresh to Silver Pines, and I think that scares some people. But you can't let their fear shape your future."

His words settled over me like a warm blanket, the weight of uncertainty lifting just enough for me to breathe. "Thank you, Ethan. I needed to hear that."

He smiled, a genuine expression that lit up his eyes. "Anytime. Just remember, I'm in your corner."

I nodded, feeling the bond between us grow stronger, fortified by the challenges ahead. Together, we could navigate this unpredictable terrain, facing whatever came our way with resilience and a shared purpose. The journey ahead felt daunting, but as I stood there with Ethan, I knew I was ready to defend my heart, my dreams, and my place in Silver Pines.

The following morning, the sun spilled over Silver Pines like honey, golden light dappling the streets and softening the edges of the day. It was a town that looked picturesque on the surface, but beneath its charming façade lurked whispered resentments and hidden agendas, a duality I was beginning to understand all too well. I moved through my morning routine with a sense of purpose, each ritual grounding me as I prepared to face whatever new challenges awaited me.

As I stepped out of my cottage, the crisp air brushed against my cheeks, a gentle reminder that fall was inching closer. Leaves danced in the wind, painting the sidewalks with hues of amber and crimson. I paused for a moment, letting the serenity of the morning wash over me, but it was short-lived. Claire's lingering presence in town hung over me like a cloud, and I couldn't shake the feeling that her motives weren't as straightforward as they seemed. She was back, and her intentions felt tangled, like the ivy creeping up the walls of my cottage.

Deciding I needed a distraction, I made my way to the community center, a hub for classes, meetings, and events. The building itself was an old church, repurposed with rustic charm—exposed beams, stained glass, and a wide porch adorned with flower boxes overflowing with vibrant blooms. Inside, I was greeted by the familiar sounds of laughter and chatter, a comforting hum that reminded me why I loved this town.

As I wandered through the hall, I spotted a flyer for an upcoming town fair. The annual event was a beloved tradition, bringing together locals and newcomers alike to celebrate the changing seasons. My heart quickened at the thought. This could be my chance to truly integrate into the community, to show everyone that I wasn't just a passing phase but a vital thread in the fabric of Silver Pines.

"Planning on being the belle of the ball?" a voice teased, jolting me from my thoughts. I turned to see Mia, the town's unofficial social butterfly, her enthusiasm always infectious. She had a way of lighting up a room, her laughter bubbling like champagne.

"More like the wallflower, I think," I replied, a smile creeping onto my face despite my earlier worries. "Just trying to find a way to fit in."

"Forget fitting in; it's all about standing out!" Mia waved the flyer in front of me. "You should definitely sign up for a booth. Showcase those fabulous baking skills of yours! You'll win hearts and stomachs."

I chuckled, considering the idea. "A baking booth? That's ambitious."

"Ambitious is my middle name," she quipped, her eyes sparkling with mischief. "Imagine it—people lining up for your pastries, raving about how delicious they are. You'll have the entire town eating out of your hands."

"Is that how you make friends around here?" I teased back. "By stuffing them with sweets?"

"Hey, it's worked for me so far," she shot back, crossing her arms with mock seriousness. "But seriously, this fair is your chance. Get involved! We need more fresh faces and flavors around here."

I glanced at the flyer again, my mind racing with possibilities. The idea of baking for the town fair felt both exhilarating and terrifying. Could I really do it? It would be a way to reclaim my narrative, to shift the focus from Diane's whispers to my own accomplishments.

"I'll think about it," I finally said, tucking the flyer under my arm. "But only if you promise to help me set up."

"Deal!" she grinned, and I couldn't help but feel a rush of warmth at the thought of having allies in this place.

The day rolled on, filled with preparations and a newfound sense of purpose. I dove into my baking, the rhythmic mixing of ingredients grounding me in a way I hadn't anticipated. The kitchen filled with the comforting scent of cinnamon and vanilla, memories of family gatherings surfacing like old friends. Each whisk of the batter felt like an act of defiance against the negativity swirling around me.

That evening, as the sun began to dip below the horizon, painting the sky in hues of orange and pink, I received a text from Ethan. "Want to join me for a sunset walk? I promise I won't bring any wood this time," it read, followed by a winking emoji.

With a grin, I replied, "As long as you keep the tools at home, I'm in."

Meeting him at the park, I felt a flutter of anticipation, my heart racing slightly at the thought of our time together. He was waiting for me by the old oak tree, the one where kids had carved their initials and dreams into the bark.

"Hey," he said, a genuine smile lighting up his face as I approached. "How was your day?"

I leaned against the tree, the rough bark digging pleasantly into my back. "Busy. I think I'm going to participate in the town fair. I might even try my hand at baking for a booth."

Ethan's eyes widened, a spark of admiration flaring within them. "You? Baking? I can't wait to see what you whip up. You'll have the whole town buzzing."

"Only if I don't burn down the kitchen first," I joked, though a twinge of anxiety crept in. "What if no one likes my baking?"

"Then they're clearly wrong," he replied, stepping closer. "But they will love it. You have a way of making everything special."

The sincerity in his voice made me feel lighter, as if all the weight of Diane's words and Claire's looming presence had begun to dissipate. We started walking, the path winding through the park, our conversation flowing as easily as the breeze rustling the leaves above us.

"So, what's your secret ingredient?" he asked playfully, turning the conversation to his own fondness for cooking.

I raised an eyebrow. "If I told you, it wouldn't be a secret anymore."

"Fair point," he chuckled, glancing at me sideways. "But really, cooking is an art. It's all about passion. What drives you?"

A moment of silence hung in the air as I considered his question. "I guess it's about creating something that brings people together. Food has a way of doing that, of breaking down barriers and building connections."

Ethan nodded, his expression thoughtful. "And that's exactly what you're doing here, in your own way. You're creating connections, not just with food but with your presence."

"Flattery won't get you anywhere," I teased, but I felt a warmth bloom in my chest, a connection deepening between us.

Just then, a shout echoed through the park, cutting through our moment. We turned to see a group of children running toward us, their laughter ringing like bells in the air. They barreled past, chasing after a rogue soccer ball that had escaped its owner. In the midst of their chaos, one little girl tripped, stumbling to the ground, and I felt a surge of instinct kick in.

"Hey!" I called out, darting forward.

Ethan followed, his presence solid and reassuring as we reached her side. "Are you okay?" I asked gently, kneeling beside the girl as she brushed dirt from her scraped knee.

"I'm fine," she huffed, though tears glistened in her eyes.

"See? You're tougher than you look," Ethan chimed in, a playful grin softening the moment. "But we should probably get you a band-aid just to be safe."

"Yeah!" she exclaimed, her mood shifting as she stood, her bravado returning.

As we helped her back to her friends, the tension of the day melted away, replaced by laughter and the sweet, messy chaos of childhood. In that moment, surrounded by the warmth of the park and the joy of connection, I felt a sense of belonging beginning to take root. I wasn't just fighting against the darkness; I was crafting something beautiful, and with Ethan by my side, it felt like the first step toward finding my place in this vibrant tapestry of life.

The days that followed the confrontation with Diane unfurled with a mix of anticipation and anxiety. My thoughts danced between the excitement of the upcoming town fair and the simmering tension surrounding Claire's return. Each morning, I awoke with a fire in my belly, fueled by the desire to prove myself, to carve out a space where I belonged amidst the whispers and stares. The town fair felt like a pivotal moment—a chance to shift the narrative from outsider to integral part of Silver Pines.

With every passing hour, I immersed myself in baking, testing recipes that seemed like old friends emerging from the depths of my memory. Flour dusted the counters like a light snowfall, and the air thickened with the sweet scents of cinnamon and vanilla. My kitchen transformed into a haven of creativity, where I poured my heart into every cookie, pie, and pastry. Mia had agreed to help, her bubbly energy complementing my focus. Together, we spent long evenings assembling colorful treats, our laughter mixing with the clatter of pans and the hum of the oven.

As the fair approached, the excitement buzzed around town like the gentle thrum of bees in a blooming garden. I found myself setting up the booth the day before, the sight of my freshly baked goods displayed like treasures beneath the canopy. Mia bounced beside me, her enthusiasm contagious as she arranged everything just so, ensuring our booth radiated warmth and charm.

"Look at this spread!" she exclaimed, stepping back to admire our handiwork. "People will be flocking here like moths to a flame."

"Or like kids to a candy store," I replied, unable to hide my smile. The thought of sharing my creations with the community filled me with a mix of pride and nerves. "I hope they like my baking."

"They will," Mia insisted, her confidence unwavering. "Just remember: it's not just about the treats. It's about the heart you put into them."

As the fair began the next morning, the sun rose in a brilliant display of color, casting everything in a golden glow. The park buzzed with life—children darting around with balloons, vendors calling out their wares, and laughter spilling into the air like confetti. I stood behind the booth, heart racing, nerves tingling as the first attendees approached.

"Look at this!" a young girl exclaimed, eyes wide as she pointed to the vibrant array of cookies and pies. "Can I have one?"

"Of course!" I responded, handing her a chocolate chip cookie that melted in the mouth. Watching her face light up was like witnessing a small miracle.

As the day unfolded, people lined up, drawn not just by the sweet treats but by the warmth radiating from our booth. Every compliment felt like a balm, soothing the insecurities that had plagued me since I arrived in Silver Pines. I was more than an outsider; I was becoming part of the tapestry of this community.

"See?" Mia nudged me, her excitement palpable. "You're a hit! They love you!"

Just then, a familiar figure approached, and my heart dropped. Claire, with her perfectly styled hair and practiced smile, walked toward our booth, an air of confidence surrounding her like a force field. My stomach twisted. Was she here to stir the pot again, or was she genuinely interested in what I was doing?

"Nice spread you've got here," she said, a hint of sarcasm lacing her words. "I didn't realize you were so... domestic."

I forced a smile, refusing to let her jab get under my skin. "Thank you! It's been a labor of love. Would you like to try something?"

Her eyes flicked over the baked goods, a calculated gaze as she picked up a lemon tart. "This looks interesting," she said, her tone dripping with feigned interest. "I suppose this is what happens when you let the newcomer play housewife."

I felt the warmth of the fair slip away, the laughter around me fading into a dull thrum. "This isn't just about being a housewife, Claire. I'm contributing to the community, trying to make a name for myself here."

She laughed lightly, the sound sharp and unyielding. "Oh, sweetie, the name you make is your own doing. But don't forget—some people might not take kindly to your little attempts to fit in."

Before I could respond, a voice called from the edge of the crowd. "Claire! Over here!" A man waved, his presence commanding attention. He was tall, with dark hair and a charming smile, and he seemed to radiate charisma.

"Oh, there's Jason," Claire said, her demeanor shifting like the wind. "I should catch up with him. Enjoy your little fair, won't you?" She turned on her heel and walked away, leaving me feeling like a puppet whose strings had been cut.

"What was that about?" Mia asked, her voice tinged with concern as she watched Claire go. "She's like a storm cloud hovering over your sunshine."

"I know," I sighed, shaking off the unsettling feeling that Claire's words had ignited. "But I won't let her ruin this. Not today."

As the day wore on, I poured my heart into every interaction, buoyed by the growing crowd around our booth. Laughter mingled with the sweet aroma of baked goods, and I found myself feeling lighter, more at home than I had since moving to Silver Pines. With each satisfied customer, the last remnants of doubt faded, and for the first time, I felt a sense of belonging begin to blossom.

As evening approached, the fair transformed into a tapestry of twinkling lights and vibrant sounds. I stepped away from the booth for a moment, needing air to clear my head. The park shimmered with lanterns strung between trees, casting a soft glow that danced on the faces of the festival-goers. I spotted Ethan across the way, laughing with a group of friends, and my heart did a little flip. He caught my eye and waved, his smile drawing me in like a magnet.

"I thought you might need a break," he said, joining me as I leaned against a nearby tree, the bark cool against my back.

"I can't believe how well it's gone," I confessed, a mixture of relief and exhilaration coursing through me. "I really felt like I connected with people today."

"That's because you did," he replied, the warmth of his gaze making my cheeks heat. "You've got something special, and it shines through when you're doing what you love."

"Thanks, but it's hard to shake the feeling that some people will never accept me," I admitted, glancing toward the crowds. "Especially when Claire's lurking around."

"Let her try," Ethan said with a hint of defiance. "You've got the community behind you now. Don't let anyone dim your light."

Just then, a commotion erupted at the edge of the park, drawing our attention. A group of teenagers had gathered, their voices rising in excitement. I squinted through the crowd, trying to see what was happening. Suddenly, a flash of commotion erupted, and I caught a glimpse of Claire, her face contorted in anger as she confronted Jason.

"What's going on?" I murmured, the unease creeping back into my gut.

Ethan frowned, his brows furrowing with concern. "Let's check it out."

As we moved closer, the scene unfolded like a slow-motion movie. Claire's voice cut through the air, sharp and accusing, her finger jabbing at Jason. "You can't just walk away like that! You're supposed to be on my side!"

Jason's expression was a mixture of annoyance and confusion. "I never agreed to your plan, Claire. This isn't how you handle things."

"What plan?" I whispered to Ethan, feeling a knot tighten in my stomach.

"Maybe we should get out of here," he suggested, but I felt compelled to stay, the magnetism of the unfolding drama too strong to resist.

Claire's voice escalated, drawing more attention. "You're making a mistake! You don't understand what's at stake!"

At that moment, I felt the collective gasp of the crowd as Claire's words hung in the air. Something pivotal was happening, something that could change everything. The atmosphere crackled with tension, and I found myself rooted in place, unwilling to look away.

Before I could process it all, Claire turned, her eyes locking onto mine, a storm brewing behind them. "You think you can just waltz into my life and take what's mine?" she shouted, her voice dripping with venom. "You have no idea what you're getting into."

A wave of shock washed over me, the implications of her words slamming into me like a freight train. The air felt charged, electric, and I knew in that moment that whatever had been set in motion was far more complicated than I had ever imagined. As the crowd held its breath, I realized I was on the precipice of something monumental, and there was no turning back.

Chapter 23: A Winter's Chill

A sharp breeze swept through Silver Pines, weaving through the streets and sending a flurry of golden leaves skittering like excited children across the cobblestone paths. I wrapped my scarf tighter, the wool soft against my skin, the earthy scent of damp earth and woodsmoke lingering in the air, reminding me that winter was inching closer. The town had begun its transformation, not just in the weather but in spirit, the once-vibrant hues of autumn giving way to a canvas of shimmering white lights strung across shopfronts, twinkling like stars captured in glass. The town square, usually a humble gathering place, was morphing into a festive wonderland, and I was determined to make the most of it.

At the café, the scent of fresh-brewed coffee and cinnamon wafted through the air, mingling with the laughter of patrons and the clatter of dishes. I stood behind the counter, stirring a pot of spiced apple cider that bubbled cheerfully on the stove. The steam curled upward, curling around my face like a warm embrace, yet the warmth in my heart was overshadowed by a chill of uncertainty. Claire had returned to town, her presence a mix of nostalgia and dread, and her unwavering insistence that I should leave with her gnawed at my resolve. As if the universe conspired against me, the more I tried to focus on the market preparations, the more my mind drifted toward her imploring eyes.

"Evelyn, I swear you could make a fortune just selling this cider alone," Ethan remarked, his voice smooth like the honey we'd poured into the mix. He leaned against the counter, his dark curls catching the light, framing a face that I found both comforting and infuriating at times. His smile was infectious, but right now, it didn't reach his eyes, which danced with concern.

"Not as much as you'd make if you'd just put those new pastries on the menu," I shot back playfully, though the joke felt thin, a veil over the tension that lurked beneath our surface interactions. His enthusiasm for his baking experiments had always brought life to our café, but today, that spark felt dimmed.

"Maybe you should just leave everything behind and come with me," Claire chimed in, her voice carrying across the bustling café like an unwelcome guest crashing a party. She leaned over the counter, her bright lipstick a stark contrast to my weary demeanor. "You could be so much more than this. The city has endless opportunities, and you deserve more than this quaint little café."

"Claire," I sighed, my heart aching at her words. They felt like both a lifeline and an anchor, tethering me to my own insecurities. "This place, these people—this is home. I'm happy here."

Her eyes narrowed slightly, disappointment mingling with her ambition. "Are you? Because it feels like you're holding back. I can see it, Evelyn. You have dreams bigger than this town, but you keep pushing them aside."

"Sometimes dreams evolve, Claire," I said, frustration creeping into my tone. "This café is my dream now. And if you would just let me focus on the winter market without trying to pull me away, I might actually get somewhere."

Ethan shifted beside me, his brow furrowing. "Maybe we need to find a way to work together instead of against each other." The tension that hung between us crackled like static electricity, the unspoken words adding weight to the air. I could see the way his patience was thinning, fraying at the edges like the well-loved quilt we kept in the café for chilly days.

"We can work together," I said quickly, a hint of desperation creeping into my voice. "We'll have the best winter market Silver Pines has ever seen. Just imagine it! Local artisans, food trucks, carolers singing by the fountain. We'll bring the community together." My enthusiasm felt feeble, like a flame struggling against the wind.

"Sounds great, but if we're going to do this, we need to actually communicate," Ethan replied, his tone serious. "You can't just keep avoiding the difficult conversations."

"I'm not avoiding—"

"Then why do you keep dodging the issue with Claire? It's like you're afraid of what it means to really choose." His words struck deep, reverberating in the silence that followed. The café bustled around us, laughter and chatter blurring into a background noise as the world outside faded into insignificance.

"Choose what, Ethan?" I shot back, frustration bubbling to the surface. "What do you want me to choose? My home, my life, or the fantasy of something bigger that you and Claire seem so eager to shove down my throat?"

"Evelyn," he said softly, his gaze unwavering, "I just want you to be honest with yourself. And with me."

In that moment, I could see the hurt behind his bravado, a deep-seated fear that he might lose me to the pull of the outside world. The truth hung heavily between us like a curtain, the warmth of our connection shivering beneath the frost of unspoken words. I wanted to tell him that I didn't want to leave; that the café was my heart, my safe haven amidst the uncertainty that threatened to engulf me. Yet Claire's incessant whispers in my ear sowed seeds of doubt, and I was scared of what admitting that might mean.

"I'll think about it," I said finally, my voice barely above a whisper. The words tasted bitter, like unripe fruit, but they hung in the air like a fragile truce.

The café felt smaller as the weight of our unsaid feelings lingered, and the once bright laughter felt muted, a reminder that sometimes, the hardest battles were fought in silence. As the sun dipped lower in the sky, casting long shadows across the floor, I was left grappling with the reality that the choices ahead would shape more than just the upcoming winter market—they would define who I was, who I wanted to be, and what I truly desired from this life I had built, piece by piece, in the heart of Silver Pines.

The winter market was a mere whisper of an idea that had grown into a full-fledged dream, and as I busied myself with the preparations, the café felt like a stage set for a play I wasn't quite ready to perform. Each morning, I arrived early, wrapping my hands around steaming mugs of coffee, letting the warmth seep into my fingers while I mentally choreographed the festivities. Pine boughs adorned the café, their evergreen scent mingling with the sugary sweetness of gingerbread cookies. I imagined the bustling stalls filled with local crafts, the laughter of children chasing after the scents of cinnamon and nutmeg, and the glow of lanterns twinkling in the twilight.

Ethan flitted in and out, his baking magic infusing the air with the smell of fresh pastries that could make anyone swoon. He'd whip up trays of flaky croissants or decadent brownies, each creation a testament to his talent and passion. Watching him work, I found myself admiring the way his hands moved, the ease with which he transformed simple ingredients into something extraordinary. And yet, the deeper I fell into my plans for the market, the more it felt like we were standing on opposite shores of a widening chasm.

"Hey, I think I nailed the recipe for that spiced mulled wine we talked about," Ethan said one morning, his eyes bright with enthusiasm as he flourished a wooden spoon like a baton. "Just a pinch more of that secret ingredient, and it's perfection."

"Secret ingredient? Is that what we're calling the leftover cinnamon from last year?" I teased, unable to suppress a grin.

"Touché. But still, it's going to be amazing. Just picture it: warm wine, laughter, and twinkling lights—pure magic," he replied, his voice a melodic blend of hope and excitement.

I couldn't deny the allure of his vision, but my heart felt heavy with the weight of unresolved tension. Claire's relentless encouragement hung over me like a cloud threatening rain, her words echoing in the corners of my mind. "You could have everything you want if you just take that leap," she had said, her tone imploring. Yet, what did "everything" even mean in a place where I had forged my identity?

As the days rolled on, I juggled the planning with an exhausting fervor, balancing family obligations and the constant pull of Claire's ambitions. I found myself retreating into my thoughts while trying to navigate conversations with Ethan, each dialogue becoming a delicate dance of unspoken emotions. His gentle nudges felt like invitations to share my worries, but I held back, hesitant to let him see how deeply Claire's influence pricked at my insecurities.

One particularly chilly afternoon, as snowflakes began to flutter down like lazy feathers from the sky, I found myself sitting across from Ethan at our tiny café table, the warmth of the coffee shop contrasting sharply with the frost creeping along the windows. I could hear the soft chatter of customers and the gentle hiss of the espresso machine, but it all felt muffled, as if the world had dimmed around us.

"Evelyn," he started, his brow furrowed with concern. "Can we talk about this? I feel like you're distancing yourself from me. Is it Claire? Is it the market? What's going on?" His words poured out, an earnest plea for connection that tugged at my heartstrings.

"I'm fine," I replied a bit too quickly, my gaze darting toward the window. Outside, snowflakes whirled like tiny dancers caught in a winter waltz, and I focused on their chaotic beauty instead of confronting the storm brewing between us.

"Fine is never a good sign," Ethan shot back, crossing his arms over his chest. "Look, I get that you're trying to juggle everything. I really do. But I need you to be honest with me. If you're feeling overwhelmed, just say it. Don't hide behind a smile and pretend everything's okay."

His eyes bore into mine, a mix of frustration and concern that felt both familiar and frightening. I could see the warmth of his heart beneath that rugged exterior, the tenderness that had drawn me to him in the first place. But opening up felt like peeling back layers of an onion, each layer revealing more of the truth but also bringing tears to my eyes.

"I just want this market to be perfect," I admitted, my voice barely a whisper. "I want to bring the town together, and I'm terrified of letting anyone down. Especially you."

"Why would you let me down? You're the one making this happen! I'm just here to support you," Ethan said, his voice softening. "But I can't help if you keep me in the dark."

I swallowed hard, trying to push back the wave of emotion that threatened to spill over. "It's not just the market, Ethan. It's everything. Claire is making me question if I'm making the right choices. I mean, what if there's a bigger world out there waiting for me, and I'm just sitting here? What if I'm squandering my chances?"

"Evelyn, listen to me," he said, leaning forward, his elbows resting on the table, urgency etching lines on his face. "You are not squandering anything. You're building a community. You're building a life here, with me, with the café. The world isn't going anywhere. It'll always be there, and you can explore it anytime. But this—what we have—this is special."

His words settled over me like a blanket, heavy yet comforting, igniting a flicker of hope in the shadows of doubt. But just as I began to feel the warmth seep into my bones, a loud crash broke the moment, sending my heart racing.

The door to the café swung open violently, a gust of wind forcing its way inside, bringing with it a flurry of snowflakes and an uninvited chill. My gaze shot toward the entrance as Claire burst in, her cheeks flushed from the cold, her hair wild and windblown, looking every bit the tempest that had just interrupted our fragile moment.

"Evelyn! You'll never believe what I just found out!" she exclaimed, her eyes sparkling with excitement, oblivious to the tension that had just been building.

I exchanged a look with Ethan, a silent acknowledgment of our interrupted conversation. The moment we had been building—a bridge forged through honesty—now felt as fragile as the snowflakes swirling around us, drifting away with the promise of something more.

"What is it?" I asked, forcing a smile, trying to shake off the unease that had settled in my chest.

"There's a huge opportunity for vendors at the city-wide winter festival! It's exactly what you need to really launch this market. You've got to join!" Claire's voice was infectious, a rush of enthusiasm that could fill the room, but beneath her excitement lay a familiar undertone of urgency, a push for me to step beyond the boundaries I had so carefully constructed.

Ethan's expression shifted, the warmth in his gaze momentarily clouded by something else—was it frustration? Concern? It was hard to tell, but the atmosphere grew thick with unspoken words once again.

"Yeah, a city-wide festival sounds amazing, Claire," I replied, my heart thumping against my ribs. "But I have this market to think about first."

Claire waved her hand dismissively, her excitement palpable. "You can handle both! Just think of the exposure! The café could be the talk of the town! You could be the talk of the town!"

With each word, I felt the weight of expectation press down, the urge to please rising within me. But amid the swirl of her enthusiasm, I couldn't shake the nagging feeling that the very fabric of what I was building—my life, my connection with Ethan—might unravel if

I stepped too far into the unknown. And as I glanced at Ethan, his expression unreadable, I realized that this moment held the potential to change everything.

The moment Claire barged into the café with her whirlwind of excitement, I could feel the carefully constructed walls I had been building around my life start to tremble. Her eyes sparkled with the kind of fervor that could only come from dreams being reimagined at high speed, and while part of me wanted to embrace that energy, another part felt like a startled rabbit cornered by the hounds.

"Evelyn, you need to seize this opportunity!" Claire exclaimed, her hands flailing in animated gestures as she painted vivid pictures of bustling crowds and colorful stalls. "Imagine the café adorned with holiday cheer, and people lining up to get a taste of your famous cider and Ethan's pastries. It'll be the event of the season!"

I forced a smile, trying to catch the edge of her enthusiasm, but the thought of participating in the city-wide festival felt overwhelming. "It sounds amazing, Claire, but I don't want to overcommit. I'm already juggling so much with the winter market planning."

"Overcommit? Come on! You thrive under pressure! Besides, we're in a small town. How often do we get a chance like this?" Her voice was filled with urgency, and I could sense the unyielding determination behind her words. "Think of the exposure! This could be the moment when the café breaks out of the cozy little corner it's been tucked into."

Ethan's expression shifted as he listened to Claire's fervor. His brows furrowed, and I could almost see the gears in his head turning, weighing the pros and cons of what she proposed. "I get where you're coming from, Claire," he interjected, trying to keep his tone steady, "but we need to focus on making the winter market a success first. If we start spreading ourselves too thin, we risk losing everything we've worked for."

A wave of relief washed over me at his support, but Claire wouldn't be deterred. "Oh, come on! We can handle both! I mean, who doesn't love a little chaos in their lives? You two are practically the dynamic duo!" She flashed a smile, her eyes brightening at the thought of all of us working together, but the edges of her enthusiasm felt jagged to me.

"Maybe we're not the dynamic duo you think we are," I muttered under my breath, irritation bubbling up like the cider on the stove.

"What's that?" Claire asked, her attention darting back to me, curiosity piqued.

"Nothing." I waved it away, feeling a flush creeping up my cheeks. "I just think we need to consider what we can realistically manage."

"Exactly!" Ethan chimed in, his voice filled with a mix of passion and reason. "I don't want to burn out before the market even begins. We have something special here, and I want to ensure we do it right."

A tense silence settled between us, the air crackling with unsaid words. Claire shifted uncomfortably, and I could see the conflict brewing in her eyes. She was used to taking risks, to pushing boundaries, while Ethan and I were trying to carve out something stable amidst our ever-changing landscape.

"Look," Claire said, her voice dropping slightly, "I just want what's best for you, Evelyn. I know you've got big dreams. I can see them flickering beneath the surface. Don't let fear hold you back."

Her words, meant to be encouraging, sliced through the air like a cold wind. It was true that I felt trapped between what I wanted and what was expected of me, but was stepping into the unknown really the answer? Or would it pull me further away from everything I'd built?

"Sometimes dreams need nurturing, not just reckless pursuit," I replied, my voice steadier than I felt. "I appreciate your enthusiasm, but maybe it's time to let this café shine in its own right, without jumping into every opportunity that comes our way."

Claire's face fell, a hint of hurt flashing across her features before she masked it with a forced smile. "Fine. I just thought you'd want more. I thought you'd be ready to take the plunge."

As she turned away, the tension in the room was palpable. I glanced at Ethan, searching for reassurance, but his gaze was fixed on Claire's retreating figure.

"Do you think she's right?" I asked, my voice barely above a whisper. "Am I holding myself back?"

"Evelyn, it's not about what others think," Ethan replied, his voice softening as he placed a hand over mine. "It's about what you truly want. You have to choose what's right for you, not what others expect you to do."

I took a deep breath, trying to absorb his words. But the uncertainty swirled around me like the snowflakes outside, each one a reminder of the choices waiting to be made.

A soft chime from the café door pulled my attention. In walked a group of familiar faces, all wrapped in layers of winter gear, laughing and chatting as they entered the warm embrace of the café. My heart lifted at the sight of my loyal customers, the people who made this café feel like home, but that warmth was quickly overshadowed by the sudden rush of anxiety bubbling up in my chest.

"Hey, Evelyn! Is the winter market still on?" one of the regulars called out, his cheeks rosy from the cold. "We can't wait to see what you've planned!"

"Yeah! What about those festive treats you mentioned?" another chimed in, excitement brightening her eyes.

Their eagerness washed over me, and for a moment, the weight of my inner turmoil lightened. "Of course! We're going to have everything—crafts, food, music. It's going to be great!" My voice held a note of enthusiasm, but deep down, I felt the cracks starting to widen.

As the customers settled into the warmth, filling the café with the sound of laughter, Ethan caught my eye. "You know you can do this, right?" he said quietly, his voice barely cutting through the chatter.

"I want to believe that," I admitted, feeling the weight of his gaze on me. "But the pressure—it's intense."

"Then let's take it one step at a time," he offered. "You don't have to carry it all alone."

The warmth of his hand over mine was grounding, yet I felt a familiar itch of uncertainty creeping back in. Just as I was about to respond, the door swung open again, a sudden gust of wind carrying in the cold and the sound of hurried footsteps. I turned to see Claire's silhouette framed against the snow-dusted street, her expression grave.

"Evelyn! We need to talk. Now!"

The urgency in her tone sent a jolt through me, igniting a rush of adrenaline that drowned out the café's warm laughter. I exchanged a glance with Ethan, who looked equally startled. The air shifted as Claire stepped closer, breathless and wide-eyed, and all the questions I had been grappling with surged back to the surface, twisting and knotting in my stomach.

"What's going on?" I asked, my heart racing.

Claire opened her mouth to respond, but before she could speak, the sound of a loud crash reverberated through the café, rattling the windows and sending everyone into a startled silence. My pulse quickened as I turned to face the commotion, dread pooling in the pit of my stomach.

From outside, a figure burst into the café, a tall silhouette shrouded in snow and shadows, carrying an air of uncertainty that sent shivers racing down my spine. I barely had time to register the sight before everything in the café shifted, and the warmth I had felt moments ago dissipated, replaced by a tension so thick I could hardly breathe.

What had just stepped into my life?

Chapter 24: Choices and Consequences

The winter market sprawled out before me, a kaleidoscope of twinkling lights and vibrant stalls, each one bursting with the promise of seasonal cheer. Frost hung delicately in the air, curling around my breath like an icy ribbon, while the sweet scent of roasted chestnuts mingled with the spicy aroma of mulled cider. Children dashed past, their laughter echoing in the frosty evening, hands clutching colorful candies and wooden toys that clacked together in jubilant symphony. I stood at the edge of the chaos, feeling less like a participant and more like a spectator, ensnared by a swirling current of emotions that left me breathless.

Claire's voice echoed in my mind, a relentless tide urging me to return home, to the familiarity and comfort of a life I had once deemed my own. But every time I thought of it, my stomach twisted in knots. I could still hear her pleading tone, tinged with desperation, reminding me of the duties I had fled. Did she think I was made of sterner stuff? That I could simply pack up my dreams and take the next train back to where expectations loomed like dark clouds overhead? The weight of her expectations bore down on me like an iron shackle, chaining me to a past I was trying to escape.

As I turned to search for Ethan among the throngs of familiar faces, a pang of jealousy clawed at my insides. There he was, leaning casually against a stall, his smile radiating warmth that seemed to draw the townsfolk toward him like moths to a flame. He chatted animatedly with Mrs. Callahan, who always baked the best apple pies, and waved to little Timmy, who was proudly showcasing his hand-painted ornament. My heart ached, a bitter twist of longing and anxiety. I had fought too hard to carve out a place for myself here, only to feel like an interloper in a world where he thrived.

Taking a deep breath, I made my way through the crowd, the festive spirit swirling around me, but it felt suffocating rather than uplifting. I needed to talk to Ethan, to lay bare the turmoil churning within me, but the closer I got, the more the words tangled in my throat. When I finally reached him, I pulled him aside, desperate to bridge the growing chasm between us.

"Ethan, can we talk?" I asked, my voice barely rising above the din of laughter and music surrounding us.

He turned, the light from the nearby stall reflecting off his deep-set eyes, revealing a flicker of concern. "Of course. What's up?" He smiled, but it didn't quite reach his eyes, and my heart sank.

"I just—this whole thing, the market, everyone's so happy. It's hard not to feel..." I trailed off, searching for the right words, but they slipped through my fingers like grains of sand. "It's hard not to feel out of place."

His brow furrowed, a crease forming that made him look more serious than I wanted. "Out of place? You've been part of this community for months now. You're one of us, or at least you can be."

The sharpness in his tone stung, and I felt the heat rise in my cheeks. "But am I really? Every time I see you fitting in so easily, it just reminds me how far I've wandered from what I once knew. And I can't shake the feeling that you'd be better off without me, that you might be happier with someone who doesn't hesitate." My voice trembled, the admission hanging between us like a fragile ornament on a fraying string.

His expression shifted, pain flashing in his eyes. "Is this about me? Because I thought we were building something here, together. I thought you wanted to be with me."

"I do! I just—" The frustration bubbled over, and I struggled to keep my emotions in check. "I want to be with you, but I can't ignore the fact that I'm not sure I belong here. I worry that I'm pulling you down with me."

The air around us thickened, tension coiling tighter than the colorful lights strung above us. He stepped back, running a hand through his hair, a gesture of exasperation I'd seen before. "So what's your plan? Are you just going to retreat? Every time things get tough, you want to run? Do you even see what you're doing?"

"I'm not trying to run! I'm trying to figure this out!" My voice rose, drawing glances from those nearby, and a knot of embarrassment twisted in my stomach. "I thought talking to you would help, but all I'm doing is making things worse."

"Maybe if you let me in instead of shutting me out, we wouldn't be having this conversation." His words were sharp, but there was hurt behind them, a vulnerability that made my heart ache for him.

The chaotic market faded into the background, the lively atmosphere dulling to a whisper. We stood in a bubble of silence, where all the laughter and warmth seemed to seep away, leaving only us, raw and exposed. I realized I'd been building walls to shield myself from the very love I craved, thinking it would protect me. But all it did was create distance between us, pushing him away when I needed him closest.

"I'm scared, Ethan," I finally admitted, my voice a quiet whisper. "Scared that if I let go of these fears, I'll lose everything. You. This place. What if it all slips away?"

He stepped closer, the anger fading from his eyes, replaced by a deep understanding. "I can't promise it won't hurt. Life is messy, and so are we. But I'm here. I want to help you face those fears, not just run away from them."

In that moment, surrounded by the twinkling lights and the bustling market, I felt the walls I had carefully constructed begin to crumble. Maybe it was time to stop running, to embrace the uncertainty instead of fearing it. I took a shaky breath, the air thick with possibilities, and dared to hope that perhaps, together, we could navigate whatever came next.

The moment hung in the air, thick with unspoken words and unresolved emotions. Ethan's gaze bore into mine, and for a heartbeat, I wondered if the warmth of the market could thaw the ice that had formed between us. It was strange how quickly a scene filled with laughter and merriment could turn solemn, how the lights strung overhead felt more like interrogation lamps than festive decor. I opened my mouth, ready to offer an apology or an explanation, but the words tangled in my throat. Instead, silence reigned, wrapping us in an awkward cocoon.

"What if we... go for a walk?" he suggested, the tension in his voice softening as he motioned towards a quieter lane that wound away from the crowd. I nodded, relief flooding through me. Maybe a change of scenery could help untangle the mess we found ourselves in.

As we walked, the night enveloped us like a warm blanket, the distant sounds of the market fading into a comforting hush. The snow crunched under our feet, each step a rhythmic reminder of the chill in the air, contrasting sharply with the heat radiating from our earlier confrontation. I took a deep breath, filling my lungs with the crisp winter air, hoping it would also clear my mind.

"I didn't mean to upset you," I started, the words tumbling out before I could filter them. "I guess I'm just... confused."

He looked at me, a hint of softness returning to his expression. "Confusion is okay, you know. But it feels like you've been confused about us for a while now. You pull back just as I start to think we're getting somewhere."

"Isn't that the irony of it all? I want to be closer to you, yet I feel like I'm standing on the edge of a cliff, looking down into an abyss." The honesty startled me, but it felt freeing, a release valve for the pressure that had built up inside.

Ethan stopped walking, turning to face me, his expression serious. "What do you see when you look down?"

"Fear," I admitted, feeling my heart race. "Fear of falling, of getting hurt. I've been burned before, and I thought if I shielded myself, I could keep it from happening again." The words poured out, each one laden with the weight of past experiences that shaped my hesitation.

He reached for my hand, warm and grounding. "But you're not standing alone on that cliff, are you? I'm right here beside you. And if you do fall, I want to be the one who catches you."

His declaration sent a shiver down my spine, igniting a spark of hope in the deep recesses of my heart. Yet, the specter of Claire's voice loomed large, reminding me of the life waiting for me back home—the expectations, the family, the plans meticulously laid out before me. I struggled to reconcile my desire for adventure with the loyalty I felt toward those I loved.

"I don't know how to balance it all," I confessed, pulling my hand away as if I could physically distance myself from the truth. "There's this part of me that wants to stay and forge a new path, but Claire... she's family. She's always counted on me."

"Family shouldn't weigh you down; they should lift you up," he replied, his tone a mixture of understanding and frustration. "I get that there's history there, but it shouldn't define your future. You're not a pawn in someone else's game."

I met his gaze, searching for something solid to hold onto, but his words shook me to my core. Maybe he was right. I had let the fear of disappointing others dictate my choices for far too long. It was time to take ownership of my own story, to write a narrative that didn't just revolve around everyone else's expectations.

"What if I choose wrong?" I whispered, my voice laced with vulnerability. "What if I decide to stay, and it's a mistake? What if I go back, and I miss out on... on us?"

"Life's a series of choices, and none of them come with guarantees." His voice was steady, as if he had been preparing this speech for a while. "You can't let fear dictate your decisions. You have to go with what feels right for you. Besides, if you choose to stay and we don't work out, we can still be friends, right?"

Friends. The word hung in the air, a bittersweet reminder of what we might lose if things didn't go as planned. "You're sure about that?" I asked, a hint of disbelief coloring my voice.

"Of course. But I'd rather take the risk of being more than friends." He smirked, a playful glint in his eye that made my heart flutter. "After all, who wouldn't want a front-row seat to your life? It's bound to be an adventure."

His humor lifted the heaviness, reminding me of why I was drawn to him in the first place. "Adventure, huh? So you're saying I'm the thrilling rollercoaster you've always wanted?"

"More like the unpredictable storm that leaves you breathless and slightly terrified, but also wanting more." His laughter warmed the air between us, a counterpoint to the chill of the winter night.

I chuckled, the tension easing just a bit. "I'll take that as a compliment. But what happens when the storm passes and the sun comes out?"

"Then we ride the waves together," he replied, a sincerity in his voice that made my heart race. "We weather the storms and bask in the sunlight. But you need to decide if you want to be part of this journey, with all its uncertainties."

His words resonated within me, each syllable igniting a spark of defiance against the shadows of doubt that had loomed over my heart. The idea of seizing my own narrative, of stepping off that cliff with him by my side, began to feel less terrifying and more exhilarating.

With a newfound clarity, I took a deep breath, allowing the cold air to fill my lungs and chase away the lingering fears. "Okay. Let's see where this adventure takes us. But just know, if we do crash and burn, you're the one who suggested it."

He laughed, that rich, infectious sound that made me feel like I had just stepped into the light. "I'll take full responsibility. But trust me, I have a feeling we're going to soar."

As we stood there beneath the blanket of stars, the world around us faded into insignificance. What mattered was the path ahead, the choices we would make together, and the promises whispered in the winter air.

The cold nipped at my cheeks, but the warmth radiating from Ethan kept my spirits buoyed as we continued down the quiet path. The festive music from the market had faded into a soft hum, allowing our conversation to fill the space with a surprising intimacy. I had taken the plunge, opening myself up to the possibility of a future beyond the familiar ties of my past, and the anticipation surged within me like the first warmth of spring breaking through a long winter.

Ethan's fingers intertwined with mine as we strolled, his touch a steadying force against the uncertainty swirling in my mind. "So, what's our first adventure then? You know, since we're soaring now," he teased, a playful glint in his eye.

I shot him a sidelong glance, my heart fluttering at the prospect of spontaneity. "How about we start with some hot chocolate? I hear Mrs. Callahan makes a mean cup, with marshmallows that could rival any fluffy cloud."

"Hot chocolate it is. But we have to make it a competition: first one to finish buys the next round of drinks."

"Oh, you're on!" I laughed, the thrill of the challenge sparking a sense of camaraderie I had yearned for. We picked up our pace, heading back toward the market, my heart lighter than it had been in weeks. The sound of laughter grew louder, and as we neared the bustling stalls again, the festive spirit enveloped us like a cozy blanket.

When we reached Mrs. Callahan's stand, the aroma of rich chocolate wafted toward us, a siren song that promised warmth and indulgence. The elderly woman greeted us with a broad smile, her hands steady despite the chill, and before long, we were clutching steaming mugs, the heat radiating through our gloves.

"I've seen you two around," she said, her eyes twinkling with mischief as she leaned closer. "You're always so wrapped up in each other. Just don't let that passion turn into a snowball fight, or I might have to intervene!"

I felt the heat rise in my cheeks as I exchanged a glance with Ethan, who raised an eyebrow in playful challenge. "I make no promises, Mrs. Callahan," he replied, his voice dripping with feigned innocence. "But I can assure you, if a snowball fight does break out, it will be entirely her fault."

Mrs. Callahan chuckled, a rich sound that seemed to blend perfectly with the laughter of children and the festive music in the background. "Ah, young love. Just don't forget to enjoy it; life's too short to let it pass you by."

"Wise words," I murmured, taking a sip of my hot chocolate. The warmth spread through me, and for a moment, I let myself be fully present in the moment, letting go of the shadows that had clouded my mind.

Ethan nudged me playfully, bringing me back to reality. "So, what's the verdict? Is it the best hot chocolate in town?"

"Definitely a contender," I grinned, savoring the creamy richness. "But I might need a second cup to be sure."

"Just as I suspected. A scientist at heart," he said, shaking his head in mock seriousness. "I knew that degree in mixology would pay off."

The teasing banter felt familiar and comforting, like an old sweater I had forgotten how much I loved. But as we continued sipping our drinks, a shadow flitted across my mind, a reminder of the unresolved tension surrounding my choices. I wanted to tell him about Claire's insistence, about the weight of familial expectations that still tugged at my heart. Yet, something held me back, the fear that voicing those concerns might ruin the magic of this moment.

As we wandered through the market, I caught sight of Claire's familiar figure in the crowd, her vibrant scarf a beacon that drew my gaze like a moth to a flame. My heart dropped. The last thing I wanted was for her to interrupt this fragile peace I had managed to cultivate with Ethan. But as I watched, she waved enthusiastically at someone—someone I recognized. A chill crept up my spine as I noticed Jason, my old friend from home, stepping into view.

"What's he doing here?" I muttered, my heart racing as memories of past arguments and unresolved tensions flooded my mind.

"Who?" Ethan asked, his brows knitting together in confusion.

I nodded toward the pair, my stomach churning as Claire's laughter rang out like a bell, cheerful and bright, echoing in stark contrast to the turmoil building inside me. "Jason. He's... someone from home."

Ethan turned to look, and I could see the moment recognition dawned on him. "The one who always tried to convince you to come back?"

"Yeah. And the last person I wanted to see tonight," I replied, trying to keep my voice steady despite the rising panic within me.

Ethan frowned, his protective instincts kicking in. "Do you want to go talk to her? Maybe get some answers?"

"No!" The word escaped my lips too quickly, too forcefully, and I felt a surge of guilt for snapping at him. "I just... I want to enjoy this night, but I can't shake the feeling that she's going to try to pull me back into that life."

Ethan regarded me, a flicker of understanding in his eyes. "I get that. But you can't let her dictate your choices. It's your life, and you need to decide what you want."

I nodded, though the weight of my indecision felt heavier than ever. But before I could respond, Jason and Claire started walking toward us, their expressions brightening at the sight of us.

"There you are!" Claire exclaimed, her voice jubilant as she approached. "I was hoping to find you! Jason just got in town, and we were hoping to catch up."

Ethan's grip tightened around my hand, a silent reassurance as Jason's eyes met mine, a flash of surprise crossing his face. "Hey! I didn't expect to see you here," he said, his tone friendly but laced with an underlying tension.

"Yeah, well, I'm... enjoying the market," I said, forcing a smile that felt more like a grimace.

Claire, oblivious to the tension, beamed at Ethan. "I'm so glad you're here too! We were just talking about how the market's better with friends. You should join us!"

My heart raced as I exchanged glances with Ethan, who wore a mask of neutrality but the tightness in his jaw revealed his discomfort.

"Actually, we were just—" Ethan began, but Jason cut him off, his enthusiasm bubbling over.

"Great idea! Let's all hang out together. The more, the merrier, right?"

As Jason's words hung in the air, I felt a sudden urge to bolt. The path I had just begun to forge with Ethan was now shrouded in uncertainty, a minefield of emotions and expectations. The tension spiraled, and I could feel the precariousness of my situation.

What if this encounter shifted everything? What if Claire convinced me to return home, leaving Ethan and this newfound connection behind? The questions spiraled like snowflakes caught in a tempest, and I fought against the rising tide of panic.

Ethan's eyes held mine, a silent question flickering between us. Would we stand firm against this unexpected reunion, or would I allow the shadows of my past to swallow the light of our present? I could feel the choice pressing upon me, heavy as the winter sky above, and as Jason's eager voice continued to ring in my ears, I realized that this night could change everything.

"Okay," I finally said, the decision weighing on my heart. "Let's see where this goes."

But as I turned to face the group, a sudden commotion erupted nearby, drawing my attention. I glanced back toward the crowd, and what I saw sent a jolt of panic through my veins: a group of townspeople had gathered, pointing and gasping, their faces pale as they turned toward the source of their shock.

What had happened? And why did I have a sinking feeling that whatever it was, it would change everything I had just fought to embrace?

Chapter 25: Unraveling Threads

The vibrant colors of the market swirl around me, bright banners dancing in the crisp winter air, but I'm numb to their allure. Laughter erupts like the crackling of a fire, yet it feels distant, as if I'm peering through a glass wall at a world I can't quite access. People mill about, their cheeks flushed from the cold and excitement, arms laden with crafts and baked goods. The sweet scent of cinnamon wafts past, promising warmth and nostalgia, but it does little to break the chill in my heart. I wander aimlessly, the sound of cheerful chatter a stark contrast to the turmoil brewing inside me.

Ethan's words from our argument replay in my mind like an old record stuck on a loop, each repetition deepening the groove of my anxiety. "You're too wrapped up in this place," he had said, his voice steady but tinged with frustration. "You need to look beyond Silver Pines." I can still see the way his brow furrowed, those familiar blue eyes reflecting a mix of concern and something else—something that felt suspiciously like doubt. A pang of regret stabs at me, sharp and merciless. What if he was right? What if I had let this quaint town become a prison, its charm a gilded cage?

Shaking off the heaviness that clings to me like a wet blanket, I make my way toward Clara's café, its inviting sign swaying gently in the breeze. The moment I step inside, the warmth wraps around me like a favorite sweater, and the low hum of conversation creates a cocoon of safety. Clara stands behind the counter, her apron dusted with flour and a friendly smile lighting up her face. She waves me over, and I can't help but feel a sense of relief wash over me.

"Hey, you," she says, her voice a soothing balm. "What's got you looking like a snowman that just got hit by a bus?" She pours a generous cup of steaming coffee and slides it across the counter, her eyes sparkling with concern.

"Just the usual existential crisis," I say, attempting to infuse my tone with humor, though it falls flat. I wrap my hands around the warm mug, letting the heat seep into my chilled fingers. "Ethan and I... we had a bit of a falling out."

"Ah, the infamous winter market love quarrel," she replies with a knowing nod, leaning against the counter. "What was it this time? You want to stay in Silver Pines, and he wants to take you to the big city?"

"Something like that," I murmur, staring into the rich, dark depths of my coffee. "It's just... I don't know if he sees how much this place means to me. It's not just a town; it's home. My roots are here."

Clara studies me for a moment, her expression softening. "And what if your roots could grow in other places too?"

I'm caught off guard by her question. "You mean like being uprooted? That sounds terrifying. What if I can't flourish somewhere else?"

"Or what if you could? You could be a wildflower blooming in unexpected places," she counters, her voice gentle but insistent. "Just because you love this town doesn't mean you have to confine yourself to it. Growth can happen anywhere."

Her words hang in the air, and I take a sip of coffee, allowing the warmth to chase away some of the chill that has settled deep in my bones. "You sound like you've been thinking about this for a while," I say, a touch of curiosity piquing my interest.

Clara shrugs, her gaze turning contemplative. "Maybe. I mean, this café has always been my dream, but sometimes I wonder if I'm just running away from something. I love it here, but there are days when I feel the walls closing in."

"Really? You?" I say, surprise lacing my tone. Clara is the embodiment of warmth and security in this town, her laughter a guiding light for so many. "What do you mean by that?"

She leans in closer, lowering her voice as if sharing a secret. "I guess I'm afraid that I'm not living up to my potential. That this café is all I'll ever be. Sometimes I think about moving to a bigger city where I could open a chain or do something else entirely."

"Clara, you're amazing! This café is a piece of you, and it brings joy to so many," I insist, my heart swelling with admiration for her dream. "But what if you could expand that joy without leaving?"

Her eyes glimmer with intrigue, and for the first time, I see a spark of something more in her. "What do you mean?"

"Why not hold workshops? Teach people how to bake or run their own cafés? You could host events—get people excited about the community!" My enthusiasm bubbles over, and I can almost see her wheels turning. "You'd be sharing your passion, and it would still be rooted in Silver Pines. You could grow without leaving."

Clara's face brightens, a flicker of hope dancing in her eyes. "You might be onto something there."

Just then, the bell above the door jingles, and a familiar voice calls out, breaking our moment. "Clara! Is that coffee I smell?" Ethan strides in, shaking off snowflakes that cling to his coat. My stomach twists into a knot at the sight of him, and I can't help but feel the weight of unresolved tension between us.

"Clara! Is that coffee I smell?" Ethan strides in, shaking off snowflakes that cling to his coat. My stomach twists into a knot at the sight of him, and I can't help but feel the weight of unresolved tension between us. His cheeks are flushed, not just from the cold but from an undeniable energy that always seems to light up a room—especially when he's surrounded by the aroma of freshly brewed coffee.

"Ethan!" Clara beams, a hint of mischief dancing in her eyes as she pours him a cup. The air suddenly feels electric, charged with an undercurrent I can't quite place. I watch them share a moment, the ease between them contrasting sharply with the tension tightening around my chest. "Just the way you like it—extra strong, like your opinions," she teases, and he laughs, a sound that usually fills me with warmth but today cuts like a knife.

"Careful, Clara. I might just steal your secret recipe," he shoots back, flashing that disarming grin that has always made my heart skip. Yet now, it feels like a challenge rather than an invitation. I can't help but feel like an interloper in their banter, a stranger in the very space I once felt at home.

Clara glances between us, her smile fading just a touch as she senses the unspoken words hanging heavy in the air. "So, what brings you here, Ethan? Looking for a fix or trying to make peace with the winter market gods?"

He turns his attention to me, the playfulness melting away into something more serious. "I came to check on you," he says, his voice dropping a notch, pulling me in like a moth to a flame. "I didn't mean what I said earlier. It came out wrong."

"Did it?" I reply, unable to keep the bite from my tone. "Because it felt pretty clear to me."

Ethan shifts, running a hand through his hair, the movement both familiar and frustrating. "Can we not do this here? Not in front of Clara?"

Clara raises an eyebrow, her playful demeanor now replaced with keen awareness. "You know I can hear you, right? And I happen to be an excellent mediator."

"Not the kind of mediation I'm looking for," Ethan replies, crossing his arms defensively. "I just think we need to talk without an audience."

"Right, because avoiding the topic has worked so well for you so far," I shoot back, feeling the heat rising in my cheeks. "What, are you worried I'll be too emotional in front of Clara?"

"Not at all! I just—"

"—think you'll get defensive," Clara interjects, her tone matter-of-fact. "Look, if you're going to hash it out, I have a full house of people waiting for coffee. Let me know when you need a refuel." She hands Ethan his cup, and with a wink, she walks away, leaving us in an uncomfortable silence.

I take a deep breath, fighting the urge to either laugh or cry. "Great, just us then. What do you want to say?"

Ethan leans against the counter, his expression softening. "I want you to know that I care about you. This isn't about Silver Pines. It's about us—what we want for our future."

"Right, and what do you want? A future that doesn't include this place?" I challenge, feeling a mix of anger and hurt rising to the surface. "It's like you don't see me at all. You see this quaint little town with its winding streets and friendly neighbors, but you don't see me. You only see a ticket out."

"That's not true!" he exclaims, and his eyes widen, as if I've struck a nerve. "I love this place because I love you. But I also want to explore, to experience more than what's right in front of us."

"Maybe I don't want to explore! Maybe I'm content here!" My voice rises, drawing a few curious glances from other customers. I lower my tone, but the heat of my passion doesn't dim. "I'm not a bird that needs to fly the coop, Ethan. I'm a tree that's grown roots here."

His shoulders slump slightly, the fight leaving his body as he meets my gaze. "I didn't mean to suggest that you're trapped. I just—"

"Want me to be someone else," I finish for him, the bitterness in my words tasting like ash. "You think you know what's best for me, but you're not listening. You're projecting your dreams onto me."

"Maybe you're projecting your fears onto me," he counters, his voice low, the tension crackling between us like a winter storm. "What if you're scared to leave?"

"Why would I be scared?" I fire back, but even I can hear the tremor in my voice. The truth is a murky mess I'm not ready to unpack in front of him. "I love Silver Pines, but I also want to feel like I'm living, not just existing."

"Then let's figure it out together," he implores, stepping closer. "Don't shut me out. I want to be part of your journey, not just the destination."

Just as I'm about to respond, Clara reappears, carrying a tray piled high with warm pastries. "So, who wants a croissant? Trust me, it's the best therapy."

I can't help but smile at her attempt to lighten the mood. "I'm good, thanks," I say, forcing a grin that feels more like a grimace.

"Suit yourself," she replies with a knowing smile, glancing between us. "But if you need to vent, I'm all ears. Just don't involve the pastries. They're not ready for that kind of drama."

Ethan chuckles, breaking the tension momentarily. "I think we've had enough drama for one day, don't you?"

"Ethan, this isn't just a casual conversation. It's—"

"Real," he interjects, his voice firm yet soft. "And it's okay to feel lost sometimes. Just don't lose yourself in the process."

"Easier said than done," I mutter, my heart racing as I grapple with his words. The coffee shop feels both like a sanctuary and a cage, with the walls closing in as we confront the truth of our relationship. I want to be brave, but the fear of stepping outside the familiar terrifies me.

In that moment, I realize that what we're navigating is more than just a disagreement; it's a crossroads, and I must decide which path to take.

The aroma of freshly baked pastries envelops the café, but the warmth doesn't quite reach the cold knot in my stomach. I force a smile for Clara, who is watching us with keen interest, like a cat preparing to pounce. The tension between Ethan and me simmers beneath the surface, our words ricocheting around the intimate space as if they have a life of their own.

"Listen," I begin, my voice quieter now, searching for the right words. "I appreciate that you want to be involved, but I need to figure this out on my own. I don't want you to feel like you have to solve everything for me."

His brow furrows, and the corner of his mouth twitches downward. "It's not about solving things; it's about being together in this. You don't have to shoulder it all alone."

"Together? Is that what we are?" The question slips out, sharp and unyielding. I catch a flicker of hurt in his eyes, but I can't help it. The uncertainty gnaws at me, a little worm burrowing deeper into my psyche. "You seem to want different things. I want to stay here, Ethan. I want to grow my roots deeper. But you—"

"I'm not asking you to change!" he bursts out, frustration lacing his tone. "I'm asking you to consider a future that could include more than just Silver Pines. I'm trying to give us options, to think big."

I take a deep breath, my mind racing as I consider what he's saying. His dreams feel like a distant constellation, beautiful but unreachable. "You make it sound so easy," I say, my voice trembling slightly. "But moving away from everything I know? It feels like jumping off a cliff without knowing if there's water at the bottom."

"Maybe the water's there, just waiting for you to leap," he responds, his eyes earnest, and I see the glimmer of something hopeful in his gaze. But my heart twists at the thought. How can I take that leap when I'm terrified of heights?

"Do you ever think that maybe this place, this community, is worth sticking around for?" I ask, my tone softening. "I mean, it's not just about what we want as individuals. We're in this together, and I don't want to lose that. But what does that even look like if you leave?"

Ethan studies me, and I can almost hear the gears grinding in his head as he processes my words. "I want to be with you, but I also want to explore the world with you. This town won't vanish if we take a break from it. Sometimes you have to step outside to see the beauty inside."

The café buzzes with the laughter and chatter of patrons enjoying their morning, but I feel oddly detached from it all, as if I'm watching life unfold through a foggy window. "I don't want to be the person who holds you back," I admit, my voice barely above a whisper.

"Then don't," he replies, his voice steady. "Just be you. The you I love. I'm not looking to escape; I'm looking to expand, to share it with you. You're not a weight, you're my partner."

In that moment, I can feel the heavy mantle of expectations shifting. It's terrifying, exhilarating. "You make it sound easy, but…"

"Nothing worth having is easy," he interjects, his eyes searching mine. "And that's where the beauty lies."

Clara returns, her arms laden with a fresh batch of croissants. "Okay, enough about existential crises for today. Who wants to indulge?"

"Can I get one of those with a side of emotional support?" I say, trying to inject a bit of humor into the air, but it falls flat, the weight of our conversation still thick between us.

"Coming right up!" she chirps, seemingly oblivious to the undercurrents swirling around us. "I'll even throw in some jam because I can tell you both need a little sweetness."

Ethan and I exchange a glance, and for a brief moment, I see a flicker of something in his eyes—a shared understanding, a quiet acknowledgment of the storm we're weathering together.

"Thanks, Clara," he says, a hint of warmth returning to his tone. "You always know how to lighten the mood."

As Clara walks away, I catch Ethan's gaze, and a familiar tension builds again, wrapping around us like a thick fog. "So, where do we go from here?" I ask, a mixture of hope and fear creeping into my voice.

He takes a step closer, his gaze unwavering. "Let's take it one day at a time. You're not losing me unless you want to, and I'm not going anywhere without you."

My heart races at his words, a fragile flicker of hope igniting within me. "Okay," I say softly, "but I need you to promise that you'll really listen. I want us to communicate openly about what we both need, even if it's scary."

"Promise," he replies, extending a hand. "To be honest, even when it hurts."

I place my hand in his, feeling the warmth radiate through our connection. It's a small gesture, but in this moment, it feels monumental. Just as I start to breathe easier, the café door swings open with a jingle, and an icy gust of wind sweeps in, sending shivers through me.

A figure strides in, silhouetted against the bright light outside. As they step further into the café, I freeze, my breath catching in my throat. It's Ethan's brother, Jack, his presence commanding and unexpected.

"Ethan!" Jack calls out, his voice booming, cutting through the chatter of the café. "We need to talk."

Ethan's expression shifts from warmth to concern in an instant, and I feel a tightening in my chest. The look on Jack's face is serious, a weight of urgency that hangs heavy in the air. I glance between the two of them, uncertainty flooding my mind.

"What's going on?" I ask, but the words are swallowed by the tension thickening around us. The café, once a haven, now feels like a stage where an unexpected play is about to unfold, and I'm not sure if I'm ready for the next act.

Chapter 26: The Tipping Point

The morning sun filters through the frost-laden window, casting delicate patterns of light that dance across the room. The air feels heavy, laden with the remnants of last night's revelries and the echoes of laughter that now seem like ghosts. I blink against the sunlight, the warmth of the bed failing to chase away the chill that has settled in my bones. The silence is unnerving, a stark contrast to the symphony of voices that had filled the winter market. I stretch, pulling the quilt tighter around my shoulders, but even its familiar weight does little to comfort me. Ethan's absence gnaws at my insides, a hungry little beast demanding attention.

Slipping out of bed, I wrap my arms around myself, my fingers grazing the wooden banister as I navigate the creaking floorboards. Each step is a reminder of the uncertainty swirling around me like the dust motes caught in the morning light. I head to the café, the scent of fresh-brewed coffee drawing me like a moth to a flame. But as I open the door, I am met with the dissonance of murmurs. The usually warm embrace of the Maple Leaf feels cold today, charged with a tension I can't quite place.

Diane stands at the counter, her voice sharp and penetrating, slicing through the cozy atmosphere like a knife. I can't help but notice how her words twist and turn, dripping with the venom of malice. "And you see," she says, her tone laden with feigned concern, "if we allow her to take over the café, who knows what will happen next? This place has always belonged to us. We can't let outsiders change that." The room falls silent, and I sense the shift in the air, the way a predator senses its prey.

My heart pounds as I step deeper into the café, the warmth of the coffee machine now feeling like a barrier between me and the gathering storm. I catch the eyes of the townsfolk, their expressions a mix of curiosity and doubt. Diane's accusations hang in the air, thick and suffocating, and I can't let them linger unchallenged. "Diane," I say, my voice trembling but rising to the challenge, "you know that's not true. I'm not here to take anything from anyone. I love this place and everything it stands for."

"Oh please, don't pretend you're some kind of martyr," she retorts, her laughter laced with mockery. "You're here to capitalize on our traditions, aren't you? This café was our refuge before you swooped in like a hawk, ready to feast on our misfortunes."

The accusation stings, and for a moment, I feel the room closing in around me. But beneath the sting is a bubbling determination, a fire ignited by the thought of Ethan and all he means to me. "You don't understand," I press on, my voice stronger now. "This café isn't just a business to me; it's a community, a home. And I want to help it thrive, not tear it down. We can make it better together, but only if we stop this divisive nonsense."

The murmurs begin to swell, a low tide of uncertainty as the townsfolk exchange glances. I can see the wheels turning in their minds, the conflict between loyalty and truth playing out like an old film reel. Just as I think I might have swayed them, a familiar face pushes through the door—Ethan, his expression a mix of confusion and hurt that slices through me like a cold winter wind. He hesitates at the threshold, and for a split second, it feels as though the world has stopped.

"Ethan!" I call out, a wave of relief washing over me, but it quickly dissipates as I see him step back, almost as if he's recoiling from an unseen force. My heart sinks deeper than I thought possible. He turns away, avoiding my gaze, and I can feel the weight of judgment in the room intensify.

"Look at her, Ethan," Diane presses, her voice dripping with saccharine sweetness. "Is this really the woman you want to trust? Can you honestly say she has your best interests at heart?"

"Diane, that's enough," he snaps, his tone sharper than I've ever heard it. But the damage is done; I can see it in the lines of tension etched across his forehead. He's caught between the reality of our connection and the venomous seeds Diane has planted.

"Ethan, please," I implore, stepping forward, my heart racing with a mix of hope and dread. "I love this town, and I love you. I'm not trying to change anything; I just want to contribute, to be part of this community. Can't you see that?"

His gaze falters, and for a fleeting moment, I think I see the flicker of something—understanding, perhaps. But then it vanishes, replaced by a shadow of doubt. "You say that, but you're not the one who has to live with the consequences. It's easy for you to stand there and make grand declarations."

The crowd around us shifts, and I feel their eyes like burning coals, judging, weighing. My stomach knots, and I can hardly breathe. "I don't want to be an outsider," I whisper, the sincerity in my voice cutting through the tension. "I want to be here, with you, with everyone."

But my words seem to float into the void, unheard. The doubt in his eyes mirrors the skepticism of the townsfolk, and my heart fractures as I watch him retreat. I am left standing in the middle of the café, the warmth of the space now turned to ice. The vibrant colors of the winter market seem to fade, the laughter turning to a dull echo, and as I look around, I realize I am fighting not just for myself but for a love that feels precariously balanced on the edge of a knife.

The silence in the café swells, a palpable thing that wraps around me tighter than a winter scarf. I glance around at the familiar faces—friends and neighbors who have become so much more than mere acquaintances. But today, their expressions are shrouded in suspicion, a barrier between us that feels insurmountable. Diane, triumphant and smug, seems to drink in the chaos she's created. Her lips curl in a way that suggests she relishes the spectacle, as if each whisper, each furrowed brow, feeds her insatiable need for control.

"Ethan, wait!" I call again, pushing past the dense knot of townsfolk who now seem to form a living wall between us. He's still standing at the entrance, a silhouette against the daylight, and my heart races at the thought of him slipping away entirely. I can't let that happen; not now, not after everything we've built.

"You want to explain yourself, or are we just supposed to take your word for it?" Diane's taunt cuts through the crowd like a razor. "This is about more than just your feelings, sweetheart. This is our home."

"Your home?" I challenge, the fire in my belly igniting. "I'm not here to take anything from you. I'm here to give back. Have you forgotten how much the Maple Leaf means to all of us?"

"Give back?" she scoffs, crossing her arms as if bracing for an attack. "What exactly do you plan to give us? Fancy new recipes that only serve to line your pockets?"

"Oh, for heaven's sake, Diane," I say, exasperation bubbling over. "This isn't about me making money. It's about the community coming together, finding new ways to thrive. You think adding a couple of lattes to the menu is going to destroy Silver Pines? You're smarter than that."

But the doubts hang in the air like fog, thick and suffocating. I can see some of the townsfolk nodding along with her, their conviction firm as if they've never heard my side at all. There's a pang of betrayal in my chest as I watch the very people I wanted to unite divide themselves further, with me standing in the middle of the battlefield, clutching my heart like a shield.

Ethan shifts, his shoulders tensing as though he's caught in a tug-of-war between loyalty and truth. I take a breath, willing my voice to steady. "What do you want from me, Diane? To crawl back to where I came from?" I sweep my arm wide, gesturing to the café.

"I want to be here, to belong. But I can't fight this alone. We can do this together."

"Maybe we should ask Ethan what he thinks," she replies, the smirk returning to her face. "After all, he's the one who invited you into our lives. Isn't that right, Ethan?"

He hesitates, and in that moment, I can see the struggle in his eyes. The way his lips press together suggests he's grappling with a tidal wave of emotions, trying to balance his affection for me with the loyalty he feels toward his friends and family. "I..." he starts, but the words catch in his throat, and my heart sinks further.

Before I can respond, one of the older ladies, Mrs. Wilkins, steps forward. "I remember when this café was a gathering place," she says, her voice a warm melody amid the discord. "We'd share stories over coffee, comfort food that felt like a hug. It was our heart. But now..." She shakes her head, a sad smile breaking through. "We're forgetting what makes us family."

Diane rolls her eyes, but Mrs. Wilkins has struck a chord. "We're not family anymore," Diane retorts, desperation dripping from her voice. "Not if we let someone like her in."

The murmurs swell again, and I can feel my pulse quicken. I know that if I want to turn this tide, I have to confront the fear, the baseless rumors swirling in the air like snowflakes caught in a storm. "Family isn't about blood," I interject. "It's about choice. It's about standing together when things get tough."

"And what if I choose to protect what's mine?" Diane snaps, stepping closer, her eyes narrowing like a hawk ready to strike. "You think you can waltz in here and change everything without consequence? You think we'll just sit back and let it happen?"

"I'm not asking you to sit back," I counter, my voice ringing out like a bell. "I'm asking you to join me. To trust that I want the same things you do. To honor the legacy of this place instead of turning it into a battleground. We can modernize without losing our roots."

The air grows heavier, and the words hang like snowflakes poised to fall. I take a deep breath, searching Ethan's eyes for a flicker of understanding, a sign that he's with me. "Ethan," I plead softly, "you know me. You know my heart. I would never betray the Maple Leaf or anyone here. I just want us all to succeed together."

But he stands silent, his face a mask of conflict. The crackling energy between us feels more potent than ever, a web of unresolved emotions that threatens to snap. Just then, a voice cuts through the tension, one I recognize instantly.

"Is this what we've become?" Sarah steps forward, her brow furrowed in confusion. "A place where we turn on each other? I've seen what you're doing here, and I don't think it's fair to paint her as the villain, Diane. She's trying to help us all."

A collective gasp ripples through the crowd. The tide shifts, the murmurs rising in fervor. Diane, cornered and indignant, sputters, "You don't know her like I do!"

But Sarah holds her ground. "No, but I know you, and I've seen what this town can be. We should be banding together, not tearing each other apart. I believe in what she's trying to do."

In that moment, the tension fractures, allowing a glimmer of hope to seep through the cracks. I feel my chest expand, the warmth of camaraderie rising, pushing against the chill of doubt.

"Let's give her a chance," Sarah continues, her voice steady. "What's the worst that could happen? More lattes?"

I can't help but smile at the absurdity of it all. Maybe the tide is finally turning. Maybe we can transform the Maple Leaf into something that embodies our past while also embracing the future.

Diane's expression darkens, and I brace for her retaliation. But before she can speak, Ethan steps forward, taking a breath as if he's finally found his voice amidst the cacophony. "I want to support her," he says, his eyes locking onto mine, and for a moment, the world around us falls away. "I believe in her vision for Silver Pines."

My heart soars, buoyed by the affirmation I so desperately needed. The crowd stirs, the judgmental gazes beginning to soften. A crack in the ice, and maybe—just maybe—a way forward.

Ethan's declaration settles over the room like a gentle snowfall, transforming the cacophony into a whisper of possibility. The crowd's murmurs shift from hostility to curiosity, their eyes darting between us, searching for clarity amid the confusion. I can feel the pulse of hope flickering, but Diane's dark scowl reminds me that the battle is far from over. "You really think she'll bring anything good to this town?" she retorts, a sharp edge to her voice. "You don't know her like I do. She'll ruin everything!"

I open my mouth, ready to retort, but Ethan holds up a hand. "No, Diane. I do know her. She's passionate, she cares about this community, and she wants to see it thrive. Why can't you just—" His voice falters, frustration evident in the tightening of his jaw.

"Because we've built something here," she snaps, eyes flashing. "We've fought for every inch of this town, and now you want to hand it over to someone who doesn't understand our struggles?"

"Maybe that's exactly the point," I interject, trying to regain control of the narrative. "I'm not here to dismantle what you've built. I want to enhance it, to help it grow into something that can sustain itself for generations to come." The sincerity in my voice seems to hang in the air, suspended like the breathless moment before a storm.

Silence follows, thick and heavy, punctuated only by the faint clatter of cups and the quiet shuffle of feet. Then Sarah steps forward, the fire in her eyes unwavering. "You talk about preserving what we have, Diane, but isn't it worth exploring new ideas? We can honor our past without being shackled to it."

A ripple of agreement stirs among the crowd, but Diane stands resolute, her arms crossed tightly over her chest as though bracing against a harsh wind. "And what if her ideas lead us to ruin? You'll all be left wondering why you trusted an outsider."

A breathless tension envelops us. I glance at Ethan, who is watching Diane with a mixture of concern and exasperation. His eyes dart back to mine, and in that instant, I see a flicker of what we once shared—trust, laughter, the easy banter that once flowed like a river between us. But now, it feels dammed, held back by misunderstandings and outside influences.

"Enough!" I finally say, frustration erupting like a firework in the stillness. "This isn't just about me or you, Diane. It's about all of us. If we can't find a way to come together, we're just going to keep fracturing. You think I want to walk into a place that's divided? I want the Maple Leaf to be a haven, a symbol of everything we cherish. But we can't do that while we're tearing each other apart."

The words hang in the air, electrifying the space between us. I take a step forward, determination igniting within me like a flame in the dark. "You all have a choice to make. You can stand with me and create something beautiful, or you can stay locked in this endless cycle of suspicion and fear. I can't do this alone, and frankly, I don't want to."

Mrs. Wilkins nods again, her age-creased face softening. "Maybe it's time we let someone new bring their perspective. We've become so set in our ways that we've forgotten what it means to be open to change."

Encouraged by her support, I continue. "Imagine hosting events that attract people from neighboring towns, workshops that bring in fresh ideas, seasonal festivals that celebrate our heritage while inviting new traditions. We can create a space where everyone feels welcome—if we let go of our fears."

As the murmurs begin to shift towards contemplation, I catch a glimpse of Ethan's expression softening, a shadow of hope replacing the uncertainty. But Diane steps forward, her lips pressed into a thin line, eyes narrowing as though she's weighing her next move. "And what if your vision fails? What then? Will you take the blame when this place crumbles?"

I can feel the pulse of the room quicken, the stakes rising like the tide. "If we don't try, we're guaranteed failure," I respond, my voice steady. "Isn't that scarier? The idea of staying stagnant, letting fear dictate our future? I'd rather risk failure than live in a world of what-ifs."

Just as Diane opens her mouth to reply, a sudden commotion at the café entrance draws our attention. The door bursts open, and in strides a figure cloaked in a thick winter coat, breathless and frantic. It's Emily, her usually bright eyes clouded with distress.

"I'm sorry to interrupt," she gasps, the words spilling from her lips like the snowflakes cascading from her hair. "But you all need to see this."

"What is it?" I ask, anxiety creeping into my voice, and a knot twists in my stomach.

She steps closer, her expression a mixture of urgency and fear. "It's about the Maple Leaf. There's a group of developers in town. They're looking to buy up the land, including this café, to build a new shopping complex. They're moving quickly, and if we don't act fast..."

The air becomes charged with disbelief, the weight of her revelation settling over us like a shroud. Gasps ripple through the crowd, and I feel my heart plummet. Diane's face pales, the color draining as the reality sinks in.

"No, this can't be happening," she whispers, and for the first time, I see a crack in her armor.

"We need to rally everyone," Emily insists, her voice rising above the chaos. "If we don't unite, we'll lose everything we've fought for."

I glance at Ethan, whose eyes are wide with shock. The tension that had held us captive moments ago evaporates, replaced by a rush of adrenaline and the urgency of action. "We can't let this happen,"

I declare, determination swelling within me. "We'll fight for the Maple Leaf and for our home. Together."

The crowd begins to stir, a newfound sense of purpose igniting among them, but just as I feel a glimmer of hope, the door swings open once more, and a man in a crisp suit steps inside, a smug smile plastered on his face. "Ladies and gentlemen," he calls, his voice smooth as silk, "I believe you've all heard about the incredible opportunity that awaits you. The Maple Leaf has been chosen as the prime location for our newest shopping complex…"

The words hang in the air, dark and ominous, and as realization dawns, I see the tide shifting once again, but this time, it feels more perilous than ever. The fight for our home has begun, and the stakes are higher than I ever imagined.

Chapter 27: Bridging the Divide

The scent of freshly brewed coffee mingled with the sweet aroma of cinnamon rolls as I prepared for the first book club meeting at Silver Pines Café. It was a quaint place, the kind where the walls were lined with mismatched bookshelves, each brimming with tales waiting to be discovered. I had envisioned this moment as a gathering of like-minded souls, but with each tick of the clock, my enthusiasm began to wane, replaced by an uneasy flutter in my stomach.

"Did you really think this would be easy?" I muttered to myself, straightening the stack of books I'd chosen for discussion. Traveling Mercies had seemed a perfect fit for a town that felt somewhat isolated from the outside world, its stories about journeys and redemption mirroring the paths I hoped we'd forge together. Yet, doubts clouded my mind, making me question my ability to bridge the divide that had long separated me from the townsfolk.

I glanced around the café, the dim lighting casting a warm glow over the tables, each adorned with handmade coasters and well-loved mugs. Laughter drifted in from a nearby group, their conversations interspersed with the occasional burst of music from a vintage record player in the corner. The contrast between their ease and my anxiety felt stark, as if I were an outsider peering into a world I desperately wanted to be a part of.

My heart raced as I rehearsed my opening remarks in my mind. I had practiced them in front of my mirror, pretending to be confident, charismatic even. "Welcome, everyone! Let's embark on a literary adventure together!" It sounded so much better in my head. Would they laugh? Would they care? Would Diane, with her polished demeanor and practiced charm, swoop in like a hawk to reclaim her territory?

Just as the clock chimed, the door swung open, and a gust of chilly wind followed. I turned, my breath hitching. Ethan stepped inside, his cheeks slightly flushed from the cold, and a wide grin spread across his face. "I thought I'd find you here, organizing your literary coup," he quipped, his eyes sparkling with mischief.

"Coup? I'm merely trying to overthrow the tyranny of boredom," I replied, my tension easing just a bit.

He chuckled, shaking off his coat. "Well, in that case, I'm fully supportive of your revolution."

As the other attendees filtered in—some hesitant, others curious—the warmth of Ethan's presence wrapped around me like a cozy blanket, banishing my insecurities. We started with small talk, discussing our favorite travel destinations and the books that had inspired us. The café soon filled with the sounds of laughter and spirited debate, voices rising and falling like waves, crashing against the shore of our collective enthusiasm.

"Okay, so if you could travel anywhere in the world right now, where would it be?" I asked, my heart racing at the thought of their answers.

"Definitely Japan," said a woman with vibrant red hair and a penchant for quirky accessories. "The culture, the food! Plus, I've always wanted to try an authentic ramen experience."

"Ramen? That's all well and good," Ethan chimed in, "but what about the cherry blossoms? I'd fly there just to see that pink explosion of beauty. It's nature's confetti."

A ripple of laughter flowed through the room, and suddenly I felt as though we were all sharing the same air, breathing in each other's dreams and aspirations.

"I'd love to hike the Inca Trail," I added, trying to keep the conversation alive. "I can almost picture it—the ancient ruins peeking through the clouds, the satisfaction of reaching Machu Picchu. There's something magical about a journey that challenges you, don't you think?"

The group nodded, their expressions lighting up with shared excitement. The barriers of skepticism and reserve began to crumble, replaced by a burgeoning sense of community that left me feeling buoyant.

"Speaking of challenges," Ethan said, leaning forward, "what about the challenge of reading a book that changes your perspective? What's a book that did that for you?"

That question hung in the air, inviting reflection. One by one, the members shared stories of books that had shifted their understanding of the world. A young man spoke about The Alchemist, describing how it inspired him to pursue his own dreams against all odds. An elderly woman recounted the heartache and wisdom of The Grapes of Wrath, her voice rich with the weight of history and emotion.

As the stories unfolded, I felt an exhilarating sense of belonging. My fears about Diane dissipated into the ether, leaving only the warmth of camaraderie in their place. There was no battle to be fought here, no need for competition. Instead, we were weaving a tapestry of experiences, each thread unique yet intricately intertwined.

Time slipped away, hours seeming like mere moments, and as I glanced at the clock, I realized the meeting had extended well beyond my original plan. Yet nobody seemed to notice or care. They were too engaged, lost in the vibrant discussions and laughter that filled the space.

As we wrapped up, I couldn't help but smile at Ethan, who leaned against the café counter, a satisfied grin plastered across his face. "You were amazing," he said, his voice low and sincere. "I think you've officially won them over."

"Really? You think so?" My heart swelled at the compliment.

"Definitely. They were practically eating out of your hand," he teased, but I could see the pride in his eyes.

"Well, maybe I should take that as an invitation to make this a regular thing," I replied, my confidence blossoming with each word.

"I'd be honored to be your sidekick in this literary escapade," he declared, mockingly placing a hand over his heart.

As we exchanged playful banter, I felt a shift within me, a promise that the connection I'd fostered in this quaint café would only continue to deepen. Little did I know that the stories shared today would serve as the foundation for something far more profound, a bond that could bridge any divide—real or imagined.

As the days rolled into weeks, the book club blossomed like the first flowers of spring, unfurling their petals toward the sun. Each gathering drew more faces, a blend of curious newcomers and familiar regulars. The café had become a sanctuary, a cozy haven where laughter mingled with the rich scent of brewed coffee and baked goods. On Tuesday evenings, I could count on a tapestry of voices discussing characters, plotting twists, and dissecting themes as passionately as if we were debating the fate of the world.

Ethan's presence was a constant delight, and his clever remarks kept the atmosphere light, even when the topics grew heavy. "Is it just me, or do the protagonists in these novels need a serious lesson in decision-making?" he quipped one night after a particularly tense discussion about a character who made one poor choice after another. The group erupted in laughter, and I couldn't help but admire how he effortlessly wove himself into the fabric of our little community.

One evening, as I set out the snacks—a mélange of fruit, cheese, and an embarrassing number of chocolate chip cookies—I noticed Diane lurking at the edge of the café, her sharp features casting a long shadow. Her arrival had become something of a shadow over my newfound confidence, a specter of my past that I thought I had laid to rest. She waved, her smile wide yet curiously empty, as if she were testing the waters of a pool she didn't quite want to dive into.

"Care to join us?" I called, my voice tinged with equal parts enthusiasm and trepidation.

"Oh, I wouldn't want to interrupt your little book club," she replied, her tone dripping with sweetness that felt oddly artificial.

"Not little at all! We're making literary history here," I shot back, my mouth running faster than my brain. "The next great novel could be inspired right here in this very café."

With a playful roll of her eyes, she approached the table, and my heart raced. I was acutely aware of how her mere presence seemed to chill the atmosphere. "What are you discussing tonight? Something deep and philosophical, I hope?"

"Actually, we're delving into The Night Circus," I replied, gesturing to the group. "You should stay. I think you'd enjoy it."

She hesitated, and I could practically hear the gears turning in her head. "Maybe I'll drop by later," she said, not committing either way.

As she retreated to a corner table, I felt a pang of annoyance mixed with pity. She had been a formidable figure in my past, a relentless critic who thrived on undermining others. Yet, seeing her alone in the bustling café reminded me of the importance of connection, something she seemed to be struggling with.

"Don't let her get to you," Ethan whispered, sidling up next to me. "You've built something beautiful here. Diane is just a storm cloud in a sky full of sunshine."

"Is that your way of calling me a ray of sunshine?" I shot back, smirking.

"Only on your best days," he teased, and the warmth in his gaze pushed my worries aside, if only for a moment.

The conversation flowed freely that evening, a delightful dance of words and ideas. The group became animated, exploring the magic of the circus within the novel, marveling at its enchanting atmosphere. "Can you imagine the sights, the sounds?" a woman exclaimed, her eyes alight with wonder. "It's like walking into a dream!"

As discussions deepened, I noticed Diane inching closer, her interest piqued. She was like a cat eyeing a mouse, stealthy yet full of intent. I took a breath and pressed on, weaving a narrative that captivated everyone, including her. "Imagine stepping into a world where reality bends and the impossible becomes possible," I said, my voice carrying the weight of my passion. "Every turn is a chance to be swept off your feet, to discover something that could change your life forever."

I locked eyes with Diane, challenging her to join the conversation. "What do you think, Diane? Do you believe in the magic of stories?"

Her lips curled into a smirk, the kind that promised a playful jab. "I believe stories are best when they reflect reality. Magic is all well and good until you have to deal with the consequences."

"Fair point," I acknowledged, refusing to let her dim the light of the gathering. "But isn't it the escapism that we crave? It's the reminder that there's more out there, beyond our own realities."

The room buzzed with agreement, and even Diane seemed to falter, her confidence wavering against the tide of shared enthusiasm.

As the evening progressed, laughter filled the air, and the sense of community felt thicker, almost tangible. The conversation flowed like the wine we had shared, rich and intoxicating. It was invigorating to see the barriers crumbling, to witness connections forming between people who had once been strangers.

After the meeting, as attendees trickled out, Ethan lingered, a playful glint in his eye. "So, what's next? A reading of Moby Dick? Because I'm not sure I'm ready to dive into existential dread yet."

"Ah, but think of the whaling lore! The profound metaphors!" I countered, grinning. "I could whip up a sea-themed cheese platter to accompany it."

"Now you're talking," he replied, his tone conspiratorial. "Count me in for the existential dread, as long as there's cheese."

In that moment, with the warm glow of the café lights surrounding us, I felt an overwhelming sense of gratitude. "You know, I couldn't have done this without your support. You've made this whole experience feel... well, less terrifying."

Ethan shrugged, a modest smile dancing on his lips. "Just doing my part to help you conquer the literary world, one cookie at a time."

As we both laughed, the door swung open, and to my surprise, Diane stepped back in, a hesitant expression on her face. "I... um, I just wanted to say I enjoyed tonight," she said, her voice softer than I'd ever heard it. "You really captured everyone's interest."

I raised an eyebrow, unsure whether to accept her compliment or brace myself for the inevitable criticism. "Thank you, Diane. It was a collaborative effort. Everyone brought something special to the table."

She nodded, a flicker of sincerity crossing her features. "Maybe I misjudged this whole book club thing. It's not half bad."

"Only half?" I teased, the banter slipping effortlessly into place.

With a ghost of a smile, she replied, "Alright, it's quite good. I'll consider joining more often."

As she retreated, I turned to Ethan, a mix of disbelief and elation bubbling within me. "Did that just happen? Did Diane just compliment me?"

"Looks like the winds are changing," he said, his tone light yet reflective.

Perhaps this was a turning point, a moment where we could all learn to embrace our vulnerabilities and find strength in connection. As I packed up the remaining snacks, a hopeful warmth spread through me, promising that the journey ahead might be filled with unexpected revelations.

With each passing week, the book club blossomed, like vibrant petals unfurling under the tender gaze of the sun. The café transformed into a community hub, where laughter danced in the air and conversations flowed as freely as the coffee. The walls, once mere backdrops for mismatched furniture and rustic decor, seemed to pulse with the energy of shared stories and burgeoning friendships. I felt myself sinking deeper into the warm embrace of Silver Pines, the once intimidating town slowly becoming a patchwork of familiarity and connection.

Ethan remained a steadfast presence, his banter and charm weaving effortlessly into our gatherings. "If only we could book a one-way ticket to the fictional worlds we read about," he mused one evening, leaning back in his chair, a mischievous glint in his eyes. "I'd definitely choose to live in the Harry Potter universe—free Hogwarts education? Yes, please!"

"Only if I get to be a Ravenclaw," I shot back, crossing my arms with mock seriousness. "I'm not settling for Hufflepuff just because I enjoy a good snack."

"Aw, come on! Hufflepuffs are the life of the party!" he laughed, shaking his head.

The conversations unfolded like the pages of a well-loved novel, filled with intrigue and unexpected turns. Yet, just as I began to feel truly at home, life threw me a curveball. A chilling reminder of my insecurities arrived one crisp afternoon, bringing with it the scent of freshly fallen snow. I walked into the café, ready for our latest gathering, only to find Diane already seated, sipping a cup of tea as if she belonged there.

The sight of her sent an uneasy tremor through my carefully constructed world. She was flipping through one of the books we had read, her brow furrowed in concentration, and I felt an inexplicable sense of dread wash over me.

"Hey, look who it is!" Ethan's cheerful voice broke through my spiraling thoughts as he entered, his presence a welcome balm. "Ready for another epic discussion?"

Diane looked up, her expression inscrutable. "I've decided to give this book club a fair shot," she announced, her voice light yet edged with a challenge.

"Great! The more, the merrier!" I replied, plastering on a smile that felt more like a mask.

As the others trickled in, I couldn't shake the feeling that Diane's presence would overshadow the warmth we'd cultivated. The discussion began, but I found myself glancing at her, watching her reactions like a hawk. She asked insightful questions, skillfully dissecting our discussions with a clarity that was both impressive and unnerving. Each time I tried to steer the conversation back to our shared joys, she deftly redirected it, her charm slipping effortlessly into the crevices of our camaraderie.

"Do you really think that an author's background influences their work?" Diane posed, her gaze penetrating as she directed the question to me. "Or do you think it's merely a reflection of their imagination?"

I swallowed hard, feeling the collective gaze of the group shift toward me, curiosity woven with apprehension. "Well, I think it's a bit of both," I said, trying to regain my footing. "An author's experiences shape their narrative, but the imagination is a wild beast that can lead to unexpected paths."

"Interesting. So you're suggesting that imagination is somehow more powerful than lived experience?" She leaned forward, and I could almost hear the gears turning in her mind, poised to pounce on my every word.

Before I could formulate a proper response, Ethan interjected, his tone lighthearted. "I think imagination is the key to creating a world that resonates with others. Look at how much we've all connected through stories—none of us share the same background, yet here we are, bonded by books!"

"True, but sometimes those backgrounds can create a lens that's hard to see past," Diane countered, a hint of challenge sparking in her eyes.

The conversation became an unexpected duel, and I felt the weight of her scrutiny as she held my every word to the fire. I was ready to pivot, to steer the group back toward laughter and camaraderie, but it felt like an uphill battle against the tide of her influence.

"Maybe we should pick a book with a controversial background next time, see how it shakes things up!" someone suggested, attempting to lighten the mood.

"Or we could read something entirely imaginative and escape from reality altogether," I added, hoping to shift the energy.

"Let's face it," Diane chimed in, her smile almost predatory. "Not everyone can escape their realities, can they? Some of us are tied to the past."

Her words hung in the air, heavy with implications that stirred something deep within me. The room fell silent for a heartbeat, and I could feel the tension coiling like a spring. Just as I was about to respond, a loud crash erupted from the entrance, sending a shockwave through our cozy gathering.

The door swung open with such force that it slammed against the wall, and in walked a figure I hadn't seen in ages—my ex-boyfriend, Max. The winter wind whipped in behind him, scattering napkins and stirring the aroma of coffee into a frenzied dance. He was disheveled, his hair tousled, and his eyes wild with an urgency I had long thought buried beneath layers of time and distance.

"Sorry to barge in like this," he panted, his gaze darting around the room before landing on me. "But I need to talk to you. It's important."

Gasps filled the café as the group turned to witness this unexpected intrusion, eyes wide with intrigue. I felt my heart drop, the warm ambiance of the evening shifting to a tense uncertainty. The last thing I wanted was for my past to crash into my carefully constructed present, threatening the fragile threads of connection I had woven with the people around me.

Ethan's expression shifted from amusement to concern, his protective instincts surfacing as he stepped closer to me. "Maybe now isn't the best time?" he said, his tone firm yet gentle.

Max shook his head, an intensity in his eyes that made the air crackle. "No, you don't understand. This can't wait."

I took a step back, my mind racing, trying to comprehend the whirlwind of emotions now swirling in the room. "What do you mean?"

Before he could respond, Diane smirked, clearly reveling in the chaos unfolding. "Looks like you're not the only one with a complicated past," she said, her voice smooth as silk.

As I faced Max, the world around us faded into a blur, the laughter and warmth of the café becoming distant echoes. His presence was a reminder of all I had tried to leave behind, and suddenly, everything I had built in Silver Pines felt precarious, teetering on the edge of uncertainty.

"Why are you here?" I demanded, my voice barely above a whisper, the weight of his gaze pinning me in place.

And then, just as the room fell silent, as I stood poised on the precipice of a revelation, the door swung open again, bringing with it the heavy scent of impending change, a storm brewing on the horizon. The figure that entered next sent shockwaves through my already tumultuous heart, and I braced myself for whatever was about to unfold, knowing that the ties binding my past and present were about to unravel in ways I could never have imagined.

Chapter 28: A Light in the Dark

The snowflakes danced whimsically outside The Maple Leaf, each one unique, delicate, and fleeting, like moments I was beginning to cherish. The air inside the café was warm and fragrant, filled with the rich aroma of freshly brewed coffee and sweet pastries that wrapped around us like a cozy blanket. I had spent hours crafting a festive atmosphere: garlands of evergreen adorned the windows, and twinkling lights flickered like stars captured in glass. As the last remnants of the winter market faded, the holiday spirit filled the air with a promise of renewal, a fresh start almost palpable in the chilly winds outside.

The café was a symphony of chatter and laughter, the hum of life buzzing around us. Regulars chatted amiably, their faces illuminated by the soft glow of candlelight. I found comfort in the rhythm of my routine, each day blending seamlessly into the next. It was here, among the clinking of mugs and the soft laughter, that I began to feel a sense of belonging—a feeling that had evaded me for far too long.

But as I looked across the crowded room, my gaze found Ethan. He stood behind the counter, his hands expertly crafting a latte, his fingers dancing over the steaming milk with an ease that made my heart flutter. The fire crackled in the corner, casting flickering shadows across his handsome face. There was a lightness in his demeanor, a playful grin that hinted at mischief. I leaned against the counter, a teasing smile playing on my lips.

"Careful there, hot stuff," I quipped, arching an eyebrow. "You might just melt all the snowflakes with that charm."

He glanced up, laughter brightening his eyes. "Only if you promise to catch them before they hit the ground. I wouldn't want them to be left out in the cold."

I felt a warmth bloom within me at our banter, a lightness that made the world outside seem distant, the snow and wind mere whispers compared to the electric energy sparking between us. For a moment, nothing else mattered; it was just Ethan and me, cocooned in our own little universe.

As the evening wore on, the café began to empty, leaving just a handful of stragglers nursing their drinks. I found myself stealing glances at Ethan as he wiped down the counter, the way the muscles in his arms flexed effortlessly caught my attention, but it was the look in his eyes when he turned to meet my gaze that truly captivated me. It was a spark, a connection that felt both thrilling and terrifying.

"Come here," he beckoned, his voice a low murmur, drawing me closer. I stepped around the counter, my heart racing as I slid onto a barstool. The fire crackled behind us, filling the room with a gentle warmth that seemed to reflect the feelings swirling inside me. I reached for his hand, fingers intertwining as he leaned closer, our breaths mingling in the space between us.

"I've been thinking…" he started, his voice barely above a whisper, and I felt the anticipation build like the tension before a storm. I was ready for this moment, ready for us, and as I leaned in, the world around us faded into the background. But just as I opened my mouth to respond, the door swung open with a gust of cold air, and in walked Claire, my whirlwind of a sister.

"Guess who just scored us a Christmas dinner reservation at the hottest restaurant in town!" she announced, her voice bright with excitement, but the gleam in her eyes held a hint of mischief that sent a shiver down my spine. I let go of Ethan's hand, feeling the warmth of our moment dissipate as Claire approached, unaware of the storm she was about to unleash.

"Oh, you're going to love it, Grace! And I've already told them you'd be there with me," she continued, her enthusiasm bubbling over. My heart sank; the last thing I wanted was to have my plans laid out for me by Claire, the sister who always seemed to have my life mapped out better than I did.

"Claire," I began, my voice a mixture of disbelief and irritation, "I appreciate the thought, but I'd really like to decide these things for myself."

She waved her hand dismissively, her smile still bright but slightly tinged with confusion. "But this is perfect! You've been feeling lost, and this will be a great opportunity for you. It's a fancy place, and you need to meet new people!"

"Meet new people?" I repeated, my tone sharp. "Claire, I just want to enjoy the holiday season without a master plan. I'm finally starting to feel like I belong here, and I want to explore that—on my terms."

Ethan stepped in, a protective glint in his eye. "Claire, maybe it would be better to let Grace figure things out on her own. She's doing amazing things here."

For a moment, I reveled in the warmth of Ethan's support, but the air felt thick with tension as Claire's expression shifted from excitement to disappointment. "You two are really going to go this route, aren't you? Grace, you know I just want what's best for you. I thought you'd be thrilled about this."

I took a deep breath, feeling my resolve strengthen. "What's best for me is to have a say in my own life. I want to make my own choices, Claire."

Claire's eyes narrowed slightly, the flicker of surprise morphing into something I couldn't quite place. "Fine," she said, her tone cool, "but don't say I didn't try to help." With that, she turned on her heel and left, the door slamming behind her with an echoing thud that felt like a finality.

The silence that followed was heavy, and I glanced at Ethan, who was watching me with an intensity that both comforted and unsettled me. "That was... something," he said, breaking the stillness, a half-smile tugging at his lips.

"Yeah, something I didn't ask for," I replied, my voice more shaky than I intended. "But thanks for backing me up."

"Always," he said softly, leaning closer again, and I felt the electric pull of our connection return, igniting the space between us. But as I searched his eyes for reassurance, I realized that while I was battling external pressures, the internal war of what I truly wanted was just beginning. The warmth of the café, the festive decorations, and the swirling snow outside couldn't shield me from the uncertainty lurking just beneath the surface.

But as Ethan's fingers brushed against mine, I knew one thing for certain: I was ready to face whatever came next.

The air in The Maple Leaf crackled with an unspoken tension, the remnants of Claire's unexpected arrival still hanging like a stubborn cloud. As I stared at the door through which she had just exited, I felt a familiar tug-of-war within me. On one hand, there was the thrill of newfound independence, and on the other, the nagging voice of my sister, which had spent years dictating the playbook of my life. I turned to Ethan, who was leaning against the counter, a hint of concern etched across his face.

"Is it too late to send her a fruit basket? Or maybe a gift card to that place where they teach yoga to goats?" I quipped, trying to lighten the heavy atmosphere.

His laughter broke the tension, rich and full. "I think the goat yoga trend might be too avant-garde for Claire. She's more of a 'let's plan your wedding before you've even met the right guy' type."

"Exactly!" I exclaimed, feeling a rush of camaraderie. "At this rate, she'll be drafting a prenup before I even finish my coffee." The warmth in Ethan's eyes made my insides flutter. "So, where do we go from here?"

"Simple," he said, straightening up and crossing his arms, his grin teasing. "We indulge in some major Christmas cheer. I happen to know a great place that serves hot chocolate so rich it practically wears a tuxedo."

"Lead the way, tuxedo chocolate," I said, smiling back at him as he gestured toward the door.

We stepped outside into the crisp night air, the world around us transformed into a winter wonderland. Snowflakes fluttered like tiny stars, drifting down to blanket the streets in soft, white powder. The glow of streetlamps reflected off the pristine surface, creating a magical ambiance that made me feel like we had stepped into a holiday card.

"I love this time of year," I mused as we walked, the crunch of snow beneath our feet punctuating the serene silence. "Everything feels so alive, like the world is holding its breath, waiting for something wonderful to happen."

"Or waiting for the next family drama to unfold," he replied, a playful smirk playing on his lips. "You're going to need a solid plan to handle Claire. Maybe we should create a flowchart."

"Flowchart? Sounds a bit formal for sibling drama, don't you think? Perhaps a pie chart would be more appropriate—'Percentage of My Life Planned by Claire' versus 'Percentage of My Life That Is Actually Mine.'"

We both laughed, and as we rounded the corner, the glow of a quaint little café came into view, its windows fogged and inviting. It was there that the air was filled with the unmistakable scent of chocolate, mingling with freshly baked pastries.

As we settled into a cozy nook, steaming mugs in hand, I felt the weight of the evening's earlier tension begin to lift. "This is perfect," I said, savoring the rich cocoa as it slid down my throat like a warm hug. "I don't think I ever want to leave."

Ethan leaned back, watching me with an intensity that made my heart race. "You know, sometimes it takes a little chaos to realize what you truly want. Maybe Claire's plans are just the nudge you need."

"Or a brick wall," I countered, biting into a decadent chocolate croissant. "I love her, but I don't want to be her life-sized doll, you know? I want to be the one calling the shots, even if it means making mistakes."

He nodded, his gaze steady and encouraging. "Mistakes are just a sign that you're living, Grace. Just make sure you don't lose yourself in the process. You're too wonderful to let anyone else dictate who you should be."

His words settled deep in my chest, a comforting weight I hadn't known I needed. The warmth between us simmered just beneath the surface, a slow-burning ember that promised more if we dared to explore it. Just then, my phone buzzed on the table, shattering the moment. It was a text from Claire: Don't forget about dinner plans on Thursday!

I sighed, rolling my eyes at the screen. "Speaking of plans, Claire just reminded me about our dinner. Apparently, I need to be reminded of my own schedule."

"Would it help if I came along?" Ethan offered, his expression thoughtful. "You know, just in case things get too 'overly planned'?"

"Actually, yes," I said, surprised by how much I liked the idea. "You could be my buffer. Plus, you're much better at handling her charm than I am. Just make sure you have your best 'sister's boyfriend' face ready."

"Consider it done. I'll practice my surprised-but-pleased expression while I'm at it. Nothing like a little family dinner to test the waters."

The conversation flowed easily, each laugh bridging the gap between uncertainty and the exciting unknown. But just as I felt a sense of clarity beginning to settle in, the door swung open, sending a chill through the café. In walked a figure I hadn't expected to see—a tall man with dark hair and a confident stride, dressed in a fitted coat that accentuated his sharp features. He scanned the room until his eyes landed on me, and for a moment, time stood still.

"Grace?" His voice was smooth, carrying a hint of disbelief, as though we were old friends unexpectedly reunited.

My stomach twisted, caught off guard. "Caleb?"

He approached our table, his expression a mix of surprise and something unreadable. "It's been ages. I didn't expect to find you here."

Ethan's body tensed beside me, the air suddenly thick with unspoken words. I had almost forgotten about Caleb, the boy from my past who had slipped into my life like a fleeting summer breeze. Our friendship had faded as life pulled us in different directions, but seeing him again stirred a whirlpool of emotions I thought I had buried long ago.

"Yeah, well, life has a funny way of keeping us on our toes," I replied, trying to mask the surprise with a casual demeanor.

"I've heard you're running this charming little café now. It looks amazing," he said, gesturing around.

"Thanks! It's a labor of love," I replied, my voice steadying. "What brings you back to town?"

"I'm working on a project nearby," he said, glancing at Ethan, who was still silent, his expression unreadable. "I didn't mean to interrupt."

"Oh, you're not interrupting at all. This is my—uh—friend, Ethan," I stammered, awkwardly gesturing between the two of them.

Ethan finally spoke, his voice smooth but guarded. "Nice to meet you, Caleb."

The tension in the air crackled like static electricity. Caleb offered a polite smile, but I could sense the competition brewing beneath the surface. "You too," he said, and the undercurrent of unspoken rivalry hung between us like an unwelcome guest.

As the conversation meandered, I felt a sense of disarray swirling inside me. The warmth I had found with Ethan suddenly felt threatened by the presence of Caleb, whose return was a reminder of everything I had tried to leave behind. Yet amidst the confusion, I realized one thing for certain: life was about to get a lot more complicated.

Caleb's unexpected arrival sent a ripple of confusion through the café, and I could almost hear the tension tightening around us like an invisible noose. Ethan's posture had shifted, his body language becoming a fortress, and I sensed the need to bridge the growing chasm between past and present.

"So, you're back in town?" I asked Caleb, trying to reclaim the lightness that had been so abruptly snatched away. "What's the project?"

He leaned against the table, casual yet somehow poised, as if he were the one in control. "I'm working on a documentary about local artisans. I heard The Maple Leaf is one of the best places in the area. Thought I'd stop by and see it for myself."

"A documentary, huh? Sounds impressive," I replied, forcing a smile. "You'll have to let us know when it's airing so we can all tune in and cheer you on."

"Of course. I'd love to feature the café," he said, his eyes sparkling with enthusiasm. "And you, of course. Your story would add a personal touch."

Ethan cleared his throat, his voice steady yet underlined with an edge. "Grace has a lot on her plate right now. I don't think she'll have time for a film crew."

Caleb's brow furrowed slightly, and I could see the wheels turning in his head, calculating how to maneuver through the thickening atmosphere. "Surely she can spare a few minutes. I wouldn't want to make it too burdensome. It'll be all fun and creativity."

"Yeah, because nothing says fun like having a camera following you around while you try to figure out your own life," I shot back, an involuntary bite creeping into my tone. "I think I'll pass on the behind-the-scenes drama for now."

Ethan nodded, a hint of approval flickering in his expression, and I felt a rush of adrenaline. It was a small victory, a reminder that I had people in my corner.

Caleb raised an eyebrow, a smirk tugging at the corners of his mouth. "Fair enough, Grace. But you know, some people thrive under pressure. They find their true selves when the spotlight is on them."

"Or they collapse under the weight of expectations," I retorted, feeling emboldened. "I've had my fair share of that."

Ethan leaned closer, the warmth of his presence enveloping me like a shield. "You've done just fine on your own, despite all the drama. You should embrace that independence."

I smiled at him, my heart fluttering. The camaraderie between us felt like a secret we were sharing, one that pushed back against the unease rising from Caleb's sudden intrusion. "Thanks. Maybe I'll take your advice to heart. But as for your documentary, Caleb, I think you might need to find another subject—one that isn't so caught up in family expectations."

The banter hung in the air, and for a moment, it felt like we were dancing around an unspoken truth. Caleb's expression shifted, and I caught a glimmer of frustration lurking beneath his charming veneer. "Alright, I get it. It seems the local café scene is off-limits. I can respect that. Just know that I'm not the enemy here. I've always thought you had potential, Grace."

"Thanks, I think?" I replied, my confusion evident. "But potential doesn't exactly pay the bills or resolve family drama."

He shrugged, a flicker of empathy crossing his face. "Life's complicated, isn't it? You never know where your path will lead you, but I think you're on the verge of something big."

Just then, the door swung open again, and the familiar jingle of bells accompanied a gust of icy air. Claire burst in, her cheeks flushed from the cold and her eyes sparkling with excitement, oblivious to the tension that had settled like a thick fog. "There you are! I've been looking everywhere for you!" She paused, taking in the sight of Caleb and Ethan, her expression flickering between confusion and intrigue.

"Claire, this is Caleb, an old friend," I said, forcing a smile. "He's back in town doing some sort of documentary."

Her eyebrows shot up. "Oh, how wonderful! We should definitely have a conversation about that, Caleb." She turned her gaze to me, a mischievous twinkle in her eye. "You're not going to be too busy, are you? I still need your input on our dinner plans."

I felt my pulse quicken at the mention of dinner, the familiar weight of Claire's expectations creeping back in. "Actually, I think I can manage my own schedule just fine," I replied, trying to sound more confident than I felt.

Ethan placed his hand on my shoulder, a grounding force amidst the whirlwind. "I'm here to help, remember? We'll figure out the details later."

"Perfect!" Claire exclaimed, completely missing the underlying tension. "Caleb, I can't wait to hear more about your project. Grace is going to be my star! We can make it a grand event."

I shot Ethan a pleading look, silently begging for a lifeline. "Um, Claire, I really don't think I'm ready to dive into anything that big right now."

"Oh, come on," she insisted, waving her hand dismissively. "It'll be fun! And besides, everyone loves a good story. Yours is practically begging to be told."

I opened my mouth to protest, but the words were trapped in my throat, tangled in the web of my conflicting feelings. Just when I thought I had a grip on my life, Claire was there, pulling at the threads and unraveling my carefully woven plans.

Caleb stepped forward, a look of genuine concern replacing his earlier bravado. "If you need some space, Grace, I totally understand. I don't want to pressure you into anything you're not comfortable with."

The sincerity in his tone caught me off guard. "Thanks, Caleb. I appreciate that."

Ethan's fingers tightened around my shoulder, and I could feel the support radiating from him. "Let's not rush things," he said, his voice steady. "Grace has enough on her plate."

Claire rolled her eyes playfully. "You two sound like an old married couple. Relax! It's supposed to be a good time. But I do think we should plan a little something special for you, Grace. Maybe a surprise party?"

"A surprise party?" I echoed, panic surging through me. "What about that screams 'I want to be in the spotlight'?"

"Exactly!" Claire laughed, oblivious to my discomfort. "You'll love it. Trust me!"

Before I could voice my concerns, Caleb chimed in, his eyes gleaming with excitement. "Count me in! I'd love to help. A surprise party sounds like a perfect way to celebrate the holidays and get to know the real Grace again."

Ethan's expression darkened slightly, but I caught his eye, pleading silently for him to intervene. "No, wait. I—"

Just then, my phone buzzed again, vibrating violently against the table. I glanced down to see a text from an unknown number, the message bold and direct: We need to talk. Tonight. Don't ignore this.

My heart raced, panic lacing my thoughts. Who could it be? The sense of unease that had been simmering beneath the surface suddenly erupted, drowning out all the cheerful banter around me.

"What's wrong?" Claire asked, her brow furrowed with concern.

"I... I don't know," I stammered, my fingers trembling as I stared at the screen. "But I think I might need to take this."

"Grace, wait—" Ethan started, but I was already standing, the sudden urgency propelling me toward the door.

As I stepped outside, the cold air hit me like a slap, sharp and invigorating. The snow crunched beneath my feet, and I looked back, finding Ethan's worried gaze lingering on me from inside. The weight of the text pressed against me like an anchor, and I couldn't shake the feeling that I was teetering on the edge of something significant—something that could change everything.

And in that moment, I realized that whatever was waiting for me outside was about to unravel my carefully constructed world once and for all.

Chapter 29: Torn Asunder

The Maple Leaf buzzed with a familiar warmth, the kind that wraps around you like a favorite blanket on a chilly evening. Sunlight streamed through the large bay windows, illuminating the rows of mismatched tables and chairs, their surfaces worn from years of conversation and laughter. The aroma of freshly brewed coffee mingled with the sweet scent of cinnamon rolls, an intoxicating blend that made my stomach growl. I had settled into this small-town life, relishing every lazy afternoon and impromptu gathering, but today felt different. Today, a storm brewed just beneath the surface.

I spotted Claire as soon as she entered, her presence slicing through the cozy atmosphere like a knife. The chatter around me quieted, and eyes darted toward her with a mix of curiosity and concern. Her blonde hair shone with an uncharacteristic vibrancy, but it was the frown etched across her brow that sent a ripple of unease through the room. She spotted me almost immediately, her gaze locking onto mine like a heat-seeking missile. I felt the air grow heavy, thickening with tension.

"What are you doing here?" she demanded, marching toward me with purpose. I could hear the soft thud of my heart in my ears, an anxious drumroll signaling an impending confrontation. "This isn't where you belong."

Her words sliced through the warmth of the café, chilling me despite the sun streaming through the windows. I swallowed hard, searching for my voice, but it seemed lost in the weight of her accusation. It was as if she'd dropped a boulder in the peaceful pond of my existence, sending ripples of doubt and confusion crashing against the walls I had built so carefully.

"Claire, this is my home," I finally managed to say, my voice steadier than I felt. "I've made a life for myself here."

"Made a life?" she scoffed, crossing her arms. "You mean, you're playing house in a town that's stuck in the past while you waste your potential. You're talented, Sarah! You could be doing so much more than this."

Her words stung, igniting insecurities I had fought so hard to bury. Every small success, every triumphant moment of self-discovery I had celebrated felt suddenly trivial under her harsh scrutiny. I glanced at Ethan, sitting at the bar with a furrowed brow, his fingers tapping anxiously against the counter. The loyalty in his eyes flickered, an unspoken understanding passing between us that made my heart ache.

"Is that what you really think?" I asked, my voice softer now, the edge of hurt creeping in. "That I'm wasting my life?"

Claire's expression shifted, the momentary vulnerability eclipsed by the urgency of her mission. "You can't keep hiding here. You've got your degree, your connections—don't throw them away for this quaint little town and its silly charm. You belong in the city, doing big things. You're wasting your gifts!"

Around us, the clatter of cups and murmurs of conversation faded into a distant hum. The townsfolk watched, their curiosity palpable, their collective gaze a spotlight illuminating our family discord. I could feel the heat of their attention, a thousand silent judgments hanging in the air, making it impossible to breathe. What would they think of me, standing here as Claire laid bare our family drama? A sense of vulnerability washed over me, making my cheeks burn.

"Maybe I don't want to be that person anymore," I replied, my voice gaining strength as I pushed through the uncertainty. "I've worked hard to build something here that makes me happy. Isn't that enough?"

"But it's not just about you!" Claire shot back, her frustration spilling over. "It's about your future, your career. What will Mom and

Dad think? They expect more from you, Sarah. You're not living up to your potential, and I'm here to help you see that."

At that moment, I felt as if the ground beneath me was shifting. The life I had painstakingly constructed in this town, the friendships I had nurtured, the quiet moments that had become my refuge, all felt threatened by her words. I had spent so long striving to be who I truly was, to break free from the expectations that had suffocated me in the past. Yet here she was, wielding those very expectations like weapons.

Ethan's chair scraped against the wooden floor as he stood, his expression torn between the urge to defend me and the desire to avoid escalating the situation. "Claire, you're not helping," he said quietly, but his voice carried a weight that silenced the café for a brief moment.

"Oh, please, Ethan," she shot back, dismissive. "This isn't about you. This is about Sarah waking up from her self-imposed slumber and realizing what she's throwing away. You might be okay with mediocrity, but I'm not."

The room fell into a heavy silence, the tension palpable, each breath drawn feeling like an act of defiance. I glanced around, taking in the faces of my friends and neighbors, wondering if they saw me as Claire did—a dreamer lost in a whimsical fantasy—or as the woman I had become, strong and resolute in my choices. The question gnawed at me, a burr in my heart, but as I caught Ethan's gaze, I felt a flicker of defiance.

"Maybe I don't need saving," I said, my voice steadying. "Maybe I'm exactly where I'm meant to be."

Claire's eyes widened, disbelief flashing across her face. The intensity of our confrontation had reached a fever pitch, each word crackling in the air between us like static. It was as if we stood on the edge of a precipice, and I could feel the pull of the abyss beneath us, a dark chasm threatening to swallow our relationship whole.

The silence stretched, taut and electric, each of us waiting for the other to make a move. I inhaled deeply, the scent of coffee and pastries enveloping me, grounding me in the moment. I had to choose—between the sister I loved and the life I had forged with my own two hands. I felt the walls I had built begin to tremble, but in that moment, something within me solidified. I would not let her words tear me asunder.

The silence in The Maple Leaf lingered, thick with unsaid words and unexpressed emotions, as I stood there, poised between Claire's fierce determination and my own simmering resolve. The café felt like an arena, with the townsfolk acting as the quiet audience, each pair of eyes weighing the gravity of our standoff. I could practically hear the popcorn crunching as they leaned in, waiting for the next round.

"Do you think this is all just... a phase?" Claire's voice was sharp, laced with disbelief, as if she were confronting a particularly stubborn child refusing to eat their vegetables. "That someday you'll wake up and realize how far you've fallen from what you could be?"

I crossed my arms, a defensive move, but I didn't care. "And what exactly do you think I'm doing here? Building a sandcastle at the beach? This is my life, Claire. I'm not waiting for a prince to come and rescue me. I've built my own castle, one brick at a time."

She let out a short laugh, a sound tinged with frustration and disbelief. "You call this a castle? Sarah, come on. You're a glorified barista in a town where the biggest event is the annual pie-eating contest!"

The words struck me harder than I cared to admit, rattling my self-image like a windstorm through the trees. "It's not just about the job," I countered, my voice firmer than before. "It's about the community I've found here. The friendships I've nurtured. This place is more than a temporary pit stop—it's a home."

Ethan shifted uncomfortably, his presence a steady anchor amid the tempest swirling between us. "She's right, Claire," he said softly, but firmly, "You can't just judge someone's happiness by their career choice. Sarah's not the only one who loves this place. We all do."

"See? Even he agrees!" Claire's voice rose slightly, the air crackling with tension. "You're all settling for something less than what you deserve. You think this is happiness? It's complacency!"

A wave of heat surged through me, not just from anger but from the sting of her truth. Maybe I was settling. Maybe I wasn't living the ambitious life everyone expected of me. But what she saw as complacency felt like contentment. I had never been happier than in these moments, sipping coffee with friends and sharing stories. What she labeled as mediocrity was my everyday joy.

"I'm not here for everyone else's expectations," I shot back, voice quaking but resolute. "If you think I'm going to uproot my life because it doesn't fit your vision of success, then you've completely misunderstood me."

Claire took a step back, her eyes narrowing as if she were trying to decode a particularly tricky puzzle. "So, what? You're just going to give up on everything we've worked for? On Mom and Dad's dreams for you?"

The mention of our parents stung, a reminder of the weight of family legacy pressing down on me. "It's not giving up if I'm choosing my own path. I appreciate what they want for me, but I have to live my own life."

Claire opened her mouth, ready to counter, but I held up a hand. "You need to understand something. I didn't come to Maplewood just to hide. I came here to find myself, to discover who I am outside of your shadow. It's not a failure to find peace in simplicity."

The tension in the room shifted. It was a delicate balance, a tightrope walk between the familiar and the unknown. I could feel the townsfolk leaning in, sensing the undercurrents of emotion swirling between us. A grandmother with silver hair and a gnarled cane caught my eye, her gaze filled with a mix of sympathy and understanding. She had known her share of struggles, and I wondered if she had once faced down a sister or a mother who thought they knew best.

"Don't you see?" Claire's tone softened slightly, though the sharpness remained. "You're wasting your potential, Sarah. You have a gift, and it's like you're burying it out here. You could be making a difference—"

"I'm making a difference here!" I interrupted, my heart racing. "I mentor kids at the community center. I help the local business owners with their marketing strategies. I organize events that bring us all together. This isn't a wasteland, Claire. It's thriving, just like me!"

The words hung in the air, defiance and vulnerability intertwining like vines around a tree. Claire's expression shifted, a flicker of something—perhaps recognition—crossing her features. But then, just as quickly, it was gone, replaced by that familiar stubbornness.

"Maybe I just don't understand your version of happiness," she admitted, frustration coloring her tone. "But what happens when you wake up one day and realize you're... stuck? What then?"

"Then I'll figure it out," I said, my voice steady, determination igniting within me. "Just like I have every day since I moved here. I'm not afraid of change; I'm afraid of living a life that isn't mine."

The air around us felt electric, the potential for reconciliation and fracture dancing just out of reach. Claire opened her mouth to respond, but before she could find her words, a loud crash erupted from the kitchen. We all turned to see a tray of mugs tumbling to the floor, coffee splattering like miniature geysers. Laughter erupted from a group of regulars, the tension breaking like a fragile bubble.

"Well, that's one way to get attention," I murmured, half-smiling, and Claire snorted in response, the edges of her anger softening. The unexpected humor cut through the chaos, a reminder that life continued despite our clashes.

"You're lucky you're cute," Claire said, an exasperated grin breaking through her frustration. "I swear, if you weren't my sister, I'd be rolling my eyes right now."

"Just admit you love me and we can end this dramatic scene," I teased, relief flooding through me as the tension began to ease.

"Oh, please," Claire shot back, but the smile in her eyes told a different story. "I tolerate you because you're family. That's about it."

"Lucky for you, I've made myself incredibly tolerable," I replied, my heart swelling with hope. "Just don't tell Mom."

The warmth of our shared laughter wrapped around us, momentarily mending the rift that had threatened to tear us apart. We weren't finished; there were still conversations to be had, truths to confront. But in that moment, amid the chaos and the scent of coffee, I felt a flicker of understanding, the first step toward bridging the gap between us. Claire might never fully grasp the life I had chosen, but maybe—just maybe—she could learn to accept it, one laughter-filled moment at a time.

Laughter had begun to ripple through the café like a soft breeze, carrying with it the promise of understanding, however fleeting. As the clattering of dishes settled, I found a thread of hope weaving itself through the tension. Claire and I stood across from each other, the remnants of our argument hanging in the air, but for the first time in what felt like ages, there was a flicker of warmth behind her eyes, a hesitant recognition of the bond we shared.

Ethan, still perched at the bar, glanced between us, a cautious smile playing on his lips. "Well, if nothing else, at least we've provided the morning entertainment," he quipped, gesturing toward the still-chuckling regulars. I could see a few familiar faces nodding in agreement, the old-timers leaning in to catch the latest family drama.

"Right?" I chuckled, my relief palpable as I raised my coffee cup in a mock toast. "To family bonding over caffeine and chaos!"

"More like a family circus," Claire retorted, crossing her arms but unable to suppress her grin. "I mean, what are we, a reality TV show now?"

"Only if the producers are looking for emotional breakdowns and existential crises," I shot back, feeling lighter. It was an absurd moment, but we needed that levity like a plant craves sunlight.

A heavy sigh escaped Claire's lips, her expression softening as she leaned against the counter. "You know I just want what's best for you, right? I can't help but feel like I'm watching you throw your potential away."

"Maybe it's time to redefine what 'best' looks like for me," I replied, keeping my tone light even as a serious weight underpinned my words. "What you see as potential is just one path, and I'm exploring my own."

The warmth in Claire's eyes flickered, like a candle fighting against the wind. "I get that. I really do. But sometimes, I just wish you'd see it from my perspective."

"Perspective is subjective, Claire," I said gently, feeling a wave of sisterly love surge through me. "You've lived your life, and I've lived mine. Just because we're different doesn't mean one of us is wrong."

She opened her mouth to respond, but the sudden blare of a siren outside caught our attention. The quaint sound of Maplewood faded as the reality of the world rushed back in, thickening the air once more. The sound faded into the background as I caught Ethan's eye; he raised an eyebrow, the concern etched on his face palpable.

"Should we go check that out?" he asked, glancing towards the door, where a few of the patrons had begun to congregate, their whispers rising in hushed urgency.

"Maybe it's just a minor incident," I suggested, though my heart raced. Still, curiosity gnawed at me. The sirens were a jarring contrast to the cozy atmosphere of the café.

"I don't like the look of it," Claire murmured, peering out the window. "Looks like it's coming from the direction of the old mill."

My stomach dropped. The old mill had been abandoned for years, its creaking bones and decaying walls telling stories of a time long past. It was the kind of place that sparked ghost tales among the kids in town, the kind you dared each other to approach on a dare.

"Let's see what's going on," I said, suddenly needing to step outside, as if the very air in the café had become too thick to breathe.

As we emerged into the sunlight, the warmth enveloped me, yet I felt the tension coiling tighter in my stomach. A crowd had gathered, their murmurs vibrating like an unsteady heartbeat. I could see the flashing lights of the fire trucks reflecting off the nearby buildings, casting an eerie glow on the faces around us.

"Is there a fire?" Claire asked, her voice edged with anxiety.

"Looks like it," Ethan replied, moving to get a better view. I followed, pushing through the throng of onlookers, my heart thumping like a drum. The familiar sight of the old mill loomed ahead, its silhouette stark against the sky, the smoke curling into the air like a serpent rising from the depths.

"Everyone stay back!" a voice called out, cutting through the noise. A fire chief, his uniform crisp and authoritative, waved his hands to clear the crowd. "We need space to work!"

"What happened?" someone shouted from the back, but I couldn't see who it was.

"The old mill caught fire! It's going to take a while to get it under control," he replied, his voice steady, but the hint of urgency lingered.

A wave of dread washed over me as I stood frozen, unable to tear my gaze away from the billowing smoke. Memories rushed through my mind—the times I'd explored the mill with friends, its eerie charm evoking laughter and shivers in equal measure. It had always felt like a ghost of our town, a reminder of days gone by, but now it was alive in a terrifying way.

"Hey, are you okay?" Ethan's voice cut through my reverie, and I turned to him, seeing concern etched on his handsome features.

"I'm fine," I lied, but the truth was heavier. "Just... shocked. It's such an old place."

"I know," he said, squeezing my arm reassuringly. "But it's just a building. You've made your memories, and those can't be burned away."

Before I could respond, Claire spoke up, her voice shaking slightly. "We should get everyone out of here. People need to know they shouldn't be close."

I nodded, my heart racing as I scanned the crowd, taking note of the families and children who had gathered, their faces painted with curiosity and concern. "Let's help."

As we stepped forward, I felt a flicker of determination sparking in my chest. It was time to take action, to transform this moment of crisis into something more. The day had started with an argument, but perhaps it could end with solidarity.

We began to work our way through the crowd, urging people to step back, to keep their distance from the chaos. Just as I reached a small group huddled together, a loud crack echoed from the mill, the sound sharp enough to pierce the air. I turned, my stomach dropping as flames erupted from a window, bright and fierce.

"Everyone back!" the fire chief shouted again, his voice now tinged with urgency.

The crowd recoiled, a collective gasp rising as a shadow moved in the smoke, barely visible. I squinted, trying to make out what I saw. My heart raced, pounding loudly in my ears. Was that...?

"Someone's in there!" I screamed, pointing toward the mill, panic gripping my chest as the truth hit me like a brick.

Ethan stepped forward, eyes wide. "No! They can't be!"

But as the figure stumbled out from the smoky abyss, the truth became painfully clear. It was a woman, her silhouette faltering as she emerged, struggling against the darkness that clung to her. The crowd erupted into chaos, and I found myself stepping closer, drawn by a force I couldn't resist.

"Help her!" I shouted, my voice rising above the chaos.

The fire chief motioned for his team, but I knew the urgency of the moment. I felt adrenaline surge through me, a rush of purpose mingled with fear as I surged forward, determined to reach her before it was too late.

Just as I reached the edge of the crowd, the woman's eyes locked onto mine, wide and terrified, as she crumpled to the ground. A knot formed in my stomach, something dark and foreboding, and I realized with a sickening jolt that this wasn't just a fire. This was the beginning of something much larger, a revelation that would tear through the fragile peace we had fought to build in Maplewood.

"Stay with me!" I shouted, rushing toward her, the world around me blurring into a cacophony of noise and fear.

And in that moment, I understood that everything was about to change.

Milton Keynes UK
Ingram Content Group UK Ltd.
UKHW020756231024
450026UK00001B/64